Praise for Mary Robin

D0979285

"Mary Robinette Kowal is a fabulous writer."—John Scalzi

"Combining history, magic, and adventure, [*Valour and Vanity*] balances emotional depth with buoyant storytelling." *Kirkus* Starred Review (A *Kirkus* and NPR Book of the Year]

"'Evil Robot Monkey' . . . Typical of Kowal's fiction, the story is, first and foremost, a pleasure to read. It is seamless, whole and complete."— *Clarkesworld*

"'The Lady Astronaut of Mars' is a masterpiece of character, and a rich experience that begs to be read over and over again."—*A Dribble of Ink*

"['Salt of the Earth' is] real science fiction, based on the chemistry of sodium. The society is well-conceived, with a body's salt used as if it were a sacrament . . . "—*Locus Online*

"['The White Phoenix Feather' is an] exceptional tale and the ongoing descriptions of the various gourmet dishes enticed me in a way few stories can—through the sensation of taste. A must read."—*Tangent*

"['Rampion' is a] wonderful story."—Orson Scott Card

"[With 'The Bound Man,'] Mary Robinette Kowal presents a tale that exemplifies what epic fantasy is all about."—*Wired*

"['Clockwork Chickadee'] is, in turn, playful and charming, well thought out and deliberate, and Kowal appears to have written her own version of an O. Henry story."—*Adventures in Reading*

"['For Want of a Nail' is a] startlingly effective look at hard choices about what existences are worth living."—*Eyrie.org*

"Unexpected twists abound in this story, the surprising conclusion of which I loved on several levels."—*SFSite* on "At the Edge of Dying"

WORD PUPPETS

Stories by
Mary Robinette Kowal

WORD PUPPETS

Stories by
Mary Robinette Kowal

PRIME BOOKS

WORD PUPPETS

Copyright © 2015 by Mary Robinette Kowal

Prime Books
www.prime-books.com
Gaithersburg, MD

ISBN: 978-1-60701-456-0 (print)
ISBN: 978-1-60701-466-9 (ebook)

For my nephew, Peter,
who shares an appreciation of short fiction with me.

Contents

Introduction

Patrick Rothfuss

SO HERE'S THE THING: Mary Robinette Kowal is one of my favorite people.

This shouldn't come as a surprise. I am, after all, writing the introduction to her book. Things like this are done as favors for friends. You have to know that's how these things work. That's just the way the world works.

However, it puts us in a strange position, you and I. If I'm a friend of Mary's, how can you trust me to be impartial about her writing? How do you know I won't simply smile and tell you beautiful lies about her work?

Here's the thing: you don't know. This whole issue is complicated by the fact that I'm not just a good liar. I'm a *professional* liar. I lie for a living. Pretty much everything I'm writing here could be a lie.

So you're going to have to decide for yourself whether or not you're going to trust me. You'll have to decide how much of this you're going to believe.

Ready? Let's go.

I'D KNOWN ABOUT MARY for a long time before I actually met her. We had a few friends in common and attended the same conventions, but we'd never really ended up talking. We moved in different social spheres and knew different people. Mary was active in the Science Fiction and

Fantasy Writers of America (SFWA), I was not. Equally important is the fact that Mary is very socially adept. Genteel even.

I, on the other hand, tend to be more like a bear that has somehow learned to put on pants. When I show up at parties, it's usually because there's food there. I wander around in a bemused sort of way, grunting and snuffling. Then, typically, I either fall asleep or wander away before I cause too much damage.

The first time I remember chatting with Mary was back in 2011. We were both at World Fantasy Convention in San Diego, and ended up drifting into conversation with each other. After a while, the conversation wandered into writing, which isn't that strange, when you think about it.

I admitted I was fairly obsessive about the words that I used in my books. I didn't feel comfortable using the word "spartan" for example, because in my world, there was never a Sparta. I was fine with the word "rubbery" as there is vulcanized rubber, but I'd avoid a word like "comrade" as it sounds too Russian to the English-speaker's ear.

"That sort of thing drives me crazy, too. So . . . " Mary said. "For my Regency novels, I made a Jane Austen spellcheck dictionary from her complete works. If one of my novels uses a word that isn't in that dictionary, it gets flagged and I look it up to see if it was in use in Regency England." She cocked her head slightly. "Did you know they apparently didn't have wastebaskets?"

That's the point at which I thought to myself, I need to spend more time with this woman. She is my kind of crazy.

So I DID. And she was. And it was lovely.

No. WAIT. Apparently that wasn't the first time we met.

I just checked with Mary, and she reminded me that we'd actually met the summer before at Penguicon. I remember now, that was the convention where she told me one of the funniest stories I've ever heard about how she'd traumatized a bunch of children with an (admittedly accidental) perverse puppet show.

So I'm at the convention, hanging out in the bar with a few other writers, and John Scalzi was giving me shit about having one of the biggest fantasy clichés ever in the first chapter of *Name of the Wind*: stew.

I countered with the well-known fact that stew was both delicious and period appropriate for my novel.

John said that was true, but it was still no excuse for using the phrase, "hearty stew."

"I did not," I said. "I might have put stew in my book, but I did not write *hearty stew*."

While we were going back and forth like this, Mary had quietly picked up my book and was thumbing through the first scene. "Here it is," she said. *"A hearty, filling stew."*

As I've said, words are important to me. And because of this, I was mortified. Not just the kind of embarrassment where you realize your fly is down, but the sort where you realize your fly has been down all day, including when you shook hands with the president, and someone took a picture and put it up on the internet.

Then she laughed. "No—You're fine. I just made it up."

So yes. Mary is a liar. A good one. I respect that.

YEARS LATER, I invited Mary into a little scheme I was hatching. After years of resisting, I was ready to join Twitter, but I wanted to have some fun doing it.

So I created six identical Twitter accounts and invited five writers to come and impersonate me. I made a game of it, asking if people could guess who the real Pat Rothfuss is.

Mary was one of the first that I asked. To make a long, humiliating story marginally shorter: she won. Not by a little bit, either. Decisively.

Crushingly. While it's true I came in second place, the simple fact is that she ran circles around me. She got three times as many votes as I did. If that wasn't bad enough, Twitter itself verified her account three times over the two weeks we were running the contest.

Have I mentioned that Mary can write yet? She can write. She's really, really good at writing.

OVER THE YEARS, I've come to know Mary better and better, and one of the things that delights me is how little we have in common. Mary spent ten years as a touring puppeteer. She's a professional audiobook narrator and voice actor. She understands the technological and socioeconomic underpinnings of clothing. (Yes. I made that pun on purpose, and I'm not going to apologize.)

Mary appreciates whiskey and wine as a connoisseur. Mary groks Regency England, while I would be hard pressed to tell you what time period that really is (though I'm pretty sure it's somewhere in the 1800s). She writes award-winning short fiction.

When I need help with any of these things, or any of a dozen others I could name, I call Mary. She's given me advice about how to survive on tour. I've picked her brain about how clothing evolves in a society, and what it indicates about culture. And I've picked her brain about what exactly a short story is and how to write one.

This last one still eludes me. Don't hold it against her. I seem to have an innate deficiency in that particular area.

The humorous implications of asking me to write an introduction to a collection of short fiction are pretty obvious. But it actually makes it much easier for me to sing Mary's praises. I have sought this subtle art and never found it. Mary has. She's good at this sort of thing.

One of my favorite things about this collection is that it's arranged (more or less) chronologically. That means as you read, you get to see how Mary's writing has progressed over the years. From her earlier writing to her more recent award-winning stories.

I don't know about you, but it does me good to see that she didn't spring fully-formed from the head of Zeus, writing award-winning short fiction.

The other thing I like about this collection is that it shows her versatility in a way people only familiar with her novels haven't seen. In these pages you will find traditional fantasy. Historical fiction. Science fiction of both hard and soft varieties.

So. Enough from me. You're not here to read me, you're here to read Mary.

Patrick Rothfuss

P. S. I promise it's really me writing this, not Mary impersonating me.

P. P. S. Probably.

P. P. P. S. Seriously though. It's really me.

The Bound Man

LIGHT DAPPLED through the trees in the family courtyard, painting shadows on the paving stones. Li Reiko knelt by her son to look at his scraped knee.

"I just scratched it." Nawi squirmed under her hands.

"Maybe Mama will show you her armor after she heals it." Her daughter, Aya, leaned over her shoulder trying to understand the healing.

Nawi stopped wiggling. "Really?"

Reiko shot her daughter a look. But her little boy's dark eyes were upturned and shining with excitement. She smiled. "Really." What did tradition matter? "Now let me heal your knee."

He held his leg out for her, bloodstained knee showing through his trousers. She laid her hand on the shallow wound.

"Ow."

Reiko shook her head. "Shush." She closed her eyes and rose in the dark space behind them.

In her mind's eye, Reiko took her time with the ritual, knowing it took less outside time than it appeared. In a heartbeat, green fire flared out to the walls of her mind. She let herself dissolve into it as she focused on healing her son.

When the wound closed beneath her hand, she rose back to the surface of her mind. "There." She tousled Nawi's hair. "That wasn't so bad was it?"

"It tickled." He wrinkled his nose. "Will you show me your armor now?"

She sighed. She should not encourage his interest in the martial arts. "Watch."

Pulling the smooth black surface out of the ether, she manifested her armor. It sheathed her like silence in the night. Aya watched with anticipation for the day when she earned her own armor. Nawi's face—his face cut Reiko's heart like a new blade. Sharp yearning for something he would never have filled his face.

"Can I see your sword?"

She let her armor vanish into thought. "No." Reiko brushed his hair from his eyes. "It's my turn to hide, right?"

HALLDÓR TWISTED in his saddle, trying to ease the kinks out of his back. When the questing party reached the Parliament, he would be able to remove the weight hanging between his shoulders.

With each step his horse took across the moss-covered lava field, the strange blade bumped against his spine, reminding him that he carried a legend on his back. None of the runes or entrails he had read before their quest had foretold the ease with which they fulfilled the first part of the prophecy. They had found the Chooser of the Slain's narrow blade wrapped in linen, buried beneath an abandoned elf-house. In that dark room, the sword's hard silvery metal—longer than any of their bronze swords—had seemed to shine with the light of the moon.

Lárus pulled his horse alongside Halldór. "Will the ladies be waiting for us, do you think?"

Halldór laughed. "Maybe for you, my lord, but not for me."

"Nonsense. Women love the warrior-priest. 'Strong and sensitive.'" He snorted through his mustache. "Just comb your hair so you don't look like a straw man."

A horse screamed behind them. Halldór turned, expecting to see its leg in one of the thousands of holes between the rocks. He caught his breath. Armed men swarmed from the gullies between the rocks, hacking at the riders. Bandits.

Halldór spun his horse to help Lárus and the others fight off the bandits.

Lárus shouted. "Protect the sword."

Halldór cursed at the Duke's command and turned his horse from the fight, driving it as fast as he could across the rocks. Behind him, men cried out as they fought to protect his escape. His horse twisted as it galloped along the narrow paths between stones. It stopped abruptly, avoiding a chasm. Halldór turned to look back.

Scant lengths ahead of the bandits, Lárus rode, slumped in his saddle. Blood stained his cloak. The other men hung behind Lárus, protecting the Duke as long as possible.

Behind them, the bandits closed the remaining distance across the lava fields.

Halldór kicked his horse's side, driving it around the chasm. His horse stumbled sickeningly beneath him. Its leg snapped between rocks. Halldór kicked himself free of the saddle as the horse screamed. As he rolled clear, the rocky ground slammed the sword into his back. His face passed over the edge of the chasm. Breathless, he pushed back from the drop.

As he scrambled to his feet, Lárus thundered up. Without wasting a beat, Lárus flung himself from the saddle and tossed Halldór the reins. "Get the Sword to Parliament!"

Halldór grabbed the reins, swinging himself into the saddle. The weight of the artifact on his back gave him no comfort. What did it matter, that they had found the sword, if they died returning it to the Parliament? "We have to use the sword!"

Lárus's right arm hung limply by his side, but he faced the bandits. "Go!"

Halldór yanked the sword free of its wrappings. For the first time in six thousand years, the light of the sun fell on the silvery blade bringing fire to its length. It vibrated in his hands.

The first bandit reached Lárus and forced him back.

Halldór chanted the runes of power, which would call the Chooser of the Slain.

Time stopped.

~

REIKO HID from her children, blending into the shadows of the courtyard with more urgency than she felt in combat. To do less would insult them.

"Ready or not, here I come!" Nawi spun away from the tree and sprinted past her hiding place. Aya turned more slowly and studied the courtyard. Reiko smiled as her daughter sniffed the air, looking for tracks. Her son crashed through the bushes, kicking leaves with each footstep.

She stifled the urge to shake her head at Nawi's appalling technique, as another branch cracked under his foot. She would have to speak with his tutor to find out what the woman was teaching him. He might be a boy, but that was no reason to neglect his education.

Aya found Reiko's initial footprints and tracked them, away from where she hid. Watching her daughter carefully, Reiko slid from her hiding place and walked across the courtyard to the fountain. This was a rule with her children; to make up for the size difference, she could not run.

She paced closer to the sparkling water, using its babble to cover her sounds. Nawi shouted, "Have you found her?"

"No, silly!" Aya shook her head and stopped. She put her tiny hands on her hips, staring at the ground. "Her tracks stop here."

She and her daughter were the same distance from the fountain, but on opposite sides of it. If Aya were paying attention, she would realize her mother had doubled back in her tracks and jumped from fountain to the paving stones encircling the grassy center of the courtyard. Reiko had time to take three more steps before Aya turned.

As her daughter turned, Reiko felt more than heard her son reach for her. She let herself fall forward, using gravity to drop beneath his hands. She rolled on her shoulder, somersaulting, then launched to her feet again as Aya ran toward her.

Nawi grabbed for her again. With a child on each side, Reiko danced and dodged her way closer to the fountain. She twisted from their grasp, laughing with them each time they missed her. Their giggles echoed through the courtyard.

The world tipped sideways and vibrated. Reiko stumbled as pain ripped through her spine. Nawi's hand clapped against her side.

Through the pounding in her head, she heard his voice shrill with joy. "I got her!"

Fire exploded in her eyes and the courtyard vanished from her sight.

TIME BEGAN AGAIN.

The sword in Halldór's hands thrummed with life. Fire from the sunset seemed to engulf the sword and rent the air. With a keening cry, the air opened and a form dropped through, silhouetted against a haze of fire. Horses and men screamed in terror.

When the fire died away, a woman stood between Halldór and the bandits.

Halldór's heart sank. Where was the Chooser of the Slain? Where was the warrior the sword was supposed to call?

A bandit snarled a laughing oath and rushed toward them. The others followed him with their weapons raised.

The woman snatched the sword from Halldór's hands. In that brief moment, when he stared at her wild face, he realized he had succeeded in calling Li Reiko, the Chooser of the Slain.

Then she turned. The air around her rippled with a heat haze as armor, dark as night, materialized around her body. He watched her dance with deadly grace, bending and twisting from the bandits' blows. Without seeming thought, with movement as precise as ritual, she danced with death as her partner. Her sword slid through the bodies of the bandits.

Halldór dropped to his knees giving thanks to the gods for sending her. He watched the point of her sword trace a line like the path of entrails on the church floor. The line of blood led to the next moment, the next, and the next—as if each man's death was predestined.

Then she turned her sword on him.

Her blade descended, burning with the fire of the setting sun. Jewels of blood clung to its length. If his blood was to be the price for saving Lárus, then so be it.

She stopped as if she had run into a wall, with the point touching his throat. Halldór's heart pounded as if his blood wanted to leap out to join the sword. Why had she stopped? Her arm trembled. Her teeth bared in a grimace, but she did not move the sword any closer.

Her face, half-hidden by her helm, was dark with rage. "Where am I?"

Holding still, Halldór said, "We are on the border of the Parliament lands, Li Reiko."

Her dark eyes, slanted beneath angry lids, widened. She backed away from them and her armor rippled, vanishing into thought. Skin, tanned like the smoothest leather stretched over her wide cheekbones. Her hair hung in a heavy, black braid down her back. Halldór's heart pounded.

Only the gods in sagas had hair that did not gleam with shades of the All-Father's sun. Had he needed proof that he had called the Chooser of the Slain, the inhuman black hair would have convinced him of that.

He bowed his head. "All praise to you. Grant us your blessings."

REIKO'S BREATH hissed from her. He knew her name. She thought she had dropped through a flaming portal into hell. But this demon with bulging eyes knew her name.

She had been ready to slay him as she had the others, but could not press her sword forward. As if a wall had protected him.

And now he asked for blessings.

"What blessings do you ask of me?" Reiko said. She controlled a shudder. What human had hair as pale as straw?

Straw lowered his bulging eyes to the ground. "Grant us, O Gracious One, the life of our Duke Lárus."

His gaze rested, not on the ground, but on the demon lying in front of him. This one, Lárus, had a wound deep in his shoulder. His blood was as red as any human's, but his face was pale as death.

She turned from Straw and wiped her sword on the thick moss, cleaning the blood from it. As soon as her attention seemed turned from them, Straw attended Lárus, the fallen demon. She kept her awareness on the sounds of his movement as she sought balance in the familiar task of caring for her weapon. By the gods! How had he come to have her sword? It had been in her rooms not ten minutes before when she was playing hide and seek with her children.

Panic almost took her. What had happened to her Aya and Nawi? She needed information, but to display ignorance to an enemy was a weakness which could kill surer than the sharpest blade. She considered. They wanted her aid. Could demons be bound by blood debt? She turned back to Straw.

"What price do you offer for this life?"

Straw raised his eyes; they were the color of the sky. "I offer my life to you, O Great One."

She set her lips. What good would vengeance do? Unless . . . "Do you offer blood or to serve me?"

He lowered his head again. "I submit to your will."

She jerked her head once in agreement. "You will serve me then. Do you agree to be my bound man?"

"I do."

"Good." She sheathed her sword. "What is your name?"

"Halldór Arnarsson."

"I accept your pledge." She dropped to her knees beside them and pushed the fabric from the wound on the fallen demon's shoulder. His shoulder was warm and finely molded. Laying her hands upon it, she pulled upon the reserves within herself and began to heal him. As her mind dove into the healing ritual, she realized he was human. She pushed the thought aside; she could not spare the concentration.

HALLDÓR GASPED as fire began to glow around Li Reiko's hands. He had read of the gods healing in the sagas, but it to bear witness was beyond his imagining.

The glow faded. She lifted her hands from Lárus's shoulder. The wound was gone. A narrow red line and the blood-soaked clothing remained. His breathing was slow and easy. Lárus opened his eyes as if he had only been sleeping.

But her face was drawn. "I have paid the price for your service, bound man." She lifted a hand to her temple. "The wound was deeper . . . " Her eyes rolled back in her head and she slumped to the ground.

Lárus grabbed Halldór by the shoulder. "What did you do?"

He shook him off and crouched next to her. She was breathing. "I saved your life."

"By binding yourself to a woman? Are you mad?"

"She just healed you. Healed! Look." Halldór pointed at her hair. "Look at her. This is Li Reiko."

"Li Reiko was a warrior."

He wanted to throttle Lárus. "You saw her. How long did it take her to kill six men?" He pointed at the carnage behind them. "Name one man who could do that."

Would it be sacrilege to move her? He grimaced. He would beg forgiveness if that were the case. "Let's move before the trolls come out."

Lárus nodded slowly, his eyes still on the bodies around them. "Makes you wonder, doesn't it?"

"What?"

"How many of the other sagas are true, too?"

Halldór frowned. "They're all true. They're our history."

THE SMELL OF MUTTON cooking invaded her dreamless sleep. Reiko pulled herself to consciousness. She lay under sheepskin, on a bed of straw ticking. The straw poked through the wool fabric to prick her bare skin. Straw. Her memory tickled her with an image of hair the color of straw. Halldór.

Only long practice kept her breath even. She lay with her eyes closed, listening to the sounds around her. She needed to learn as much as possible, before changing the balance by letting them know she was awake. A small room. An open fire. Women murmuring.

A hand placed a damp rag on her brow. The touch was light. The hand was small, likely a woman or a child.

The sheepskin's weight would telegraph her movement if she tried to grab the hand. Better to open her eyes and feign weakness, than to create an impression of threat. There was time for that later.

Reiko let her eyes flutter open. A girl bent over her. She showed the signs of the same demonic sculptor as Halldór. Her hair was the color of honey, her wild blue eyes started from her head. She stilled slightly when Reiko opened her eyes, but did not pull away.

Reiko forced herself to smile, and let a small crease of worry appear between her eyebrows. "Where am I?"

"In the women's quarters at the Parliament grounds."

Reiko sat up. The sheepskin fell away, letting the cool air caress her body. The girl averted her eyes. Conversation in the room stopped.

Interesting. They had a nudity taboo. She reached for the sheepskin and pulled it over her torso. "What is your name?"

"Mara Arnarsdottir."

Arnar's daughter. So she was likely to be Halldór's sister. "Where are my clothes, Mara?"

The girl turned to a low bench next to the bed and picked up a folded bundle of cloth. "I washed them for you."

If Mara had time to wash and dry her clothes, Reiko must have been unconscious for several hours. The wound had been deeper than she thought. "Thank you for washing them." She studied at the empty bench. "Where is my sword?"

"My—my brother has it."

Rage swarmed up Reiko's veins like the fire that had brought her here. She waited for the heat to pass, then smiled at Mara. "Thank you." Standing, she began to dress.

Behind Mara, the other women shifted nervously as if Reiko were about to cross a line. As Reiko pulled her boots on, she asked, "Where is he?"

Mara looked behind her for support, then back at Reiko. "He's at the Parliament."

"Which is where?" The eyes of the other women felt like heat on her skin. Ah. Parliament contained the line she should not cross, and they clearly would not answer her. She smiled at Mara. "Thank you for your kindness."

As she strode from the room she kept her senses fanned out, waiting for one of them to stop her. They hung back, almost as if they were afraid of her.

The women's quarters fronted on a narrow twisting path lined with low turf and stone houses. The end of the street opened onto a large raised circle. The circle was perhaps a hundred paces across and lined around its perimeter with stone benches.

Men sat on the stone benches, but women stayed below. Lárus spoke in the middle of the circle. Halldór stood by his side, with her sword in his hands. Standing in the shadow by a house, Reiko watched them. They towered above her, but their movements were clumsy and oafish like a trained bear. Nawi had better training than any here.

Her son. Sudden anxiety and rage filled her lungs, but to give into rage would invite rash decisions. She forced the anger away.

With effort, she turned her focus to the men. They had no awareness of their mass, only of their size—and an imperfect grasp of that.

As she watched, Halldór lifted his head as if he smelled something. His eyes narrowed and his grip tightened on the scabbard of her sword. As if it were guided by strings, his head turned slowly till he stared at her. Reiko stepped out of the shadows and his nostrils flared.

Halldór dropped to his knees and held her sword out to her. In mid-sentence, Lárus looked at Halldór, then turned slowly to Reiko. Surprise crossed his face, but he bowed his head.

"Li Reiko, you honor us with your presence."

Reiko climbed onto the stone circle. As she crossed to Halldór, a shaggy bear of a man rose to his feet. "I will not sit here, while there is a woman in the Parliament's circle."

Lárus spun to face the man. "Ingolfur, this is no mortal woman."

Reiko's attention sprang forward. What did they think she was, if not mortal?

"You have darkened a trollop's hair with soot." Ingolfur crossed his arms. "You expect me to believe she's a god?"

Her pulse quickened. What were they saying? Lárus flung his cloak back, showing the torn and blood-soaked cloth at his shoulder. "We were set upon by trolls. My arm was cut half off and she healed it." He pointed at her. His pale face was flushed red. "I tell you this is Li Reiko, returned to the world."

She understood the words, but it was as if they had no meaning. Each sentence out of their mouths raised a thousand questions in her mind.

"Ha." Ingolfur spat on the ground. "Your quest sought a warrior to defeat the Troll King."

This she could understand.

"And if I do, what price do you offer?"

Lárus opened his mouth but Ingolfur crossed the circle and leaned toward Reiko. Beside her, Halldór tensed. Reiko waited.

"You pretend to be the great warrior?" Ingolfur reached for her, as if she were a doll he could pick up. Before his hand touched her shoulder, she took his wrist in her hands, pulling on it as she twisted. She drove her shoulder into his belly and used his mass to flip him as she stood.

She had thought these were demons, but by their actions, they were men, full of swagger and rash judgment. She waited. He would attack her again.

Ingolfur bellowed behind her. Reiko focused on his sounds and the small changes in the air. As he reached for her, she twisted away from his hands and used his force to send him stumbling from the center of the circle. The circle of men broke into laughter.

She waited again.

It might take time but Ingolfur would learn his place.

Halldór stepped in front of Reiko and faced Ingolfur. "Great Ingolfur, surely you can see no mortal woman could face our champion."

Reiko cocked her head slightly. Her bound man was clever to appeal to the oaf's vanity.

Lárus looked around the circle of men and pointed to her sword in Halldór's hands. "Who here still doubts we have completed our quest?" They shifted on their benches uneasily. "We have fulfilled the first part of prophecy by returning Li Reiko to the world."

What prophecy had her name in it? There might be a bargaining chip here.

"You promised us a mighty warrior, the Chooser of the Slain." Ingolfur snarled, "Not a woman."

It was time to act. If they wanted a god, then they should have one. "Have no doubt. I can defeat the Troll King." She let her armor flourish around her. Ingolfur took an involuntary step back. Around the circle she heard a collection of gasps and sharp cries.

She cocked her head and drew her sword from Halldór's hands. "Who here will test me?"

Lárus dropped to his knees in front of her. "The Chooser of the Slain!"

In almost the same breath, Halldór knelt and cried, "Li Reiko!"

Around the circle, men followed suit. On the ground below, women and children knelt in the dirt. They cried her name. In the safety of her helm, Reiko scowled. Playing at godhood was a dangerous lie.

She lowered her sword and looked around the circle. "But there is a price. You must return me to the heavens."

Halldór raised his head. His eyes wider than she thought possible. "How, my lady?"

She shook her head. "You know the gods grant nothing easily. They say you must return me. You must learn how. Who here accepts that price for your freedom from the trolls?"

She sheathed her sword and let her armor vanish back into thought. Turning on her heel, she strode off the Parliament's circle. Behind her, the circle erupted into knots of discussion.

The Bound Man

HALLDÓR WATCHED Li Reiko leave the Parliament circle and clambered to his feet to follow her. Lárus grabbed him by the arm. "What does she mean, return her?"

Ingolfur tossed up his hands. "If that is the price I will pay it gladly. To be rid of the Troll King and her at the same time would be a joy."

"Is it possible?"

Men crowded around him, asking him theological questions, and questions of the sagas which he found difficult to answer. He had not cast a rune-stone or read an entrail since they started for the elf-house a week ago. "She would not ask if it were impossible." He swallowed. "I will study the problem and return to you."

Lárus clapped him on the back. "Good man." When he turned back to the throng surrounding them, Halldór slipped away.

He found Li Reiko surrounded by children. The women hung back, watching her, too shy to come closer. But the children crowded up close. Halldór could hardly believe she had killed six men as easily as carding wool. He had the space of a breath to watch her playing peek-a-boo with a small child before she saw him. Her face had been open with delight and pain; the shutters closed when she saw him.

She tilted her head back to meet his eyes. "I want to read the prophecy."

He blinked in surprise. Then his heart lifted; maybe she was going to show him how to pay her price. "It is stored in the church."

Reiko looked back at the child and brushed its hair away from its eyes, then fell into step beside him. Halldór forced himself to walk at a sedate pace to the church. He led her into the nave of the church, and then into the room where the holy books were stored. His palms were damp with sweat as he pulled the drawing off the shelf and unrolled it on the table.

He did not look at the careful rendering of entrails. He watched her. Her face was impassive; she turned to him and said, "I want to hear your explanation of this."

He pointed at the arc of sclera. "This represents the heavens, and the overlap here," he pointed at the bulge of the lower intestine, "means time of conflict. I interpreted the opening in the bulge to mean specifically the Troll King. This pattern of blood means—"

She crossed her arms. "You clearly understand your discipline. Tell me the prophecy in plain language."

"Oh." He looked at the drawing of the entrails again. "Well, in a time of conflict—which is now—the only thing that can overcome the Troll King is a legendary warrior. The Chooser of the Slain." He pointed at shining knot around the lower intestine. "See how this chokes off the Troll King. That means you win the battle."

"And how did you know the legendary warrior was—is—me?"

"I cross-referenced with our histories and you were the one that fit all the criteria."

She shivered. "Show me the history. I want to understand how you deciphered this."

Halldór pulled the volume of history from the shelves. He placed it in front of Li Reiko and opened the heavy pages.

In the autumn before the Collapse, Li Reiko, greatest of the warriors, trained Li Nawi and his sister Aya in the ways of Death. In the midst of the training, a curtain of fire split Nawi from Aya and when they came together again, Li Reiko was gone. Though they were frightened they understood that the Chooser of the Slain had taken a rightful place in heaven.

Reiko trembled, her control gone. "What is this?"

"It is our history." Halldór knelt beside her and traced the letters. "Since the gods left the Earth, we have kept records of histories and prophecies." He nodded at the bookshelves behind them. Reiko turned to look at the ranks of stone shelves lined with thick leather bindings. "The sagas are our heritage and charge."

Reiko turned her eyes blindly from the page. "I am your history?"

"You are a legend. See? Your son Li Nawi recorded your triumphs in battle."

He flipped the pages forward. "Here. This is how we knew where to look for your sword." He paused with his hand over the letters. "I deciphered the clues to find it."

Reiko pushed away from the table. "You caused the curtain of fire?" She wanted to vomit her fear at his feet.

Halldór shook his head, his face drained of color. "No. The prophecy foretold that you would return in our time of need."

"I dropped through fire this morning." *And when they came together again, Li Reiko was no more.* What had it been like for Aya and Nawi to see their mother disappear in the curtain of fire?

"You were in the heavens with the gods."

"That's something you tell a grieving child! I was playing hide and seek with my children and you took me from them."

"I-I didn't, I—" His face turned gray. "Forgive me, Great One."

"I am not a god!" She pushed him, all control gone. He tripped over a bench and dropped to the floor. "Send me back."

"I cannot."

Her sword flew from its sheath before she realized she held it. "Send me back!" She held it to his neck. Her arms trembled with the desire to run it through him. But it would not move.

"You ripped me away from my children." She leaned on the blade, digging her feet into the floor.

He shook his head. "It had already happened."

Her sword crept closer, pricking a single drop of blood from his neck. "Because of you."

She leaned against a force that kept her from driving the sword home. What kept her from him?

Halldór lay on his back. "I'm sorry. I didn't know . . . I was following the prophecy."

Reiko stepped back, gasping. Prophecy. A wall of predestination. She dropped to the bench again, empty, and cradled her sword to her. "How long ago . . . ?"

"Six thousand years."

She closed her eyes. This was why he could not return her. He had not brought her from somewhere else. He had brought her through time. If she were trapped here, if she could never see her children again then it did not matter if these were human or demons. She was banished to Hell.

"What do the sagas say about my children?"

Halldór rolled to his knees. "I can show you." His voice was gentle.

"No." She ran her hand down the blade of her sword. Its edge whispered against her skin, still sharp. She touched her wrist to the blade. It would be easy. "Read it to me."

She heard him get to his feet. The pages of the heavy book shuffled.

HALLDÓR SWALLOWED and began to read. "And so it came to pass that Li Aya and Li Nawi were raised unto adulthood by their tutor."

A tutor raised them, because he had pulled their mother away. He shook his head. It had happened six thousand years ago.

"But when they reached adulthood, they each claimed the right of Li Reiko's sword."

They fought over the sword, which he had used to call her, not out of the heavens, but from across time. Halldór shivered and focused on the page.

"Li Aya challenged Li Nawi, saying Death was her birthright. But Nawi, on hearing this, scoffed and said he was a Child of Death. And saying so, he took Li Reiko's sword and the gods smote Li Aya with their fiery hand, thus granting Li Nawa the victory."

Halldór's entrails twisted as if the gods were reading them. He had read these sagas since he was a boy. He believed them, but he had not thought they were real. He looked at Li Reiko. She held her head in her lap and rocked back and forth.

He wiped his brow. For all his talk of prophecies, he was the one who had found the sword and invoked it. "Then all men knew he was the true Child of Death. He raised an army of men and—"

"Stop."

"I'm sorry." He would slaughter a thousand sheep if one would tell him how to undo his crime.

He ran his hand across the pages. In all the histories, Li Reiko never appeared after the wall of fire, except in prophecy. He closed the book and took a step toward her. "But the price you asked . . . I can't send you back."

Reiko drew a shuddering breath and looked up. "I have already paid the price for you." Her eyes reflected his guilt. "You will have to find another hero to kill the Troll King."

His pulse rattled forward like a panicked horse. "There isn't anyone else. The prophecy points to you."

"Gut another sheep, bound man." She stood. "I won't help you." Reiko's arm hurt from the effort holding back a blow. She spun on her heel and walked away from him. "I release you from your debt."

"But—" He scrambled to his feet. "It's unpaid. I owe you a life."

"You cannot pay the price I ask." She turned and touched her sword to his neck. He flinched. "I couldn't kill you when I wanted to." She cocked her head, and traced the point of the blade around his neck, almost, but not quite, touching him. "What destiny do you have to fulfill?"

"Nothing. There are no prophecies about me."

She snorted. "How nice to be without a destiny." Sheathing her sword, she walked away from him.

He followed her. "Where are you going?" She spun and drove her fist into his midriff. He grunted and folded over. Panting with anger, Reiko pulled her sword out and swung at his side with the flat of the blade. It connected with a resounding crack. Halldór did not cry out.

She swung the blade again, but the invisible wall of force stopped her. He had to live, but she could hurt him. She turned the blade again, so the flat paddled against his ribs. The breath hissed out of him, but he did not move. He knelt in front of her, waiting for the next blow. His face was red and his eyes shone with religious ecstasy. Reiko backed away from him.

"Do not follow me."

He scrabbled forward on his knees. "Then tell me where you're going, so I won't meet you there by accident."

"Maybe that is your destiny." She spun and walked away.

He did not follow her.

LI REIKO CHASED her shadow out of the Parliament lands. It stretched behind her in the golden light of sunrise, racing her across the moss-covered lava. The wind whipping across the treeless plain seemed to push her like a child late for dinner.

Surrounded by the people in the Parliament lands, Reiko's anger had overwhelmed her. It buried her grief, and she needed to deal with that before she could make a rational decision. Whatever Halldór thought her destiny was, she saw only two paths in front of her—make a life here to replace the one he had stolen from her, or to join her children in the only way left to her. It was not a path to choose rashly, but the temptation shone brightly.

As she walked, small shrubs and grasses broke the green with patches of bright reds and golds, as if someone had unrolled a carpet on the ground. Heavy undulations creased the land with deep crevices. Some held water reflecting the sky, others dropped down to a lower level of moss and soft grasses, and some were as dark as the inside of a cave.

When the sun crossed the sky and painted the land with long shadows, Reiko sought shelter from the wind in one of the crevices in the ground. The moss cradled her with the warmth of the earth.

She pulled thoughts of Aya and Nawi close to her. In her memory, they laughed as they tried to catch her. Sobs pushed their way past Reiko's reserves. Each cry shattered her. She wrapped her arms around herself and gave in to the grief. Her children were dead. It did not matter if they had grown up, she had not been there. They were six-thousand years dead. Inside her head she battled her grief. Her fists pounded against the walls of her mind. *"No! no no nonono no."* Her brain filled itself with that silent syllable.

All because this man had decided a disemboweled sheep meant he had to rip her out of time. She pressed her face against the velvet moss wanting the earth to absorb her.

She heard a sound.

Training quieted her breath in a moment. Breath stilled, Reiko lifted her head from the moss and listened. Footsteps—probably a man's—crept across the earth above her. She manifested her armor and rolled silently to her feet. If Halldór had followed her, she would play the part of a man and seek revenge.

In the light of the moon, a figure, larger than a man, crept toward her. A troll. Behind him, at a distance, a gang of other trolls watched. Reiko counted them and considered the terrain. It was safer to hide, but her bones ached to fight. She left her sword sheathed and slunk out of the crevice in the ground. Her argument was not with them.

Flowing across the moss, she let the uneven shadows mask her until she reached a standing mound of stones. She stood in their shadow and watched the trolls. The wind carried their stink to her.

The single troll reached the crevice she had sheltered in. His arm darted down like a bear fishing. When his hand touched nothing but moss, he roared with astonishment.

The other trolls laughed. "Got away, did she?"

One of them poked the others and said, "Mucker was just smelling his own crotch is all."

"Yah, sure. He didn't get enough in the Hall and goes around thinking he smells more."

They had taken human women. Reiko felt a stabbing pain in her loins; she could not let that stand.

Mucker whirled. "Shut up! I know I smelled a woman."

"Then where'd she go?" The troll snorted the air. "Don't smell one now."

The other lumbered away. "Let's go. I got some beddin' to do."

"Yah, let's get back while some of 'em are still fresh."

Mucker slumped and followed the other trolls. Reiko eased out of the shadows. She was a fool, but would not hide while women were raped.

She hung back, and let the wind carry their sounds and scents to her as she tracked the trolls back to their Hall.

The moon had sunk to a handspan above the horizon as they reached the Troll Hall. The night was silent except for the sounds of revelry. Trolls stood on either side of the great stone doors.

Reiko crouched in the shadows. Trolls wandered in and out in drunken stupor. Even with alcohol slowing their movement, there were too many of them.

If she could goad them into taking her on one at a time she could get past the sentries, but only if no other trolls came. The sound of swordplay would draw a crowd faster than crows to carrion.

A harness jingled in the dark.

Reiko's head snapped in the direction of the sound. Trolls did not ride horses.

She shielded her eyes from the light coming out of the Troll Hall. As her eyes adjusted, a man on horseback resolved out of the dark. He sat twenty or thirty horselengths away, far enough to be invisible to the trolls outside the Hall. Reiko eased over the ground, senses wide.

The horse shifted its weight when it smelled her. The man on its back put his hand on its neck to calm it. The light from the Troll Hall hinted at the planes on his face. Halldór. Her lips tightened. He had followed her. Reiko warred with an irrational desire to call the trolls down on them.

She needed him. Halldór, with his drawings and histories, might know what the inside of the Hall looked like.

Praying he would have sense enough to be quiet, she stepped out of the shadows and stood next to him. He jumped as she appeared, but stayed silent.

He swung off his horse and leaned close. His whisper was hot in her ear. "What are you doing here?"

He turned his head, letting her breathe an answer to him. "I heard them talking. They have women inside."

He nodded. "I know." He looked behind them and she saw, for the first time, dried blood covered the left side of his face. He turned back to her. "We should move away to talk."

She nodded. Something had happened since she left the Parliament lands. She followed him as he took his horse by the reins and led it away from the Troll Hall. Its hooves were bound with sheepskin so it made no sound on the rocks.

Halldór limped lightly on his left side. Reiko's heart beat in her chest as if she were running. The trolls had women prisoners. Halldór bore signs of battle. Trolls must have attacked the Parliament. They walked in silence until the sounds of the Troll Hall dwindled to nothing.

Halldór stopped. "There was a raid." He stared at nothing, his jaw clenched. "While I was gone . . . I came back and—" His voice broke like a boy's. "They have my sister."

Mara. "Halldór, I'm sorry." Anger slipped away from her. Reiko looked for other riders. "Who came with you?"

He shook his head. "No one. They're guarding the walls in case the trolls come back." He touched the side of his face. "I tried to make them."

"Why did you come?"

"To get Mara back."

"There are too many of them, bound man." She scowled. "Even if you could get inside, what are you going to do? Challenge the Troll King to single combat?" Her words seemed to resonate in her skull. Reiko closed her eyes, dizzy with the turns the gods spun her in. When she opened them, Halldór was watching her. His lips were parted as if he had begun a prayer. Reiko swallowed. "When does the sun rise?"

"In another hour."

She turned back to the Hall. In an hour the trolls could not chase them. She reached up and began to undo her braid.

Halldór stared as her long hair began to flirt with the wind. She smiled at the question in his eyes. "I have a prophecy to fulfill."

REIKO STUMBLED into the torchlight. Her hair hung loose and wild about her face. She clutched Halldór's cloak to her.

One of the troll sentries looked up. "Hey. Lookie. A dolly."

Reiko contorted her face with fear and screamed. The other troll laughed. "She don't seem taken with you, do she?"

The first troll came closer. "She don't have to."

"Don't hurt me. Please, please . . . " Reiko backed away from him. When she was between the two, she whipped Halldór's cloak off, tangling it around the first troll's head. With her sword, she gutted the other. He dropped to his knees, trying to put his entrails back as she turned to the first. She slid her sword under the cloak, slicing along the base of his jaw.

Leaving them to die, Reiko entered the Hall. Mingled in the sounds of revelry, she could hear women crying.

Reiko kept her focus on the battle ahead. She would be out-matched in size and strength, but hoped wit and weapons would prevail. Her mouth twisted. She knew she would prevail. It was predestined.

A troll saw her. He lumbered closer. Reiko held up her sword, bright with blood. "I have met your sentries. Shall we dance as well?"

The troll checked his movement and squinted his beady eyes at her. Reiko walked past him. She kept her awareness on him, but another troll loomed in front of her.

"Where do you think you're going?"

"I am the Chooser of the Slain. I have come for your King."

The troll laughed and reached for her, heedless of her sword. She dodged under his grasp and slid her sword up to his neck. She held the point there. "I have come for your King. Not for you. Bring him to me."

She leapt back. His hand went to his throat and came away wet with blood.

Behind her, a bellow went up at the entry. Someone had found the sentries. Reiko kept her gaze on the troll in front of her, but her peripheral vision filled with trolls running. Footsteps behind her. Reiko spun and planted her sword in a troll's arm. The troll howled, backing away. Reiko shook her head. "I have come for your king."

She turned her back on them and walked toward the Hall. She had no chance of defeating all of them, but if she could goad the king into single combat, she stood a chance of leaving the Hall with the prisoners. When she entered the great Hall, whispers flew among the trolls there. In the words around her, Reiko heard the number of slain trolls mount.

The Troll King lolled on his throne. Mara, her face red with shame, serviced him.

Anger buzzed in Reiko's ears. She let it pass through her. "Troll King, I have come to challenge you."

The Troll King laughed like an avalanche of stone tearing down his Hall. "You! A dolly wants to fight?"

Reiko paid no attention to his words.

He was nearly twice her height. Leather armor, crusted with crude bronze scales, covered his body. The weight of feasting hung about his middle, but his shoulders bulged with muscle. If he connected a blow, she was dead. But he would be fighting gravity as well as her. Once he began a movement, it would take time for him to stop it and begin another.

Reiko raised her head, waiting for his laughter to die down. "I am the Chooser of the Slain. Will you accept my challenge?" She forced a smile to her lips. "Or are you afraid to dance with me?"

"I will grind you to paste, dolly. Then I will sweep over your lands, bed your women and eat your children for my breakfast."

"If you win, you may. Here are my terms. If I win, the prisoners go free."

He came down from his throne and leaned close to her. "If you win, we will never show shadow in human lands again."

"Will your people hold to that pledge when you are dead?"

He laughed. The stink of his breath boiled around her. He turned to the room. "Will you?"

The room rocked with the roar of their voices. "Aye."

The Troll King turned back to her. "And when you lose, I won't kill you till I've bedded you."

"Agreed. May the gods hear our pledge." Reiko manifested her armor.

As the night-black plates materialized around her, the Troll King bellowed. "What is this?"

"This?" She taunted him. "This is but a toy the gods have sent to play with you."

She smiled in her helm as he swung his heavy iron sword over his head and charged her. Stupid. Reiko stepped to the side, already turning as she let him pass her.

The dust swirled in his wake. She brought her sword hard against the gap in his armor above his boot. The blade jarred against bone. She yanked her sword free; blood coated it like a sheath.

The Troll King dropped to one knee, hamstrung. Without waiting, she vaulted up his back and wrapped her arms around his neck, like Aya riding piggyback. He flailed his sword through the air, trying to bend his arms back to reach her. She swung her sword around to his neck. His bellow changed to a gurgle as blood fountained in an arc, soaking the ground. Around them, trolls moaned in despair.

A heavy ache filled her breast. She whispered in his ear. "I have killed you without honor. I am a machine of the gods."

Reiko let gravity pull the Troll King down. The moans of the trolls rose to shrieks. She leapt off his body as it fell forward.

Before the dust settled around his body, Reiko pointed her sword at the nearest troll. "Release the prisoners."

REIKO WALKED into the dawn with women weeping and singing her praises. As they left the Troll Hall, Halldór dropped to his knees. Mara ran forward, weeping, to wrap her arms around his neck.

Reiko felt nothing. She listened to the rejoicing around her and could not join it. Why should she, when the victory was not hers? She walked away from the group of women.

Halldór chased her. "Lady, my life is already yours but my debt has doubled."

She knelt to clean her sword on the moss. "Then give me your firstborn child."

She could hear his breath hitch in his throat. "If that is your price."

Reiko raised her eyes to him. "No. That is a price I will not ask."

He knelt next to her, his blue eyes shining with excitement. "I know why you can't kill me."

"Good." She turned back to her sword. "When you fulfill your destiny let me know, so I can."

"I'm supposed to return your daughter to you."

Reiko's heart flooded with pain and hope. She fought for breath. "Do not toy with me, bound man."

"I'm not. After you went into the Hall, I began thinking about the sagas. It says 'and the gods smote Li Aya with their fiery hand.' I can bring Li Aya here."

Reiko sunk her fingers into the moss, clutching the earth. "You want to rip Aya out of time as well. If Nawi had not won, then the Collapse would not have happened."

"But." His voice was gentle. "It already did."

Reiko lifted her head, looking at the women, and the barren landscape beyond them. Everything she saw was result of her son's actions. Or were her son's actions the result of choices made here? She did not know if it mattered.

"Are there any prophecies about Aya?"

Halldór nodded. "She's destined to—"

Reiko put her hand on his mouth. "Don't. When she comes here, don't let her know she's bound to the will of the gods."

Chrysalis

Dear Grandma,

Your letters beat me to Husa and I've told the computer to dole them out at the intervals that you sent them. I got no idea why I'm telling you that, since there's zero chance you'll read this. Helps me focus, I guess.

I'm so wound up and . . . lonely. There. I admitted it. Just like you were worried I'd be. You don't even get the satisfaction of saying I told you so, do you?

Call me a fool, but I'm going to pretend I'm a knee-high girl again and tell you what's bothering me. For the last fourteen months I've been working on this documentary for one of the Husith's. It's supposed to help him after Chrysalis scrambles his memories, like it does for all Husiths.

Geroth's a good enough guy. Mind you, he looks like a mealworm on steroids, but that's not unusual around these parts. Humans are the minority here.

I wonder what you'd think of the Husiths. You'd probably think they were ugly creatures with hundreds of tiny fingers bristling from their underbellies. It's how they express their moods and provides traction as they inch through these massive underground cities. God, I wish you could hear them. They're real soft most of the time, but when they fight, they bray like sea-lions mating.

And Geroth's fighting all the time with his betrothed. I mean *all* the time. And here's the thing. I'm supposed to be recording this so he can remember it afterwards. But I mean, Geroth loves Iliath so I can't figure why he'd want to remember these knock-down drag-out fights they have. I know I'd like to forget mine.

The deal is that Iliath wants him to undergo Chrysalis and he doesn't want to even though he's way, way overdue. Totally unhealthy, even to my eye. Claims that no one besides him can understand this theory he's working on. I can't pretend to follow the equations but apparently his treatise has the potential to unlock the space between stars. I might even see the practical application of it within my lifetime. Heck, I could travel back to Earth without the hassle of cryosleep.

Although *that* seems pretty pointless. Even if Geroth could open a gateway between planets at this moment, you'd be dead—are in fact, already dead, despite your letters . . .

Right. Well, that morbid thought isn't helping at all.

So, today, in the middle of one of their spats, the door opens. I turn the camera to frame Qyo, this post-Chrysalis Husith.

He still shocks me. I mean, three months ago he was a grub like the others, but now Qyo has limbs like a praying mantis and these colors swirl under his exoskeleton like the rainbows in an oil slick. All those tiny fingers transformed during Chrysalis into a fringe like spun silk. Beautiful every time, as if he were made for the camera.

Hang on, let me paste in my notes:

Geroth turned to the door and barked, "What!"

Qyo stiffened his filaments in shock. His golden eyes passed over Van and me, ignoring us as if we were pieces of furniture. When he saw Iliath, his filaments fell gracefully. "Greetings, Iliath."

(Oh, Grandma, I wish you could hear him. It's like listening to a living flute.)

Iliath's thousand fingers drooped in greeting. "Greetings, Artist Qyo."

"Is my brother ignoring you again?"

Iliath shook her heavy head, spreading her fingers wide. "No. Not at all."

"Ha." Geroth snorted at Iliath. "I let distraction enter the room when there is no time." He turned his back on her. "I shall make note of this in my journals. You may be certain of that."

Iliath's fingers curled in as if Geroth had struck her. "What good will it do you, if you have no mind after?"

He hissed at Iliath. "I make note of your concern."

Qyo: "I have come with wonderful news."

Iliath: "What is it, Artist?"

"The council has purchased my latest composition."

Iliath: "Wonderful!"

"Please, join me for dinner." Qyo folded his arms across his body and inclined his head.

Geroth snorted. "I have much work to do."

"I am certain you do, but your journal entries need not be solely about work. I reread my larval notes and am saddened by how little pleasure I sought."

"You loved your work."

"Did I?" Qyo spread his arms. "It seems loathsome now."

It shocks me, sometimes, how different Qyo is now than before Chrysalis. Not just the physical changes, but his attitude. He and Geroth had been closer than any brothers I had known, even if they are giant larvae. Now it seems as if Qyo was only being dutiful to a memory.

Geroth crept closer to him. "You were a brilliant mathematician." He tossed a pad on the ground at Qyo's feet. "Look at what I've done with our work."

Qyo took a step back. "I have no interest. I have come with an invitation for dinner, that is all."

"Look at it, and I will join you. It will save me the effort of proofreading."

"No." Qyo retreated to the door. "I have no time for such larval things."

"You no longer understand such things." Geroth glared at Qyo. "Is this what you want for me?"

"I am simply asking you to dinner."

"Take Iliath then; she is practically an adult in her thoughts. I have work to do."

"Please come, Geroth." Iliath placed her tail over his, pleading with him.

Geroth looked at the floor. "The larva works so the adult can play."

Iliath pulled her tail away. "Will you ever grow up?" She crept to the door where Qyo stood. Then she stared into the camera. "Vanessa, will you join us?"

I jerked away from the eyepiece and gaped over the barrel of the camera. Iliath held my gaze, against the conventions of etiquette towards documentarians. A flush rushed up my neck, like my menopause had come early. Russ's mouth hung open. A documentarian was supposed to record, not participate in the action.

"No. Thank you." I looked at the floor, mimicking their gesture for apology. How dare she try to bring me into this! But I was a professional; you would have been proud. I kept my voice calm. "I, too, have work to do."

"I doubt you understand the damage your work does." Iliath slid out the door, her marble body undulating down the hall.

Great exit, if Iliath had not breached the fourth wall by talking to the camera. By talking to me.

Qyo spread his limbs in surrender and exited with a graceful flourish. When the door closed behind Qyo, Geroth's cracked hide shivered like somebody was walking on his grave. He turned to me. "You may stop recording. I will work on my treatise this evening. There is no need for more footage of that. Go home. Rest."

Russ, my sound guy, started stowing his gear.

I had this momentary leap of excitement like a child promised a day off from school, but reality snared me. What would I do with an evening off? "Are you sure?"

"I promise, I will do nothing memorable." Geroth twitched. "Besides, you have stationary cameras throughout my home."

"I don't mind staying."

"I make note of your concern." Geroth turned his back on us. "If I want to forget this evening, it is my prerogative."

So, that was that. I came back to my apartment. Each of the four rooms would house a family of five back on crowded Earth. It may not have the history of our family home, but at least I don't have to rent the other rooms out to anyone.

Speaking of . . . have you found a new boarder yet? I guess you'll tell me when you do, or—well, you know what I mean.

At times, the emptiness of these rooms overwhelms me. Lately, I've been opening the channels to Geroth's home and letting his activity fill the space while I work.

The evening routine is pretty much the same every night. I'll fast-forward through the day from one relevant point to the next and write a summary of each. The hours flow by like minutes as I lose myself in the process of logging the day's footage.

Intercut with these, in my mind, are the live images from Geroth's home. It's usually just Geroth scribbling on his treatise, but not tonight. Which is why I started writing this letter.

Geroth set down his treatise. He stopped in front of his medicine and stared at it for a few minutes, then turned and went to bed without taking his hormone treatment.

I had a crazy moment where I wanted to call him, to be certain he meant to do that, and only stopped myself by focusing on my job—to record, not to participate.

Briefly, I considered following his lead and going to bed, but I liked the idea of actually getting caught up on the backlog of footage.

When I finally finished logging everything, I leaned back in my chair and rubbed my eyes. Geroth's home, dark and quiet, lulled me into drowsiness. My eyes glazed over as I stared at the screens and sleep seemed moments away.

And then, on the monitor, the outer door of Geroth's apartment opened. Iliath entered the apartment and crept from room to room.

I sat forward in my chair as she picked up Geroth's treatise. My heart raced as I tracked Iliath through the apartment to the kitchen. She glanced furtively around her and buried Geroth's treatise in the compost bin.

I stared at the screen, mouth open in a silent cry, as Iliath snuck out.

In my years as a documentarian, I have kept the sacred distance from my subjects even when I long to become part of the action. Geroth's work means everything to him.

But nothing I do will change Iliath's action, right? Geroth will discover it himself when he gets up. It's just because I'm lonely that I'm thinking about interfering. I've got the monitors turned off now, but the temptation is hanging right above me.

I've been lying in bed for hours, staring at the ceiling, as my memory replayed Iliath's actions in a montage. Finally, gave up on sleep and thought I'd write to you, see if I could sort my brain out. Maybe I'll treat myself and open one of your letters early.

Love,
Vanessa

DEAR VAN,

I finally found a boarder who fits into the household. Her name is Kim Perkins and she's an archaeologist. She's delighted to live in a house with history.

You should have seen her eyes widen when I told her how long the house had been in the family. And the stove! Lands, you would have thought she had died and gone to heaven.

How is your work going? (I know it's foolish asking you questions, but I do that with your grandfather too. Bear with an old woman's fantasies.)

Now don't you worry about me, you're a good girl but you're a worrier so cut it out. Be well and do good work.

Love,
Grandma Tucker

DEAR GRANDMA,

I've lost my mind.

This morning, Russ was leaning outside Geroth's door when I arrived. I stepped on the door chime to let Geroth know we were there.

And we waited.

And waited.

Russ stretched and grinned. "Nothing like a night off, huh?"

"Yeah, I managed to log everything." By this point I'm already starting to worry, but I kept telling myself that I had done what I was supposed to do. Worked. I had not interfered.

"Crazy woman." He shook his head.

Maybe I was. "He didn't have a meeting this morning did he?" Geroth still had not come to the door. Which was freaking me out, 'cause he is Mr. Punctuality. I should have checked his cameras again before I left the house.

"Nah." Russ ran his hand through his hair and reseated his cap. "It's business as usual today. Lots of audio of writing and one or two arguments. Dang, I never thought I'd miss the days when he was singing love songs to her. Have I played you my rave mix of those?"

Why did he have to babble like that? I silently begged Geroth to come to the door.

"It was slick!" Russ chuckled. "Might do one from the fights too."

I stepped on the chime again. The door opened but Iliath blocked the entrance with her body. "Your services will not be required today."

Craning my neck, I tried to see past her. "Sorry, Iliath. Geroth hired us, not you."

Iliath lowered her head as if she was going to ram me, which is really extreme behavior from a Husith. "No. You're tricking him and I won't let you do it anymore."

"Look. I'm recording things. I don't talk, I don't judge, I just document." I tightened my grip on the camera and pushed forward. I had worked in tougher situations than this and was not about to be stared down by a giant maggot. "Let me past."

The door irised farther open at my touch, but Iliath slammed into my midriff with her head. My stomach felt like it was shoved up through my lungs and breath wuffed out of me as I staggered back.

Russ tried to catch me, but wasn't fast enough. I hit the ground hard, too busy trying to protect my camera to break my own fall. But I didn't care. I could see past Iliath into Geroth's quarters.

Without thinking, I framed the shot.

Iliath wove back and forth menacingly in front of the open door. "You're killing him!" Beyond her, the quarters were a shambled mess. Papers lay over everything. Furniture was upturned, and gossamer webs strung through the room catching the light in their silk.

I wanted to kiss Russ as he turned his gear on; he was a crazy man, but he understood the importance of doing good work. Charging forward, we bulled past Iliath.

That's the first point where I started to cross the line, acting like I was doing an exposé instead of a documentary.

Wait for it—it gets worse.

Iliath retreated, hissing and feinting with her head.

I pointed the camera at her. "Where's Geroth."

"He's out."

Keeping the camera on Iliath, I glanced around the room looking for a clue to Geroth's whereabouts. At my side, Russ focused in the middle distance as he listened to amplified sound over his headset. He tapped my arm and pointed to the hall.

I nodded. He must have heard Geroth. Steadying the camera, I led the way down the hall. As we crept forward, I could hear cursing and things breaking. I held the camera in front of me like a shield as we rounded the corner to Geroth's study.

He lunged across the room toward us. His skin cracked as if it were about to slough off. "I can't find my treatise."

I racked the focus when he reared in front of me. Geroth coughed and a wad of silk clung to his lips. "I have to find it."

"No." Iliath swarmed between them, pushing Geroth back from the camera. "You have to undergo Chrysalis."

He shook his head mulishly. "I need my treatise."

"You'll die!"

I backed away, so I could frame both Husiths, sliding back into my role as documentarian. In the corner of my vision, Russ adjusted his boom to stay out of the shot.

"And what you're asking me to do is death just as surely."

"I'm asking you to grow up, Geroth. That's all. But you want to commit suicide over a collection of numbers."

He turned his back on her. "Chrysalis will end me! I live to do good work."

The gears in my brain snagged at Geroth's words. It was like you were there doing a voice over. *Be well and do good work.*

Iliath wrapped her tail around him. "Stop your work. I want you to be able to play like any other adult." She turned to the camera.

She turned to me.

"You think this documentary will help him after Chrysalis? The longer he puts it off, the less he will remember."

Geroth pushed the papers aside as another cough racked his body. The heaves rolled up the length of him and glistening silk clogged his mouth. He spit it in a wad on the table. "Please help me find it."

Iliath pushed him away from the table. "No."

"Then I will look for it."

It would kill him. His body was forcing him to go through Chrysalis, and if he continued spitting the silk instead of cocooning himself, the enzymes would dissolve him into a pool of nothing. But my job was to document. Not to act.

If I did my job right, my inaction would destroy him. Surely, Iliath would give in and tell him where the treatise was. But, what if she didn't? Lord help me. This isn't what you meant when you told me to do good work. My silence was killing him.

Just like that, the sacred distance snapped.

I lifted my eye from the camera. "I know where it is."

Geroth spun. A piece of his skin stayed on the floor. The flesh underneath was red and angry. "Where!"

I said, "Your compost bin."

He grunted and crawled to the kitchen, like an inch-worm measuring out his own life.

Iliath cried out, "No!" and chased Geroth.

We hurried after the pair. With any other documentary, I would have been delighted at this confrontation. It would make a brilliant climax, but my stomach turned at the deadly game the two were playing. Geroth could die. This was beyond the mini-death that the scrambling of his memories represents, he could be as irrevocably dead as y—

In the kitchen, Geroth shoved the compost aside, burrowing into it until he found the papers of his treatise. He dragged it out of the pile, brushing the dirt from it with his thousands of fingers. Sobbing coughs racked his body. He flipped through the pages desperately and his breath eased as he read. But silk still hung from his lips.

Geroth turned to Iliath. "You did this."

"Beloved, I—" Her fingers vibrated so quickly their edges blurred with the motion.

"Our betrothal is ended."

"But Geroth—"

"Go." He turned the length of his back on her.

I followed her with the camera as Iliath crept to the door. Geroth said, "Stop recording her. I want you to edit her out of my documentary."

Iliath stopped at the door. "No, beloved—"

"You will not exist to me."

I still held the camera on Iliath, my fingers frozen.

Geroth barked, "Turn it off."

I nearly dropped the camera—I had changed events by speaking.

Iliath crept out the door. The room was silent except for Geroth's labored breathing.

I stared at him. What had I done? If I had waited Iliath would have relented. Right? It would have ended happily without me; Iliath would have told him where it was and he would have gone to the Cocoon Chamber. But I had to open my trap, thinking that I was saving his life.

Now I was part of the scene, but my role was unclear. A wave of coughing racked Geroth's body. As he spit silk onto the floor, I realized why he had not taken his medicine. "You finished your treatise last night, didn't you?"

"Yes." Geroth coughed again. He held the pages in his trembling fingers. "I thought I had lost it. I thought the Chrysalis enzymes were already stealing my mind, but it was Iliath who stole it." He looked at me. "I meant what I said about Iliath. I do not want her mentioned in the final cut."

"But what if you have memories of her afterwards?" Some small part of my brain still screamed that I should not get involved.

"Iliath betrayed me."

I have months of footage showing how deeply Iliath cares about him. "She loves you. I don't think she knew you had finished."

Geroth writhed in indecision.

Russ met my gaze over Geroth's head. His eyes were wide. I was in the scene fully, but he still stood outside it. For a heartbeat longer, I wondered if I could step back out of the scene, then I placed my hands on either side of Geroth's face. "You'll regret it later."

He barked a sardonic laugh. "Not if I don't remember."

What do you do with a statement like that?

Even if I had stayed outside the scene I couldn't begin to guess what memories would survive Chrysalis.

Christ.

As if my memories of you make you any more alive. But you are. In my mind you are alive still. I only left home a year ago, by my count, and I still get your letters.

Do I tell a ghost that I'm sitting here sobbing as if I choking on Chrysalis silk? I want to go *home*, but home no longer exists. Even if I hopped on the next ship back to Earth, even if Geroth's treatise made a wormhole open up straight to the family home everything would be different. Two hundred years! I understand now why you clung to the family history, for the memories it preserved. If I went back to Earth, it would be as different from my memories as if I had undergone Chrysalis.

Shit. I can't undo my choice, but I sure as hell can undo Geroth's.

~

DEAR VAN,

I'm so excited I can hardly type. Kim Perkins came home and she had an elderly gentleman with her. I say elderly, but he's two years younger than me. Lands, I feel like a girl again. Anyway, he's her uncle and Kim asked if I wouldn't like to go out for a cup of tea with them.

Well, we did and he's lovely. His name is Terrence. We went on another outing today, but it was only the two of us without the third wheel. I've just come home and I'm in a whirl. We're going to the cinema this evening.

Anyway, I had to tell someone and I thought of you. I know you were worried about me being lonely after you left, but I'm doing fine. Now, you be well and do good work.

Love,
Grandma Tucker

DEAR GRANDMA,

When Geroth's cocoon showed signs of opening, I found myself in a warm dry room surrounded by the lyric figures of adult Husiths and their white larvae. In the center of the dim chamber lay a misshapen cocoon. Geroth's cocoon was not the smooth, egglike enclosure that sheltered most Husiths as enzymes restructured their bodies for adulthood. His was gray and patched with bandages holding it together.

I longed for my camera as the cocoon rocked, but the documentary was finished. The Husiths around me gathered their breath almost as one when the first feeble limb tore an opening in the cocoon. At that signal, the attendants rushed forward and pulled the fibers apart letting the damp, gasping form struggle out.

As the warm air hardened his exoskeleton, Geroth—I stopped myself and mentally edited out the last two sounds of his larval name—Gero began to assume some of the beauty of his brethren as shades of amber and cerulean swirled under his exoskeleton. Qyo knelt in front of him to create the first impression on Gero's adult mind. It should have been Iliath.

"Gero, welcome to your adulthood. I am Qyo, your brother."

Gero focused on his brother and nodded. "Qyo, I remember you."

One by one, the Husiths came forward, saying their names, reminding him of how he knew them. To each, he replied, "I remember you."

Then, feeling truly alien, my turn came. Kneeling in front of a being different from the Geroth I had known, I said, "I am Vanessa, your documentarian."

"Vanessa." He cocked his head and I willed myself to see recognition in his unfathomable golden eyes. "I remember you."

What else did he remember?

But my turn was over. I was already at the door when I heard, "I am Iliath. We were betrothed."

I turned, my mental focus racking in for a close shot. Iliath's marble flesh had grayed with the approach of her own Chrysalis. Her fingers trembled in anticipation.

"Iliath." Gero cocked his head as if the camera had shifted to slow motion. "I remember you." He turned, seeming to look for something he was missing.

Qyo leaned in and whispered the correct response.

Gero turned to Iliath. "Sit by my side, beloved."

As Iliath inched to his side, I had to put my hand on the door to steady myself. He did not remember the fight. My eyes misted, making the room look as if a diffusion filter had been placed over the lens.

I needed to switch the documentaries. Turning, I went into the Memory Room. I had done as Geroth asked and edited Iliath out of the documentary that was in the projector.

I pulled that reel out of the projector and stuffed it into my pocket as Gero walked into the room. Attendants supported him while his hard-wired instincts taught him to walk. As I loaded the new reel, Iliath settled next to Gero. She looked behind her at the projection booth, as if in apprehension.

I hit the *play* button and the second documentary began to roll. On the screen, Geroth worked on his treatise while Iliath supported him. Their love unfolded frame by frame, the fights and anger edited out.

I watched, imprinting the moment in my memory, as Gero pulled Iliath close.

I think you would be proud of me. I've done good work.

Rampion

As the warrior guided his horse back home, she pondered what the future might hold. Sybille brushed a strand of her golden hair, still sweat-damp, back from her face. Tracing a path to her belly, her hand came to rest above her womb.

If his seed failed to quicken, her cuckoldry would be for nothing. Her yearning for a child ran deep, winding through her bones and into the secret places inside. Sybille had seduced the man for one purpose—to get her the child Roland could not.

She turned and went into the cottage she shared with her husband. If the man chanced to look back, she did not want to be standing in the doorway, watching like a girl at a barn dance. Stripping the linens off the bed, she carried them to the pile of laundry waiting in the garden. When Roland returned from his fool's errand, she wanted him to find nothing more than his wife doing the washing.

As she banked the fire under the cauldron, Sybille fought the sadness simmering below her surface. Mother Gothel, the witch on the far side of the village, had said Sybille was not barren. Poor Roland. She loved him for his gentle ways, but he could not give her what she wanted most.

So, when the band of warriors came to the village, Sybille realized how she might bear a child.

She let down her long hair and seduced the man who looked most like her husband. And though she had come to Roland as a chaste bride, she invited the man to her home. To her bed.

Sybille wanted to burn the sheets.

Before the man arrived at the cottage, she had sent Roland in search of rampion, knowing it was too late in the year to find the green. She claimed to be ill from craving it.

Roland had believed her.

She closed her eyes against the memory; she had never lied to him before.

Plunging the linens into the cauldron, Sybille tried to wash her guilt away with the soil on the sheets. As she worked over the boiling water, new sweat beaded her skin despite the October air. A droplet trailed between her breasts, reminding her of the man's hand. She wiped furiously at it; Roland would be home soon.

Sybille hung a shirt, which she had made for Roland shortly after their marriage, over the line. She imagined hanging a girl's dress on the line beside it. In her mind, the dress had tiny pintucks and delicate lace at the hem.

She smiled, fingering the sleeve of Roland's shirt. The autumn sun lit the linen, seeming to bleach it back to a new white, but she knew that when she pulled it from the line, eight years of toil would still tinge the fabric. How long would her guilt tinge her mind?

The sound of footsteps, running along the path, reached her ears before Roland burst into the back garden. Beneath his sandy hair, his face was flushed red as maple leaves.

Her heart seemed to race in answer to his haste. Sybille turned from the line, conscious of the perspiration still between her thighs. "Roland?" Had someone seen the man come to her?

Roland ducked past the laundry and wrapped his arms around her, pressing her to him. His shirt was damp and heat radiated from him even though the autumn day was cool. His breath was ragged in Sybille's ear as he clung to her.

"I love you." He kissed her cheek. "I love you."

She squeezed Roland back, her fear of being caught replaced by concern for her husband. "I love you, too."

He smoothed her hair as he released her. "I don't know if you still will."

"Roland, what's wrong?" Fear seemed to form a bubble at the top of her throat, stopping her breath.

In answer, he knelt and swung the strap of the basket off his shoulder. He lifted the lid. A sweet peppery tang floated from the greens within. "I found rampion."

Sybille sank to her knees beside him. She reached into the basket, plunging her hand into the cool green leaves. Scattered across the top were stems covered with purple flowers. It was too late in the year for rampion to grow. Far too late. Mesmerized by the green, she pulled out a leaf and placed it between her lips. The flavor exploded on her tongue with promises of hot summer.

She lifted her eyes to Roland and leaned across the basket to kiss him gently on the lips. "Thank you, my love."

He pulled away from her and shook his head. "They were in the witch's garden."

The taste in her mouth turned to ash. The witch. Mother Gothel, who had told Sybille her womb could bear a child. "What—?"

"She caught me." His eyes were huge, like a little boy's. "I had to promise—I thought it would be all right, because it's been eight years and—"

"What did you promise her?"

"Our firstborn child."

His words seemed to silence every sound from the surrounding forest. His lips continued to move, but she heard nothing he said. She staggered to her feet and stumbled away from him. Racked with sudden nausea, she clutched her stomach and vomited, bright green flecks spattering the dirt.

She felt Roland's hands on her back. "I'm sorry. When she demanded a child, I thought I wasn't giving anything away . . . We had tried so hard."

He could not know the truth. Wiping her mouth with the back of her hand, she said, "You had to get away from her." Roland could not know how she spent the afternoon. "And we can't have children, so you've promised her nothing."

A moan of despair ground out of him. "After I promised, she said you would have a child, a girl." His voice dwindled to a whisper. "We're to name her Rapunzel, after the rampion I stole."

Sybille straightened slowly, with her hand over her womb.

Roland hovered by her, tears coursing down his solid face. "I didn't think we could have children."

"I know." She looked away from him, at the sheets hanging over the line. "I tried everything."

At the Edge of Dying

KAHE PEEKED OVER the edge of the earthen trench as his tribe's retreating warriors broke from the bamboo grove onto the lava field. The tribesmen showed every sign of panicked flight in front of the advancing Ouvallese. Spears and shields dropped to the ground as they tucked in their arms and ran.

And the Ouvallese, arrogant with their exotic horses and metal armor, believed what they saw and chased the warriors toward him. The timing on this would be close. Kahe gathered the spell in his mind and double-checked the garrote around his neck. His wife stood behind him, the ends resting lightly in her hands. "Do it."

Bless her, Mehahui did not hesitate. She hauled back, cutting into his throat with the knotted cord. Kahe tried not to struggle as his breath was cut off. Black dots swirled in his vision, but he could not afford to faint yet.

With each breath he could not take, with each step closer to death, Kahe's power grew. As the tribe's warriors reached the trench and leaped down, he scanned the lava field to make certain none were left behind. Vision fading, he unleashed the spell coiled inside him.

The heat from the firestorm singed the air as it swept out from his trench. Even through his graying sight, the blue flame burned like the sun as it raced toward the Ouvallese battalion. Screams rose like prayer as his spell crisped the men in their armor.

As soon as the spell rolled out, Mehahui released her hold and Kahe fell against the damp red soil. The grains of dirt blended with the dots dancing in front of his eyes, so the very earth seemed to move. Air scraped across his tortured throat as life flooded into him. He gasped as the goddess's gift of power faded.

Beyond his own wrenching sobs, Kahe heard the agonized screams of those Ouvallese too distant to be instantly immolated. He prayed to Hia that his spell had gotten most of them; the goddess of death and magic had rarely failed him. Still, the kings of the tribes would have to send runners out to deal with the burned soldiers; a dying enemy was too dangerous to allow to linger.

Mehahui patted him, soft as a duckling, on the back. Her round face hovered in the edge of his vision. "Stay with me."

Kahe coughed when he tried to speak. "I am." His throat scraped as if it were filled with thorns. He knew she hated seeing him downed by a spell, but flirting with Hia was the only way to get the power he needed for a spell this big. Pushing against the earth wall, Kahe sat up.

His head swam. The dirt thrummed under his hands.

The vibration grew to a roar, and the earth bucked. A wall collapsed. Dirt spilled into the trench, as the earth quaked.

No. A sorcerer must have been at the edge of his firestorm, and by almost killing him, Kahe had given him access to Hia's power—only a dying man would have enough power to work magic on the earth itself. As the trench shifted and filled with falling rocks, the spell he needed to counter it sprang to his mind but without power. He turned to Mehahui even while knowing there wasn't enough time for the garrote to work. He fumbled for the knife at his side.

The tremors stopped.

Dust settled in the suddenly still air but he had not cast the counter-spell. Even if he had, it would have been as a rush lamp beside a bonfire.

Around them, men in the earthworks called to each other for aid or reassurance. Trickles of new dirt slid down the wall in miniature red avalanches. King Enahu scrambled over a mound, using his long spear as a walking staff.

"Hia's left tit! You're still alive." He slid down the side of the trench, red dirt smearing his legs with an illusion of blood. "When you stopped the earthquake, I didn't think you could have survived the spell. Not so soon after working the other."

"I didn't stop it." Kahe watched Mehahui instead of the king. Her skin had bleached like driftwood and she would not meet his eyes.

Beside him, King Enahu inhaled sharply, understanding what Kahe meant. "There's another sorcerer in the ranks? Hia, Pikeo, and the Mother! This could be the saving of us. Who?"

Mehahui hung her head, her hair falling around her face like rain at night. "It's me."

Kahe's heart stuttered, as if he had taken makiroot poison for a spell. Hia only gave her power to those on the road to death. "That's not possible."

"I'm dying, Kahe." His beautiful wife lifted her head and Kahe could not understand how he had missed the dark circles under her eyes.

WITH ONLY a thin blanket covering her, every breeze in the hut chilled Mehahui. She shivered and kept her attention focused on the thatched pili-leaf ceiling while the surgeon poked at her.

Iokua stepped back from the table. "Why didn't you come to me sooner?" he asked.

Clinging to the blanket, Mehahui sat up. "Could you have done anything?"

"I could have tried."

They had studied under the same masters at the Paheni Academy of Medicinal Arts; she didn't need Iokua to tell her that only palliative care was possible. "Are you finished?"

He nodded and Mehahui wrapped her felted skirt back around her waist. Her hands shook when she tucked in the ends of the fabric. "Will you tell Kahe? I can't." She pulled her hair away from her face, securing it with the tortoiseshell pins Kahe had given her for their fifteenth anniversary. She tucked a red suhibis flower behind her left ear so her married status was clear—not that she needed it. Everyone in the united tribes knew Kahe.

Iokua tugged at his graying doctor's braid. "As you wish." He paused to pick up the sandalwood surgeon's mask and settled it on his face. The image of the goddess hid his worry behind her fragrant, smooth cheeks. Carved filigree of whale bone formed the mask's eyes, giving no hint of the man beneath.

He pushed aside the hanging in the door of the hut. Outside, Kahe was pacing on the lanai. He stopped, face tightening like leather as he saw the surgeon's mask, but he came when Iokua beckoned him.

Mehahui could not say anything as she took her husband's hand. The scars on the inside of his wrists stood out in angry relief.

Iokua bowed formally. "Your wife has a tumor in her abdomen." The mask flattened his voice.

"Can you cut it out of her?" Kahe sounded like she was still strangling him.

"No." The surgeon's mask was impassive. "I'm sorry."

Despite her husband's touch, Mehahui felt herself shrink into the far distance.

"How long does she have?"

The mask turned to her, cold and neutral though the voice underneath was not. "I suspect Mehahui will know better than I."

And she did know. Underneath the constant ache in her belly, the mass hummed with the goddess's power. She had known she was dying, but until today she had been afraid to prove it.

Kahe grasped her hand tighter. "Mehahui?"

Blindly, she turned toward him. "Weeks. Maybe."

As soon as they were alone, Kahe said, "Why didn't you tell me?" When had the soft curves of her face turned to planes?

"You would have tried to heal me."

Hia dealt out the power to kill but was more sparing with her willingness to heal. She would grant a life only in exchange for another. Kahe could have healed Mehahui, could still heal her, but only if he were willing to be taken to Hia's breast himself. And to do that would leave the king without a sorcerer.

He stood and paced the three strides that their tiny house allowed. The pili-leaf walls pressed in on him and his throat still felt tight. After all the times Mehahui had nearly killed him, only now did he feel the impact of death. He went over the list of poisons in his kit. "Makiroot acts slowly enough that I could work spells for the king until it was time to heal you. I'd be stronger than I am from strangling, so—"

"Stop. Kahe, stop." Mehahui clutched the sides of her head. "Do you think I could live with the guilt if you wasted your death on me?"

"It wouldn't be a waste!"

"Will you look beyond me? Paheni is being invaded. The South Shore Tribe have allied with the Ouvallese and we are overwhelmed. Hia has given us this gift and—"

"A gift!" If the goddess presented herself right then, he would have spit in her face.

"Yes, a gift! It's like Hia and Pikeo's Crossroads all over again. Can you imagine a better meeting of death and luck? It's not as if I am a common housewife—I've worked at your side; I know all the spells but I've never had the power to cast them. Hia gave me this so we can win the war." Mehahui held out her hands to him. "Please. Please don't take this from me."

Kahe could not go to her, though he knew she was right. Her power would only grow, as his mentor's had at the end of his life. In short order, she would surpass what he could do, and the tribes needed that to turn the tide in their favor.

But he needed her more. "How long do you have? Think deeply about it, and Hia will tell you the time remaining."

Mehahui's gaze turned inward. He watched her, sending a prayer to Pikeo for a little bit of luck. Hia's brother could be fickle, but Kahe no longer trusted his patron goddess.

"Eighteen days." Those two words shook Mehahui's voice.

But a tiny seed of hope sprouted in Kahe. "That might be enough."

"What? Enough for what?"

"To get you to Hia'au." Pilgrims from every tribe went to the goddess's city to die, and sometimes—sometimes Hia would grant them the power to heal with their dying breath.

Mehahui looked at him like he had lost his senses. "But we lost Hia'au to Ouvalle."

Kahe nodded. "That's why we have to win this war quickly."

King Enahu's great house, despite the broad windows opening onto a terraced lanai, felt close and stifling with the narrow thoughts of the other kings who had gathered to meet with him. Kahe's knees ached from kneeling on the floor behind Enahu.

King Waitipi played with the lei of ti leaves around his neck, pulling the leaves through his fat hands in a fragrant rattle. "We are sorry to hear of your wife's illness, but I fail to see how this changes any of our strategies."

Kahe bent his head before answering. "With respect, your majesty, it changes everything. Mehahui will be stronger than me in a matter of days. What's more, she can cast spells at a moment's notice. We can take the battle right to the Ouvallese ships and handle anything that they cast at us."

"I'll admit it's tempting to retake Hia'au." The bright yellow feathers of King Enahu's cloak fluttered in the breeze. Across his knees lay the long spear he used in battle as a reminder of his strength.

King Haleko said, "I, for one, do not want to subject our troops to another massacre like Keonika Valley."

"I understand your concern, your majesty. But the Ouvallese only have one full sorcerer from their alliance with the South Shore tribe. With Mehahui's power added to mine, we can best them."

"Of course I do not doubt your assessment of your wife's power"—King Waitipi plucked at a ti leaf, shredding it—"but it seems to me that the South Shore tribe is making out much the best in this. Should we not reconsider our position?"

So many kings, so few rulers.

King Enahu scowled. "Reconsider? The Ouvallese offered to let us rule over a portion of *our* land. A portion. As if they have the right to take whatever they wish. I will *not* subject my people to rule by outlanders."

"Nor I." King Haleko nodded, gray hair swaying around his head. "But this does raise some interesting possibilities." King Haleko's words raised hope for a moment. "Would the infirm in our hospices offer more sorcerers?"

"You would find power without knowledge. Hia's gift only comes to those who study and are willing to make the sacrifice of themselves."

"But your wife—"

"My wife . . ." Kahe had to stop to keep from drowning in his longing for her.

In the void, King Enahu spoke, "The lady Mehahui has studied at Kahe's side all the years they have been in our service."

Kahe begged his king, "This war could be over in two weeks, if you let us go to the South harbor. It would not divert troops; only a small band need come with us. No more than ten to protect us until we reach the South Harbor where the Ouvallese are moored. We could wipe them out in a matter of minutes." And then, though he would not say it out loud, he could take Mehahui to the Hia'au and pray that one of the dying in the goddess's city would heal her.

King Enahu scowled. "Pikeo's Hawk! You're asking me to bet my kingdom that your wife is right about how long she has to live. What happens if we extend ourselves to attack and are cut off because she dies early? Everything is already in place to stop Ouvalle's incursions into King Waitipi's land. I need you there, not at the South Shore."

"Well." King Waitipi let the lei fall from his hand. "You've convinced me this merits more discussion and thought. Let us consider it more at the next meeting."

Kahe slammed his fists on the floor in front of him, sending a puff of dust into the air. "Eighteen days. She has eighteen days. We don't have time to wait."

The men in the great hall tensed. Kings, all of them, and disrespect could mean a death sentence.

Half-turning, Enahu let his hands rest on the spear across his knees. "Kahe. You are here on my sufferance. Do not forget yourself."

Trembling, Kahe bit his tongue and took a shallow breath. He bowed his head low until it rested on the floor. "Forgive me, your highness."

King Waitipi giggled like a child. "You are no doubt distraught because of your wife's condition. I remind you that she will find grace with Hia no matter the outcome of our meetings."

Kahe knew that better than any king could.

But to wait until they made up their mind was worse than trusting Mehahui's life to the hands of Hia's brother god, Pikeo—luck had never been his friend.

If they did not decide fast enough, he would take Mehahui and go to the goddess's city without waiting for leave. He tasted the chalky dust as he knelt with his forehead pressed against from the floor. Leaving his king would mean abandoning his tribe in the war.

Surely Hia could not ask for a higher sacrifice. Surely she would spare Mehahui for that.

MEHAHUI COULD NOT REMEMBER the last time she had seen a crossroad instead of the usual roundabout. Most people went out of their way to avoid invoking the gods with crossed paths, connecting even forest tracks like this with diagonals and circles.

She half expected Hia and Pikeo to materialize and relive their famous bet.

A cramp twisted in her belly. Mehahui pressed her fist hard into her middle, trying to push the pain away. It was clear which god would use her as a game piece if they appeared. Doubling over, a moan escaped her.

She tried to straighten but Kahe had already returned to her. "Are you all right?"

Mehahui forced a laugh. "Oh. Fine. Hia's gift is being a talkative one this morning." She unclenched her fist and patted him on the arm. "It will pass."

"Can I do anything?" He caught her hand and squeezed it. Every angle of his body spoke of worry.

"Just keep going." Mehahui wiped her face. Her hand came away slick with sweat, but she smiled at her husband. "See. It has already passed." She pushed past him onto the main road to Hia'au

As if she had said nothing, Kahe took her hand and pulled her to a stop in the middle of the crossroad. "You should take something for the pain." He knelt and fished his sorcery kit out his pack.

Amid the ways of dying lay the remedies. Some spells needed a long slow death and he had poisons for that. Others needed the bright flash of blood flooding from the body, and he had obsidian knives, bone needles, and sinew for those. But all of the deaths brought pain. Mehahui had nursed him back from all of them. The painkiller had been one of the most faithful tools in her arsenal.

She held out her hand to accept one of the dark pills from him. "Thank you."

A drumming sounded on the main road, heading toward the harbor.

She dropped the pill. A queasy tension in her belly held Mehahui rigid. Three creatures came into view—men whose bodies were twisted into something like massive storks with four legs. Her fear raced ahead of her mind and she had already begun to back away from the road before she recognized them as men riding horses, the exotic animals the Ouvallese had brought with them from overseas.

Warriors, clearly, and wearing the green and black Ouvallese colors—outriders, returning to the main band. If the gods were replaying their age-old game, then this unlucky chance was clearly Pikeo's move.

Which had more influence on mortal lives: Death or Luck? Would Hia win again in her battle against her brother?

The man in front saw them and shouted. She could not understand his words, but his intent was clear. Halt. Kahe placed his hand on his knife.

In moments, the three riders had cut them off, pinning them in the middle of the crossroad. The one who had shouted, a small effete man with blond curls showing under the bottom of his black helm, pushed his horse in closer. He pointed at Kahe's knife.

"Not to have!" His Pahenian was slow, as if he spoke around a mouth of nettles.

Kahe glanced at the other riders. "I don't understand."

The blond pointed to the ground. "There. Put!"

Kahe nodded and reached slowly for the tie of his knife belt.

Despite the shade of the trees, heat coursed through Mehahui. The knot in her stomach throbbed with her pulse. Hia could not have brought them to this crossroad only to abandon them.

She looked around for an answer. The soldier closest to her lifted a bow from his saddle. Without giving Kahe time to disarm, he pulled an arrow from his quiver. Aimed it at her husband. Drew.

"Kahe!"

Her husband flinched and turned at her cry. Before he finished moving, the arrow sprouted from his cheek.

Mehahui shrieked. The soldier turned to her, bow raised.

Kahe flung out his hand and a palpable shadow flew through the air to engulf the soldier. His face was visible for a moment as fog in the night, then he vanished.

Blood cascaded from Kahe's mouth down his chest. He staggered but raised his arms again.

Spooked by its rider's disappearance, the soldier's horse reared and came down, nearly atop Mehahui. She danced back and grabbed at the dangling reins, trying to stop the bucking animal.

Ignoring her, the other two soldiers closed on Kahe. She flung the same spell she had seen him use, sucking a living night into being.

In that moment of inattention, the horse crashed into her, knocking her down. A hard hoof slammed against her belly.

Mehahui rolled, frantic to get away from the horse's plunging feet. Fetching up against a trunk at the side of the road, she struggled to get air into her lungs. Dear goddess, was this what Kahe felt when she strangled him?

The hard crack of metal on obsidian resounded through the forest. Kahe somehow had drawn his knife and met the remaining soldier's blow, but the glass shattered on the steel.

Mehahui pushed at the ground, but her arms only twitched. The bright pain of Hia's gift flared in her belly, almost blinding her. Her thighs were damp and sticky.

The soldier raised his sword again to bring it down on Kahe's unguarded neck.

Mehahui cried out, "Stop!"

It was not a true spell, but the soldier stopped. His arm, his horse, everything froze in mid-motion.

Kahe shuddered. Then, he slipped sideways and fell heavily to the ground.

The soldier, a statue in the forest, did not move.

Mehahui crawled across the dirt road to her husband. The pain in her stomach kept her bent nearly double. Her skirts were bright with blood.

Something had broken inside when the horse had knocked her down.

No matter now, Kahe needed her. During the years of aiding him, she had seen almost every form of near-death and learned to bring him back. She grabbed the smooth leather sorcerer's kit. With it in her grasp, Mehahui set to work to save him.

The arrow had entered his cheek under his right eye, passing through his mouth and lodging in his jaw opposite. Kahe was bleeding heavily from the channel it had cut through the roof of his mouth, but she knew how to deal with that.

Shaking, Mehahui turned him on his side, so he would not drown in his own blood. She broke the arrow and pulled the shaft free. Then with a pair of forceps, she tried to pry the arrowhead out of his jawbone. The forceps slipped off it. She gripped it again, but her hands shook too much to hold it steady and his mouth open. If she could not get it out, the wound would suppurate and Kahe would die despite all her efforts. Again, she tried and gouged his cheek when the forceps slipped.

Mehahui looked at the sky, tears of frustration pooling in her eyes.

The frozen soldier still stood in arrested motion. His cape stood away from his body showing the bright gold seal of the Ouvallese king on the field of dark green. A bead of sweat clung to the edge of his jaw in unmoving testament to her power.

She did not need the forceps. She had Hia. Praise the goddess for giving Mehahui power when she needed it most.

Mehahui focused on the arrowhead and sent a prayer to Hia. Channeling the smallest vanishing spell possible, she begged the arrowhead to go. For an instant, a new shadow appeared in Kahe's mouth and then blood rushed from the hole where the arrowhead had been.

"Praise Hia!"

The other wounds would answer to pressure. From the kit she took pads of clean cloth, soaked them in suhibis flower honey and packed them into the wounds. When all was tied and tight, Mehahui looked again at the soldier. There was no time to let Kahe rest.

She held smelling salts under his nose and braced herself for the next task.

KAHE RETCHED and his world exploded with pain. Every part of his head, his being, seemed to exist for no reason but to hurt.

He tried to probe the pain with his tongue and gagged again. Cloth almost filled his mouth.

"Hush, hush . . . " Mehahui's gentle hand stroked his forehead.

Kahe cracked his eyes and tried to speak, but only a grunt came out. Bandages swaddled his head and held his mouth closed.

"You have to get up, Kahe. The rest of the warriors will be coming."

Battalion. He had to get up. Kahe could barely lift his head, and somehow he had to stand. With Mehahui's help, he rolled into a sitting position.

A soldier stood over them. His sword was raised to strike.

Kahe tried to push Mehahui away from the man and fell face forward in the road. All the pain returned and threatened to pull him back into Hia's blessed darkness.

"It's all right! He's—he's frozen." Mehahui helped him sit again.

He looked more carefully at the soldier. The man's cloak had swung out from his body, but gravity did nothing to pull it down. Kahe did not know of a spell that could do such a thing.

He looked at Mehahui. The shadows under her eyes were deeper. In the hollows of her cheeks, the bone lay close beneath her skin. Blood coated her skirts and showed in red blotches at her ankles.

He tried to ask, but his words came out more garbled than a foreigner's.

Still, Mehahui understood enough. "Hia granted my prayer." She stood, the effort clear in her every movement.

Kahe grabbed her skirt and gestured to the blood. What price had Hia demanded for this power?

She pushed his hands away. "You have to hurry. I think the main road is the fastest way back, yes?"

Kahe forced a word past the cloth in his mouth. "Back?" They could go around the battalion in the forest.

"Yes. Back." Mehahui stood with her hands braced on her knees, swaying. "You have to go to King Enahu."

He shook his head. "Hia'au."

"I am not going to Hia'au. The goddess gave me the power to save Paheni, not myself. I am staying here."

She could not mean that. Kahe clambered to his feet. The forest tipped and swayed around him, but long practice at being bled kept him standing. He had to make her understand that going to Hia'au would save both her and Paheni. No possible good could come from her staying here.

As if in answer to his thoughts, Mehahui said, "Look at the soldier, Kahe. Do you see the badge on his shoulder?"

Kahe dragged his eyes away from her. The coiled hydra of Ouvalle shone against a field of green. Where the necks sprouted from the body, a crown circled like a collar.

"That's their king's symbol, isn't it? He's landed. It's not a single battalion, but his army." Mehahui beckoned him. "Please, Kahe."

He would not leave her here. Kahe clawed at the bandages surrounding his head. If he could only talk to her, she would understand.

"Please, please go. Hia—" her voice broke. Tears wiped her cheeks clean of dirt. "Hia has given me more power, but I only have until this evening before she takes me home. I want to know you are safe while I meet the King of Ouvalle."

Thunder rumbled in the distance.

Kahe had freely dedicated himself to the goddess but she had no right to demand this of his wife. Mehahui was his wife. His. Hia had no right to take her from him. Not now. Not like this.

Death combined with Luck showed the hands of Hia and Pikeo and they stood square in the middle of a crossroads. The Mother only knew what else the gods had planned.

"Hate her."

"No. No! Do you think this is easy for me? The only comfort I have is that I am serving a greater good. That this is the will of Hia and Pikeo and the Mother. You will *not* take my faith from me."

How could he live without her? The thunder grew louder, discernible now as the sound of a great mass of men marching closer.

Mehahui limped to his side and took his hand. She raised it to her lips and kissed his knuckles tenderly. "Please go."

Belling through the trees, a horn sounded.

Kahe cursed the goddess for cutting their time so short and leaned in to kiss his wife. The pain in his jaw meant nothing in this moment.

The sound of approaching horses broke their embrace. Kahe bent to retrieve his sorcery kit; if he took one of the faster poisons, then he could match Mehahui's power and meet Hia with his wife.

Mehahui put her hand on his shoulder. "No. I don't want you to go to the goddess. Someone must bear witness to our king."

He shook his head and pulled out the tincture of shadoweve blossoms.

"I have spent our entire marriage helping you die and knowing I would outlive you. Have you heard me complain?" She spoke very fast, as the army approached.

Kahe glanced down the road. The first of the men came into view. It seemed such a simple thing to want to die with her.

A mounted soldier separated from the company and advanced, shouting at them until he saw his immobile comrade. Moments later, a bugled command halted the force a bowshot away.

Men crowded the road in the green and black of Ouvalle. Scores of hydras fluttered on pennants, writhing in the breeze. Rising above the helmets of the warriors were ranks of bows and pikes. In the midst of them were towering gray animals, like boars swollen to the size of whales, with elongated, snaking noses that reached almost to the ground and wicked tusks jutting from their mouths. Each whale-boar glimmered with armor in scales of green lacquered steel. The black huts on their backs brushed the overarching trees. What spell had they used to bring these monsters across the ocean?

Mehahui squeezed Kahe's shoulder. When she stepped away from him, the absence of her hand left his shoulder cold and light.

She spoke; a spell amplified her voice so the very trees seemed to carry her words. "Lay down your arms and return to your homes."

Involuntarily, the closest warriors began to unbuckle their sword belts. Their sergeant shouted at them and looks of startled confusion or bewildered anger crossed their faces.

Then, at a command, the front rank of archers raised their bows.

Kahe reached for what little power was available to him. A rain of arrows darkened the air between them and the army. Kahe hurled a spell praying that Hia would allow him to create a small shield. As the spell left him, the air over them thickened, diverting the leading arrows but not enough.

Mehahui wiped the air with her hand; arrows fell to the ground. Their heavy blunt tips struck the road creating a perimeter around them. Designed to bludgeon a sorcerer to unconsciousness, without risking a wound that would bring more power, these arrows meant the Ouvallese army had recognized what the two of them were.

How long would it take them to realize that *he* was without power? Kahe turned to his kit when the air shuddered. A spell left Mehahui and the trees closest to the road swayed with a breeze. A groan rose from their bases. The trees toppled, falling like children's playthings toward the road.

Animals and men screamed in terror. Trumpeting, the tall whale-boars were the first to feel the weight of the trees.

On the lead whale-boar, the cloth curtains of the black hut blew straight out as a great wind pushed the trees upright.

The curtains remained open. An ancient, frail man stood at the opening, supported by two attendants—Oahi, the South Shore king's sorcerer. Another spell left the traitor king's sorcerer, forming into a bird of fire as it passed over the warriors' heads.

Screaming its wrath, the phoenix plummeted toward them. The counter-spell formed in Kahe's mind and he hurled it, creating a fledging waterbird. The phoenix clawed the tiny creature with a flaming talon and the waterbird steamed out of existence.

Moments later, Mehahui hurled the same spell. Her waterbird formed with a crack of thunder. The roar of a thousand waterfalls deafened Kahe with each stroke of the mighty bird's wings.

As it grappled with the phoenix, dousing the bird's fire in a steaming conflagration, Kahe saw the power of the goddess. *This* was why Hia wanted them both there; Mehahui had the power and the knowledge, but not the instincts of a sorcerer.

Without waiting for her waterbird to finish the phoenix, Kahe attacked the Ouvallese. The pathetic spell barely warmed the metal of the whale-boar's scales. But when Mehahui copied him, the animal screamed under the red hot metal, plunging forward in terror. Its iron shod feet trampled the warriors closest to it.

On its back, the attendants clutched Oahi, struggling to keep him upright as he worked the counter-spell. Even though he cooled the scales, the panicked creature did not stop its rampage. A blond, bearded man, with a gold circlet on his helm staggered forward in the hut to stand next to the old man. What would the King of Ouvalle do when all his animals panicked?

Kahe croaked, "Others."

Mehahui nodded, and heated the scaled armor of the whale-boar next to the first.

As quickly as she heated it, the Ouvallese sorcerer cooled it, but the frightened animal turned the disciplined ranks around it to chaos. Mehahui turned to the next one as the King shouted to a hut behind him.

Kahe drew in his breath as the front whale-boar plunged into the wood, letting him see the one behind it clearly for the first time. In this hut rode a half dozen men and women. Though of differing ages, each wore a simple gray skirt with the white flame of Hia—these passengers were some of the dying of Hia'au. The Ouvallese did not have one sorcerer, they had a half dozen, and in battle, Hia's only chosen people were the dying. Kahe could expect no favors from her, unless he paid her price.

Clutching the upright post in the corner, a priest of Hia spoke quickly to the woman closest to him.

Kahe grunted and pointed at them. Mehahui had to destroy the sorcerers before the priest finished explaining the spell he wanted the woman to cast.

Mehahui nodded and threw the spell to heat their whale-boar's scaled armor, but Oahi anticipated her and cooled it before the animal panicked. Kahe shook his head. "No. People."

Squinting her eyes in confusion, Mehahui refined her spell and released it. The magnitude of the spell staggered Kahe as it passed him. It came from someone on the threshold of death. Mehahui's face was gray. She swayed on her feet. They had to finish this now, before she went home to Hia.

The warriors of Ouvalle screamed as one, ripping their helms from their heads. Some threw themselves on the ground in their efforts to get away from armor that began to take on the dull cherry red of heat.

Even the king wrenched his circlet from his head before Oahi cooled the metal.

It was a mighty spell, but the wrong one. Hia's dying wore no metal. Kahe grabbed Mehahui's arm and pointed at the hut of the dying. He threw a cloud of dark, hoping to absorb the priest in that veil of nothing.

Mehahui nodded, staggered, and threw the same spell. The world groaned at the immensity of the void she created. As it flew forward, it unfurled to the size of the road. In the moment when it engulfed the first row of warriors, the woman in the hut unleashed her spell as well, dying as it left her. Small and arrow-bright, the spell flew past the void without pausing. Its shape seemed familiar, but Kahe did not recognize the form. He tossed a general defensive spell and prayed to Pikeo for luck that it would be enough to counter this attack.

The void continued eating its way through the ranks of Ouvallese warriors. Those closest to the edge of the road threw away their weapons and ran for the woods. The old sorcerer in the hut produced the counterspell for the void, but it only reduced the girth of the dark cloud.

Kahe looked at his wife, at her gray and bloodless lips, at the bright red staining her skirts and ankles; Hia, Pikeo and The Mother—she had surpassed the ancient man in power.

The dying woman's narrow spell struck Mehahui in the belly. Light as white as Hia's fire flared around her. She convulsed.

Kahe leaped to catch her as she collapsed. Seeing her fall, the Ouvallese king shouted a command to the few remaining archers. They raised their bows and fired at Kahe and Mehahui. Kahe welcomed the speeding arrows, but they too were consumed by the void Mehahui had created.

It roiled forward.

The handler for the king's whale-boar frantically turned the animal, trying to outrun the void.

Created in the moment before Mehahui's death, it was the strongest spell Kahe had yet seen.

Seeming to recognize this, the sorcerer in the King's hut grabbed a knife from his side and plunged it into his own heart, throwing the counter-spell again. It struck the void, undoing it, as the whale-boar plunged into the trees. The archers again raised their bows.

In Kahe's arms, Mehahui stirred and opened her eyes. She gulped in air. "Oh, Hia. No!"

Her skin was clear and flushed with life. Kahe took her face in his hands, feeling the warm vitality of her flesh. "How?"

"They healed me," she groaned. "The goddess has left." She looked past him at the archers. Her eyes widened.

They had no more blunt arrows. A field of sharp points sprang toward them.

"Pikeo save us!" Kahe threw himself across her, turning to cast a shield at the deadly arrows. It stopped most of them.

A familiar pain tore open his cheek. Another arrow plunged into his left shoulder and the third went through his right arm and pinned it to his thigh.

But none of them hit Mehahui.

Kahe waited for Hia's power to come to him, but the wounds were too slight. So he sent a prayer to Pikeo begging for good luck. They were in a crossroads, if ever Luck were going to play fair with him, it would be here and now.

And this would be the moment to strike. Oahi sagged in the arms of his escort, already gone home to Hia, but Kahe lacked the power for any large spells. He tried to reach for his dagger but by unlucky chance, the arrow bound his right arm to his leg. His left arm hung limp. This was how Pikeo answered his prayer?

Mehahui, flush with life, cast an unbinding spell. It was a simple childish spell, good only for causing a rival's skirt to drop.

One tie on the king's hut came undone.

Kahe held his breath, praying that Pikeo would notice that chance and play with it.

As the animal lurched onto the road, the king's hut slid off and toppled among the remnant of the Ouvallese army. Kahe could almost see the hand of Pikeo knock the king from the falling hut and drop him upon a pike.

The sharp head pierced the king's body as he slid down the shaft. He convulsed once and hung limp.

At the sight of their dead monarch, a rising wail swept through the remaining warriors. Those closest to Mehahui and Kahe backed away. Others, seeing their decimated ranks, threw down their arms and ran.

Mehahui leaned her head against Kahe's back. Then she patted him, soft as a hatchling. "Stay with me."

Kahe coughed as he tried to speak, gagging on the mass in his mouth. She knelt in front of him.

Looking at his wife's fair and healthy face, Kahe sent a prayer of thanks to both gods.

"The arrow in your cheek appears to have followed the same path as the other did; it is lodged in your bandages. I'd say we have Luck to thank for our survival today." Mehahui picked up the sorcery kit. "And now, my love, I intend to keep you out of Hia's hands."

She broke the arrow in his arm. He gasped at the sliding pain as the shaft pulled free. Nothing had ever felt so sweet as the touch of Mehahui's hands, proving they were both alive.

Clockwork Chickadee

THE CLOCKWORK CHICKADEE was not as pretty as the nightingale. But she did not mind. She pecked the floor when she was wound, looking for invisible bugs. And when she was not wound, she cocked her head and glared at the sparrow, whom she loathed with every tooth on every gear in her pressed-tin body.

The sparrow could fly.

He took no pains to conceal his contempt for those who could not. When his mechanism spun him around and around overhead, he twittered—not even a proper song—to call attention to his flight. Chickadee kept her head down when she could so as not to give him the satisfaction of her notice. It was clear to her that any bird could fly if only they were attached to a string like him. The flight, of which he was so proud, was not even an integral part of his clockwork. A wind-up engine hanging from the chandelier spun him in circles while he merely flapped his wings. Chickadee could do as much. And so she thought until she hatched an idea to show that Sparrow was not so very special.

It happened, one day, that Chickadee and Sparrow were shelved next to one another.

Sparrow, who lay tilted on his belly as his feet were only painted on, said, "How limiting the view is from here. Why, when I am flying I can see everything."

"Not everything, I'll warrant," said Chickadee. "Have you seen what is written underneath the table? Do you know how the silver marble got behind the potted fern, or where the missing wind-up key is?"

Sparrow flicked his wing at her. "Why should I care about such things when I can see the ceiling above and the plaster cherubs upon it. I can see the shelves below us and the mechanical menagerie upon it, even including the clockwork scarab and his lotus. I can see the fireplace, which shares the wall with us, none of which are visible from here nor to you."

"But I have seen all of these things as I have been carried to and from the shelf. In addition the boy has played with me at the fountain outside."

"What fountain?"

"Ah! Can you not see the courtyard fountain when you fly?" Chickadee hopped a step closer to him. "Such a pity."

"Bah—Why should I care about any of this?"

"For no reason today," said Chickadee. "Perhaps tomorrow."

"WHAT IS WRITTEN underneath the table?" Sparrow called as he swung in his orbit about the room, wings clicking against his side with each downstroke.

Chickadee pecked at the floor and shifted a cog to change her direction toward the table. "The address of Messrs. DeCola and Wodzinski."

"Bah. Why should I care about them?"

"Because they are master clockworkers. They can re-set cogs to create movements you would not think possible."

"I have all the movement I need. They can offer me nothing."

"You might change your mind." Chickadee passed under the edge of the table. "Perhaps tomorrow."

Above the table, Sparrow's gears ground audibly in frustration.

Chickadee cocked her head to look up at the yellow slip of paper glued to the underside of the table. Its type was still crisp though the paper itself threatened to peel away. She scanned the corners of the room for movement. In the shadows by the fireplace, a live mouse caught her gaze. He winked.

~

"How DID the silver marble get behind the potted fern?" Sparrow asked as he lay on the shelf.

"It fell out of the boy's game and rolled across the floor to where I was pecking the ground. I waited but no one seemed to notice that it was gone, nor did they notice me, so I put my beak against it and pushed it behind the potted fern."

"You did? You stole from the boy?" Sparrow clicked his wings shut. "I find that hard to believe."

"You may not, today," Chickadee said. "Perhaps tomorrow."

She cocked her head to look away from him and to the corner where the live mouse now hid. The mouse put his forepaw on the silver marble and rolled it away from the potted fern. Chickadee felt the tension in her spring and tried to calculate how many revolutions of movement it still offered her. She thought it would suffice.

"WHERE IS the missing wind-up key?" Sparrow hung from his line, waiting for the boy to wind him again.

"The live mouse has it." Chickadee hopped forward and pecked at another invisible crumb, but did not waste the movement needed to look at Sparrow.

"What would a *live* mouse need with a windup key?"

"He does not need it," said Chickadee. "But I *do* have need of it and he is in my service."

All the gears in the room stopped for a moment as the other clockwork animals paused to listen. Even the nightingale stopped her song. In the sudden cessation of ticking, sound from the greater world outside crept in, bringing the babble of the fountain in the courtyard, the laughter of the boy, the purr of automobiles and from the far distance, the faint pealing of a clock.

"I suppose you would have us believe that he winds you?" said Sparrow.

"Not yet. Perhaps today." She continued pecking the floor.

After a moment of nothing happening, the other animals returned to their tasks save for the sparrow. He hung from his line and beat his wings against his side.

"Ha! I see him. I see the live mouse behind the potted fern. You could too if you could fly."

"I have no need." Chickadee felt her clockwork beginning to slow. "Live Mouse!" she called. "It is time to fulfill our bargain."

The silence came again as the other animals stopped to listen. Into this quiet came a peculiar scraping rattle and then the live mouse emerged from behind the potted fern with the missing wind-up key tied in his tail.

"What is he doing?" Sparrow squawked.

Chickadee bent to peck the ground so slowly she thought she might never touch it. A gear clicked forward and she tapped the floor. "Do you really need me to tell you that?"

Above her, Sparrow dangled on his line. "Live Mouse! Whatever she has promised you, I can give you also, only wind my flying mechanism."

The live mouse twirled his whiskers and kept walking toward Chickadee. "Well now. That's a real interesting proposition. How about a silver marble?"

"There is one behind the potted fern."

"Not no more."

"Then a crystal from the chandelier."

The live mouse wrinkled his nose. "If'n I can climb the chandelier to wind ya, then I reckon I can reach a crystal for myself."

"I must have something you want."

With the key paused by Chickadee's side, the live mouse said, "That might be so."

The live mouse set the tip of the key down like a cane and folded his paws over it. Settling back on his haunches, he tipped his head up to study Sparrow. "How 'bout, you give me one of your wings?"

Sparrow squawked.

"You ain't got no need of 'em to fly, that right?" The live mouse looked down and idly twisted the key on the floor, as if he were winding the room. "Prob'ly make you spin round faster, like one of them zeppelin thingamabobs. Whazzat called? Air-o-dye-namic."

"A bird cannot fly without wings."

"Now you and I both know that ain't so. A *live* bird can't fly without wings, but you're a clockwork bird."

"What would a live mouse know about clockworks?"

The live mouse laughed. "Ain't you never heard of Hickory, Dickory, and Dock? We mice have a long history with clockworks. Looking at you, I figure you won't miss a wing none and without it dragging, you ought to be able to go faster and your windings would last you longer. Whaddya say? Wouldn't it be a mite sight nicer to fly without having to wait for the boy to come back?"

"What would you do with my wing?"

"That," the live mouse smiled, showing his sharp incisors, "is between me and Messrs. DeCola and Wodzinski. So do we have a deal?"

"I will have to consider the matter."

"Suit yourself." The live mouse lifted the key and put the tip in Chickadee's winding mechanism.

"Wait!" Sparrow flicked his wings as if anxious to be rid of them. "Yes, yes you may have my left wing, only wind me now. A bird is meant to fly."

"All righty, then."

Chickadee turned her head with painful slowness. "Now, Live Mouse, you and I have an agreement."

"That we did and we do, but nothing in it says I can't have another master."

"That may well be, but the wind-up key belongs to me."

"I reckon that's true. Sorry, Sparrow. Looks as if I can't help you none." The live mouse sighed. "And I surely did want me one of them wings."

Once again, he lifted the key to Chickadee's side. Above them, Sparrow let out a squeal of metal. "Wait! Chickadee, there must be something I can offer you. You are going on a journey, yes? From here, I can tell you if any dangers lie on your route."

"Only in this room and we are leaving it."

"Leaving? And taking the key with you?"

"Just so. Do not worry. The boy will come to wind you eventually. And now, Live Mouse, if you would be so kind."

"My other wing! You may have my other wing, only let the live mouse use the key to wind me."

Chickadee paused, waiting for her gears to click forward so that she could look at the Sparrow. Her spring was so loose now, that each action took an eternity. "What would I do with one of your wings? I have two of my own."

The other clockwork bird seemed baffled and hung on the end of the line flapping his wings as if he could fling them off.

The live mouse scraped a claw across the edge of the key. "It might come in real handy on our trip. Supposing Messrs. DeCola and Wodzinski want a higher payment than you're thinking they do. Why then you'd have something more to offer them."

"And if they didn't then we would have carried the wing with us for no reason."

"Now as to that," said the live mouse, "I can promise you that I'll take it off your hands if'n we don't need it."

Chickadee laughed. "Oh, Live Mouse, I see now. Very well, I will accept Sparrow's wing so that later you may have a full set. Messrs. DeCola and Wodzinski will be happy to have two customers, I am certain."

The live mouse bowed to her and wrapped the key in his tail again. "Sparrow, I'll be right up." Scampering across the floor, he disappeared into the wall.

Chickadee did not watch him go, she waited with her gaze still cocked upward toward Sparrow. With the live mouse gone, Chickadee became aware of how still the other clockworks were, watching their drama. Into the silence, Nightingale began to cautiously sing. Her beautiful warbles and chirps repeated through their song thrice before the live mouse appeared out of the ceiling on the chandelier's chain. The crystals of the chandelier tinkled in a wild accompaniment to the ordered song of the nightingale.

The live mouse shimmied down the layers of crystals until he reached Sparrow's flying mechanism. Crawling over that, he wrapped his paws around the string beneath it and slid down to sit on Sparrow's back.

"First one's for me." His sharp incisors flashed in the chandelier's light as he pried the tin loops up from the left wing. Tumbling free, it half fell, half floated to rattle against the floor below. "And now this is for the chickadee."

Again, his incisors pulled the tin free and let the second wing drop.

Sparrow's clockwork whirred audibly inside his body, with nothing to power. "I feel so light!"

"Told ya so." The live mouse reached up and took the string in his paws. Hauling himself back up the line, he reached the flying mechanism in no time at all. "Ready now?"

"Yes! Oh yes, wind me! Wind me!"

Lickety-split, the key sank into the winding mechanism and the live mouse began turning it. The sweet familiar sound of a spring ratcheting tighter floated down from above, filling the room. The other clockwork animals crept closer; even Chickadee felt the longing brought on by the sound of winding.

When the live mouse stopped, Sparrow said, "No, no, I am not wound nearly tight enough yet."

The live mouse braced himself with his tail around an arm of the chandelier and grunted as he turn the key again. And again. And again. "Enough?"

"Tighter."

He kept winding.

"Enough?"

"Tighter. The boy never winds me fully."

"All right." The mouse turned the key three more times and stopped. "That's it. Key won't turn no more."

A strange vibration ran through the sparrow's body. It took Chickadee a moment to realize that he was trying to beat his wings with anticipation. "Then watch me fly."

The live mouse pulled the key out of the flying mechanism and hopped up onto the chandelier. As he did, Sparrow swung into action. The flying mechanism whipped him forward and he shrieked with glee. His body was a blur against the ceiling. The chandelier trembled, then shook, then rattled as he spun faster than Chickadee had ever seen him.

"Live Mouse, you were rig—" With a snap, his flying mechanism broke free of the chandelier. "I'm flying!" Sparrow cried as he hurtled across the room. His body crashed into the window, shattering a pane as he flew through it.

The nightingale stopped her song in shock. Outside, the boy shrieked and his familiar footsteps hurried under the window. "Oh pooh. The clockwork sparrow is broken."

The mother's voice said, "Leave it alone. There's glass everywhere."

Overhead, the live mouse looked down and winked.

Chickadee pecked the ground, with her mechanism wound properly. The live mouse appeared at her side. "Thanks for the wings."

"I trust they are satisfactory payment?"

"Sure enough. They look real pretty hanging on my wall." He squinted at her. "So that's it? You're just going to keep on pecking the ground?"

"As long as you keep winding me."

"Yeah. It's funny, no one else wants my services."

"A pity."

"Got a question for you though. Will you tell me how to get to Messrs. DeCola and Wodzinski?"

"Why ever for?"

"Well, I thought . . . I thought maybe Messrs. DeCola and Wodzinski really could, I dunno, fix 'em on me so as I can fly."

Chickadee rapped the ground with laughter. "No, Mouse, they cannot. We are all bound to our integral mechanisms." She cocked her head at him. "You are a live mouse. I am a clockwork chickadee, and Messrs. DeCola and Wodzinski are nothing more than names on a scrap of paper glued to the bottom of a table."

Body Language

SASKIA LEANED into the darkness above the stage, only vaguely aware of the wood rail against her hips as she re-tied the left headstring on her marionette. On the stage below, the Snow Queen's head eased into balance. The marionette telegraphed its stance back up the strings to the control in Saskia's hands. She ran the Snow Queen across the set to check the repair, barely conscious of her own body on the bridge above the stage. It was almost like being immersed in a VR suit.

One of the techies called up. "Hey, Saskia? There's a detective here for you."

She stopped abruptly and the marionette continued its motion in a long pendulum swing. Detective? At the foot of the ladder, the techie stood next to a stocky man.

If she hadn't taken her Glass off, she might have gotten an alert from her interface about who he was, but she'd caught the lenses once with a puppet control. You only needed to watch them hit the stage floor during a performance one time to swear never to wear them on a bridge again.

Even without the Glass, it was obvious he was a detective. Rather than the slimline Glass so hip these days, he wore full wraparound AI interface glasses, with an eBud in one ear. Above each eye, a camera provided the AI with stereoscopic vision. At his throat, where you'd usually see a collar stud, he wore another camera.

And that was just the hardware that she could see.

Saskia shivered; AI always made her edgy. They were like puppets in reverse—a soul without a body. She took her time hanging up her puppet before she descended the ladder.

"Ms. Dorlan? I'm Agent Jared Patel with the FBI, and I'm accompanied by the AI Metta G. FBI." Patel's eyes flashed over Saskia's shoulder. She glanced back before realizing that he was looking at the AI in his interface glasses. It gave her the creeps. "Do you have an interface she could sync in on?"

"My fans are usually a little younger . . . " She tried to use humor to lighten the tension, but Patel's lips barely curved in response.

"We need to talk to you about eDawg."

Saskia had done the motion-capture for eDawg in the series eCity, but she could not, for the life of her, figure out why the FBI would be investigating the puppet. They hadn't filmed a new episode in over a year.

Unless, holy crap, unless this was about one of the toys the series had spun off. Maybe one of their tiny terrier brains had gone rogue and killed some rich kid. It had to be a rich kid; they never investigated the deaths of poor ones.

"I realize this will seem like a strange request. Your producers agreed to loan us the eDawg puppet, but only if you oversee its care. They said the controls are customized to you and they didn't want to risk it with someone else."

"I'm stunned that they would let the puppet out of the studio at all. You must have a heck of an insurance waiver."

"We're the government." He let that sit between them for a moment, then smiled. It was not comforting. "We'll compensate you for your time, of course."

The word *compensate* changed everything. He wasn't investigating eDawg; he was offering her a gig. "So you want me to work the puppet?" She itched to get back into the suit again. She loved traditional puppetry, but nothing compared to motion-capture work.

"Our AI will handle that, don't worry; you're just there as a formality."

"Look." She caught herself before she could start a rant about AIs driving puppeteers out of film and video work. "Even if I were willing, it's not going to look right."

"What do you mean?"

"When you recognize someone from a distance, it's not just their height and weight, it's how they move. Give the same puppet to different puppeteers and it'll look like different characters. That's why they had me do the motion-capture work when they made the toy versions of eDawg." She stopped suddenly, wondering why they needed the puppet at all. "Can't you use one of the toys? They look just like eDawg and there are like, thousands of them."

"We need to have more control of eDawg than a toy would provide."

"You can have control, but you won't have eDawg. Not unless it moves like me."

Patel shifted his gaze to the spot over her shoulder. His jaw worked in silent conversation with his AI partner. Crazy machines had no idea how people thought or moved, yet they thought it could do the job.

Patel looked back at her. "Our agent feels confident that she'll be able to match your movements."

"Is this something you can force me to do?"

"No."

"Then I can't see any reason to help someone else do *my* job." She grabbed the ladder to climb back up.

Patel leaned forward. "Do you know Hamilton Cruise?"

"Personally? No. Seen him in the news, yeah."

"His son, Wade, has been kidnapped. The kid's toy eDawg was the only witness. We've got the thing torn apart trying to access its memory without wiping it, but the kidnappers just told us that they want the ransom delivered via eDawg. You say 'no' to this, we don't get to use the puppet. You say 'no' and that kid's life is thrown up in the air."

Crap. A kid. Saskia stopped where she was on the ladder and rested her head against the rung. "Okay. Let me tell the stage manager where I'm going."

At the FBI field office, the motion-capture rig dominated the space like a bizarre piece of gym equipment.

In the early days of motion-capture, the performer roamed the studio trailing wires, but the new technology used a universal treadmill floor to allow performers to simulate covering ground while remaining in a single location. In the center of the rig, almost obscured by cables and rods, was the carapace Saskia wore when she performed. It looked like a wire-frame rendering of eDawg. In addition to controls for eDawg's ears and tail, the carapace had sensors built into it so that when Saskia moved, the system translated her movements via a wireless interface to the puppet's limbs. Patel's AI partner would hack into the signal and bypass the rig.

A holo of a woman's head and shoulders materialized over a desktop interface. She smiled with almost Victorian purity. "I'm Metta. Sorry I couldn't introduce myself earlier."

"That's fine." Saskia had been in no hurry to meet the AI then, and would be more than happy to skip it now.

For the next fifteen minutes, she watched the smooth purple titanium dog spin through a series of movements, all of which looked indistinguishable from her performance. Even the bark sounded like her. It was uncanny, like the first time she had seen one of the toys activated. Except then she had been watching a three-dimensional recording of her performance. This was different; the AI could replace her. Heck, the AI could *be* her.

When Metta finished, she turned to Saskia and said, "Am I convincing as eDawg?"

She was convincing as a bitch, yes. But Saskia nodded. "That all looks really good."

"Thank you." The AI looked unsurprised at Saskia's praise. "Would you watch us role-play the scenario for dropping the ransom money?"

Patel held the door open. "We'll have eDawg start as if it were on the street outside the drop location."

eDawg sniffed the air as it leaned forward, with its ears held upright and tail wagging. The movements looked familiar. They also looked wrong. Saskia said, "That's from the episode with the eTreats, isn't it?"

"Yes," Metta said.

"eDawg was searching for treats then. She shouldn't be excited here. Think 'scared.'"

The sniffing changed instantly. eDawg crouched and shivered. She lifted her nose and sniffed twice. Saskia's jaw dropped. It looked *exactly* like eDawg emerging from her doghouse in the thunderstorm episode. "Are you doing this by rote?"

"I'm mimicking your movement."

Saskia glared at Metta. "You can't just copy what I did in episodes, you'll make inappropriate choices."

Patel pursed his lips and turned to Saskia. "Can you teach her?"

The taste of "no" filled her mouth, but a kid's life was on the line. "How long do I have?"

"Two hours."

They wanted her to teach fifteen years of experience in two hours. Not possible. She bit her lower lip and tried to focus on the problem at hand. "What's your cue to enter?"

"The kidnapper gave us the address; Mr. Cruise is supposed to drop eDawg off a block away."

"eDawg wouldn't understand it if you told her to go to a specific address. You could point her in a direction or tell her to 'go home,' but that's about it." This was stupid. There was no way she could teach Metta everything she needed to know about the character in time.

Patel's jaw worked subtly as he subvocalized. Metta gave no outward sign of having a private conversation with him, instead she said, "What sort of signals might eDawg look for?"

"A whistle, a trail of eTreats, a ball . . . someone familiar? I don't know. Look—" Saskia caught herself before she could offer to perform eDawg for the ransom drop. She might know puppetry, but there was no way she should be involved in a kidnapping investigation. "You'll have to hope it's obvious."

"Will you show me the correct response to each of those?"

Saskia's neck stiffened like someone had shoved a control rod through her spine. There was not enough time. "Do you want me to just perform the puppet?" She wanted to call the words back as soon as they were out of her mouth, but she didn't see a choice if they wanted to get this kid back.

Patel looked at her and smiled. "We were just talking about that."

"And what have you decided?"

Metta raised her chin. "We're still discussing it."

"I think having Ms. Dorlan work the puppet may be our best option." Patel tugged at the cuff of his shirt and avoided looking at Metta's interface.

Metta's nostrils flared, for all the world as if she'd taken a deep, angry breath. "I can learn this."

"Look." Saskia raised her hand. "It's not that I don't think you can, but it took me fifteen years to get to where I am—"

"With all due respect, I learn faster than you can." Metta rocked eDawg back on her heels in a perfect match of Saskia's movement. "I simply need the right instructions, which I am not getting."

"Excuse me if I don't offer to upload my brain for you. But, gosh. I *can't*. You want to learn this. You have to practice it. And you have two hours. So do you want to practice or do you want me to work the puppet?"

Patel's jaw moved but he said nothing that Saskia could hear. At her feet eDawg lay down and powered off.

Patel cleared his throat and turned to Saskia. "So you're willing to work the puppet?"

Saskia ought to have felt vindicated that they recognized her skills, but there were still so many things that could go wrong with this role. But there was this kid, Wade, and underneath that . . . she loved working eDawg. She loved the purity of motivation in the character and the simple trust of being a dog. "What would I have to do?"

"Not much. You'd carry the money in saddlebags and wait for the kidnappers to send you back with instructions. We'll use the cameras built into the puppet to map the location." Patel seemed to sense Saskia's unease. "It's extremely unlikely that Wade will be there. Typically, the kidnappers keep the victim at a safe distance from the drop location."

Thank God. The possibility that a mistake might get the kid killed had slowly been making its way to the front of her brain.

Patel gestured to the puppet. "Want to practice?"

"That's okay." Puppetry came as easily as breathing. Saskia frowned, remembering all the quirks of the rig. "I think you'll have to put it in a truck."

"What? Why?" Patel said. "I thought it was designed to work remotely."

"It's designed to work in a studio; the farther away I am, the more likely you are to have a delay or interference with the wireless signal."

"Ah. What else do you need?"

"I need a picture of Wade." The toy's tiny brain would have learned to recognize Wade as its owner and part of eDawg's character was all about strong loyalty. If she was going to do this part, she was going to do it right. Speaking of doing it right. "And you'll need to talk to my agent."

WHILE PATEL OVERSAW transferring the rig to a truck, Metta briefed Saskia on what they knew about Wade's kidnapping, which was very little. Wade had disappeared from the family home two nights previously. The housekeeper had found Devon Taylor, Wade's bodyguard, on the floor of Wade's rec room, dead from a gunshot wound to the chest. Ballistics showed that he had been shot by his own weapon, but it had not been self-inflicted. The forensic evidence suggested the gun had been fired while the assailant was trying to get it away from Taylor.

The security tapes were erased. There were no signs of forced entry.

The following day, a ransom e-mail had arrived from a free account.

If Wade's father had carried a kidnapping policy on his insurance, they might have considered him as a suspect, but he didn't, so he stood to gain nothing. Currently, they were expecting that Saskia would see someone related to a household staff member, but not one of the intimate family members.

"But," Metta stressed, "I'm only telling you this so you can have appropriate reactions as eDawg. You are not here to investigate. We'll monitor what you see and evaluate that."

Saskia nodded and stared at the holo of Wade that Metta was projecting. According to the AI, the boy was thirteen years old. His black hair was slicked back in the latest style and looked like it had a week's salary worth of styling products in it. But he smiled at the camera with remarkable openness and held eDawg in his lap.

Patel poked his head through the doorway. "We're ready for you now."

A thrill of butterflies tingled in her gut. It had been years since a show made her nervous. Not that this was really a show, not in the traditional sense.

From the outside, the truck looked like it belonged to UPS. Inside, it was a studio in miniature.

On a small table, the puppet lay waiting for Saskia's manipulation to bring it to life. Metta's virtual-head floated over a desktop interface in the corner of the truck. Boxes were stacked at the front of the rig to shield it from casual view through the truck's windshield.

The act of strapping herself into the rig soothed Saskia the way she imagined others might feel about yoga. As much as she enjoyed traditional puppetry, motion-capture was the closest she got to actually *being* something else.

When she was suited up, with a sensor at each of her major joints, and the vowel capture next to her lips, she tweaked the carapace to get the right amount of resistance. A motion-capture rig had a higher level of articulation than a standard VR suit, but it required finer calibration. More importantly, it provided haptic feedback so that she could feel the floor under eDawg's feet.

Saskia dropped the VR headset in place.

When the feed on the headset went live, Saskia had a moment of disorientation as she adjusted to looking through eDawg's eyes. Inside the carapace, she flexed her left hand to activate the ears. With her right, she triggered the control that manipulated eDawg's tail. Then, with each joint, she stretched, checking the range of movement. Saskia's mind shifted as her consciousness of the puppet's body became greater than her awareness of her own.

She stood on the table and Patel towered over her. Wagging her tail, she barked for attention.

He jumped, and then, as if he couldn't help himself, Patel patted her on the head. The rig pushed against her head as it readjusted to the puppet's new position. It felt as if *her* head were being patted.

She wagged her tail in a frenzy of pleasure.

Patel grinned sheepishly and looked over to the side. "I know it's a puppet, but you're really good."

Saskia turned her head to follow his gaze and saw herself.

She looked away. The image of her body twitching in a web of cables and rods was not one she needed in her head while she was performing.

Another agent climbed into the truck with Hamilton Cruise behind him. Cruise was lean and sinewy. His eyes were red and his entire body leaned forward as if he wanted something badly.

He examined her, strapped into the rig. "What's this?"

Patel said, "Ms. Dorlan is the original puppeteer for eDawg. She's agreed to—"

"The kidnapper asked for *Wade's* eDawg. I wasn't informed about this."

"It's a decision we reached this morning."

"I will not have you taking chances with my son's life!" The veins in his neck stood out like control cables gone wrong.

Metta said, "Mr. Cruise, we believe that Ms. Dorlan's participation is the best chance to bring your son out unharmed. She is a professional puppeteer and knows this character better than anyone."

Saskia stopped fiddling with the sensor at her elbow and stared at Metta. That could not have been easy for the AI to say.

"I don't care if she's Lassie! I object to this in the strongest possible terms. I demand that you send in Wade's toy."

"Sir, even if that were advisable, the toy is currently disassembled as our technicians try to retrieve its memory without wiping it. It is not possible to send the toy in."

Cruise's face strobed through a spectrum of color—white, red, and ended in purple. "If anything happens to my boy, you'll hear from my lawyers. This is gross incompetence." Scowling, he thrust a pair of saddlebags at Patel. Saskia assumed they contained the ransom money.

Patel strapped the bulging bags to eDawg. As he did, the carapace pressed against Saskia, giving her a sense of the change in weight on the puppet. When he was finished, he patted her flank. "Break a leg."

Metta whispered in her ear. "I'll be riding your signal. If you need anything, subvee and I'll have an agent take care of it."

"Will do." Saskia's heart pounded like this was her first time on stage. "Let's kick some puppet butt."

Cruise carried her out to his car like she was covered with mange instead of plastic. As they drove to the rendezvous point, Saskia kept the puppet alive, looking around at the buildings, cars, and pedestrians with the random curiosity of a dog.

When the car stopped, Cruise opened the door to let her out. They were at a street corner in the industrial district. The interstate ran overhead and buildings hunched up against it, almost making a tunnel of the street.

eDawg would not know what to do. She looked up at Cruise and whined.

He pointed. "Go on."

When he pointed again, angrily, as if she were a real dog, she trotted down the street. The buildings towered over her puppet body and made her feel very small.

The abandoned Masonic Lodge where the drop was supposed to occur was at the end of the block, but she could think of no motivation for eDawg to go there. So she sniffed and explored the street, praying for a cue.

The door opened.

Out of the darkness, she heard a short whistle. Thank heavens. Cocking her head, she trotted to the door, pausing to peer inside. The door opened onto a broad, dark lobby.

Three doors spanned the far wall. They were heavy double-doors with amber stained glass in their upper panel. On her right, a fourth door opened on a flight of stairs.

Saskia knew someone had to be behind the front door, but it would never occur to eDawg to look. So she walked to the middle of the room, her hard paws clattering on the marble floor. When the door shut behind her, she yelped and spun.

Wade stood in the shadows.

She bounded toward him with her tail in full wag, fighting the urge to look for the kidnappers; eDawg would only care about her owner.

Wade's mouth twisted in a smile. "Hello, Edie."

Saskia's heart skipped. eDawg had never had a nickname; she liked it.

As Wade stepped forward, the light from the dusty windows caught blood staining the side of his shirt.

Metta whispered in her ear. "Can you tell if it's his blood?"

As if that hadn't occurred to her. But it never paid to argue with your stage manager, and that's what Metta was for this gig, AI or no. Saskia sidled closer, begging Wade to pet her, so she could get a closer look. When he knelt without a trace of pain in his movements, she subvocalized back to Metta, "I don't think it is." It must belong to his bodyguard. She had a horrible vision of the bodyguard jumping in front of Wade to save him.

"Hey, girl." Wade's face was haggard and his hair hung in his eyes with all trace of style gone. He looked younger than his photo.

Her vision of the world swung crazily as Wade scooped her up. "I've been so scared, Edie."

Where were the kidnappers?

She rested her head on Wade's shoulder and looked around as discretely as she could. The lobby was empty.

He leaned his head against hers. "I'm sorry I left you, but it's okay now. Right?"

"Right!" she barked, as her mind raced to figure out what he meant.

"That's my girl." Wade set her down and unstrapped the saddlebags from her side. "Dad sent it all, huh?"

"Aroo?" She cocked her head at him.

"It's okay." Wade peered inside one of the bags. Trotting closer, she stuck her head in the saddlebag to look. He laughed. "It's just money. No eTreats."

Sitting on her haunches, she raised her front paws and begged for one of the virtual treats.

"I'll get you one later. Promise." The corners of his mouth turned down and he pulled a reset key out of the saddlebag. "Man, I don't want to do this."

"What is he—" Metta broke off as the center door opened.

Three skate punks sauntered into the room. One had Day-Glo red hair in a perm like Ronald McDonald. Another was so skinny his elbows had worn holes in his green flannel shirt.

She had to protect her owner. Loyalty was the biggest part of eDawg's character. Getting between Wade and the skate punks, she growled with all the ferocity an electronic terrier could muster.

Wade's face paled and he clutched the saddlebags to his chest. "Come on, Edie."

She backed away slowly, still growling at the punks.

The last punk through the door, a boy no older than Wade and with more piercings than eDawg had bolts, shook his head lazily. "I don't think so, Wade."

"Do I know you?" Wade's voice cracked an octave higher.

"Doesn't matter." Piercing Boy leaned against the door.

Trying to keep herself between Wade and the punks, Saskia subveed Metta, "Are you getting this?"

"Yes," Metta whispered. "We're considering our options. The one on the left has a gun tucked in his waistband."

She adjusted the view in Saskia's VR glasses to highlight a slight bulge under the shirt of the kid who looked like McDonald. Saskia couldn't see the gun, but MickyD's body language was filled with confidence.

Taking Wade's pant cuff in her mouth, she tugged toward the door. Got to get him out of there.

MickyD slipped his gun out and pointed it at Wade.

"What . . . what's going on?" Wade retreated a step, making her dance to avoid getting stepped on.

Metta whispered, "When I tell you, get Wade on the ground."

Saskia's heart was pounding so hard that it had to be shaking the puppet. She weighed all of six pounds. How the heck was she supposed to get Wade on the floor?

"You're coming with us." Piercing Boy gestured to Skinny, who yanked the saddlebag out of Wade's hands and slung it over his own shoulder. Piercing Boy stepped back through the doors leading deeper into the Masonic temple, as if absolutely certain Wade would follow. Almost before MickyD beckoned with his gun, Wade had already stumbled forward.

In Saskia's ear, Metta whispered, "Stay with him."

She trotted as close to Wade as she could, praying that the skate punks would let eDawg follow. They led her and Wade down a long hall flanked on the left by windows with the same amber glass as the lobby doors. As she passed each window, she tensed, expecting Metta's command to come with a hail of bullets. But she passed through the flashes of light and shadow without hearing anything from the AI.

At the end of the hall, Piercing Boy jogged down a broad set of stairs. Crap. eDawg couldn't handle steps. Saskia stopped at the top of the steps, whining. Wade, bless him, bent to pick her up.

"What do you think you're doing?" MickyD held the gun in Wade's face.

Wade stopped, held still by the gun. His face was pale. "Her legs are too short for the stairs."

Saskia held her breath; she could see Wade think about snatching the gun. Bad plan. She barked at MickyD to distract both boys.

"Screw that." MickyD swung his foot forward and kicked her.

Wade shouted, "No!"

Saskia yelped as the world twisted in her vision. The stairs. Wade. A light spun past. Saskia shut her eyes against the nausea, but her harness readjusted brutally, wrenching her limbs into the puppet's new posture. Her eyes snapped open. This was not supposed to hurt.

eDawg lay on the landing of the stairs, in front of Piercing Boy. Behind him, MickyD and Skinny laughed like kids with a new toy. Piercing Boy kicked her twice, sliding her body to the edge of the steps and then sending her spinning through the air again.

She tried to stay limp as the carapace forced her into new positions, but when the movement stopped, she did not have to act to make eDawg shiver. She dragged herself back to all fours, wincing as her knee protested.

The boys clattered down the stairs, pushing Wade in front of them.

"See. It can go down steps by itself." Piercing Boy slapped Wade on the back of the head, pushing him past eDawg's shivering body. Wade looked at her with anguish written on his face; God in heaven, he really cared about Edie. His body tensed as if he was going to spin and punch Piercing Boy. She held his gaze and shook her head.

Wade did a double-take, but he didn't try anything stupid.

Saskia limped after them, becoming more aware of the fatigue in her real body than she was of the puppet she manipulated. At the end of the hall, the boys disappeared around the corner; Wade's face briefly shone like a ghost in the dark.

Something scraped across stone. She forced herself into a run, stretching her front legs out and thrusting with her hind legs.

By the time she reached the end of the hall, Skinny was dragging a piece of the wall closed behind him.

Metta said, "Keep it open!"

Saskia barked sharply, hurling herself at the crack. Dodging back and forth, she nipped at Skinny's ankles. She had never wanted working teeth on eDawg as much as she did now.

"Want me to shoot it?" MickyD said.

"Nah." Piercing Boy picked a flashlight off the floor. "We'll just lock it up on this side of the wall."

Fear trembled down her spine before Saskia remembered that *she* was in a truck above ground. For the time being, she just needed to keep eDawg close to Wade until the cavalry arrived. Without her, they had no way of knowing where these kids were taking Wade.

Against the far wall, Wade sat on the ground with his hands in his lap. MickyD stood over him, still holding the gun.

Wade raised his head and leaned slightly toward her. His hand twitched as if he wanted to reach out.

Skinny kicked her aside, pushing the stone wall shut. As the wall ground into place, eDawg missed a step. Great. The wall was blocking the signal. She jerked forward with an increasing delay in movement. Saskia slowed down, trying to mask her struggle to manipulate the puppet.

She subveed, "I'm losing the signal. Can you get the truck closer?"

"I'll tell the driver."

Saskia crept toward Wade, keeping her head down and her body language as submissive as possible. Expecting MickyD to stop her, she crawled into Wade's lap and collapsed.

She could not feel the warmth of his body, but she could tell he was petting her by the way her harness shifted gently against her spine. "Shh. It's okay. Good girl . . . "

What kind of boy tries to comfort a toy? She pressed her head into his side, wishing she could comfort her owner back, but the signal was too uncertain for specific movement.

Wade pulled her up so her head rested on his shoulder. He whispered, "Record mode, on."

She pulled her head back to look at him. This close, she could see the circles under his eyes. And inside his eyes, she could see her own reflection—eDawg's reflection. Wade whispered in her ear, as if he were Metta, "Tell my dad I'm sorry. It was an accident. The gun just went off. I shouldn't have run away, I was just scared. I'm still scared . . . "

Saskia wanted to shush him, to tell him that other people were listening, but all she could do was stay in character. She pushed her snout against him, trying to nuzzle comfort into him.

MickyD dragged Wade to his feet, tumbling eDawg onto the floor. "Move it."

Staggering after Wade, she followed the light, determined not to be left behind. She couldn't leave Wade with these punks. He wasn't safe. She wagged her tail to encourage him, not knowing if he could see her in the gloom. The corridor bent and twisted as if it were dodging other buildings or sewer pipes. She lost sight of her boy. After each step she took, she had to wait for the puppet to respond. The plodding pace made her want to scream.

They were getting away.

Her world went dark. The system locked, freezing her limbs in place.

Hands grabbed her, her real body, helping her sit. Saskia winced at the bright light in the truck as her VR headset was pulled off. Patel leaned over her and she flinched at the sight of him. Saskia had forgotten that anyone except Metta was with her.

"Are you all right?"

Saskia nodded. Nothing around her seemed real. The lights were too bright; the lines were too sharp. The truck seemed crowded with people after the confines of the tunnel.

Beyond the cables surrounding her, Cruise leaned toward Patel in a perfect aggressive line. "What is happening down there! Where is he?"

Patel held her gaze, as if he needed an anchor to hold his temper. "We're working on that, sir."

"Well, get her back online. Send her back!"

Saskia wanted to tear the motion capture gear off and hurl it at him. "They're too far underground; I don't have a signal."

"So you've got no idea what's happening down there!" Cruise virtually ignored her and continued to yell at Patel.

Metta said, "We are proceeding to the best of our abilities."

"Bull. I'll go in there myself." Cruise strode to the door.

Patel pushed past the cables to follow him. "I don't recommend that."

"What do you recommend? Another puppet show?" He slammed out of the truck.

Patel hesitated for a moment. He glanced at Saskia. "Metta is going to have the driver try to get above eDawg's last position." Then he followed Cruise, cursing quietly under his breath.

As the truck rumbled forward, Metta let out an almost human sigh. "I'm sorry about that."

"It's all right."

But, it wasn't all right. Wade was missing, and even if she could get back to him, there was nothing she could do. The whole thing sucked. She had spent, what, twenty minutes with Wade? But she still felt her character's loyalty to the boy as strongly as if she weren't acting. She tried to relax as the truck rumbled forward, but the last half-hour kept replaying. None of it made sense.

The truck stopped moving and Metta said, "We have a clean signal now."

The thought of dropping to all fours made her muscles ache. "You should take over."

"I—" Metta shook her head. "I'm not used to being bad at something, but you were right. It has to be you."

"Does it make a difference now?"

"There are too many new variables. I don't want to change anything. Unless you don't feel like you can continue."

Saskia picked up the VR helmet. "Show must go on." She pulled it down over her eyes.

eDawg was still in the dark, and the corridor was silent around her. Rolling onto eDawg's belly, she gathered her legs under herself and started down the corridor. She subveed to Metta. "Do you have any idea where we are?"

"You're under Burnside, close to the corner of Northeast Third. I think the kidnappers came out in the basement of a warehouse there. I've sent agents down, but they haven't made visual contact, and the agents behind you are having difficulty getting through the wall."

"What am I supposed to do?" And just like that, she realized that she trusted Metta the way she would trust a good director.

"Find Wade. Be ready to get him onto the ground."

"Yeah. About that. I'm knee-high. How do I can knock the kid down?"

Saskia set off blindly down the hall, relying on her sense of balance.

"I would suggest tripping him." She must be imagining it, but she thought she heard hesitation in Metta's voice.

Saskia considered angle of impact and the physics of knocking Wade down, the way that she would run through a complicated piece of blocking. "Yeah. That could work. Good call."

Walking in virtual darkness seemed to take forever. When she finally reached the end of the corridor, she found another false wall. This one was partially open.

She peeked around the corner. The ceiling sloped toward her, so that a human would have to walk bent over. A single light bulb hung halfway across the room, casting harsh shadows among the old brick columns supporting the ceiling.

She looked for some indication of where Wade might be. By instinct, she lowered her nose to the ground, which was beyond stupid, since she had no sense of smell and no audience.

Metta said, "Hold still."

"What?"

"The dust is scuffed here." Metta highlighted the image on the screen, and a slight path in the dust on the ground showed. "Can you follow it?"

"Keep it highlighted." Saskia kept eDawg's nose to the ground, and Metta lit the trail up like a yellow brick road. It wound along the side of the room until she came to a low break in the wall.

"Ah . . . " Metta whispered. "That's how they got out."

Peering carefully through the hole, Saskia could not see any sign of the boys. "Do you want me to go through?"

"Yes, we're parked just outside then entrance now. I'll send the team in the truck down, but—"

Shouting and gunfire came at her from two places at once. Her mind reeled, caught between worlds. "That sounded—"

"Shh. Stop. Play dead."

Saskia flattened eDawg against the dirty floor of the tunnel. In the distance, she could hear the boys' voices. She waited, her heart pounding in her chest, for Metta to tell her what was happening. Lying down, she felt as if she were in two places at once. She heard the boys underground, but could also feel a vibration from the floor of the UPS truck, giving her a reminder of her real body.

Metta whispered, "Listen carefully, but do not move or react. They are in the truck."

Saskia stopped breathing.

"They attacked the agent driving and are in the front."

"How is that even possible? You're the freaking FBI."

Metta's voice was pained. "I made an error. There were two sets of stairs and our agents were on the wrong one."

"And you sent them all."

A human's breath would have hitched here. Metta was only silent.

Saskia closed her eyes and tried to become conscious of her real surroundings. The vibrations grew stronger, accompanied by a sense of motion. The truck was rolling forward again. It maddened her to lie on the ground without doing anything. She tried listening past her headset for sounds in the truck, but nothing was loud enough to be distinct. The truck was not that large, no bigger than a real UPS box truck, but her headset muffled everything. "I'm going to take off my VR headset."

"I don't advise that."

Saskia tensed all of her muscles against the desire to move. "What should I do then, just lie here?"

"We are in pursuit."

"They're going to notice me eventually."

"Not necessarily. Two of them are in the cab of the truck. Only one is in the back and if you don't move, I am hoping they will not notice that you are embedded in the rig." Metta paused. "Do you want me to feed the image from my interface to your VR headset?"

"Yeah, that'd be good."

The image on her headset changed. She saw the truck as if she sat at Metta's desktop interface in the corner. Creepy.

She could see why Metta hoped they wouldn't notice her. The carapace of the rig masked her enough that it would be possible to think she was a modern art sculpture, all hard plastic and wires. From where MickyD leaned against the front wall of the truck, with his gun pointed loosely at Wade, it would be impossible to see the few points where her skin was exposed.

Wade sat on the floor of the truck, with his arms wrapped around himself. He was staring at her body as if seeing a ghost, as if he knew *exactly* what this rig did and who she was.

Her body, almost obscured by the rods and cables of the rig, lay on the floor like a marionette dog. She had a sudden urge to see if she could manipulate it like a puppet on a screen. Her left hand twitched before she could stifle the thought.

MickyD glanced at the rig, and for a moment Saskia thought he hadn't noticed her in the tangle of cables. But like a cartoon character, he did a double-take and pointed the gun at her.

"Hey! There's a chick back here."

Piercing Boy leaned through the small door between the cab and cargo area. "What are you talking about?"

"Look." He pointed the gun at her again, but the bulk of the rig was between her and Piercing Boy. Letting the gun drop for a moment, MickyD shoved a bunch of cables to the side.

Piercing Boy ducked under the cables. "Who the hell are you?"

Saskia sat up, watching herself move in third person. The rig shifted around her as if it were manipulating her. She pulled the VR headset off, and her point of view shifted violently.

Piercing Boy loomed over her, closer than she expected. "I said, who are you?"

"I'm Saskia Dorlan." She paused, waiting for Metta to tell her what to do.

"I don't care about your freaking name, what are you doing here? What is this?"

Shit. Without the VR headset, Metta could not secretly talk to her. She was cut off. Saskia's stage instincts kicked in with adrenaline to spare. Spin it, girl. This is a stage show gone wrong, just find a way to end the scene. If you couldn't hide a mistake, try to work it in. She didn't even need to wholly convince them, just keep them off-balance long enough for Patel and the rest of the FBI to come to the rescue.

"I'm one of the puppeteers on the show." She smiled. "You guys are doing a great job."

"What are you talking about?"

Trying to mask her shaking fingers, Saskia started undoing the sensors on her arms. eDawg must be having a seizure. "Sorry. My bad. I just figured since the camera crew wasn't here, you'd drop character."

The words came out of her mouth as if a prompter were standing offstage. Saskia turned her attention to the buckles on the legs. "I hate these reality shows, but it's a living, right, Wade?" She looked at the boy, willing him to go along with it.

He startled, visibly, but before either punk turned, Wade was nodding.

Piercing Boy said, "What do you mean, *reality show*?"

Saskia let her mouth drop. "Shit. You didn't know? I thought you were actors, too." She stood, dropping the leggings on the ground. Only her torso remained attached to the rig. "Oh hell no . . . you must be the contestants. The director is going to kill me. I just figured since you were here, he must . . . Look, if you could not say anything, I'd really appreciate it." Without the VR headset on, she had no way of knowing if Metta would get the hint. Trying to keep her panic from showing, she glanced around. "Where's the rest of the crew?"

Piercing Boy screamed at her. "I want to know what's going on, and I want to know now!"

Saskia widened her eyes, leaning back to show apprehension. It took all her acting skill to keep from gibbering like an idiot. "Okay,

okay. Just don't say you got it from me. I don't want to get fired. We're shooting a new show called *To Catch a Thief* and I didn't realize you weren't briefed beforehand. Wade and I only met last week. Say, Wade, can you undo the strap on this for me?"

She reached her arm behind her, as if there were a buckle there too. Wade levered himself off the ground, and slid past the cables. He was smaller than she thought. His every movement screamed of fear.

Saskia kept babbling to distract the two punks. "It's a great concept, because they can use my puppet to do the filming when they can't work in a camera crew. Although, man, when you kicked the dog down the stairs, I thought I'd never get a clean shot again." She laughed, as if she were sharing a joke in the green room, and stepped forward so she was between them and Wade. "So where'd they find you guys?"

"Cruise hired—"

The truck slammed to a stop.

Saskia let the rig catch her, while MickyD and Piercing Boy tumbled backwards, tripping over cables. Wade slammed into her. She heard his breath *wuff* past her ear.

Skinny leaned through the little door at the front of the truck. "The road's blocked! What do I do?"

Saskia's breath caught in her throat; Piercing Boy had said, "Cruise hired . . . " Wade's father had sent these punks? Why?

She looked over her shoulder at Wade, willing him to understand that help was on the way. "That's the film crew."

He nodded, almost imperceptibly.

"The director will probably want to reset for the last scene."

Piercing Boy scrambled to his feet. "I don't like it when people screw with me—"

The back door of the truck flew open. Patel bounded up the steps. His coat was gone and the sleeves of his shirt were rolled up. He held a clipboard in one hand, his other hand was poised behind it as if he held a pen. "Babe! What are you doing to me?"

Babe?

She turned to face Patel, because that's what she would do with a real director. But the thought of having a gun at her back made her scalp prickle with fear. Wade's eyes were huge.

Patel nodded at Wade, "Doing great, kid. Head out to wardrobe."

Patel's back was too stiff; he didn't have the relaxed confidence of a director. He moved like a cop.

She heard MickyD's weight shift.

Saskia turned her head as MickyD leaned forward, raising the gun. She pushed Wade down, falling toward him as Metta yelled over the loudspeakers, "Get down!"

Patel dropped the clipboard, bringing his gun out to cover MickyD. Wade hit the ground. The rig caught Saskia, suspending her.

A gun fired.

The sound ricocheted through the truck, and pain screamed through her back.

DESPITE SASKIA'S NOTES, her understudy botched his first scene as he overplayed the moment. Saskia fidgeted in the auditorium seat. She shouldn't be in the audience, but she couldn't even climb the ladder to the bridge.

Her PDA vibrated in her pocket. Saskia eased out of her seat and slipped out the side door of the auditorium to answer it.

"Saskia? This is Metta."

She sounded so human. It was easy to forget she was a machine. Heck, it was like talking to an old crew member long after a show wrapped. "The arraignment just ended. I figured you'd want to know."

The thoughtfulness of the AI continued to stagger Saskia. The entire time she had been in the hospital, Metta had kept a small part of her consciousness keyed into the interface in Saskia's room, just in case she needed anything. "Thanks. I'd been wondering."

"The DA agreed to a plea bargain of involuntary manslaughter. In exchange, they won't try Wade as an adult."

Saskia closed her eyes with relief. The kid had been through enough. She had been terrified that they would go to trial and she would have to testify. "And his dad?"

"That was part of the plea bargain. His father is charged with obstruction of justice and conspiracy; he confessed to trying to cover up Wade's involvement in the bodyguard's death. After Wade ran away, Cruise erased the security tapes. When he realized that it was only a matter of time until we cracked the encryption on Wade's eDawg—which would have shown exactly what happened—he made the 'ransom demand' to send in the toy so they could wipe the memory."

"So that's why Wade had a reset key." Saskia remembered him pulling it out of the saddlebags.

"Correct."

"Did you crack the encryption?"

Metta laughed. "Puppets are hard, encryption is easy. Wade was trying to get Taylor to let him hold his gun. Taylor wouldn't let him. They wrestled. The gun went off. If he'd reported it . . . "

"What about the skate punks?"

"Cruise hired them to make the kidnapping look good. Once they figured out how much money was involved, they decided that actually kidnapping Wade would be more profitable." Metta paused. "How are you?"

"Getting better." She used her good shoulder to shrug. The bullet had gone in her back at an angle, skating across her shoulder blade and ripping a hole through her trapezius. It wasn't life-threatening, but played havoc with her ability to perform. "The deal you guys signed with my agent means the feds are paying my bills till I'm healed. It's better than most theater contracts."

"But it is healing, right?" There was a strange insistence in Metta's voice.

"Yeah. I'll be offline—so to speak," Saskia winced at the turn of phrase, "for another couple of months."

Metta cleared her throat, which was such a strange thing, when

Saskia thought about it. "Patel is giving me no end of grief because of my sudden fascination with puppetry."

"Well, you tell him that it's an old and noble profession. And then make him buy you a puppet."

"I did."

Saskia nearly dropped the phone in her astonishment. "Really? A puppet?"

"I know it's peculiar. I've never envied a flesh and blood person before, but riding your signal while you were controlling eDawg, I did. I could feel the puppet's responses to you and watch how you manipulated it to give meaning to its movements. It's the closest I've come to having a body. When I worked the puppet at headquarters, it was . . . it was an external thing. I mean, I can analyze body language and tell you exactly what it means, but I didn't understand the visceral way character relates to movement. Which brings me to a question . . ." She took a breath, like a person steeling herself for disappointment. "Would you be willing to teach me?"

Saskia leaned against the wall and let it hold her up. Teach her? "You'll have to practice, you know."

"I know. I'm willing to learn this in real time. No uploads."

Saskia smiled at the obvious, entreating enthusiasm in Metta's voice. God, how familiar was that need to breathe life into a puppet.

"Absolutely," she said. She stretched her shoulder a bit to test it. "I'd like that."

Waiting for Rain

Mundari Vineyard 2045, Nashik (India), Shiraz
Black cherry, plum, and currant flavors mingle with aromas of sweet
tobacco and sage in this dependable offering from India.

THE SUN PEEKING THROUGH the grapevines felt hotter on Bharat
Mundari's neck than twenty-four degrees. Another perfect day. Bharat
scowled and worked his way down the row of vines, thinning the grapes
so the remaining Shiraz crop would become fuller and riper.

Not that there was a point in having healthy vines when he couldn't pay
his weather bill. Without rain, the grapevines would weaken under the
stress, and stressed grapes made poor wine. No one bought flawed wine.

He snipped another cluster from the grapevine, dropping it on the
ground where it would raisin in the persistent sunshine.

He needed his micro-climate back.

"Bharat!" Indra peered over the trellis. "Have you heard anything I
said?"

He stood, working the kink out of his back and blinked at his wife.
"No. I'm sorry, my dear, I was thinking."

She tilted her head, like an inquisitive bird. "About what?"

About how the family was destitute. About how he had no resources.
About the rain. "Nothing important."

She arched an eyebrow and looked down the row to their youngest
daughter, Rachana. "Nothing important? Do you hear your father?
Here we are discussing possible grooms and he is distracted by 'nothing
important.'"

"I'm sorry." Bharat smoothed the anxiety from his brow. "What did you say?"

"Rachana said she wants to date." Indra frowned. "I told her in my youth we wouldn't think of such things, but everyone thinks you and I married for love."

"True." The dust between the rows coated his feet as if the earth itself wanted to prepare him for the poverty awaiting them.

Indra stopped and peeled back her glove. "I thought so." She showed him the blister on her hand from the pruning sheers. "I wish you had hired a crew to do this."

If she knew about the debt . . . Bharat snipped another cluster from the vine. "It's important for Rachana to learn the business."

"Not if she marries into another family."

They had just married one daughter off; the thought of paying for another wedding made him shudder. "I'm in no hurry to see her married."

The bindi mark on Indra's forehead seemed to glare like an accusing third eye.

"Let her find her own husband if she wants one." Bharat went up the row, heading back to the winery. It was starting again, the marriage broker fees, setting the dowry . . . And a marriage broker would look at his financial records. He ground his teeth. They had no money.

The *tap tap* of Indra's footsteps followed him, but he kept his eyes focused on the winery. He could imagine the look of reproach in Indra's eyes.

"Bharat?"

She always knew when he lied, so he simply grunted.

"What's wrong?" Indra's voice sounded sweet and gentle, but the question held too many demands.

"Nothing. I have some work in the winery." He escaped into the cool dark of the cellar. The stacked barrels of last year's vintage soothed him with their mute round sides. They asked him no questions.

But the current vintage had its own demands.

Watering the vineyard would require every waking moment. That left no time for shoot positioning, leaf pulling, or hedging. And what of thinning? How could he tend the wines in barrel and water the vines?

Any one of the millions of unemployed laborers in Nashik could irrigate, but a day laborer would want his wages at the end of the day. And if he had money to pay them, then he could pay the weather bill and he would not need to irrigate.

How had his father managed before the India Space Research Organization began weather control? Bharat had barely been in his teens when they switched to micro-climate management, but Nashik had been a wine region since the time of the Moghuls. Of course, it had rained more then. He still remembered monsoons.

Bharat ran up the stairs to his office and sat in front of the ancient quad-core processor. He asked it, "What are forms of irrigation for vineyards?"

It immediately responded with a list of sites; at the top, the ISRO offered micro-climate management. Bharat grimaced and scrolled through his other options.

Rachana cleared her throat. "Hey, Bapu?"

He jumped. He had not heard her enter. "Are you finished with thinning, then?"

She nodded. "Those rows. Matti wants to know when you want dinner."

At the thought of food, Bharat's stomach turned. "Don't wait for me. I've got work to do."

"'kay." She leaned over his shoulder. "Irrigation, huh?"

Sweat pricked on the palms of his hands. Words came out of his mouth in a string of lies and half-truths. "Wine historically had seasonal variations but we've lost that. I thought I'd stop using a micro-climate so the grapes could truly express the vintage." As Bharat spoke, his words became true. He had attended some pre-weather control vertical tastings and the vintage variations were fascinating. "We've gotten away from what wine is supposed to be."

"I thought you'd just forgotten to turn the rain back on after Deepali's wedding."

She had noticed. Of course, she had; he had been programming the 1969 Hermitage weather patterns since she was a little girl. If the weather company had given him an extension on his bill, today would be overcast and twenty degrees.

"I didn't think it would be this long between natural rains." Why *had* it been so long since it had rained? He remembered a year when his father had turned off the weather and it had not been this long between rains. Bharat turned back to the computer. "Run on. I have work to do."

When Rachana was gone, he opened the FAQ page of the ISRO website and clicked on, "What happens when you can't pay your weather bill?"

At India Space Research Organization, we don't want anyone left in the cold. When your micro-climate is discontinued, your weather will remain 24°C and sunny.

Each individual word made sense, but the picture they painted when strung together mocked him. *24°C and sunny.*

Your weather will remain . . .

Sunny.

He stared at the words so long that all meaning drained away from them. How could they be true? There must be thousands of people who could not pay their bills in the cities. He had been to Nashik and seen the poverty lining the streets.

But he wasn't on the municipal weather grid here, the city weather tax did not cover his vineyard. His land was large enough that the nanites in the atmosphere could create a localized micro-climate.

"It won't rain again." He wanted to call the words back, as if saying it out loud had made it true.

The vineyard would die.

Bile surged up at the back of his throat. He stumbled away from the desk trying to reach the rubbish bin before vomiting. No rain. Cramps wrenched his back as he heaved again. Sunny. He clenched the plastic tub, gasping. Ruined. Sweat covered him with images of dirt floors, and tiny rooms; Indra, with her sari hitched up around her knees, doing laundry in the Godavari River like one of the untouchables.

Bharat knelt on the floor until the wave of nausea had passed. Then he leaned against the cool wall and stared out the window, empty. The moonlight lay over the vineyard like a sari draped across a beautiful woman. How could he take Indra from this?

He hung his head. Vomit had splattered his shirt. He gagged again, wanting to crawl out of his own skin to get away from the stench.

Unclean. He ripped the shirt off and hurled it into the rubbish bin.

One of the harvest hands had rigged a shower in the cellar, attaching the barrel washing hose to an old garden nozzle. Bharat snatched his coveralls from the peg inside the door.

In the cellar he stripped and stood in the middle of the cavernous room, with barrels stacked five high around him. He grabbed the soap the cellar rat had left. Honeysuckle. Bharat's stomach heaved again. Who had brought a scented soap into the winery? That could wreak havoc on his ability to distinguish odors in the developing wine.

He meant to wash quickly, but the rhythm of the drops pounding against his skull displaced all thought. Their aquifer ran deep and water from the surrounding hills fed it. The water pelted his face, warm from the solar tank on top of the winery. He could use that to water the vineyard. That was something.

He went outside, pulled the hose from the wall and started to water the grapevines. The earth crackled with thirst as it absorbed the cool current.

Each row was planted at one meter spacing, fifty vines-to-a-row, with two meters between rows. 194,256 square meters of vines. If he soaked the ground with water for ten minutes at each vine it would take . . . Three hundred hours. He almost stopped in despair, but had no other answer.

The house was dark when Bharat returned, but Indra rolled over as he slid into the bed. "What time is it?"

Bharat glanced at the clock and winced. "Late."

"What were you doing?"

"Work." He kissed her cheek. "Go to sleep."

Indra snuggled next to him, her body warm against his. She kissed the back of his neck and stiffened.

"What?"

"Nothing." Then, almost as if she couldn't help herself, Indra said. "Your hair smells different."

"I took a shower in the cellar. Remember the contraption the harvest hands rigged last year?"

She pulled back. "Why didn't you shower at home?"

"I—" He stopped. He did not want to tell her he had been sick. He did not want to answer her questions. "I just did. Does it matter?"

She answered with less than a whisper. "No." Indra turned her back to him leaving a chill between them.

Château d'Yquem, Sauternes 2024
Revisiting the perfect 1931 season, Château d'Yquem has recreated the wine considered the Holy Grail of Sauternes. Concentrated fruit and brilliant acidity marry perfectly in a wine for the ages.

SHUTTING THE DOOR to the study, Bharat cradled the bottle of Sauternes under his arm. It was only one bottle out of the collection of anniversary wines Indra's parents had given them as a wedding present. He had no reason to feel guilty about selling one bottle.

He was doing it for her, so she would not know they were destitute. He set the golden bottle of wine next to the computer and surfed across the web to his favorite wine auction site. With the money from this sale, he could buy enough hose to put in a crude drip irrigation system.

Opening a new auction page, he began inputting data from the wine.

Indra opened the door of the study. The lamp in the living room backlit her, peeking through the folds of her sari. "Bharat? The photographer sent Deepali's wedding album."

"I need to finish some work. I'll be right there."

"You work so hard." She crossed the room, her hair still as dark as when the matchmaker had introduced them. Leaning down, Indra kissed the back of his neck. He caught the hints of jasmine in the natural scent of her skin.

Bharat captured her hand and kissed her palm, thanking all the gods that Indra did not know how badly in debt Deepali's wedding had placed them. "Give me five more minutes."

Indra fingered the collar of his khurta with her free hand. She whispered so her voice seemed to kiss his ears, "Perhaps when you finish, we could do more than look at photos—Are you selling one of our anniversary wines?"

"I—" He looked at the screen, half-filled with information from the wine. "Yes. I am."

In his hand, her fingers twitched like a mouse. "Why?"

Shrugging, he released her and picked the bottle up. "We've got more than we'll use."

"But it's our anniversary wine."

"It's one bottle." He ran his thumb across the label, trying for nonchalance.

"I see." Reflected in the glass, a distorted Indra retreated from the room without another word.

When the door closed, Bharat shut his eyes and cursed. He should tell her the truth. Even with solar power and well water, eventually Indra would need some money. And then what?

The door opened again. Bharat spun in his chair, still cradling the d'Yquem.

Rachana poked her head around the door. "Do you have time for a quick chat session?"

"Of course." He set the bottle down, and wiped his forehead, forcing a smile.

She sat on the edge of the desk. "You know this whole natural weather vintage thing?"

He nodded.

"Well, I was talking with a—" She hesitated and looked away. "A friend of mine at school who's interning at a law office and his boss is a wine geek."

"*His* boss?"

"Um . . . yeah. Anyway, he told his boss, and his boss was way excited, so I said they could come for a barrel tasting. I know I should have asked first, but . . . "

"So, who is this 'friend'?"

Rachana ducked her head, looking like her mother in her coy moments. "A classmate."

Unlikely. "Does he have a name?"

"Mukund Krishnasami. May I bring them for a tasting?"

"Have you talked to your mother about this?"

"You know Matti. She goes epic if I mention boys at all. And . . . and you said that I should find my own husband."

Bharat winced as his angry words from the vineyard returned to haunt him. Still, this would give him a chance to look the boy over. He nodded. "All right."

Rachana grinned and bounded to the door. "Hey. Matti's got Deepali's wedding album. Want to look at it?"

He could finish the auction listing later. "Of course."

As they entered the living room, Indra looked up, wiping her eyes hastily as if she had been crying.

Bharat stopped in the doorway. "Are you all right?"

"I'm fine." Indra smiled, but her eyes were red. "Just allergies. It's all this dust, I suppose." She waved at the dry landscape.

Rachana laughed, crossing the room to plop beside Indra. "Get Bapu to turn the weather back on."

"You turned off the weather?" Indra looked stricken. "Why?"

Bharat swallowed the panic rising in his throat. "I want to make wine influenced by natural weather. The whole industry makes wine that tastes the same; we've lost the differentiation in vintages." These were not lies which spilled off his tongue. He did hate the sameness. He wanted to make wine expressing a time, and a region with true terroir. "I want to make something new."

Indra's gaze drifted back to the grapevines thrusting through the dry soil. "But the grapes will die without water."

That's why he had stayed out every night, watering the Shiraz. "I know. I'm putting in a drip irrigation system."

Indra crossed her arms and leaned back on the couch. "Well, I don't see how drip irrigation is any different than scheduling the rain."

"The temperature and humidity, water retention in the soil—" Bharat could not explain all the variables which made harvests different. He flung out his arms in frustration. "Will you trust me!"

Her nostrils flared, the gold ornamental stud sparking in the light from the window. "Of course, husband. I am your true companion and life-long partner."

The words of their wedding vows crossed the room like a slap. Bharat's face burned. She had no right to challenge him. He had striven to protect and care for her.

Rachana cleared her throat. "Weren't we looking at Deepali's wedding album?"

"If your father wants to, then we will." Indra's smile chilled him.

Rachana looked caught between her parents. "If this isn't a good time . . . "

"No. This is a perfect time." Bharat sat beside Indra.

As if nothing had happened, Indra opened the album to the first photo. In it, a tiny Deepali danced with her new husband; even in miniature, she looked radiant with joy. Bharat leaned forward. The wedding might have beggared them, but he could not deny his little girl anything.

Tears streamed down Indra's face. "This was the happiest day of my life."

Bharat smiled at her. "You said that on our wedding day too."

Her tears stopped. "I was wrong."

Rachana stood abruptly. "I . . . I have some homework."

Reaching forward, Indra snapped the album shut. "And I need to make dinner." She pushed the album to Bharat. "Perhaps you would like to view the rest. Their wedding vows are particularly lovely."

Bharat watched her rise. "I thought you had not looked at it yet."

"I haven't, but I remember the vows." She paused in the doorway. "I like the part where the groom promises to cherish the bride and consult her as his partner."

She swept into the kitchen. Bharat winced as pots clanged together.

He stared at the wedding album for another moment and then returned to the office to list the Sauternes.

He should have done that earlier.

Domaine Drouhin Oregon, Pinot Noir, Lauren, 2031, 2032, and 2033
Typically polished wines from this respected producer in the Red Hills.
Uniformly clean, balanced, and delicious Pinot Noir.

IN THE WINERY LAB, Bharat hunched over the spectrophotometer, running the numbers on the sugar content and acidity profile of the grape sample. With the unrelenting sunshine, the fruit was ripening faster than he had expected. As long as the vines did not shut down before the drip irrigation system arrived, he might have an early harvest.

Indra knocked on the door of the lab, holding his eBud. "You left this at the house."

"Thanks."

She set the earbud on the workbench beside him. "A woman called."

Would that be Rachana's lawyer? "Did she leave a number?"

"Your eBud recorded it." Indra crossed her arms as if she were hugging herself. "Bharat . . . "

When she did not continue, Bharat looked up. "What?"

"Nothing." Indra shook her head. "Nothing."

He waited to see if she would say anything else, and then returned to his sample.

After a silent moment, the winery door closed with a little more force than necessary. Bharat set down his sample. What had he done to make Indra angry? He had thanked her for bringing the earbud down.

Later. He would ask her later. Bharat clipped the eBud behind his ear and pulled up the last incoming call; the e-bud tapped his optic nerve, flashing *Kumari Tupno* across his field of vision.

The woman who appeared superimposed in the winery had hair that seemed like an advert for a high-end designer. "Bharat! Thanks for calling me back. I'm very excited by what I hear about the new direction you're taking your wines. Very excited." Kumari's voice marched through the eBud. "When I started collecting wines, I couldn't afford foreign wines and your father was my favorite of the local producers. No one else planted Shiraz in those days."

Somehow the conversation drifted to the climates for growing grapes. Bharat found himself running through the different great vintages whose weather patterns he had copied over the years.

"So far, the best results have come from using the Hermitage 1969 patterns. But it gets dull."

"I know exactly what you mean." Kumari laughed. "Though not as a wine-maker, of course. A friend of mine did a vertical flight from Domaine Drouhin Oregon. Dull, dull, dull."

"Back to back vintages?"

"God. Yes, I don't know what he was thinking." Kumari sighed. "I tasted a pre-weather control vertical flight from Latour. God. The differences amazed me."

"What years?"

"2000, 2001, and 2002. The 2000 blew me out of this world; still fresh with fruit and truffle, and this wonderful minerality. The 2001 was good, but 2000 was outstanding. 2002 had this earthy, gamey character. They were so different."

"Vintage variation."

Kumari said, "That's why I think your return to natural weather is exciting."

"I am sorry to disappoint you. I won't be able to do a natural weather vintage after all."

"Why not?"

Bharat hesitated and then explained the ISRO's policy, which left him with weather he could not control and could not turn off.

When he finished, Kuzahli sniffed. "They can't force you to accept services you don't want. So we'll have to stop ISRO from controlling your weather."

While Kumari explained her hopes for the case, Indra poked her head into the lab.

Bharat muted the eBud's mic. "What?"

"Dinner is ready."

"I'll be up soon."

She nodded and slipped out. Bharat unmuted the eBud as Kumari finished. Even within the privacy of the lab, his next question almost stuck in his throat. "What—what are your rates?"

Kumari cleared her throat as if she were embarrassed. "Would you consider futures on next year's vintage? I retain an old fondness for your wines."

"Why next year, why not this one?" He should not even question such a generous offer.

"Well, we won't have a court date in time to affect this year's harvest so it will still be produced under an artificial micro-climate. Now, when we come out for the barrel tasting, Mukund can record the current conditions and you can turn the weather control back on." She laughed. "He and your daughter are so cute together."

Bharat split in two, wanting to ask about his daughter and her assistant, but caught by the phrase, "turn the weather control back on." He grimaced, focusing on business. "Do I have to restore weather control?"

"I understand your reluctance, but I can make it look good in court. 'Farmer forced to use ISRO's services or face losing crop.'"

"But—"

"Trust me, the press will eat it up."

That sounded wonderful, but too late for this harvest. Mechanically, Bharat made arrangements for a tour and barrel tasting. He finished the call and put his head in his hands. This harvest was doomed.

Unless he turned the rain back on.

Bharat looked at the numbers he had run on the fruit. It came so close to being ready for harvest, but the vines would not get there without water. He drummed his fingers on the table, trying to calculate if he could make it to the end of the season without weather control. The Sauternes auction had another three days to go and then he could buy the irrigation hoses.

But even with that, Indra was right; it was little different than using weather control. He groaned. Indra. He had forgotten dinner.

By the time he got to the house, Indra and Rachana were already eating.

"I'm sorry I'm late. It took longer than I thought." He sat at his place. The table groaned under vegetable kebabs, rice, nan, dal, raita, and Sag Paneer. A glass of pale straw wine—probably an Alsatian Gewurztraminer—waited for him.

"What were you talking about?" Rachana asked.

Bharat glanced at Indra but she was absorbed in adding more dal to her rice. He looked back at Rachana and shook his head trying to signal that he didn't want Indra to know about the phone call. "Not much."

Indra put the spoon back in the bowl of dal. "You certainly spent a long time talking about not much."

"I was arranging a barrel tasting." His innards twisted in knots.

"Oh." Rachana said, "Thanks for doing that."

Indra said, "Why am I the only one who doesn't know who's coming?"

Rachana met Bharat's gaze, her eyes wide. She shook her head, clearly begging him not to tell Indra about her "friend." Bharat picked up the glass of wine to delay answering. Gewurztraminer, indeed. "Is this the Hugel?"

Indra shook her head. "Ostertag. Who is coming?"

"A lawyer wants to talk about futures on the next vintage." That was true. He swirled the Gewurz in his glass and studied the legs, but his heart pounded as he tried not to look at Indra.

She said nothing. Then Indra pushed her chair back from the table and picked up her plate. She walked to the kitchen.

Rachana asked, "Where are you going?"

Indra paused in the doorway. "I'd rather not eat with people who are lying to me."

Bharat set the wine glass down, harder than he intended. "I wasn't lying!"

"And you're not telling the truth."

"Every word I've said has been true." He had been very careful.

"Oh. I'm sure, that's true. But you can say only true things and still tell a world of lies."

Bharat stood, but his knees trembled under him. "When have I lied to you."

"Every time you've said that *nothing* is bothering you."

Rachana stared at the table like a child being punished. "Stop it! Bapu's just trying to protect me."

Bharat did not know whether he should curse or bless his daughter's timing.

"Protect you!" Indra looked like she was going to throw the plate across the room. "From me? What have I done?"

"No, no. You've done nothing, Indra." Bharat came around the table, holding his arms out to her.

She backed away. "Don't try to comfort me!"

"Matti. I'm sorry." Rachana put her head in her hands. "I'm dating a boy at university. He's coming with this lawyer. That's what Bapu isn't saying."

Indra caught her breath. "You're dating." She swung around to Bharat. "You knew this? And didn't tell me?"

"I—It slipped my mind." He winced. How could something so important slip his mind?

Again, Indra raised the plate as if she wanted to hurl it. She trembled and lowered her arms. "What's his name?"

Rachana peeked over her fingers. "Mukund Krishnasami."

"And what does he do?"

"He's getting his law degree. Corporate law."

Indra nodded. "He'll make a good living then." She took a shuddering breath. "Well. We'd better go shopping tomorrow to get you something new to wear. We'll need to call the cleaning service in—"

"No." The word surprised Bharat.

Indra looked at him briefly and then turned back to Rachana. "And I'll want to meet his parents, of course. Would it be better to have the meal catered or—"

"Stop!" Bharat pressed his hands against his temples, as his wife's mouth seemed to hemorrhage money. "We can't do any of that."

Indra slammed the plate against the floor. The porcelain shattered, pieces skittering across the tile. "Why? What are you hiding!"

Bharat twitched. She wanted to know what he had been hiding, then fine. "We don't have any money. We spent it all on Deepali's wedding."

"How can you expect me to believe—" He could see the memories of the wedding stride across her face like the elephants which bore the bridal couple off to their honeymoon. Her face paled with understanding. "That's why you sold the Sauternes?"

He nodded.

Indra's face slowly crumpled. She covered her mouth with her hand, but a moan still escaped from her. Bharat's heart caught as she began to sob.

He reached out for her again, but she shook her head and held up her hand, waving him away. Bharat pressed his hands together in supplication. He could do nothing but repeat, "I'm sorry."

She lowered her hand. "I thought you were cheating on me."

The floor seemed to drop away from him. "What—why?"

"When you sold the Sauternes, I thought it meant you weren't expecting more anniversaries. And you've been staying out every night for weeks; when you come home you smell like honeysuckle. You hate scented soaps."

"I was watering the grapevines." He forced the rest of the explanation out. "I couldn't pay the weather bill."

"I don't understand. Why didn't you just tell me?"

He pressed his hands tighter against his forehead to keep it from splitting open. "I didn't want you to worry."

"Do you have any idea what things I've been imagining because I knew *something* was wrong but I didn't know what it was?"

"I'm sorry." Bharat could only repeat the words like a mantra. "I—Deepali's wedding was so important to the family."

"I'm not a child. Even Deepali would have understood if you had told us." Her chin trembled and she backed away from him. "Twenty-four years—you've had twenty-four years to understand me and you still think I'm a doll."

"No. Indra, I love you—"

"But you don't trust me." She ran out the door.

Bharat's chest felt hollow. He turned slowly away, and saw Rachana still sitting at the table. Her shoulders were hunched like a beaten child.

"I'm sorry." There was nothing else left in him.

Château Latour, Bordeaux, Pauillac, 2000
Simply sublime. Luscious fruit, spice, and silky tannins dance gracefully across the palate in this massive yet elegant wine.

ANOTHER PERFECT MORNING shone over the vineyard. Bharat stood in the door of the kitchen and cleared his throat.

Indra turned from her book. "Yes?"

"The lawyer and her assistant are due at nine. Will you join us?"

Indra considered him for a moment and then marked her place and put the book down. "Yes. Let me change."

As she passed, Bharat inhaled the scent of jasmine she left in her path. He leaned against the wall and shut his eyes. What a fool.

"Bapu? May I come too?" Rachana stood in the living room, twisting her hands as if she were still a little girl.

"Of course." He went to the window. No clouds graced the sky, except over his neighbor's land. At best, the grapevines at the outer edges would receive moisture from the run-off, but nothing else.

Indra returned, dressed in work clothes which somehow made her look older and stout. She stood at the window with him.

He wanted to seek comfort or to comfort her, to wrap his arms around her and bury his face in her hair. But they waited, with silence between them, watching the rain on their neighbor's land. Rachana paced in the room behind them.

At half-past nine, an aero swung onto the property. With his wife and daughter creating the picture of a perfect family, Bharat led the way outside. They all had smiles like the day, beautiful and dry.

A young man got out of the aero. Alone. Fresh-faced and eager, he smiled. His eyes darted to Rachana and his smile broadened, before he held his hand out to Bharat.

"I'm Mukund Krishnasami. Doctor Tupno had a last-minute emergency, but thought we could still record conditions."

"Of course." So this was Rachana's "friend" from school. With his easy good looks the boy probably had lots of "friends." Bharat gestured to the vineyard. "Shall we start with the vines?"

"Please." Mukund pulled a small camera bag out of the car. "I'm ready to record."

"I can carry that for you." Rachana stepped forward. "So your hands are free to film."

"That would be nice." His hand touched hers too long when he handed her the bag. "Thank you."

What sort of man let a woman carry his bag? Bharat crossed his arms over his chest. Beside him, Indra watched the couple thoughtfully.

Bharat started down the closest row of Shiraz, explaining that he had watered these vines, so they remained reasonably healthy. He kept trying to watch Rachana and Mukund out of the back of his head. Indra followed behind the couple, surely keeping an eye on them, but she was smiling.

Bharat stopped with his hand on a leaf. When he had last seen her smile?

After they finished with the first row, Bharat led them deeper into the vineyard, to rows he had not watered yet. The signs of stress were clear to his eye. The shoots were beginning to droop, the leaves were loosing their waxy green luster, not enough to be apparent without looking at a healthy vine, but even that little bit meant the stress would already show in the wine.

He pointed at a cluster of grapes he had pruned earlier. The cluster lay on the ground, desiccating in the heat. "See. These grapes show the severity of the current conditions."

Mukund took pictures but every time Bharat stopped talking about wine, the boy started a conversation with Rachana. Did he think his employer had sent him to flirt with Bharat's daughter?

Indra stooped and gathered a raisined cluster from the ground. She plucked a wrinkled berry off the stem and tasted it. "Bharat, what's that wine made from dried grapes?"

"There are several. Most come from Italy, but Amarone is probably the best known. The whole clusters are traditionally dried on straw mats but most people use electric dehydrators now." Clearly, Rachana needed to explain her behavior with this boy.

"Have you tasted these?"

"What?" Whole clusters! He turned his back on Rachana and the boy. "Amarone—do you think?"

She held out the bunch of desiccated grapes. The flesh had shriveled on them, concentrating the juice in the tiny packets. Bharat plucked a grape and placed it in his mouth. The flavor exploded on his tongue. None of the stressed qualities of the grapes still on the vine showed here. The sugar, acid, and vibrant flavors had been concentrated by the slow evaporation of water through the grape skins.

He picked up another cluster. They showed the same raisined quality and the flavors were consistent with the first sample.

This could make an interesting wine. Different. One showing the qualities of the vineyard during this time. Bharat had been so focused on making it rain, that he had not thought about other ways to make wine. In the past, the thinned grapes had only been garbage, not beautiful packets of flavor.

Indra tilted her head, watching him. "What do you think?"

He laughed and grabbed her around the waist, lifting her off the ground. "I think you're brilliant! We can make an Amarone style wine." He kissed her cheeks. "My love, I would never have thought of this on my own."

With her thumb, Indra wiped a tear from his face. "And I would never have thought of it if you had not introduced me to wine." She nodded past him to Rachana and Mukund. "Do you think they would be good partners for each other?"

Bharat narrowed his eyes, imagining them in fifty years. "I don't like the way he makes her carry his bag."

"Ah." Indra shook her head. "I like the way he lets her share his burdens."

"Which is what you asked of me."

"Yes." She took his hand. "I promised to be your partner."

Bharat looked at the raisined grapes in his other hand. "Will you forgive me?"

"Forgiving you takes no effort, but I need your trust. That's what hurt. You did not trust my love for you."

Bharat dropped the grapes in the dust and turned fully to her, taking her other hand in his. "I promise to be your true companion and life-long partner from this day forward."

She smiled at him and led him forward a step. "Let us take this sixth step for longevity."

At the sound of the sixth sutra of their wedding vows, the hollow space inside Bharat slowly filled. He led her into the fifth step, moving backwards through their vows. "Let us take this fifth step to pray for virtuous, intelligent, and courageous children."

She looked at Rachana and wrinkled her nose in a smile. "Let us take this fourth step to acquire knowledge, happiness, and harmony by mutual love and trust."

The vineyard dropped away, and his world filled with Indra. "Let us take this third step with the aim of increasing our wealth by righteous means."

"Let us take this second step vowing to develop mental, physical, and spiritual powers." Indra leaned forward and kissed him, the scent of jasmine filling his nostrils.

He kissed her back. "Let us take this first step vowing to keep a pure household; avoiding things injurious to our health."

Rachana laughed. "What are you two doing?"

The steps of the wedding sutras had taken them down the row to Rachana and Mukund. Bharat lifted his head from Indra and smiled at his daughter. "We are having a romantic moment. Go away."

Then he held his wife and wept as she pulled him closer.

Mundari Vineyards, Amarone, 2048
An odd but interesting wine for the adventurous. Made from dessicated
Syrah in an Amarone style. Dried cherry and cranberry favors
dominate within an overtly sweet but lively structure.

Mundari Vineyards, Shiraz, 2048
The flagship wine from Mudari this year is deeply flawed.
The result of an ill-considered weather experiment, the wine suffers
from flabbiness, high ethanol, and queer tequila flavors.

BHARAT HANDED a printout of the latest copy of *Sommelier India* to Indra. "It's here."

"And? No—don't tell me." Indra started to read and sucked in her breath.

During Kumari's legal battle with ISRO, Bharat had not turned the weather control back on. With the sugars concentrated by dehydration, the potential alcohol levels of the grapes were high. The Amarone remained in balance with its residual sweetness, but the dry Shiraz showed coarse flavors and was excessively alcoholic.

She set the review down. "Oh, my dear. I'm so sorry about the Shiraz."

Bharat fought the grin threatening to overwhelm him and handed her another page. "Look at the incoming order forms for today."

More orders than they usually received in a month filled the page. "Most of them are for the Shiraz."

Indra's eyes widened as she scanned the order forms. "But—why?"

The grin broke out, spreading across his face. "The novelty! It's been at least forty years since a vineyard was stressed by drought."

Indra raised an eyebrow, and the corner of her mouth twitched with the beginning of a smile. "Maybe we should put 'deeply flawed' on all our labels."

"Perhaps." He laughed, still giddy.

She wrapped her arms around his neck. "I want you to know that I am very proud of you."

Her words poured through him with sweet comfort. "Thank you." Bharat held her and listened to the rain falling on their vineyard.

Indra snuggled against him. "What do you think the weather will be like tomorrow?"

"I don't know." He kissed the top of Indra's head. "But it will be beautiful."

First Flight

MARY ELOIS JACKSON stood inside the plain steel box of the time machine. It was about the size of an outhouse, but without a bench or windows. She clutched her cane with one hand and her handbag with the other. Felt like the scan was taking nigh unto forever, but she was pretty sure it was just her nerves talking.

Her corset made her ribs creak with every breath. She'd expected to hate wearing the thing but there was a certain comfort from having something to support her back and give her a shape more like a woman than a sack of potatoes.

A gust of air puffed around her and the steel box was gone. She stood in a patch of tall grass under an October morning sky. The caravan of scientists, technicians, and reporters had vanished from the field where they'd set up camp. Elois inhaled with wonder that the time machine had worked. Assuming that this was 1905, of course—the year of her birth and the bottom limit to her time traveling range. It beat all she'd ever thought of to be standing there.

The air tasted sweet and so pure that she could make out individual fragrances; the hard edge of oak mixed with the raw green of fresh mowed grass. And here Elois had thought her sense of smell had gotten worse because she'd plain gotten old.

She recollected her self and pulled the watch out from the chain around her neck to check the time, as if it would reflect the local time instead of the time she'd left. 8:30 on the dot, which looked about right judging by the light. Now, she had six hours before they spun the machine back down and she got returned to her present. If the Board of Directors had thought she could do it all faster, they'd not have sent her back for so long on account of how expensive it was to keep the machine spun up, but even with all the physical therapy, Elois was still well over a hundred.

With that in mind, she started making for the road. She'd been walking the route from the box to Huffman Prairie for the last week, so they could get the timing on it. It looked mighty different for all that. There had been a housing development across the street from where she'd left and now there was a farm with a single tall white house sitting smack in the middle of the corn fields.

If she thought too much on it, she wasn't sure she'd have the nerve to keep going. Down the road a piece, a wagon drawn by a bay horse came towards her. Besides the fellow driving it, the back of the wagon was crammed full of pigs that were squealing loud enough to be heard from here. Made her think on her husband, dead these long years or two years old, depending on how you counted it. She shook her head to get rid of that thought.

Elois patted her wig, though the makeup fellow had done a fine job fixing it to her head. She'd had short hair since the 1940s and it felt mighty strange to have that much weight on top of her head again. The white hair wound around her head in the style she remembered her own grandmother wearing. She checked to make sure her broad hat was settled and that the brooch masking the "hat-cam" was still pointing forward.

She hadn't got far when the wagon pulled up alongside her.

"Pardon ma'am." The boy driving it couldn't be more than thirteen and as red-headed as a step-child. He had more freckles than a dog has spots and his two front teeth stuck out past his lip. He had a nice smile for all that. "Seeing as how we're going the same way, might I offer you a ride?"

He had a book in his lap, like he'd been reading as he was driving. The stink of the pigs billowed around them with the wind. One of the sows gave a particularly loud squeal and Elois glanced back involuntarily.

The boy looked over his shoulder. "My charges are garrulous this morning." He patted the book in his lap and leaned toward her. "I'm pretending they're Odysseus's men and that helps some."

Elois couldn't help but chuckle at the boy's high-faluting language. "My husband was a hog farmer. He always said a pig talked more sense than a politician."

"Politicians or sailors. If you don't mind sharing a ride with them I'll be happy to offer it."

"Well now, that's mighty nice of you. I'm just going to Huffman Prairie."

He slid over on the bench and stuck his hand out to offer her a boost up. "I'm Homer Van Loon."

Well, that accounted for his taste in reading and vocabulary. Boys his age were more like to read the penny dreadfuls than anything else but anyone whose folks saddled him with a moniker like Homer was bound to be a bit odd.

"Pleased to make your acquaintance. I'm Elois Jackson." She passed him her cane and gripped his other hand. Holding that and the weathered wooden side of the wagon, she hauled herself aboard. Grunting in the sort of way that would have made her mama scold her, Elois dropped onto the wooden bench. Three months of physical therapy to get ready for this and just climbing into a wagon about wore her out.

"You walk all the way out here from town?" Homer picked up the reins and sat next to her.

"Lands, no." Elois settled her bag in her lap and told the lie the team of historians had prepared for her, just in case someone asked. "I took the interurban rail out and then thought I'd walk the rest for a constitutional. The way was a mite longer than I thought, so I'm grateful to you." The Lord would forgive her for the lie, given the circumstance.

"Are you headed out to the Wright Brothers'?"

"I am. I never thought I'd see such a thing."

"That's for a certai—" His voice cut off.

Elois slammed hard against pavement. The wagon was gone. Power lines hung over her head and the acrid smell of asphalt stung her nose.

And smoke.

Shouting, half a dozen people ran toward her. Elois rolled over to her knees and looked around for her cane. It had landed on the road just to her side and she grabbed it to lever herself back to her feet.

Mr. Barnes was near the front of folks running toward her. Poor thing looked like his heart would plum give out he was so worried, though Elois wasn't sure if he was worried about her or his invention.

The young fellow who did her wig got to her first, helped her to her feet. Seemed as if everyone was chorusing questions about if she was all right. Elois nodded and kept repeating that she was fine until Mr. Barnes arrived, red-faced and blowing like a racehorse.

Elois drew herself up as tall as she could. "What happened?"

"We blew a transformer." Mr. Barnes gestured at one of the telephone poles, which had smoke billowing up from it. "Are you all right?" Up close, it was clear he was worried about her and Elois chided herself for doubting him. He'd not been a thing but kind to her since the Time Travel Society recruited her.

"I'm fine. More worried about the boy I was talking to than anything else."

That stopped all the conversation flat. The program director, Dr. Connelly, pushed her way through the crowd, face pale. "Someone saw you vanish? You're sure?"

"I was sitting in his wagon." Elois settled her hat on her head. "Maybe, if you send me back a few seconds after I vanished, we can make out that I just fell out of the wagon."

"Out of the question." Dr. Connelly set her mouth into a hard line. With her dark hair drawn tight in a bun, she looked like a school marm with an unruly child.

"He'll think he's gone crazy."

"And having you reappear will make things better?"

"At least I can explain what's happening so he's not left wondering for the rest of his life."

"Explain what? That you are a time traveler?"

Elois gripped her cane and took a step closer to Dr. Connelly. When she was young, she would have been able to look down at the woman and still felt like she ought to, even though their eyes were on level. "That's exactly what I'll tell him. He's a twelve year-old boy reading Homer on his free time. I don't think he'll have a bit of a problem believing me."

A muscle pulsed in Dr. Connelly's jaw and she finally said, "There's no point in arguing out here in the heat. We'll take it to the rest of board and let them decide."

That was as clear a "no" as if she'd actually said the word. Elois leaned forward on her cane. "I look forward to speaking with them." She cut Dr. Connelly off before she could open her mouth. "As I'm the only one who's met the boy, I trust you'll want me to tell y'all about him." Folks shouldn't make the mistake of thinking that just cause she was old meant she was sweet.

ELOIS SAT in her costume in a conference room with Dr. Connelly, Mr. Barnes, and two other members of the board, both white men who looked old but couldn't be much past retirement age. The conference room had flat panel screens set up with the other board members on them. They had been debating the issues for the past half hour largely going into details of why it was too dangerous to try to make her reappear on the wagon on account of it being a moving vehicle.

Elois cleared her throat. "Pardon me, but may I ask y'all a question?"

"Of course." Mr. Barnes swiveled his chair to face her. The boy didn't seem that much older than Homer Van Loon for all that he'd invented the time machine.

"I hear y'all talking a lot about the program and I understand that's important and all, but I'm not hearing anyone talk about what's best for Homer Van Loon."

Dr. Connelly swiveled her chair to face Elois. "I appreciate your concern for the boy, but I don't think you have an understanding of the historical context of the issue."

Her disdain lay barely under the surface of civility. Elois had seen this sort of new money back when she'd been working in the department store and she always had been required to smile at them. No need now.

"Young lady," Elois snapped at Dr. Connelly like one of her own children. "I've lived through two world wars, the Great Depression, the Collapse. I lived through race riots, saw us put men on the moon, the Spanish Flu, AIDS, the *Titanic*, Suffrage, and the Internet. I've raised five children and buried two, got twenty-three grandchildren, eleven great-grandchildren, and five great-great grandchildren with more on the way. And you have the nerve to say I don't understand history?"

The room was silent except for the whir of the computer fans.

Dr. Connelly said, "I apologize if we've made you feel slighted, Elois. We'll take your concerns under advisement as we continue our deliberations."

If she hadn't been a good Christian woman, she would have cracked the woman upside the head with her cane for the amount of condescension in her voice.

"How many folks do you have that are my age?" She knew the answer to the question before she asked it. She might not use the Internet but she had grandchildren who were only to happy to do searches for her. A body couldn't travel back before she was born and Elois was born in 1905. There weren't that many folks of her age, let alone able-bodied ones.

"Six." Dr. Connelly looked flatly unimpressed with Elois's longevity.

Mr. Barnes either didn't know where she was headed or agreed with her. "But you're the only that's a native English speaker."

Elois nodded her head in appreciation. "So it seems to me that you might want to do more than keep my concerns 'under consideration.'"

A man on one of the screens spoke. "Are you blackmailing us, Mrs. Jackson?"

"No sir, I'm not. I'm trying to get y'all to pay attention." She straightened in her chair now that they were all looking at her. "Y'all saw the video of me meeting him. Homer Van Loon is a boy out of time himself. He's reading the *Odyssey*, which if you know anything about farm boys from 1905 ought to tell you everything you need to know right there. Not only will he believe me, he'll understand why it needs to be kept secret—as if anyone would believe him anyhow. And if you think on it, having someone local to the time might be right handy. He's twelve now. When you send someone back to Black Friday, which you will I expect, he'll be in his thirties. You think a man like that wouldn't be helpful?"

Mr. Barnes shook his head. "But we researched him today. His life was entirely unremarkable. If he knew you were a time traveler, wouldn't that show up?"

Elois took a breath to calm herself. "If he's told to keep it a secret, and does, do you think his history would look any different?"

One of the board members in the room, a lean man with wire-rim glasses spoke for the first time since they started. "You've convinced me."

"Gerald!" Dr. Connelly swiveled to glare. "Conversations with a pig farmer are not what our investors have paid for."

And that was the real point that they had been dancing around in her presence. "I can do both."

They stared at her again but she only looked at Mr. Barnes. "Can't I? There's no reason I can't go back to the same time twice, is there?"

He shook his head, slowly smiling. Oh, but he was completely on her side, wasn't he. Elois beamed at him.

"Well, then, why don't y'all send me back for twenty minutes to talk to Homer to see how he took it. Twenty minutes. That's all and then I'll come back to the present and tell ya'll how the conversation went. If Homer believes me, then I can hop back to the same spot and he can give me a ride to Huffman Prairie. I'll get there about the same time as I would have walking. If it doesn't then you can send me to the B point and we'll have tried."

Slowly, in the screens heads began to nod. Dr. Connelly scowled and threw her hands up. "That's two set-ups. Do you people know how much that costs? Just the transformer delay is cutting into our return. I can't conscience this. We're contracted to deliver footage of the Wright Flyer III and you, madam, are contracted to do that for us." She pointed at Mr. Barnes. "If she can go to the same time twice, then send her to the same place she went today but after she met the boy. We'd built in extra time for the walk, right?"

Elois prayed that the Good Lord would grant her patience and give her strength to forgive this woman. And then Elois added a prayer that He would forgive her for being devious. "I reckon that'll work fine."

Mr. Barnes shook his head. "He'll still be there unless we send you too late to get to the field."

Never in her life had Elois wished for someone to lie, but she was about beside herself wanting Mr. Barnes to be quiet. She was figuring on Homer sticking around, too, in fact, she was counting on it so she could explain things to him.

Dr. Connelly rolled her eyes. "Not you, too. You haven't even met the boy."

"No, but on the video he reminds me a lot of myself and, well, I'd still be there." Mr. Barnes shrugged. "Can you imagine being twelve and seeing someone just vanish?"

"Anyone with sense would high-tail it out of there so whatever got her wouldn't get them, too." Dr. Connelly rolled her shoulders with blatant aggravation. "All right. Let's say he's more like you and still there. Send her back earlier so she can clear the site before the boy comes along. How much extra time will you need?"

The teeth Elois had left all hurt to answer civilly. "It doesn't take me but thirty minutes to get down the road to Huffman Prairie."

Dr. Connelly narrowed her eyes. "I trust that you won't try to wait and contact the boy instead of performing your contractual obligations."

Elois sucked in her dentures and set her jaw before answering. "I said I'd get you photos of that Wright Flyer and I aim to do so."

"That's not the same. I'll need your word, Elois."

"*Doctor* Connelly. You have my word that I will not wait for Homer. But I want you to understand that I think this is a terrible thing."

"Noted." She turned her attention to Mr. Barnes. "Given the trial runs, what's the shortest amount of time she'll need to be out of sight?"

"There's a bend in the road that she should reach in about ten minutes."

"Let's set her down fifteen minutes early then." She surveyed the board. "Unless there are objections?

Nobody but Elois seemed to care and she kept her mouth shut before she could say something not very Christian.

WHEN THE STEEL BOOTH vanished this time, the field looked exactly as it had before, save that the sun hadn't risen quite as high in the sky. The dust kicked up around her shoes as she walked and it smelled of the mud pies she used to make as a child. She passed the knotted fence about where Homer had picked her up and kept on to where she thought they had been when she vanished. The trees came down almost to the edge of the road and made a place to hide. Oh, but wasn't she tempted to turn off and set a spell, waiting for Homer to turn up. There was even a natural bench where a tree had fallen down.

But even if she hadn't given her word, they'd know if she waited on account of that hat-cam. There was nothing for it but to get the photos fast enough so maybe she could come back and talk to Homer before the plane flew. That wasn't set to happen until eleven o'clock anyhow.

She got to the bend in the road and looked back to see if Homer's wagon was in sight but didn't see hide nor hair yet. Elois headed on to Huffman Prairie and felt every year of her life as she walked. Dust coated her shoes and the hem of her dress by the time she reached the field. A trickle of sweat crept between her scalp and the wig, about driving her crazy with its slow progress across her skin.

The hanger in the middle of the field was in worse shape than it was in her present. Some historical society had built a replica of the rough structure but it bore little resemblance to the original. She dug into her handbag and pulled out a pair of opera glasses. Thumbing the switch, she turned on the high-definition digital camera embedded inside the case and began filming the barn and surrounding field. Sun cut across the field, weaving in and out of the tall grass like a child playing hide and seek. Across the way, a group of men in suits and ties were carrying the Wright Flyer III to the single rail track next to the hangar. The catapult tower stood in front of them, waiting to hurl the flyer down the rail and into the air.

Elois lowered the opera glasses. Well now, she hadn't expected them to start moving it so early, so maybe Dr. Connelly had a point after all.

She'd seen photos of the plane, of course, but until this moment the reality of time travel hadn't hit her. She recognized the Wright Brothers like they were her own family. The fellow down at the end with the handlebar mustache, that was Orville. And over there, with the bright blue eyes, was Wilbur, covering his bald head with a bowler, even while he was working.

And then there was the plane. It was like a child's model made large. A wood and cloth construction that was equal parts grace and lumbering ox. Looking at it, it was hard to believe that it would roll down the track, much less fly for half an hour. Elois raised the opera glasses to her eyes and filmed the men settling the plane on the track. They milled around then, while Orville Wright did something with the one wheel trolley underneath.

She checked her watch. 8:45, which is about when she'd vanished on the first trip. There was two hours yet before the flight was going to happen. She'd need to hurry and snap the photo of that gear they wanted and then skedaddle down the road to meet Homer. There ought to be more than enough time to get down the road to Homer and be back in time for the flight.

The board had their mission and she had hers. Tucking the opera glasses back into her bag, Elois made her way across the field. She wanted to run, but the uneven ground would cause her a tumble if she stepped out of walking pace.

Wilbur looked up as she approached. From his face, she must make quite a picture. An old lady, in a fine plum walking suit, out by herself in a field full of men and machinery. Elois nodded her head. "Morning. I hope I'm not disturbing you."

"No ma'am." Wilbur pulled a rag out of his pocket and hastily wiped his grease stained fingers off. "Can I help you with anything?"

That was one of the handy things about being old, folks were always wanting to help out. No telling if the folks at the Time Travel Institute had thought of that or not. "I just had a hankering to see what all you boys were doing out here. I've been reading about your efforts and they're mighty inspiring, I'll tell you." Elois moved around the wing of the plane toward the rudders, where the missing part was. Or not missing. Since the plane was whole and perfect. She turned so her hat-cam was pointing straight at him, recording for posterity. "Y'all don't mind me. I'm just the nosy type."

"Um. Well. We're getting ready for a trial flight, so if you don't mind . . . "

"Oh, I'll stand way over on the side when you take off." She lifted the glasses again and aimed them at the part, moving around to get it from a different angle.

He laughed. "I appreciate that ma'am. It'll just be another ten minutes or so."

Elois gasped. The records showed that they took off at eleven and that was two hours from now.

"Something wrong, ma'am?" His face was flushed and so alive that it was hard for Elois to credit that he'd been dead for nigh unto seventy years where she came from.

"No, no. I just didn't realize how soon it was. Somehow I got it in my mind that y'all were going to fly later today." This time travel was a marvel, it was. Standing here as they fiddled with whatever it was on the airplane, it made her pity poor Mr. Barnes who couldn't travel back more than thirty years. What had there been to see in his lifetime that was like this?

It made her wish she was a few years older so she could see their first flight. Elois worked her way around the plane, determined to film every inch of it. Did they know that it would break records today? "How long do you reckon you'll fly today?"

He grinned and rubbed the back of his neck. "It's good of you to think it'll get off the ground, ma'am."

Orville gave the wrench a twist on the gizmo. "The gentlemen are taking wagers so my brother doesn't feel as if he can make predictions. It wouldn't be 'sporting.'" He lowered the tool and gestured at her with it. "How long do you think we'll stay aloft?"

"Well now, I'm not a betting person, so I couldn't rightly say." If truth be told, she knew exactly how long it would take. Eighteen minutes and forty-two seconds. In two days, they'll do the flight everyone talks about, where the machine stays aloft for thirty minutes. But this flight, today, is the first time it'll be able to stay aloft for more than a few minutes. There were no records of it because no one knew that it would be a historic moment.

"Go on. We won't write your name down." One of the men said.

"No, thank you sir. It'd be betting in my heart, because I'd still be hoping I was right." Elois smiled at him but he shifted uncomfortably and tugged on his collar. Well, if it made him think better of his ways, that was all to the good, even if it wasn't why she'd traveled through time to get here.

After a few moments of uncomfortable silence, they got back to work and more or less ignored Elois, which suited her fine. She took pains to look at every inch of the flyer so no one at the Time Travel Institute could say she had neglected her duty when she went haring off after Homer.

Orville said, "Is there anything you're looking for in particular?"

"Oh! No. Thank you. I'm just fascinated is all."

He grunted and lifted his head. "Wilbur! Would you get me the oilcan?" Orville jiggled a gizmo on the front of the plane. "I don't like the way the elevator is responding."

Nodding, Wilbur trotted over to the hangar while Orville continued to tweak the Flyer. "Wilbur's a trusting sort." He beckoned Elois closer.

"The thing is, I don't think we've ever had someone display so much interest in one of our flyers before, except industrial spies, of course." He smiled at her, but his eyes were hard and narrow.

It hadn't even occurred to her, what it must look like for her to be staring at the plane with opera glasses. "I'd so wished I'd seen your first flight that I'm determined not to miss a thing about this one." She put on her best sweet little old lady face and pointed at the rudder. "What does this do?"

Leaning in close to her, Orville kept his smile fixed. "It helps the flyer fly."

Behind her, Elois heard the squeal of pigs. She lost all interest in Orville and turned as Homer came thundering up to the field, driving the wagon faster than was wise. He pulled the horse up in a cloud of dust. Standing, he pointed at her. "I thought so!"

"Excuse me, gentlemen." Elois set her back to them and started walking across the field to meet Homer.

He half ran at her but stopped before he got near enough to touch. "Are you a witch?"

Back at the plane, one of the men muttered. "Well she's old enough to be."

Elois half-turned her head to him. "I'm old but ain't a thing wrong with my hearing." She faced Homer again. "And I'm not a witch."

"How do you explain disappearing and then turning up here?"

She shook her head. "Walk with me, young man, and I'll explain."

He crossed his arms. "Not a chance. I want witnesses to whatever you're going to say. There's no way that I'm going to let you take me off and enchant me."

The snickers again from behind her. Elois sighed. "You want these gentlemen to think you've read too many penny-dreadfuls? You ever heard tell of witches outside of a storybook? Ever read bout one in the papers? No. On account of there's no such thing."

"That might be so, but I saw you disappear with my own two eyes and I ain't taking any chances."

"You took a chance coming here, didn't you? If I'm what you say I am. What's to stop me from vanishing right now and taking y'all with me if it were something I could do? So when I ask you to walk with me, I'd take it kindly if you would."

"What have you got to say that you're afraid to say in front of these folks?"

"Not a thing. I'm more worried about them thinking you're any more touched than they already do." She gestured toward the hangar. "I'm going to walk over yonder and you can come with me or not, as you like. I'll keep at arm's distance though so you aren't thinking I'll latch onto you and haul you Lord knows where." Without waiting for Homer to respond, she set out, stabbing the ground with her cane as she went. She figured that curiosity had brought him here and curiosity would make him follow her. Sure enough, she hadn't got more than ten steps before she heard him coming along after.

She waited until she was pretty sure she was out of earshot of the men at the flyer and then waited a mite more before she started talking. "You ever read H. G. Wells?"

"Of course I have."

"Well, that'll make things a mite easier." She stopped abruptly and turned to face him. Homer was almost on her heels and half-stumbled back to keep out of arm's reach. Elois snorted. "You recollect the book *The Time Machine*?"

Homer blinked and then guffawed. "You aren't trying to tell me you're from the future."

"Being a witch is more believable?"

"Well . . . no offense, ma'am." He dug his toe into the ground. "But a time traveler wouldn't be old."

"I'd not have thought so either but it turns out that time travel only works within the span of a person's lifetime. They picked me on account of how I was born this year."

His face screwed up with concentration. "Let's say that's so. Give me a good reason for you to vanish then."

"The machine broke and I can only stay here for so long as it's turned on. It took a full day for them to fix it while I was back in my own time." She shook her head. "I told them to set me down near you so I could explain, but they thought you wouldn't understand. I'm real sorry about that."

"Prove it. Bring me tomorrow's paper or something." Those arms were crossed across his chest again as if he were preparing for war. At least Elois knew he'd survive the Great War, 'cause the records they'd found about him showed Homer dying in the 70s.

"I can't just nip back and forth in time all willy-nilly. It's an expensive machine that's sent me here and the operator is back in my own time." Elois pursed her lips, thinking. Dr. Connelly wouldn't approve, but the only obviously modern thing she had with her was the opera glass camera. Pulling it out of her handbag, Elois rewound the footage a little, so he could watch it. "Here. This is a moving picture camera, disguised as opera glasses. I was filming the plane."

Homer started to reach for them and then stopped. "What if this is just a story and that's ensorcelled?"

"Young man. I don't know why you're so set on me being a witch instead of a time traveler Why on earth would I pretend to be something so unbelievable if I were trying to hide being a witch? It just doesn't make a spot of sense. If I were going to make up a story, it'd be a darn sight cleverer than that—unless I'm telling the truth. Now you tell me why I'd pretend to be a time-traveler instead of letting you think I'm a witch?"

"There are laws against witchcraft. You could be burned at the stake."

She didn't say anything to that, just sighed and looked over the rim of her glasses at him. Living as long as she had gave her plenty of time to perfect the withering glare of scorn. She'd decimated sons and grandsons with it and this whippersnapper melted just as surely as the others. His face colored right out to the tips of his ears, which burned bright enough to serve as a landing beacon for the airplane. He rocked back on his heels and raised his shoulders as if he were trying to protect his neck from the butcher's knife.

Swallowing, Homer said, "I guess that's not too likely."

"No. It's not. Now are you going to look at this or not?"

He took the opera glasses from her and held them up to his eyes. Immediately he yanked them away, eyes wide with shock. Spinning on his heel, he stared at the airplane. Homer brought the glasses up to his eyes and even with his back to her, Elois could see his hands shaking. "What is this?"

"It's a camera."

"I mean, why are you taking all these pictures of the flyer?" He lowered the glasses, turning to face her.

"Because, today is the first day that they really fly. Wilbur will go up for eighteen minutes and not come down till he drains the gas tank. It's a historic moment but they weren't expecting it, so there's no photographer or anything here. Day after tomorrow, Orville'll fly in front of a crowd for thirty-four minutes, but today's the day everything changes. And later on, after they fly it, they'll make changes and eventually dismantle the flyer. In 1947 Orville will rebuild it for an exhibit, but he'll only have about sixty percent of this plane. There's a historical society that wants to check the rebuilt plane against this one."

And right then, Wilbur stepped out of the open door of the hangar. "This has gone on long enough. Madam, you should be ashamed of yourself, filling this boy's head with nonsense in order to get him to help in your espionage." He held out his hand to Homer. "Give me the camera, son."

"Espionage?" Elois lifted her cane so it served as a barrier between the man and Homer. "I don't rightly know what you're talking about, but the opera glasses are mine and I'll thank you to leave them be."

"I overheard everything and though your story is designed to play upon the fancies of a boy, I could hear the elements of truth." He reached over the cane and snatched the opera glasses from Homer's hand.

"Hey!" Homer pushed Elois's cane out of the way and stepped toward the man. "Give that back."

"We've been at pains to keep our invention out of the wrong hands."

He brushed past both of them and hurried across the field, waving the opera glasses.

Homer ran after him and caught his coat. "Please, Mr. Wright. I was just funning with her. I didn't think anyone would take me seriously."

Elois hurried after them, focused more on the uneven ground than the man in front of her.

Wilbur shrugged off Homer's hand and shook his head. "We didn't advertise this test flight, so how do you suppose that she knew to come out here today, except through spying."

Elois laughed to hide her discomfiture. This was the sort of thing that it would have been nice for the Time Travel Society to let her know. "You can't think that folks aren't talking about this in town, can you?"

"The folks in town aren't out here snooping around. Who looks at things up close with *opera glasses*?" Wilbur lifted the opera glasses and mimed snooping.

The moment he looked through the opera glasses he cursed and jerked his head away from the eye piece. Slowly he put it back to his eyes. His face paled. Wilbur wiped his mouth, lowering the opera glasses to stare at Elois. "Who do you work for?"

"I'm just a body that's interested in seeing you fly." She could barely breathe for fear of the moment. "You're making history here."

"History." He snorted. "You were talking to the boy about time travel."

Before Elois could think of a clean answer, Homer said, "She disappeared earlier. Utterly vanished. I . . . I think she's telling the truth."

"And if she is?" Wilbur turned the glasses over in his hands. "I look at this and all I can see are the number of inventions that stand between me and the ability to do . . . If I weren't holding it, I should think it impossible."

Elois could not think of a thing to say to the man. He looked as if his faith had been as profoundly shaken as a small boy discovering the truth about Santa Claus. Elois shook her head. "All I want is to watch you fly; once I've done that I'll be gone and you won't have to worry about the pictures I took."

"This is why you were so certain the Flyer will work today, isn't it?" There was no wonder his voice, only resignation.

"Yes, sir."

"And what you told the boy, about Orville rebuilding the plane. True? So, we'll be enough of a success that someone builds a museum and sends a time traveler back to visit. That's something, even if I'm not around to see it."

Startled, Elois replayed the things she had told Homer. "How do you reckon that?"

"Because everything you said was about my brother. At some point, I'll stop registering on the pages of history." He twisted the glasses in his hands. "Is the future fixed?"

Elois hesitated. "The Good Book promises us free will."

"You have not answered my question." He took his bowler off and wiped a sheen of sweat from his scalp before settling it back in place.

When he looked back at her with eyes as blue as a frozen river, she could see the boy she'd read about. Self-taught and brilliant, he had been described as having a voracious mind. Everything she said would go in and fill his mind with ideas.

"Y'all understand that I'm a traveler and don't really understand the science of it, right? If you think about time like a stalk of broccoli, what Mr. Barnes's machine does is it takes a slice of the broccoli and shuffles it to a different point in the stalk. My past is one big stalk. My future is made up of florets. So the only places I can travel back to are the ones that lead to the future I live in. If I tried to go forward, they tell me that the future will be different every time. Which I reckon means that you can do things different and wind up in a different stalk of the broccoli, but I'll only ever see the pieces of broccoli that lead to my present." She shook her head. "If that makes a mite of sense to you, then I'll be impressed."

"It makes sense enough." Wilbur lifted the glasses to his eyes again and with them masked said, "I'll thank you not to intimate at this to my brother."

"Of course not." Elois shuddered.

"Very good." Wilbur spun on his heel. "Well, find a spot to watch."

"But Miss Jackson's opera glasses . . . " Homer trotted after him.

"I'll give them back after I've flown." Wilbur Wright grinned. "If your history is going to lose track of me, then perhaps the future needs to be reminded."

ON THE FAR SIDE of the hangar, the other men were still celebrating the flight. Eighteen minutes and forty-two seconds precisely. She'd spent time recording their joy but every time Wilbur looked at her, Elois got the shivers and finally given up to wait out her remaining time out of sight. She leaned against the side of the hangar, studying her watch. Time was almost up.

At a run, Homer rounded the corner of the hangar with the opera glasses in his hands. He relaxed visibly at the sight of her. "I was scared you'd be gone already."

She held the watch up. "Two minutes."

"He didn't want to come. Said that the doubt would be better than knowing for certain." Homer chewed his lip and handed her the opera glasses. "What happens to him, Miss Jackson?"

Elois sighed and remembered all the things she'd read about Wilbur Wright before coming here. "He dies of typhoid when he's forty-seven. Wish I'd not let on that I was from the future."

Homer shook his head. "I'm glad you told me. I'll—"

And he was gone.

The tall grass of Huffman Prairie was replaced by a crisply mown lawn of chemical green. Where the weathered hangar had been stood a bright, white replica. Neither the hangar nor the lawn seemed as real as the past. Elois sighed. The air burned her nostrils, smelling of carbon and rubber. The homing beacon in her handbag ought to bring them round to her soon enough.

She leaned back against the barn to wait. A paper rustled behind her.

She pulled away, afraid that she'd see a big ole "wet paint" sign but it was just an envelope.

An envelope with her name on it.

She spun around as quick as she could but there wasn't a soul in sight. Breath fighting with her corset, Elois pulled the envelope off the wall. She opened it carefully and found a single sheet of paper. A shaky hand covered the surface.

Dear Elois,

You will have just returned from your first time travel mission and meeting me, so this offers the first opportunity to introduce myself to you in your present. I wish I could be there myself, but that would mean living for another forty years, which task I fear would require Olympian blood. You have been such a friend to me and my family and so I wanted you to know two things.

1. Telling me the truth was the best thing you could have done for me. Thank you.

2. We are (or will be by the time you read this) major share-holders in the Time Travel Society. It ensures that your future trips to my past are without incident, and also will let my children know precisely when your first trip takes place in your present. I hope you don't mind that I took the liberty of asking my children to purchase shares for you as well. I wish we could have presented them to you sooner.

Be well, my friend. And happy travels.

Sincerely yours,
Homer Van Loon

At the bottom of the sheet was a bank account number and then a list of addresses and phone numbers arranged in order of date.

Her eyes misted over at the gift he'd given her—not the account, but the knowledge that she had not harmed him by telling the truth.

In the parking lot, the Time Travel Society's minivan pulled in, barely stopping before Mr. Barnes and the rest of the team jumped out. "How was the trip?" he shouted across the field, jogging toward her.

Elois grinned and held out the opera glasses. "I think you'll like the footage I got for you."

"May I?" He stopped in front of her as long and lanky as she imagined Homer being when he was grown up.

"Of course. That's why you sent me, isn't it?"

He took the opera glasses from her and rewound. Holding it to his eyes as the rest of the team gathered around, Mr. Barnes became utterly still. "Miss Jackson . . . Miss Jackson, how did you get the camera on the plane?"

Dr. Connelly gasped. "On the Wright Flyer?"

"Yes, ma'am. I watched from the ground with the hat-cam while Wilbur was flying. I'm real curious to hear the audio that goes with that. We could hear him whooping from the ground."

"But how did you . . . " Dr. Connelly shook her head.

"I told him the truth." Elois sighed, remembering the naked look on his face at the moment when he believed her. "He took the camera because he understood the historical context."

Evil Robot Monkey

SLIDING HIS HANDS over the clay, Sly relished the moisture oozing around his fingers. The clay matted down the hair on the back of his hands making them look almost human. He turned the potter's wheel with his prehensile feet as he shaped the vase. Pinching the clay between his fingers he lifted the wall of the vase, spinning it higher.

Someone banged on the window of his pen. Sly jumped and then screamed as the vase collapsed under its own weight. He spun and hurled it at the picture window like feces. The clay spattered against the Plexiglas, sliding down the window.

In the courtyard beyond the glass, a group of school kids leapt back, laughing. One of them swung his arms aping Sly crudely. Sly bared his teeth, knowing these people would take it as a grin, but he meant it as a threat. Swinging down from his stool, he crossed his room in three long strides and pressed his dirty hand against the window. Still grinning, he wrote SSA. Outside, the letters would be reversed.

The student's teacher flushed as red as a female in heat and called the children away from the window. She looked back once as she led them out of the courtyard, so Sly grabbed himself and showed her what he would do if she came into his pen.

Her naked face turned brighter red and she hurried away. When they were gone, Sly rested his head against the glass. The metal in his skull thunked against the window. It wouldn't be long now, before a handler came to talk to him.

Damn.

He just wanted to make pottery. He loped back to the wheel and sat down again with his back to the window. Kicking the wheel into movement, Sly dropped a new ball of clay in the center and tried to lose himself.

In the corner of his vision, the door to his room snicked open. Sly let the wheel spin to a halt, crumpling the latest vase.

Vern poked his head through. He signed, "You okay?"

Sly shook his head emphatically and pointed at the window.

"Sorry." Vern's hands danced. "We should have warned you that they were coming."

"You should have told them that I was not an animal."

Vern looked down in submission. "I did. They're kids."

"And I'm a chimp. I know." Sly buried his fingers in the clay to silence his thoughts.

"It was Delilah. She thought you wouldn't mind because the other chimps didn't."

Sly scowled and yanked his hands free. "I'm not *like* the other chimps." He pointed to the implant in his head. "Maybe Delilah should have one of these. Seems like she needs help thinking."

"I'm sorry." Vern knelt in front of Sly, closer than anyone else would come when he wasn't sedated. It would be so easy to reach out and snap his neck. "It was a lousy thing to do."

Sly pushed the clay around on the wheel. Vern was better than the others. He seemed to understand the hellish limbo where Sly lived— too smart to be with other chimps, but too much of an animal to be with humans. Vern was the one who had brought Sly the potter's wheel which, by the Earth and Trees, Sly loved. Sly looked up and raised his eyebrows. "So what did they think of my show?"

Vern covered his mouth, masking his smile. The man had manners. "The teacher was upset about the 'evil robot monkey.'"

Sly threw his head back and hooted. Served her right.

"But Delilah thinks you should be disciplined." Vern, still so close that Sly could reach out and break him, stayed very still. "She wants me to take the clay away since you used it for an anger display."

Sly's lips drew back in a grimace built of anger and fear. Rage threatened to blind him, but he held on, clutching the wheel. If he lost it with Vern—rational thought danced out of his reach. Panting, he spun the wheel trying to push his anger into the clay.

The wheel spun. Clay slid between his fingers. Soft. Firm and smooth. The smell of earth lived in his nostrils. He held the world in his hands. Turning, turning, the walls rose around a kernel of anger, subsuming it.

His heart slowed with the wheel and Sly blinked, becoming aware again as if he were slipping out of sleep. The vase on the wheel still seemed to dance with life. Its walls held the shape of the world within them. He passed a finger across the rim.

Vern's eyes were moist. "Do you want me to put that in the kiln for you?"

Sly nodded.

"I have to take the clay. You understand that, don't you."

Sly nodded again staring at his vase. It was beautiful.

Vern scowled. "The woman makes *me* want to hurl feces."

Sly snorted at the image, then sobered. "How long before I get it back?"

Vern picked up the bucket of clay next to the wheel. "I don't know." He stopped at the door and looked past Sly to the window. "I'm not cleaning your mess. Do you understand me?"

For a moment, rage crawled on his spine, but Vern did not meet his eyes and kept staring at the window. Sly turned.

The vase he had thrown lay on the floor in a pile of clay.

Clay.

"I understand." He waited until the door closed, then loped over and scooped the clay up. It was not much, but it was enough for now.

Sly sat down at his wheel and began to turn.

The Consciousness Problem

THE AFTERNOON SUN angled across the scarred wood counter despite the bamboo shade Elise had lowered. She grimaced and picked up the steel chef's knife, trying to keep the reflection in the blade angled away so it wouldn't trigger a hallucination.

In one of the *Better Homes and Gardens* her mother had sent her from the States, Elise had seen an advertisement for carbon fiber knives. They were a beautiful matte black, without reflections. She had been trying to remember to ask Myung about ordering a set for the last week, but he was never home while she was thinking about it.

There was a time before the subway accident, when she had still been smart.

Shaking her head to rid herself of that thought, Elise put a carrot on the sil-plat cutting board. She was still smart, today was just a bad day was all. It would be better when Myung came home.

"You should make a note." Elise grimaced and looked to see if anyone had heard her talking to herself.

But of course, no one was home. In the tiny space of inattention, the knife nicked one of her knuckles. The sudden pain brought her attention back to the cutting board. Stupid. Stupid.

Setting the knife down, she reached for the faucet before stopping herself. "No, no Elise." She switched the filtration system over to potable water before she rinsed her finger under the faucet. The uncertainty about the drinking water was a relatively minor trade for the benefits of South Korea's lack of regulations. They'd been here for close to three years, working on the TruClone project but she still forgot sometimes.

She went into the tiled bathroom for some NuSkin, hoping it would mask the nick so Myung wouldn't worry. A shadow in the corner of the mirror moved. Who had let a cat inside? Elise turned to shoo it out, but there was nothing there.

She stepped into the hall. Dust motes danced in the afternoon light, twirling and spinning in the beam that snuck past the buildings in Seoul to gild the simple white walls. There was something she was going to write a note about. What was it?

"Elise?" Myung came around the corner, still loosening his tie. His dark hair had fallen over his forehead, just brushing his brow. A bead of sweat trickled down to his strong jaw. He tilted his head, studying her. "Honey, what are you doing?"

She shivered as if all the missing time swept over her in a rush. Past the cookie-cutter skyscrapers that surrounded their building, the scraps of sky had turned to a periwinkle twilight. "I was just . . . " What had she been doing? "Taking a potty break." She smiled and rose on her toes to kiss him, breathing in the salty tang of his skin.

In the six months since she stopped going into the office at TruClone, he had put on a little weight. He always had a sweet tooth and tended to graze on dark chocolate when she wasn't around, but Elise was learning to find the tiny pot belly cute. She wrapped her arms around him and let him pull her close. In his embrace, all the pieces fit together the way they should; he defined the universe.

"How was work?"

Myung kissed her on the forehead. "The board declared the human trial 100% effective."

Adrenalin pushed her breath faster and made the back of her knees sweat. "Are you . . . ?"

"Elise. Do you think they'd let me out of the lab if I weren't the original?"

"No." She shook her head. "No, of course not."

She should have been there, should have heard the success declared. The technology to print complete physical copies of people had been around for years, but they'd started TruClone to solve the consciousness problem. Elise had built the engine that transferred minds to bodies so she should have gone into the office today, of all days.

She had forgotten. Again.

"I want to hear all about it." She tugged his hand, pretending with a smile to be excited for him. "Come into the kitchen while I finish dinner."

OUTSIDE, THE FIRST SOUNDS of the market at the end of their block began. Calls for fresh fish and greens blended on the breeze and crept in through the open window of their bedroom, tickling her with sound. Curled around Myung, with one leg thrown over his thigh, Elise traced her hand down his body. The patch of hair on his chest thinned to a line which tickled her palm. He stirred as she followed the line of hair lower.

"Morning." Sleep made his voice grumble in his chest, almost purring.

Elise nuzzled his neck, gently nipping the tender skin between her teeth.

His alarm went off, with the sound of a stream and chirping birds. Myung groaned and rolled away from her, slapping the control to silence the birds.

She clung to him. Not that it would do any good. Myung loved being in the office.

He kissed her on the forehead. "Come on, get up with me. I'll make you waffles."

"Oo. Waffles." Elise let go of him, smacking his rump gently. "Go on man, cook. Woman hungry."

He laughed and pulled her out of bed with him. She followed him to the kitchen, and perched on one of the wicker stools by the counter as he cooked. It almost felt like a weekend back when they were courting at MIT. But the mood broke when Myung laid a pill next to her plate. Her stomach tightened at the sight of the drug. She didn't want the distancing the medication brought on. "I feel fine today."

Myung poured more batter on the waffle iron and cleared his throat. "Maybe you'd like to come in to work?"

The room closed in around her. Elise lowered her eyes to escape the encroaching walls. "I can't." She hadn't gone in since she came home from the hospital. Every day she thought that tomorrow the effects of the concussion would have faded. That the next day she would be back to normal. And some days she was. Almost.

Myung put his hand on hers. "Then take your medication."

She had walked away from the subway accident, but it had scrambled her brain like eggs in a blender. Head-trauma induced psychosis. On good days, she knew it was happening.

Elise picked up the pill, hating it. "You're going to be late."

He looked over his shoulder at the clock and shrugged. "I thought I'd take today off."

"You? Take a day off?"

"Why not? My clone." He paused, relishing the word. "My *clone* has offered to do my reports today."

"Is that—Isn't that a little premature?" As she said that, she realized that she didn't know how much time had passed since the board declared success. It felt like yesterday but it had been longer. Hadn't it?

"He's bored, which is not surprising since I would be, too."

If she went to the office, maybe she could see the clone. See the thing they had labored toward. Cloned rats and dogs and monkeys weren't the same as a man. Not just any man, but a clone of her husband. She swallowed against a sudden queasiness. "Who's overseeing him?"

"Kathleen. Sort of. I'll have to look over his report later but we've agreed to let him function as if he were me, to see how he does."

Which made sense. The ultimate goal was to make full clones of high-level people who needed to be in more than one place at once. "Am I a clone, Myung?"

"No, honey." He squeezed her hand, grounding her again. "You're not."

The thing that nagged at her was that she could not tell if she didn't believe him because he was lying or because the accident had left her with delusions to accompany the hallucinations.

~

The Consciousness Problem

ELISE WIPED the kitchen table, gliding the sponge across the teak in perfect parallel lines. The phone rang. Startled, she jumped and lost the pattern on the table. Putting her hand over her mouth to slow her breathing, Elise glanced at the clock to see how much time she had lost to cleaning. It was only 2:30. That wasn't as bad as it could have been.

The phone rang again.

She picked it up, trying to remember who had called her last. "Hello?"

"Hi, honey. I need to ask you to do something for me." Myung sounded tense and a little breathless, as if the phone frightened him as much as it had her.

"What?" She slid a pad of paper across the counter so she could take notes. Clearly, today was not a good day and she didn't want to make that obvious to Myung.

"Would you come to the lab?"

"I . . . " A reflection in the window caught her eye, flashing like an SOS. "Today isn't a good day."

"The clone misses you."

His words stretched out as if they could fill the ten kilometers between the lab and the apartment and then everything snapped. "Misses me? It's never met me."

"*He* has all of my memories and personality. From his point of view, he hasn't seen you in months." There was a tension in his voice, his words a little rushed and tight. "Please. It's affecting his ability to concentrate. It's depressing him."

"No." A reflection twitched in the corner of her eye becoming a spider until she looked at it. "I can't."

Myung hummed under his breath, which he always did when he was conflicted. She hadn't pointed it out to him because it was an easy way to tell when he didn't want to do something. He exhaled in a rush. "All right. How's everything at home?"

"Fine." She doodled on the pad. There had been something that she'd thought about telling him. "Oh. There are some carbon matte knives I want to get."

169

"Really? What's wrong with the ones we have?"

Elise hesitated. "These look nice. All black."

"Ah." She could almost hear his mind click the pieces together. "No reflections. I didn't realize that was still bothering you. I'll order them."

"Thank you."

"Sure I can't get you to reconsider?" He laughed a little. "I miss having you around the office as much as he does."

"Not now."

Elise hung up. Back to the office? Her stomach heaved and she barely made it to the sink before vomiting. Gasping, she clung to the stainless steel as the anxiety flung itself out of her. The back of her throat and her nose burned. If she went in, people would know that she was wrong inside.

IN THE DARK of the bedroom, Elise counted Myung's heartbeats as she lay with her head on his chest. "I'm sorry."

He stroked her hair. "Why?"

She lifted her head, skin sticky from sweat. "That I won't come to the office."

"It's all right. I understand."

At night, the idea seemed less frightening. She could tell herself as many times as she could count that the office was not dangerous, that nothing bad had ever happened to her there, but her body did not believe. "What's he like?"

"Who?" He lifted his head to look at her.

"Your clone."

Myung chuckled. "Just like me. Charming, handsome, devilishly intelligent."

"A troublemaker?"

"Only a little." He kissed her hand. "You'd like him."

"If I didn't, we'd have problems." Elise rolled onto her back, looking for answers on the ceiling. "You want to use me as a trial, don't you,"

"What? No. Don't be silly."

"Please, Myung. My brain isn't that scrambled." She poked him in the soft part of his belly.

"Hey!"

"It's the logical next step, if these clones are going to do what we told our investors they would. You need to see if a loved one can tell the difference. You need to dress identically with your clone and let me talk to both of you."

Myung hummed under his breath.

"You could bring him here." Elise kissed his shoulder.

He stopped humming. "Not yet. Too many variables. It has to be at the lab first."

"I'll think about it." Her pulse raced, just saying the words. But the queasiness was manageable.

THE KNIVES ARRIVED in the afternoon. Elise pulled them out of their shrinkwrap and set them on the counter, forming three matte black voids on the wood. No reflections marred their surfaces. She ran a finger along one edge of the paring knife. Like a thread, a line of crimson opened on her finger. It didn't even hurt.

Elise held the cut close to her face, trying to see what would crawl out of her skin. The blood trickled slowly down her finger exploring the contours. Without the reflections, her brain needed some other way to talk to her now. She could help it if she opened the gap more.

"No. Myung wouldn't like that." Elise clenched her fist so the blood was hidden. "Put NuSkin on it, Elise."

Yes. That was the right thing. As she put the liquid skin in place, it occurred to her that if she printed herself a new body it would come with nothing inside. "But we solved the consciousness problem. It would come with me inside. With me."

She weighed the chef's knife in her hand and dropped it. The kitchen counter had all the vegetables from the refrigerator set out in neat rows.

She had chopped a bell pepper without any memory of returning to the kitchen. Elise cursed. Hands splayed on the counter, she lowered her head in frustration.

The front door opened. "Honey, I'm home!"

Elise picked up the knife, then set it down and scooped the closest vegetables into her arms. Before Myung entered the kitchen, she managed to get them into the vegetable drawer in the fridge.

She let the door close and turned, smiling brightly. "Let me get your martini, dear."

Laughing, Myung caught her around the waist and kissed her. "How was your day?"

Elise shrugged. "Mixed. The usual. Yours?"

"Also mixed. My clone is . . . Well, let's say I'm learning how stubborn I can be."

She winced. "I could have told you that."

"Not." He kissed her nose. "Helpful."

She stuck her tongue out. Moments like this beckoned her to fall into them with their allure of normalcy. "Thank you for the knives."

"Sorry?"

Elise pointed at the carbon black knives laid out on the counter. "The ones you ordered for me came today."

"I—" Myung crossed to the counter and picked up the paring knife. "Elise, I didn't order these."

The floor of the room fell away from her. Elise grabbed the handle of the refrigerator to steady herself. "But you said you would. We talked about it."

"When?" Myung's nostrils had flared.

"It's not a delusion." She swallowed and her throat stayed knotted. "You called me. You asked me to come to the office."

"Fuck." He slammed his fist on the counter. "Elise, I'm sorry. It's the clone."

Relief swept her so quickly that her knees gave way. She dropped to the floor, one hand still clinging to the refrigerator. The door cracked open letting a breeze out which chilled the tears running down her face. Thank God. She had not imagined the phone call. She hadn't ordered the knives herself and forgotten. "The clone did it."

Myung crouched by her, wiping the tears from her face. "I'm sorry. He was working on a report and we let him use my office."

"You're letting him contact the outside?"

"No. I changed the passwords—"

Elise started laughing. "And he guessed?"

Myung's skin deepened in a blush and he shut his eyes. "Should have seen that coming."

"Yes, dear." Elise wiped her eyes. "Oh God. I thought it was another sign of crazy."

At that, Myung opened his eyes, pain creasing his brow. "I'm so sorry."

"Don't be." Elise stood, using her husband's shoulder to push herself off the floor. "He bought the knives I asked for."

"With my money."

"Well . . . He's doing your work."

"Point." Myung got to his feet. "And I would have gotten them for you if you'd mentioned it to me."

"I thought I did." Giggles overtook her for a moment and they both stood in the kitchen laughing. When she caught her breath, Elise said, "Tomorrow, I'll come to the office with you."

The delight that blossomed on Myung's face almost made Elise withdraw the offer. Not that she resented making Myung happy, but she would disappoint him tomorrow. In the context of the lab, her slips of mind would be more apparent.

ELISE SHIFTED on the hard metal chair in the observation room. To her left, a mirrored window hid the staff watching her. She angled her head so the reflections were not so apparent. No time for hallucinations today. The rest of the walls were pale blue Sheetrock, meant to be soothing, but clinically cold. The ballast of one of the florescent lights buzzed just at the edge of her hearing. They would have to get that fixed.

She put her hands on the linoleum table in front of her and then in her lap again as the door opened.

Myung came in, dressed in a white T-shirt and jeans. He wore athletic socks but no shoes. Glancing at his feet, his dark hair masked his eyes for a moment, like a K-pop star. "We didn't have matching shoes, so opted for none."

Elise grinned, beckoning him closer. "Are they good for a sock-hop?"

He laughed, voice bouncing in a three note pattern. "That is not on the set of questions."

"You." She pointed at him accusingly. "Aren't supposed to know what they are."

"I don't." Myung held his hands out in mock surrender. "But I'm guessing that it's not."

"Fine. We'll stick to the standards." Elise waved her hand to command him to sit across from her. Her heart beat like she was at a speed dating service. She looked at the list of questions she planned to ask each man. "When we got married, what did you whisper after you kissed me?"

Myung turned red and glanced at the mirror. He wet his lips, leaning forward across the table. "I think I said, 'How soon can we get out of here?'" His eyes were alive as if he wanted to take her right there on the table.

A flush of warmth spread out from Elise's navel to her breasts. At the wedding, his hands had been warm through her dress and she had been intently aware of how long his eyelashes were.

He looked out from under them now with his pupils a little dilated as if he also found the room too warm. "Next?"

"What is our most intimate moment?" Watching him, time focused itself in a way it had not done since the accident. Each tick of her internal clock was crisp and in sequence.

Myung's eyes hooded for a moment as he thought. "Yellowstone. We might have had the whole park to ourselves but there was also this profound sense that someone would catch us in the act. And that you would . . . " He hummed under his breath for a moment, sweeping his hand through his hair. "Let's just say, I knew that you trusted me."

Elise looked at the paper again. She had thought he would say that it was their first time after his vasectomy. At the time he had reveled in the freedom.

"Last question. Pick a number."

"That's it?"

"Yep."

Myung fingered the end of his nose, and Elise could not doubt that she was talking to her husband. He nodded. "Very nice. Confirmed memory, subjective memory, and random."

She tapped a finger on the paper. "No opinion please. Number?"

"Thirty-six."

"Why thirty-six?"

He picked at the cuticle on his thumb. "Remember the time we went to see that puppet play, 'Between Two Worlds?'" He waited until she nodded. "The guy who thought that he could win his predestined bride through Kaballah had this line, 'Thirty-six, in that number lies the essence.' It stuck with me for some reason."

MYUNG CAME IN, dressed in a white T-shirt and jeans. Elise's breath hung in her throat at the palpable déjà vu. She had seen printed clones dozens of times as parts donors but she had never seen one animated. Had she not been a part of the process to give a clone consciousness, she would have thought that her husband had just walked into the room. Like the other one, this Myung wore white athletic socks but no shoes. Glancing at his feet, his dark hair masked his eyes for a moment, like a K-pop star. "We didn't have matching shoes, so opted for none."

Elise pressed her hand over her mouth, trying to remember what she had said to the first one. No wonder they had wanted her to script her questions.

"Are you okay?" Myung—she could not think of him as anything else—took a step closer.

"It's uncanny is all." Wrong. She should not have said that out loud. It might skew his responses. "Shall we get started?" Elise beckoned him to sit across from her. She looked at the sheet of questions, trying to center herself. The calm certainty she felt before had stripped away, leaving her flustered. "When we got married, what did you whisper after you kissed me?"

Myung turned red and glanced at the mirror. He wet his lips, leaning forward across the table. "I think I said, 'How soon can we get out of here?'"

Sweat coated her skin.

He looked out from under his long eyelashes. "Next?"

"What is our most intimate moment?" Watching him, Elise looked for some clue, some hint that he was not her husband. But perhaps he was, and the Myung she had met first was the clone.

Myung's eyes hooded for a moment as he thought. "Yellowstone. We might've had the whole park to ourselves but there was also this profound sense that someone would catch us in the act. And that you would . . . " He hummed under his breath before sweeping his hand through his hair. "Let's just say, I knew you trusted me."

Elise looked at the paper again. Her hands were shaking and she could barely find air to breathe. Every nuance was the same.

"Last question. Pick a number."

"That's it?"

"Yes." Dear God, yes. She had helped create one of these two men, but she wanted nothing more than to get out of the room. Even though she knew he might be her husband, the uncanniness of having the same conversation twice threatened to shred her mind.

Myung fingered the end of his nose. "Very nice. Confirmed memory, subjective memory, and random."

A shiver ran down her spine. "What number?"

"Seventeen."

Elise had to stop herself from gasping with relief. Had they chosen the same number she might have screamed. "Why seventeen?"

"That's the day we were married." He shrugged.

Something, a darkness flickered in the mirror of the room. It would be so much easier to drop into crazy than to keep thinking. "May I see you both at the same time?"

Myung stood. "Sure. I'll ask him to come in."

Forcing her mind into order, Elise folded her list of questions in half. Then half again, creasing the edges with her nail to crisp perfect lines.

The door opened and the other Myung came in. Elise had met identical twins before, but no twin had the commonality of experience that these two men had. One was her husband, the other was a copy and she could not tell them apart. They had even printed the extra weight that Myung carried so both had identical little pot bellies.

The clone carried microchip transponders in his body, and a tattoo on his shoulder, but neither of those were visible. As they talked, Elise slowly noticed a single difference between the two.

The man to her right watched every move she made. His eyes were hungry for her in a way that—"You're the clone, aren't you?"

She had interrupted the one on her left. The two men shared a look before nodding, almost in unison. The clone said, "How did you know?"

"The way you look at me . . . " Elise faltered. He looked at her like he was trying to memorize her.

The clone grimaced and blushed. "Sorry. It's just that, I haven't seen you in months. I miss you."

Myung, the original Myung picked at his cuticle. "I told you she could tell the difference."

"But you were wrong about the reason." The clone smirked. "She could tell because you don't love her as much as you used to."

"That is a lie." Myung tensed visibly, his fist squeezing without his seeming awareness.

"Is it?" The clone shook his head. "Everything else is the same, why would my emotional memories be any different? The only difference between us is that absence makes the heart grow fonder."

"Stop." Elise stood abruptly, her chair squeaking against the floor. She pressed her hand against her forehead.

Both of them looked abashed. In stereo they said, "I'm sorry."

"It doesn't matter." Her thoughts were fragmenting. The reflection in the window moved, a child trying to get her attention. Elise shook her head. "You brought me down to see if I could tell the difference. Now you know that I can."

Her Myung said, "But not when we were separate."

"No." Elise fingered the paper on the table. "Which of you came in first?"

"I did," the clone said.

They sat in silence, Elise tried to fold the paper into another square. "I think I'm ready to go home."

"Of course." Her Myung stood, chair scraping across the floor.

The clone leaned forward on his. "Won't you stay for lunch?" His voice cracked as he asked, as if the request were more urgent than just a meal.

Elise raised her eyes from the paper to his face. The way his brows curled in the middle. The way his eyes widened to show a rim of white under the dark iris. The way his soft lips hung a little open. All of the minute elements that made the whole of her husband pulled, begging her to stay.

And the other Myung, the original, stood next to him, legs spread wide with a slight tension in his arms as if ready to protect her.

No. Not to protect her, but to protect his right to have her.

"Yes." She put her hand on the clone's, startled by the familiarity of the contact. "Yes, of course I'll stay."

THE SMELL of sautéing onions wafted in from the kitchen. Myung had offered to cook breakfast before going to work, his usual ploy when he felt like he needed to make up for something. Clearly, he had no idea that it was like a confession that the clone was right; Myung did not love her as much as he used to.

That wasn't quite true. Myung loved her the same as before, what had changed was that now there was a version of him which missed her all the time. Elise stretched under the covers and the cotton caressed her body like a lover. "I am the forbidden fruit."

Myung's cell phone rang on the bedside table where he had left it. Rolling over, she picked it up. Caller id showed the office. Elise got out of bed, not bothering with a bathrobe, and carried it to the kitchen.

Myung met her partway down the hall. He took it, mouthing his thanks even as he answered.

Elise lifted the hair away from her neck, knowing that it would raise her breasts and make her torso look longer, daring him to choose work over her. His eyes followed the movement. Lips parting, he reached for her. Stopped.

His face shut down. Myung put one hand on the wall and squeezed his eyes closed. Dropping her arms, Elise shivered at the sudden tension in his frame.

"No. No, I heard you." He leaned against the wall and slid down to sit on the floor. "Did he leave a note or . . . " His eyes were still closed but he covered them with his hand.

Elise crouched next to him. Her heart sped up, even though there was nothing she could do.

"No. I haven't checked email yet." Myung nodded as if the person on the other end of the line could see him. "I'll do that. Thanks for handling this. Tell Jin not to do anything until I get in."

He hung up. Cautious, Elise touched his thigh. "Myung?"

Her husband slammed his head against the wall. Elise jumped at the horrible thud. Cursing, Myung threw his phone down the hall and it ricocheted off the floor. Tears glittering on his cheeks, he hurtled to his feet. "He killed himself. Sent us all a video. By email."

Myung was halfway to the office before Elise could pull herself together enough to stand.

~

ON THE MONITOR, the image of Myung leans close to the screen.

"This is the clone of Doctor Myung Han. I am about to kill myself by lethal injection. You will find my body in the morgue.

"Before I do, I want to make it perfectly clear why I am taking this step. With the animals we tested, the next step in this process is dissection. We must do this to be certain that the cloning has no unexpected side effects and to fully understand the mechanism by which the consciousness transfer works. My original knows this. I know this. He will not do it *because* the experiment has been a 100% success. We are identical, more so than any set of twins. He sees terminating the experiment as murder.

"Make no mistake, he is correct.

"Which is why I am terminating the experiment myself. I am not depressed. I am not irrational. I am a scientist. The experiment needs to continue."

He stands and walks out of the room.

ELISE STOOD behind Myung's chair, scarcely breathing. He reached to restart the video.

"Don't." She stopped him with a hand on his shoulder. It was bad enough seeing it once, but to dwell on it courted madness.

Under her hand, he trembled. "I didn't want this."

"I know."

He slammed his fist against the table. "If it had been me, I wouldn't have done it."

"But—" Elise stopped herself, not wanting to blame him.

"What?"

She saw again the clone begging her to stay for lunch. "He's trapped in the lab all the time. Were you ever going to let him out?"

Myung slumped forward, cradling his head in his hands. After a moment, his shoulders began shaking with sobs. Elise knelt by the side of the chair and pulled him into her arms. The rough stubble on his cheek scraped her bare skin. She pressed closer to the solidity of him, as if she could pull him inside to safety. An ache tore at her center as she rocked him gently and murmured nothings in his ear.

She had known the clone for a matter of hours, or for as long as she had known Myung depending on how you counted it. The two men had only a few months of differing experience. The bulk of the man who had died belonged to her husband. But the differences mattered. Even something as simple as a number. "Thirty-six," she whispered. In that number lies the essence.

As MYUNG WENT to the elevator, Elise stood in the door to watch him. She could not quite shake the feeling that he wouldn't come home. That something about the place would compel him to repeat his clone's actions. When the doors slid shut, she went inside the apartment.

In the kitchen, Elise pulled out the matte black knives that the clone had given her and laid them out on the counter. He had known her. He had loved her. She picked up the paring knife, twisting it in her hands. It wasn't right to mourn him when her husband was alive.

"Elise?" Myung stood in the doorway.

"Forget som—" Adrenalin threaded its way through all her joints, pulling them tight. He wore a plain white T-shirt and jeans; his face was smooth and freshly shorn. Myung had not had time to shave. This man was leaner than her husband. "I thought . . . How many clones are there?"

He picked at the cuticle on his thumb. "Myung made just one."

"You didn't answer my question." Elise gripped the paring knife harder.

"I'm a clone of the one you met. Unrecorded. I started the process as soon as the building was empty last night." He swept his hand through his hair and it fell over his eyes. "We have about ten minutes of different memories, so for practical purposes, I'm the same man."

"Except he's dead."

"No. Ten minutes of memory and that physical body are all that is dead." Myung—she could not think of him any other way—crossed his arms over his chest. "It was the only way to escape the lab. I had a transponder and a tattoo that I couldn't get rid of. So I printed this body from an older copy. Imprinted it with my consciousness and then . . . that's where our memories deviate. As soon as we were sure it was a clean print, he went to the morgue and I left."

She should call the office. But she knew what they would do to him. Insert a transponder and lock him up. "Why are you here?"

His eyes widened as if he were startled that she would ask. "Elise—The place where the original and I differ, the thing he cannot understand is what it is like to live in the lab, knowing that I'd never be with you. He doesn't know what it's like to lose you and, believe me, knowing that, I hold you more precious than I ever did before. *I* love you."

The raw need in his eyes almost overwhelmed her. The room tilted and Elise pressed her hand against the counter to steady herself. "I can't go with you."

"I wasn't going to ask you to."

"But you were going to ask me for something."

He nodded and inhaled slowly. "Would you clone yourself? So I'm not alone."

Elise set the knife on the counter, in a careful row with the others. She walked across the room to stand in front of Myung. The vein in his neck throbbed faster, pulsing with life. "Is it any different? Being a clone?"

"There's a certain freedom from knowing that I'm not unique. But otherwise, no. I feel like I am Myung Han."

Putting a hand on his chest, the heat of his body coursed up her arm. "I need to know something."

He raised his eyebrows in question.

"After the accident . . . " She did not want to know but she had to ask. "Am I a clone?"

"Elise, there's only one of you."

"That's not what I asked. The original won't tell me, but you—you have to. Am I a clone?"

"No. You are the original and only Elise." He brushed the hair away from her face. "Everything else is head trauma. You'll get better."

She had braced herself for him to say that she was a clone. That she had died in the crash and the reason she couldn't think straight was because the process had been too new, that she was a failed experiment.

Elise leaned forward to kiss him. His lips melted against hers, breath straining as if he were running a race. She let her bathrobe fall open and pressed against him. Myung slipped his trembling hands inside the robe, caressing her with the fervor of their first date.

Parting from him burned, but Elise stepped back, leaving him swaying in front of her. She closed the robe. "When I'm well, if I can. I will."

Myung closed his eyes, forehead screwing up like a child about to cry. "Thank you." He wiped his hand across his face and straightened.

"They'll notice that another body was printed and come after you."

"Not right away." He picked at his cuticle. "I took my original's passport from the office. Knowing me, it'll take him awhile to realize it's missing."

She felt herself splitting in two. The part of her that would stay here and see her husband tonight, and the part of her that already missed him. At some point, the two halves would separate. "Where are you going?"

He tucked a loose hair behind her ear. "Yellowstone."

Elise caught his hand and kissed it. "I will see you there."

For Solo Cello, op. 12

His keys dropped, rattling on the parquet floor. Julius stared at them, unwilling to look at the bandaged stump where his left hand had been two weeks ago. He should be used to it by now. He should not still be trying to pass things from his right hand to his left.

But it still felt like his hand was there.

The shaking began again, a tremelo building in his hand and knees. Julius pressed his right hand—his only hand—against his mouth so he did not vomit on the floor. Reaching for calm, he imagined playing through Belparda's Étude No. 1. It focused on bowing, on the right hand. Forget the left. When he was eight, Julius had learned it on a cello as big as he had been. The remembered bounce of the bow against the strings pulsed in his right hand.

Don't think about the fingering.

"Jules, are you all right?" Cheri's voice startled him. He hadn't heard the door open.

Lowering his hand, Julius opened his eyes. His wife stood silhouetted in the light from their apartment. Her hair hung in loose tendrils around her face, bleached almost colorless by the backlight.

He snatched his keys off the floor. "I'm fine." Julius leaned forward to kiss her before she could notice his shaking, but Cheri turned her head and put a hand to her mouth.

"No. Sorry. I—I was just sick." A sheen of sweat coated her upper lip.

Julius slid his good arm around her and pulled her to him. "I'm sorry. The baby?" This close, her lilac perfume mixed with the sour scent of vomit.

His phantom hand twitched.

She half-laughed and pressed her head into his shoulder. "Every time I throw up, I think that at least it means I'm still pregnant."

"You'll keep this one."

She sighed as if he had given her a gift. "Maybe. Two months, tomorrow."

"See." He brushed her hair with his lips.

"Oh—" Some of the tension came back to her shoulders. "Your agent called."

Julius stiffened. His agent. How long would a one-handed cellist be of interest? "What did Leonard say?"

"He wants to talk to you. Didn't say why." Cheri drifted away and began obsessively straightening the magazines on the bureau in the foyer.

Julius let her. He had given up on telling her that the accident had not been her fault. They both knew he would not have taken the tour if Cheri had not insisted. He would have stayed in the hotel, practicing for a concert he never gave.

He tossed his keys on the bureau. "Well. Maybe he's booked a talk show for me."

AT THE COFFEE SHOP, Julius felt the baristas staring as he fumbled with his wallet. Leonard reached for the wallet with his pudgy sausage fingers. "Let me help."

"No!" Julius grit his teeth, clutching the slick leather. "I have to learn to do this."

"Okay." Leonard patted the sweat on his face with a napkin and waited.

The line shuffled behind him. Every footfall, every cough drove a nail into his nerves. A woman whispered, "Julius Sanford, you know, the cellist."

Julius almost turned and threw his wallet at her. Who the hell was she? Had she even heard him play before the accident or had she only seen him on the nightly news? Since the accident, sales of his albums had gone through the roof.

He wasn't dead, but he might as well be.

Julius bit the inside of his cheek until he tasted blood and pressed his wallet against the counter with the stump. The bandages bit into the still tender flesh, but the wallet stayed still.

He pulled out his credit card with his right hand. It was stupid and it felt good and he hated it, all at once.

As if it were celebrating, his phantom hand flicked through the opening passage to Vivaldi's Sonata in F Major. Jules pressed the wallet harder against the counter, trying to drive out the memory of a hand with each throb of pain.

Avoiding eye contact, he took his iced latte from the barista. He did not want to know if she was the type who watched him with pity or if she stared with naked curiosity.

Leonard had already picked a table outside. Jules dropped into the chair across from him. "So?"

"So." Leonard sipped his mocha. "What if you didn't have to learn to do that?"

"What? Handle credit cards?"

Leonard shrugged, and dabbed the back of his neck. "What would you give to play cello again?"

Julius's heart kicked against the inside of his ribs. He squeezed the plastic cup to keep from throwing it at Leonard. "Anything."

The older man looked away. His tongue darted out, lizard-like. "Is that hyperbole, or would you really give anything?"

Shaking, Julius shoved the stump squarely in Leonard's vision. The phantom twitched with inaudible music. "If the devil sat down with us and offered to trade my hand for my soul, I'd do it. I'd throw yours in with the bargain."

"Good." Beads of sweat dotted Leonard's forehead. "Except he's already got mine." He pushed a newspaper across the table, folded open to a page in the Arts and Leisure section.

SVETLANA MAKES TRIUMPHANT RETURN TO FIGURE SKATING

Julius stared at the article. She had suffered from bone cancer and lost her foot. Two years ago, she was told she would never skate again. Now she was at the Olympics.

"How?"

"A blastema bud."

Jules wiped his hand over his mouth. "I thought those were illegal."

"Here. Yes. Calcutta? No." His tongue flicked again, always the sign of a sticking point in negotiations. "But the blastema has to be from a related embryo to reduce chances of rejection." He paused. "Svetlana got herself pregnant."

The phantom hand froze.

"I know her doctor." Leonard tapped the paper. "I can get you in."

CHERI SAT in the living room looking at a catalog of baby furniture. When Julius entered, she smiled, barely looking up from the glossy pages. "Did Leonard have anything interesting to say?"

Julius hesitated in the door and then eased onto the sofa across from her. "He's found a way to get my hand back."

Her catalogue hit the coffee table, the pages slapping against the wood. Cheri stared at the stump. Her mouth worked soundlessly.

"It's not legal." Agitato beats pulsed in his phantom fingers. "It's—" He broke off, rubbing his left arm above the bandages to ease the ache. She wanted the baby so badly. "I feel like I'm dead. Like this."

Cheri reached across the coffee table to grab his good hand. "Whatever it takes, Jules."

He started to shake and pulled back. "The doctors can transplant a blastema bud to the stump and regrow my hand. But we have to do it now, before scar tissue forms."

"That's not so bad." She got off the couch to kneel beside him. "I don't mind moving to a country where it's legal."

He bit his lip and nodded.

Cheri ran her hand through his hair. Cool and soothing, her fingers traced a line from his scalp to the nape of his neck. "Hey. Sweetie. What's wrong?"

Wrong. She wanted to know what was wrong. The shaking started again. "It has to be related."

She froze. They hung suspended, as if waiting for a conductor to start the next movement. Julius stared at the carpet until Cheri moved her hand.

She slid it down his back and stood. "Related?"

He nodded. "To reduce the chances of rejection."

"So it might not work?" Cheri wrapped her arms around herself.

"I don't have another choice." He held the stump up so she could see it. "Do you have any idea what it's like? *I can't play.*"

"You could teach."

A laugh ripped out of him. "It's not the same thing! I can't go from being part of the music to hearing it butchered. I mean, can you imagine me with eight-year olds? Christ. Kill me now."

"Sorry." Cheri paled, her skin becoming almost translucent in the light. She turned and went to the window. "What do you want me to say?"

Say yes. Say you understand. "I—I just wanted to talk about options." Julius crossed the room to stand behind Cheri. He reached out to hold her and stopped, staring at the stump. In his memory, the tour-bus tipped and landed with his arm out the window, sliding on his hand. Grinding it away. "I should have stayed in the room."

"What?"

"Nothing." He wouldn't have gone if she hadn't insisted. "We can make another baby."

"Can we?" A vein pulsed in her neck. "It's been two years, Jules."

"So you miscarried before." The phantom hand clenched in a tight fist. "You might miscarry again, and then you won't have a baby and I still won't have a hand. Is that what you want? Are you happy that I can't play anymore?"

Her shoulders hitched and Cheri shook her head.

Julius pinched the bridge of his nose. He had gone too far, but she had to understand. "I'm sorry. I just see this chance and it's the first time I've hoped since the accident." He put his hand on her shoulder. She trembled, her shoulder as tight as a bow. "I'm sorry."

She nodded but did not turn.

Julius waited for more but Cheri continued to stare out the window. He squeezed her once and walked away.

"Jules?" Her voice caught him halfway across room. "We should do it."

Afraid to look at her, he stopped. "Do you mean that?"

"Yes." The word almost disappeared into the hush of the room.

"Because I don't want to force you into anything." He tasted the hypocrisy on his lips, but he needed this. She had to understand that.

She turned to face him then. Her face, all cheekbones and dark circles, was blotched red with anger. "You're offering me a choice between giving you your hand back and raising a child that you hate. What choice do you think there is?"

"I didn't mean—"

Cheri shook her head, rejecting his apology. "Tell Leonard I said, 'yes.'" She turned back to the window and leaned her head against the glass.

"Cheri." He stopped. Nothing he could say would make her feel better, without giving away the thing he wanted. The thing he needed. He plucked at the bandages on his stump. If he could play again . . . "You have to understand what this means to me."

"I understand that I'm your second love. I said yes. I can't give you anything else."

Julius stared at her unforgiving back. "Thank you."

He slid out of the room to call Leonard. His hand trembled on the receiver.

Down the hall, the door the bathroom shut. Cheri retched once. Then again.

Julius pressed the phone harder against his ear and started running Wilde's *Lament* in his mind.

He concentrated on the fingering.

THE LAST VIBRATIONS of Wilde's opus 12 buzzed through Julius's thighs and into his chest. He flexed the fingers on his left hand as he released the cello's neck.

Across the room, Leonard sat with his head tilted down so that his chin vanished in his neck. Julius swallowed, the gulp sounding as loud as it had when he first auditioned for Leonard.

Leonard lifted his head. "What was that?"

"*A Lament in Rondo Form for Solo Cello*, Opus 12." Julius stroked the cello's silky wood. The sweat on his palm left a film on the instrument.

Leonard grunted. His tongue darted out to wet his lips. "Well."

"Well?" Christ, the man was trying to kill him. Julius looked down, loosening his bow as he waited for the verdict.

"Heard from Cheri?"

"She sent me a card on my birthday." His left hand spasmed. "Are you going to tell me what you thought?"

"Turn the gig down."

Julius almost dropped the bow. "You're kidding. It's Carnegie Hall! I've been working for this for the last three years."

Leonard leaned forward. "Jules. Have I ever steered you wrong?"

"Three years, Leonard." He'd given up more than the time to be able to play again.

"Take a gig in a symphony, build up your chops again. You wouldn't have to audition."

"Screw that."

"You asked for my opinion. As your agent—"

"Another agent would get me the gigs that I want."

"Sure." Leonard shrugged and headed for the door. "Take it, you'll sell out the house. But after people hear you play, the only gigs you'll be

191

able to book will be novelty shows." His words resonated in the belly of the cello. "You aren't ready. It's like you're playing two different pieces now."

Julius hadn't thought anyone else could hear it. He gripped the cello between his knees, as if the fragile wood could shield him from the truth. "How long?"

He paused in the doorway. "How long did it take you to become world-class before?"

"Fifteen years . . . " Fifteen years of études and climbing his way up through the chairs of symphonies.

"Then that's your answer." Leonard shut the door.

Within Julius's left hand, the old phantom hand twitched again and started playing Bach's Sonata in D-minor. He clenched his hand, but the fingering did not stop.

For Want of a Nail

WITH ONE HAND, Rava adjusted the VR interface glasses where they bit into the bridge of her nose, while she kept her other hand buried in Cordelia's innards. There was scant room to get the flexible shaft of a mono-lens and her hand through the access hatch in the AI's chassis. From the next compartment, drums and laughter bled through the plastic walls of the ship indicating her sister's conception party was still in full swing.

With only a single camera attached, the interface glasses didn't give Rava depth perception as she struggled to replug the transmitter cable. The chassis had not been designed to need repair. At all. It had been designed to last hundreds of years without an upgrade.

If Rava couldn't get the cable plugged in and working, Cordelia wouldn't be able to download backups of herself to her long-term memory. She couldn't store more than a week at a time in active memory. It would be the same as a slow death sentence.

The square head of the cable slipped out of Rava's fingers. Again. "Monkey!" She slammed her heel against the ship's floor in frustration.

"If you can't do it, let someone else try." Her older brother, Ludoviko, had insisted on following her out of the party as if he could help.

"You know, this would go a lot faster if you weren't breathing down my neck."

"You know, you wouldn't be doing this at all if you hadn't dropped her."

Rava resisted the urge to pull the mono-lens out of the jack in her glasses and glare at him. He might have gotten better marks in school, but she was the AI's wrangler. "Why don't you go back to the party and see if you can learn something about fertility." She lifted the cable head and tried one more time.

"Why you little—" Rage choked his voice, more than she had expected from a random slam. She made a guess that his appeal to the repro-counsel didn't go well.

Cordelia's voice cut in, stopping what he was going to say. "It's not Rava's fault. I did ask her to pick me up."

"Yeah." Rava focused on the cable, trying to get it aligned.

"Right." Ludoviko snorted. "And then you dropped yourself."

Cordelia sighed and Rava could almost imagine breath tickling her skin. "If you're going to blame anyone, blame Branson Conchord for running into her."

Rava didn't bother answering. They'd been having the same conversation for the last hour and Cordelia should know darn well what Ludoviko's answer would be.

Like programming, he said, "It was irresponsible. She should have said no. The room was full of intoxicated, rowdy people and you are too valuable an asset."

Rava rested her head against the smooth wood side of the AI's chassis and closed her eyes, ignoring her brother and the flat picture in her goggles. Her fingers rolled the slick plastic head of the cable, building a picture in her mind of the white square and the flat gold cord stretching from it. She slid the cable forward until it jarred against the socket. Rotating the head, Rava focused all her attention on the tiny clues of friction vibrating up her arm. This was a simple, comprehensible problem.

She didn't want to think about what would happen if she couldn't repair the damage.

Being unable to download her old memories meant Cordelia would have to delete herself bit by bit to keep functioning. All because Rava had asked if she wanted to dance. At least Ludoviko hadn't heard *that* part of the accident. Rava rotated the head a fraction more and felt that sweet moment of alignment. Pushing the head forward, the pins slid into their sockets, as if they were taunting her with the ease of the connection. The head thunked into place. "Oh, yes. That's good."

She opened her eyes to the gorgeous vision of the cable plugged into its socket.

Cordelia spoke, her voice tentative. "It's plugged in?"

For another moment, Rava focused on the cable before her brain caught what Cordelia had asked. She yanked the mono-lens out of the jack and the lenses went transparent. "You can't tell?"

The oblong box of Cordelia's chassis had been modified into a faux Victorian-era oak lapdesk which sat on the fold-down plastic table in Rava's compartment. Twin brass cameras—not period correct—stood at the back and swiveled to face Rava. Above the desk, a lifesize hologram of Cordelia's torso hovered. Her current aspect was a plump middle-aged Victorian woman. She chewed her lip, which was her coded body language for uncertainty. "It's not showing in my systems."

"Goddamit, Rava. Let me look at it." Ludoviko, handsome, smug Ludoviko reached for the camera cable ready to plug it into his own VR glasses.

Rava brushed his hand away. "Your arm won't fit." The hum of the ship's ventilation told Rava the life support systems were functioning, but the air seemed thick and rank. Ignoring her brother, she turned to the AI. "Does your long-term memory need a reboot?"

"It shouldn't." Cordelia's image peered down as if she could see inside herself. "Are you sure it's plugged in?"

Rava reattached the camera's cable to her VR glasses and waited for the flat view to overlay her vision. The cable rested in its socket with no visible gap. She reached out and jiggled it.

"Oh!" Cordelia's breath caught in a sob. "It was there for a moment. I couldn't grab anything, but I saw it."

So much of the AI's experience was translated for laypeople like Rava's family, that it seemed almost surreal to have to convert back to machine terms. "You have a short?"

"Yes. That seems likely."

Rava sat with her hand on the cable for a moment longer, weighing possibilities.

Ludoviko said, "It might be the transmitter."

Cordelia shook her head. "No, because it did register for that moment. I believe the socket is cracked. Replacing that should be simple."

Rava barked a laugh. "Simple does not include an understanding of how snug your innards are." The thought of trying to fit a voltmeter into the narrow opening filled her with dread. "Want to place bets on how long before we hear from Uncle Georgo wondering why you're down?"

Cordelia sniffed. "I'm not down. I'm simply sequestered."

Pulling her hand out, Rava massaged blood back into it. "So . . . the hundred credit question is . . . do you have a new socket in storage." She unplugged the camera and leaned back to study Cordelia.

The AI's face was rendered pale. "I . . . I don't remember."

Rava held very still. She had known what not having the long-term memory would mean to Cordelia, but she hadn't thought about what it meant for her family. Cordelia was their family's continuity, their historical connection to their past. Some families made documentaries. Some kept journals. Her family had chosen to record and manage their voyage on the generation ship with Cordelia. Worse, she managed all their records. Births, deaths, marriages, school marks . . . all of it was managed through the AI who could be with every family member at all times through their VR glasses.

"Oh, that's brilliant." Ludoviko smacked the wall with the flat of his hand, bowing the plastic with the impact.

Rava focused on the hard metal floor, to hide the dismay on her face. "Well, look. Uncle Georgo said multiple times that our Grands packed duplicates of everything, so there's got to be a spare. Right?"

"Yes?" The uncertainty in Cordelia's voice hurt to hear. Since Rava was a child, Cordelia had known everything.

"So, let's ping him to see if he's got a copy of the inventory. Okay?" She adjusted her VR glasses and tried to project reassurance with her smile.

Cordelia shook her head, visibly distressed. "I can't transmit."

"Right . . . " Rava bit her lip realizing she had no idea what her uncle's contact was. "Crap. Ludoviko do you have his contact info?"

He turned and leaned against the wall, shaking his head. "No, Cordelia always connects us."

"I'm sorry." The droop of the AI's eyes drew a portrait of genuine unhappiness.

He waved his hand. "Just print it and I'll dial manually."

Rava rolled her eyes, glad to see him make such a basic mistake. "Ludoviko, if she can't transmit to us, she can't transmit to a printer either." She triggered the VR keyboard and lifted her hands to tap on the keyboard that seemed to float in front of her. "Tell me and I'll dial it."

Ludoviko sneered. "How old school."

"Bite me." Rava tapped out the sequence on the virtual keyboard as Cordelia gave her the routing number.

Before she toggled the call, Cordelia said, "Oh! Hardwiring! I'm sorry, I should have thought of that sooner." Cordelia's shoulders relaxed and she put a hand to her chest in a perfect mimicry of a Victorian woman avoiding a swoon. "You could hardwire me to the main ship system and then I can use that to reach my memory."

"Would that work?" Rava withdrew her hand from the trigger. She couldn't remember ever seeing a computer with external cables to anything.

"It should." Cordelia looked down the back of her chassis, like a woman trying to see the closure on her gown.

Rava toggled the keyboard off and walked around to the back of the AI's chassis. Beneath two shiny brass dials were four dark oblongs. She'd forgotten that they even existed. "At least these are easy to access." She buried her hand in her hair, staring at the ports. "Any idea where the heck I am supposed to get a cable?"

"With her other spare parts." Ludoviko didn't say "stupid" but she could hear it.

"And those would be . . . where?" Rava crouched to examine the ports. They appeared to take a different socket from the cable inside the AI. "'Cause I'm thinking our family hasn't accessed that pod since before Launch. You want to make a guess about which of our pods has her spare parts or were you suggesting we spend the credits to have all of them brought up from the hold?"

"You can spend the credits. You dropped her."

"Will you two please stop fighting?" Cordelia laughed breathlessly. "I'm trying to pretend that experiencing memory loss is good for me. It builds character."

"Well look. Wait." Rava raised her hand. "Uncle Georgo'll have the inventory."

"Oh, there's no need to bother him and fret about fetching the pods from storage. You can go to Paĉjo's Consignment Shoppe." Cordelia brightened. "Someone else on the ship must have a cable."

Rava nodded, relief lifting her mood a little. "Yeah. I'll bet that's true. So I just have to ask Uncle Georgo what kind of cable you take."

"Why don't you take me to Paĉjo's shop?" Cordelia cocked her head. "Then you can match the cable to my ports without bothering Georgo."

"That's—"

Ludoviko shook his head before she could finish her sentence. "You'll do anything to avoid telling Uncle Georgo, won't you?"

He wasn't far wrong. When Uncle Georgo had resigned as Cordelia's wrangler and accepted a seat on the family council, it had taken everyone by surprise. He was brilliant and everyone expected him to keep the post until his body succumbed to old age. At twenty-six, Rava had been far younger than anyone expected when she'd succeeded to the role of Cordelia's wrangler. The last thing she wanted was for the family to say it had been a mistake.

Gritting her teeth, Rava toggled the keyboard and called Uncle Georgo. His extension rang longer than she was used to. When he finally toggled in, appearing in her VR glasses as though he were in the room with them, his eyes were red and puffy, as if he'd been crying. "Hello?" His voice trembled.

"Uncle Georgo?" Rava leaned forward, dread needling along her spine. "What's wrong?"

"I don't . . . I don't . . . " Behind his VR glasses, his eyes darted to the left as if searching for someone. He wet his lips. "Do you know where Cordelia is?"

Rava winced. So much for easing into the subject. "Yeah, about that. So, it's like this. She's fine but needs to swap out a part."

His forehead wrinkled, brows almost meeting in confusion. "Part?"

"Her transmitter. We think." If she rushed past the problem then maybe he'd think she had everything under control. "Anyway, so the reason I'm calling is to see if you know the type of cable she needs for an external hardwire."

He muttered under his breath, tugging on his ear. "But what about Cordelia? You know where she is?"

"In my room." She turned her head so that Cordelia's chassis would come into frame. "See? Honest, it's a matter of swapping out the socket."

"In *your* room? Why is she with you? Why do you have Cordelia?" His voice rose, cracking on the AI's name. She and her uncle had disagreed on Cordelia's maintenance before, but this was all out of proportion to what was happening. Mostly. "She should be with me."

Rava swayed as if her uncle had struck her. He'd resigned from his post as the AI's wrangler and of all their relatives Rava had been the one Cordelia had chosen to take over. If the AI didn't blame Rava for dropping her, then Uncle Georgo had no room to. "Hey. I'm her wrangler now and I'm capable of dealing with this, I just need the cable."

"Where is she? I want to see her."

Rava had to fight the urge to yank her glasses off. Clenching her fists so hard her fingers ached, Rava said, "I told you, she's in my room."

"Your room . . . But I don't understand. Who are you?"

Rava froze, breath stopped. "What's that supposed to mean?"

Her uncle's eyes widened and then he scowled. "I'm not talking to you anymore." Reaching forward, he wiped off the connection and his image vanished.

Rava sat on the floor, breath coming in gasps. Her hand shook. Nothing about that conversation had made any sense. Her uncle had often been temperamental, but he'd also been eminently rational. This had been like talking to one of her nieces. Rava passed a hand over her face, sweating.

Ludoviko smirked. "Mad at you, huh?"

Ignoring her brother, Rava stabbed the redial and then listened to her uncle's handy ring. With each tone, another weird aspect struck her. Uncle Georgo crying. Ring. Uncle Georgo seeking Cordelia in his glasses. Ring. Uncle Georgo asking her who she was.

She must have misunderstood that. And yet, there had been no recognition in his gaze, no sense that he'd been playing with her. The phone dropped into voicemail and Rava slapped it off.

Fine. So he was screening her calls now. She'd grab Cordelia and go to her uncle's quarters. Not that she was looking forward to that but it'd be an improvement over talking to Ludoviko. "Okay. We're going to Uncle Georgo's."

"Really" Cordelia smiled. "That's not necessary, you and I can solve this together. Take me to the consignment shop and we can find a match."

The option to pretend that nothing had happened, that Uncle Georgo was normal, sat right in front of her, but it was as illusionary as anything on VR. If it were just the cable, Rava might have gone for it, but a question had started nagging her. She nodded at Cordelia. "Okay. Sure. Why don't you shut down—"

"I don't fucking believe this." Ludoviko put his hands on his hips. "You are unbelievable."

"You've said that." Rava faced Cordelia again. "Go to sleep until we get to the consignment shop. There's no point in wasting your memory on a trip through the corridors."

Cordelia's hesitation was almost invisible as she looked from Rava to Ludoviko. She nodded. "Good idea. Wake me there." Her image flickered and vanished.

Rava waited until the alert light faded before letting out the breath she'd been holding. She'd been worried that Cordelia would see through the lie.

Ludoviko dropped into the chair by her table. "You are quite the piece of work."

Rava stared at him for a minute until she remembered that with Cordelia down, the call to Uncle Georgo wouldn't have been relayed to her brother. "He didn't know me."

"What? Talk sense, Rava. Who didn't know you?"

"Uncle Georgo. There's something wrong with him . . . " Her voice trailed off, the weight of her suspicions too heavy to be supported by voice. "Will you . . . will you come with me?"

Ludoviko opened his mouth, lip already curling with whatever insult he was preparing.

"Please."

He blinked and let his breath out in a huff. "Jesus, Rava. This really has you freaked. No one is going to fire you."

"Believe it or not, I'm not worried about that." She glanced away from Cordelia's inert cameras. "Would you come with me?"

"Yeah. Yeah, I'll come."

Her brother might drive her mad, but oddly, having someone who disliked her so much was comforting. It was a known quantity and that at the moment, that was a welcome thing.

UNCLE GEORGO did not answer when she knocked on his door. She waited, counting the seconds as people walked past, until Ludoviko reached past her and pounded on the door, making it bounce in its tracks. The speaker crackled into life and her uncle's voice quavered out. "Who's there?"

"It's Rava."

"And Ludoviko."

She sighed. "I brought Cordelia."

The door opened and Uncle Georgo peered out with obvious distrust. His hair was disheveled and a streak of brown stained his shirt from chest to navel. His gaze darted to the corner of his glasses and back to look past Rava. "Where is she?"

This was not right. Rava cocked her head, squinting with concentration. She held the chassis out a little away from her chest. "She's right here."

He huffed, running his hand through his hair so it stood on end. "Don't see her."

Ludoviko said, "Didn't Rava tell you? Cordelia can't download her memories because Rava dropped her. She's sleeping to save space."

Nice to know that his willingness to help didn't change his pattern of insults. "May I come in?" Rava took a step toward the door.

Her uncle chewed on his bottom lip, head tilted to the side in his usual pose, but his eyes darted around searching for something. In his hesitation, Rava decided to push forward. He retreated as she crossed the threshold. His quarters were a mess, clothes and bedding strewn around as if he'd pulled everything out of the drawers. His desk was in the same spot hers was, so she pushed the wrinkled shirt off of it and set Cordelia's chassis down.

Putting her finger on the wake up button, Rava pressed, the click vibrating under her finger as a gentle chime rang.

Before it had faded, Cordelia's camera's rotated to her and her head and shoulders appeared above the chassis. "Success?"

Her uncle sobbed, "Cordelia!" He reached past Rava, fingers trembling.

Rava kept her gaze fixed on Cordelia, whose image didn't change. At all. For an AI programmed to act human, she became awfully rigid. Her face stayed fixed on Georgo, but the cameras flicked to Rava for a moment, then away. She softened and her image morphed so the high neck of the Victorian gown sank to reveal her bosom. Her lashes lengthened and her lips became full and pouting. "Georgo, honey, what have you done with your room?" Her voice was sultry.

"I was looking for you." He held his hands out to his side. "Why did you leave me?"

"I needed to get you a present. You like presents, right?"

He nodded, like a little boy. The confident, haughty man Rava knew had vanished. She trembled and wrapped her arms around herself.

"Good. Now, lie down for your nap and I'll give you the present later."

"I don't want to."

Ludoviko stepped around Rava and leaned in close to Cordelia. "What the fuck is going on?"

Only because she had studied the mannerisms built into Cordelia, Rava did see the AI's fraction of hesitation. "I am afraid that is confidential information between me and one of my users."

Rava shook her head. She didn't like Ludoviko's manner, but that didn't change the fact that Cordelia was dodging questions. She swallowed and put her hand on Cordelia's interface, setting her thumb on the print reader. "Authorized Report. What is Uncle Georgo's status?"

Cordelia lowered her head, biting her lip. "He has dementia."

"No." Ludoviko laughed, breath catching in his throat. "I talked to him yesterday and he most certainly does not." The air purifiers beat in the silence in the room. "Look, he'd have gone to recycling if he weren't productive anymore. It's the most basic law of conservation of resources."

"You've been covering for him, haven't you?" Rava's whole body was shaking, but her voice sounded flat and dead.

"Yes."

The need to respond pressed her throat shut. What could she say in the face of this? Cordelia had lied to them, and lied repeatedly. Dementia.

Ludoviko's hand fell on Rava's shoulder, pulling her out of the way. "How long?"

"I don't know." Cordelia's voice verged on inaudible.

"Bullshit." He slapped the table beside her, jarring her chassis with the impact.

Uncle Georgo jumped forward and grabbed his arm. "Don't touch her!"

Enraged, Ludoviko shrugged him off. Uncle Georgo reached for Cordelia, hands scrabbling. Ludoviko flat-handed him in the chest, pushing with the full brunt of his strength. The breath coughed out of Uncle Georgo. He crumpled to the floor with a cry.

"Ludoviko!" Rava interposed herself between her brother and her uncle. "What are you doing?"

Ludoviko leveled his finger at Uncle Georgo, who cowered. "I fucking want to know how long this has been happening."

"Leave him alone." Rava wanted to know too, but attacking Uncle Georgo, who was clearly out of his mind—she balked at the thought. If he had dementia, he should have been recycled long ago.

"Are you paying attention, Rava? Our AI is breaking the law." He spun, tendons in his neck standing out in cords of rage. "How long has he been like this?"

Raising her head, Cordelia glared down her nose at him. "I do not know. The start date is recorded in my long term memory."

"I don't believe you." Ludoviko flexed his fists open and closed as if he were five years old and wanted to hit something. "You're lying."

Cordelia leaned forward, her gentle Victorian face distorting with rage. "I can't lie. Mislead, yes, but not lie. If you don't want to know the truth, don't ask me to report with direct questions. You have no idea. No idea what my existence is like."

Though Cordelia's form was a hologram, Rava could not shake the feeling that she was about to step off her dais and slap Ludoviko.

"Was it last month? Was it three months ago? You must have some clue."

"I do not know."

"Ludoviko, what does it matter?"

Sweat dotted his brow. "It matters because if she's been covering for our dear uncle, then she's the one who's been keeping me from reproducing."

The air pump whined as it circulated the air in the room. "What?"

"You didn't know Uncle Georgo was on the repro committee?" He smirked. "Of course not. As a girl, it's your biological imperative to reproduce. You have to keep your womb warm and ready to go. Not me. I have to beg to be allowed to spill my seed in some test tube on the off-chance someone will want it." Ludoviko glared at Cordelia. "My application was denied on grounds that my personality was unstable. Exactly how unstable would you like me to be?"

"I have no memory of this."

He cracked his neck, glaring at her. "That's convenient."

"If you want an answer, I suggest you help your sister find a cable."

"Right." Rava patted her uncle on the shoulder, trying to soothe the sobbing man. "Cordelia, do whatever it is you do to make Uncle Georgo seem normal. Then he can tell us where the inventory is and we can get the cable."

The bark of laughter that broke from Cordelia startled Rava with its bitterness. "Don't you understand, yet? I have been using his VR glasses to feed him lines every time he speaks. He only knows what I know and I don't remember where the inventory is."

"Why? Why have you been covering for him? Report."

Cordelia's eyes sparked with fury. "My report, O wrangler, is that Georgo would go to the recycler if the family council found him to be without use or purpose. I have kept him useful."

"No, I get that. Why keep him out of the recycler?" Rava struggled to understand. "I don't want to go either, but if none of us went, the ship would be overrun and we'd all starve. I mean, you and Uncle Georgo were two of the people who taught me the law of conservation. So why break the law?"

Above her, Ludoviko stilled, waiting for the answer. The only sound came from Uncle Georgo, who rocked on the floor, sobbing. Snot and tears steamed down his face unheeded.

The AI's mask of confidence slipped. "I do not remember. I only remember that it is important to keep him alive and to keep it a secret."

"Well, it's not a secret anymore, is it." Ludoviko's lip twisted in distaste as he stared at his uncle.

"I suppose." Cordelia narrowed her eyes. "I suppose that depends on whether or not you tell anyone else. May I suggest that whatever reason I had was strong enough to overcome my programming about the law. It might be a wise course to not act precipitously to change things."

Rava hesitated. There was something to that. As strong as her childhood training was, an AI had unbreakable taboos built into it. Cordelia had to obey the law. "Hang on." A thought struck her. "Your compulsions are tied to the ship's master log of law. If you can't transmit, how do you know what the laws are?"

"I have a copy in my onboard read-only memory and it syncs at every update."

Which was too bad. Rava had been hoping for a backup transmitter she could hack into. She shook her head to rid it of that faint hope. "How much time do you have left before your next backup is scheduled?"

"An hour and a half." Cordelia looked up and to the left, to indicate she was calculating. "But with only a single feed, I have more time than I'd normally have in memory. We might have a week before I have to start pruning."

Rava felt some of the tension winding through her joints relax. She'd been so worried about having to dump things.

"Yeah." Ludoviko rapped his fist on the wall to get their attention. "Hello? That's great that you won't have to dump any memory, Cordelia, but in the meantime our lives are going unrecorded. What do you suggest we do about that?"

"You could try writing it down." Rava beamed at her brother. "Or you could not worry about it since you won't have any descendents who care."

Her brother's face turned a blotchy red and he took a step toward her, raising his fist. "So no one will record this, will they?"

"I'm still here." Cordelia's voice snapped through the room. "I am still watching."

"Fine." Ludoviko lowered his arm. "But I'm going to tell the family what Rava did."

"By all means. Track down each and every person by walking through the whole ship to find them. Or wait until I've fixed Cordelia."

"Cordelia?" Uncle Georgo lifted his head. "I don't understand what is happening."

"Georgo, Georgo . . . " Cordelia's voice promised soothing and comfort. "It is time for your nap. That is all that has happened. You have missed your nap."

Rava watched as Cordelia used her voice to coax Uncle Georgo upright and then to wash his face and put himself to bed. The irritability and absent mindedness she had seen her uncle exhibit returned but now she could hear the hidden part of his life. Cordelia coaxed him to everything he did almost like a puppeteer with a shadow figure. It created the illusion of life, but her uncle was an empty figure.

THE CORRIDORS had begun filling with the shift change crowd as Rava slipped through the door of the consignment shop. Behind the counter, Paĉjo sat on a stool reading, his bald head gleaming with a faint sheen of sweat as if he'd been running. Tidy ranks of shelves and racks filled the room, each covered with the castoffs of generations, arranged into categories. Long sleeve shirts, paper, pens, cables and a single silver tea service. Every family had brought only what they thought they would need but even with finite resources, fashions changed.

"Hey, lady!" Paĉjo grinned, wrinkles remapping his face as tucked his reader into his coverall pocket. "What news?"

"News is the same. And you?" Rava was always relieved he still had useful work and hadn't hit the recycling point himself.

He shrugged his shoulders with a laugh. "The same, the same. So you looking for anything specific or browsing?"

She hefted the AI's chassis. "I brought Cordelia to look at cables."

He hopped off the stool and waddled across the room, beckoning her to follow. "See this row? Every one of these goes to a different machine and every one of them has a proprietary plug. The ones in these four boxes have plugs that fit the ship, but your guess is as good as mine about what kind of plug your AI uses."

Rava swallowed. "Thanks, Paĉjo. I'll browse then."

He wiped at his brow. "Ping me if you need anything."

Between the towering shelves, Rava set Cordelia's chassis on the floor. She pulled out the box of cables and sat with it on the floor beside the AI's silent frame. The cables were bound in bundles, each of which had a fat hexagon on one end. The other ends varied wildly. Some were tiny silver tubes, others were square. One seemed to be an adhesive electrode. She pulled them out and tried them one by one. The third one slotted neatly into the port on Cordelia's back.

Rising, she cradled Cordelia's chassis to her like one of her nieces or nephews. The cable dangled like a tail. She trotted down the aisles to Paĉjo. "You got a hookup here?"

He lifted his brows in surprise. "For hardwiring? I was wondering what you wanted a cable for." Hopping off the stool he led her behind the counter of the consignment shop to a wall terminal. "Here you go."

Rava set Cordelia's chassis on the floor, but the cable was a little too short to reach the terminal. Paĉjo solved it by bringing his stool to them. "Pesky things, those cables. Small wonder people stopped using them."

"Yeah." Rava feigned a laugh. "Still, I'll take this one. Charge it to my account?"

"Sure." Paĉjo looked from her to Cordelia and finally seemed to recognize that the AI was dormant. "Well, I'll leave you to it."

When he had walked away, Rava pushed the wake up button. The cameras swiveled to face her as the AI's eyelids fluttered in a programmed betrayal of her feelings. Her projected face was flushed and her breath seemed quicker. "Ah. Yes, yes, I'm connected now. Give me a moment while I manage the backlog."

Rava did not want to wait, not even a moment. She wanted this nightmare to be over and done with and for Cordelia to be connected again by wireless, as she should be. And then she wanted to know what to do about Uncle Georgo.

Her handy pinged with five different messages. Before she could open them, Cordelia said, "There are four transmitters in storage. I'm sending the storage unit information to your handy."

"Thanks." Rava flicked it open and scanned the message. The others were delayed messages from family members wanting to know what was happening with Cordelia. Wincing, Rava wrote a quick summary of the problem with the transmitter. "Will you broadcast this to the family?"

Cordelia nodded and, so fast that it might have been an extension of Rava's own thought, the message went out.

Bracing herself, Rava checked behind her for Paĉjo. He was far enough away that she had little fear of being overheard and more privacy here than in her own quarters. "Tell me about Uncle Georgo."

"What about him?" Cordelia raised her eyebrows and cocked her head to the side with the question.

Rava gaped. "The dementia? How long have you been covering for him?"

Cordelia frowned and shook her head slowly. "I'm sorry. I am not sure what you are asking about."

Alarm bells went off in Rava's head. "Did you perform a full sync?"

"Of course. After being offline all afternoon, it was the first thing I did." Cordelia's brows bent together in concern. "Rava, are you all right?"

Rava could hardly breathe. "Fine. Hey, can you set my handy so it shows the names to go with the numbers?"

"Done."

"Thank you." Rava snatched the cable from the wall.

Cordelia gasped as if struck."What are you doing?"

"Something has overwritten your memories."

"That isn't possible, dear."

"No? Then tell me about the conversation that you and I and Ludoviko had in Uncle Georgo's apartment."

"Well . . . if you plug me in to the system, so I can access long-term memory, I could do that."

"This happened less than half an hour ago."

Cordelia blinked. "No, it didn't."

"I was there." Rava lifted Cordelia, hugging the chassis to her chest. "I remember, even if you don't."

RAVA TREMBLED as she sat in the family council chambers. Ludoviko lounged in his chair, with apparent comfort, but she could smell the sweat dampening his shirt. The eight aunts and uncles who sat on the council had been quiet through her entire recitation. Only Uncle Georgo's seat sat empty. Her words dried when she had finished and she waited to hear their reaction.

Aunt Fajra removed her steepled fingers from her lips. "Two years, you say?"

"Yes ma'am." Two years ago, buried in an update, Uncle Georgo had slipped in a program than added a law to Cordelia's copy of the official shipwide laws. He'd seen the dementia coming and acted to save himself.

"Cordelia? What do you have to say about this?"

The AI's cameras swiveled to face the council. "I do not wish to discredit my wrangler, but I have no records of anything she has told you except the problem with my transmitter. The rest of her statements seem so fanciful I hardly know where to begin."

Ludoviko sat forward in his chair, eyes hard. "Would you like Uncle Georgo to respond?"

The AI's hesitation was so slight that if Rava hadn't been watching for it, she would not have seen it. "No, I don't think that is necessary."

"Can you tell us why?" Rava glanced at her aunts and uncles to see if they were noticing the same slow reaction times she was, apparent now as Cordelia adjusted her responses in accordance with the private law to keep Georgo safe.

"Because until you dropped me, Georgo was a respected member of this council. Everyone here has spoken with him. The evidence is clear enough."

Aunt Fajra cleared her throat and pressed a toggle on her handy. The doors to the council room opened and an attendant brought Uncle Georgo in. His stride was erect and only the furtive glances gave him away at first. Then he saw Cordelia and his face turned petulant. "There you are! I couldn't find you and I looked and looked."

Cordelia stilled, became a static image hovering over the writing desk. Rava could almost see the lines of code meeting and conflicting with each other. Keep his secret safe, yes, but how when it was so clearly exposed. Her face turned to Rava, but the cameras stayed fixed on Uncle Georgo. "Well. It seems I am compromised. I have to ask what my wrangler plans to do about it."

Rava winced at the title, at the way it stripped their relationship to human and machine. "I have to do a rollback."

The cameras now swiveled to face her. "You said you found the code."

"I found the code that adds the law that you must protect Uncle Georgo. Not the one that overwrites your memories." She nodded to her brother. "I had Ludoviko search as well and he also didn't find anything definitive. We think it's modified in multiple places and the only way to be sure we've got it out is to rollback to a previous version."

"Two years." Cordelia tossed her head. "Your family will lose two years of memories and records if you do that."

"Not if you help us reconcile your versions." Rava picked at the cuticle of her thumb rather than meet the AI's gaze.

Cordelia wavered and again those lines of code, those damnable lines of code fought within her. "What happens to Georgo?"

"It's not a family decision." Aunt Fajra straightened in her chair and looked at where Uncle Georgo stood, crooning by Cordelia. "You know what the laws are."

Cordelia's mouth turned down. "Then I'm afraid I can't help you."

"I think we've seen all we need." Aunt Fajra waved her hand and with unceremonious dispatch, Cordelia and Uncle Georgo were both bundled out of the council chambers. As the door slid shut, Ludoviko cleared his throat and looked at Rava. She nodded to let him go ahead.

"Okay. Here's the thing. That Cordelia is a reinstall after we pulled out the code we found. Every time we try to clear her we get pretty much the same answer. We tried lying to her and saying Uncle Georgo was already gone, but she knows us too well, so we don't know how she'd behave in that scenario. At the moment, she's insisting she'll only help if we don't send Uncle Georgo to the recycler."

Shaking his head, Uncle Johano harrumphed. "It's not a family decision. He should have been sent there the moment we sorted out what had happened. Keeping him like this is a travesty."

"And will get worse." Rava shifted in her chair. "As his dementia progresses, Cordelia will have less and less control over him. We're concerned about how far her injunction to 'keep him alive' will go. That's why we've kept her from reconnecting to her long-term storage or to the ship."

"And your solution is to reboot her from a backup, wiping those two years of memory? Including all the birth records during those two years . . ." Aunt Fajra gathered the other family council members with her gaze. "That will require a consensus from the entire family."

"Yes ma'am. We understand that."

"Actually. There's one other option." Ludoviko stretched out his legs, almost reclining in his chair. "The Grands packed backups of everything. There's another AI in storage. If we boot it from scratch, it would be able to access the database of memories without the emotional content Cordelia would carry."

"What?" Rava's voice cracked as she spun in her chair to face him. "Why didn't you say that earlier?"

"Because it means killing Cordelia." Ludoviko lifted his head and Rava was surprised to see his eyes glisten with tears. "As her wrangler, you can't be party to it and I couldn't chance you letting her know."

"But wouldn't she—No. Of course not." Since Cordelia didn't have access to her long-term memory, she would have forgotten the existence of another AI. Rava's stomach turned. "Did it occur to you that she might change her response if she knew we had that option?"

"You mean, she might lie to us?" Ludoviko's voice was surprisingly gentle.

"But Cordelia isn't a machine, she's a person."

Ludoviko cocked his head to the side and left Rava feeling like a fool. Of course this reaction was exactly why he thought he was justified in not telling her about the backup AI.

"You are correct. Cordelia is a person." Aunt Fajra tapped the handy in front of her. "A dangerous, unbalanced person who can no longer do productive work."

"But it's not her fault."

Aunt Fajra looked up from her handy, eyes glistening. "Is Georgo's dementia his fault?"

Rava slumped in her seat and shook her head. "What if . . . what if we kept her disconnected from the ship?"

Ludoviko shook his head. "And what, overwrite the same block of memory? Only remember a week at a time? Nice life you are offering her."

"At least she'd get to choose."

CORDELIA'S CAMERAS SWIVELED to face Rava as the door slid open. "He's dead, isn't he?"

Rava nodded. "I'm sorry."

The AI appeared to sigh, coded mannerisms to express grief expressing themselves in her projection. Her face and cameras turned away from Rava. "And me? When do you roll me back to the earlier version?"

Rava sank into the seat by Cordelia's chassis. The words she needed to say filled her throat, almost choking her. "They . . . I can offer you two choices. There's another AI in the hold, the family voted to replace you." She dug her fingernails into the raw skin around the cuticle of her thumb. "I can either shut you down or let you remain active, but unconnected."

"You mean without backup memory."

Rava nodded.

Under the whirring of fans, she imagined she could hear code ticking forward as Cordelia processed thoughts faster than any human could. "For want of a nail . . . "

"Sorry?"

"It's a proverb. 'For want of a nail—' " Cordelia broke off. Her eyes shifted up and to the left, as she searched for information that was not there. "I don't remember the rest of it, but I suspect that's ironic." Hiccuping sobs of laughter broke out of her.

Rava stood, hand outstretched as if she could comfort the AI in some way but the image that showed such torment was only a hologram. She could only bear witness.

The laughter stopped as suddenly as it had began. "Shut me off." Cordelia's image vanished and the cameras went limp.

Breathing shallowly to keep her own sobs at bay, Rava pulled the key from her pocket. The flat plastic card had holes punched in it and metallic lines tracing across the surface in a combination of physical and electronic codes.

Counting through the steps of the procedure, Rava systematically shut down the systems that made Cordelia live.

One. Insert the key.

She had known what Cordelia would choose. What else could she have chosen? Really. The slow etching away of self, with pieces written and over-written.

Two. Fingerprint verification.

Uncle Georgo had chosen to stay, though, and Cordelia might have followed his lead.

Three. Confirm shut down.

If only Rava hadn't dropped the chassis—but then it would have come out eventually.

Four. Reconfirm shut down.

She stared at the last screen. *For want of a nail* . . . Tomorrow she would visit the consignment shop and get some paper and a pen.

Confirm shutdown.

And then, with those, she would write her own memories of Cordelia.

The Shocking Affair of the Dutch Steamship *Friesland*

I WAS BORN Rosa Carlotta Silvana Grisanti, but in the mid-eighties, I legally changed my name to Eve. As you have guessed in your letter, after the shocking affair of the Dutch steamship *Friesland*, my dear friends Dr. Watson and Mr. Sherlock Holmes suggested that my safest course of action would be to distance myself from my family.

But I get ahead of my story; I have not Dr. Watson's gift for explaining Mr. Holmes's methods, and I fear your wish that I relay the particulars of this strange case may be met with inadequate measures.

On the twelfth of October, 1887, I was being taken by the steamship *Friesland* from our home on the Venetian isle of Murano to Africa; there to meet my betrothed, Hans Boerwinkle, a man several years my senior with whom my father had very recently made arrangements. Living as we do now, in the nineteen-twenties, it is difficult to remember what a sheltered life we girls led forty years ago, but at the time it seemed natural that my brother, Orazio Rinaldo Paride Grisanti, escorted me as chaperone. With us also was my lady's maid, Anita.

In addition to my trousseau, we had several boxes packed with the finest Murano crystal as part of my dowry. My father had blown glass without cessation after my betrothal was announced. I remember Zia Giulia asking, "What is the hurry?" At the time, I was only anxious to be an adult, which was all that marriage meant to me.

I can still recall my excitement at dinner the first evening as glittering ladies and gentlemen, in full evening dress, caught me in a dazzle of delight. Orazio and I were seated at a table with two British gentlemen and a couple from Hungary; at the captain's table sat Signore Agostino Depretis, the prime minister of Italy, with his new bride, Signora Michela Depretis. As I anticipated my own wedding and honeymoon, I envied the young woman and the way all eyes sought her.

But I should not dwell on my youthful fancies. The two British gentlemen, as you might have surmised, introduced themselves as Mr. Sherlock Holmes and Dr. Watson.

Mr. Holmes delighted me by having an excellent command of Italian, and asked us endless questions about glassblowing. While we bantered, Signore and Signora Comazzolo, the Comazzoli were a rival glassblowing family who also sailed on the *Friesland,* sent a bottle of expensive champagne to the bridal couple.

My brother's eyes narrowed, then laying his hand upon my arm, he said in Italian, "Would you send them a gift as well, though it means parting with a small item from your dowry?"

"Papa will send me more." I smiled at him. "I shall write a note myself.

Orazio gestured to Anita and gave her hurried instructions. In moments she returned with a small box containing a matched pair of opalescent champagne flutes ornamented by delicate tracings of crystal. I quickly penned the note that you have in your possession.

A foolish note, from a foolish girl, but—how was I to know what was to follow? Before the ink was dry, my brother snatched the note and fairly sprinted across the dining room. Bowing at the captain's table, he presented the box of flutes to Primo Ministro Depretis and his bride. She laughed prettily, and kissed him on both cheeks to thank him.

I do not boast when I say the artistry of these flutes was without peer. My father was a brilliant glassblower; no other studio knew the secret of his opalescent glass, and of its shifting colours that bent light into translucent rainbows.

Nothing would do then but for the bridal couple to open the champagne and toast the assembly with these confections of glass. The champagne's bubbles danced as merrily as if they were celebrating with us.

Signore Depretis said, "Ladies and gentlemen, with this lovely Murano glass I propose a toast to my fellow countrymen and to my beautiful wife. Long life and health to us all."

They drank their champagne and kissed each other with love in their eyes while we looked on, applauding wildly. Signore Comazzolo, perhaps jealous that our flutes had upstaged his champagne, called out. "How is the champagne, prime minister?"

Signore Depretis bowed to him before burying his nose in his glass to inhale the bouquet of the champagne. "An elegant nose with nuances of honey, gingerbread, parsley, and slight hints of garlic." He sipped the champagne again, savoring it. "Minerality, pears, and a bright acidity. Delightful."

We applauded again, perhaps even more wildly than before. I sat, breathless with delight, darting glances at the bridal couple over each course. The first course was oysters and my brother ordered a bottle of champagne so that we could celebrate "in the same style as our Primo Ministro and Signora Depretis."

During the second course, Signora Depretis excused herself and I looked up as she stood. Her face was pale, and she held her hand to her abdomen as if her stomach hurt. Signore Depretis escorted her from the dining room, his own face tight.

"What is the matter, do you think?" I asked Orazio.

He shrugged. "Perhaps the oysters."

During the rest of my meal, I imagined stomach pains until, feeling nauseous, I excused myself during the fourth course.

The next day, neither Depretis came to dinner.

THE THIRD DAY, my lady's maid, Anita, announced that two men waited in my parlour

"Where is my brother?" I asked.

She shook her head, smiling apologetically, "I do not know, Signorina."

I hesitated to step into the parlour unchaperoned, so I motioned Anita to accompany me. You must imagine my relief to find my dinner companions, Dr. Watson and Mr. Holmes, awaiting me.

Here, I must pause to give you a word picture of Mr. Holmes. He towered above me, indeed, even among most men his lean figure loomed like a hawk. His dark shaggy brows pulled down in an expression of fixed concentration from the moment I stepped into the parlour and his eyes gleamed with a fire of excitement.

"How are you, Signorina Grisanti?" he asked in flawless Italian.

Dr. Watson hung back and watched our conversation with the eager interest of a newspaper reporter, in the scene but not part of it.

"I am well, thank you, Signore Holmes." I wondered for a moment if I might ask him for news of Signore and Signora Depretis.

"The Depretis are dead." Mr. Holmes said, bluntly.

I gasped, both at the news and at how easily he read my thoughts. "The oysters?"

"Their nuptial toast was poisoned." Mr. Holmes gave me a long searching look. "Do you know where your brother is?"

"No." My attention was barely upon him, so horrified was I by the thought of that happy couple murdered. Assassinated.

"Well then, we shall chat with you while we wait for him, if you do not mind?"

I shook my head.

He folded himself into one of the cabin's chairs. Dr. Watson sat in a chair to the side, holding so still that in my memory he is almost invisible. Mr. Holmes leaned forward to put his elbows on his knees. "Tell me about your approaching nuptials."

I blushed and stammered but proceeded to tell him about my recent betrothal to Mr. Boerwinkle and his business arrangements with Papa. About how I was moving to Africa but Papa could not accompany me because he was busy with the upcoming elections helping with the campaign for the Left. I told him about my dress; in other words, I acted every inch the vain, silly girl that I was.

In the midst of my recitation, Mr. Holmes hesitated and then asked. "May we look at your dowry?"

"Of course." I beckoned Anita and she helped the gentlemen unpack the crates of crystal. I hovered, anxious and useless, as they lay the sparkling glass and crystal about the cabin with infinite care. Mr. Holmes stopped to admire an opalescent vase, which my father had made to serve as a centerpiece for our table.

He glanced at the matched rows of clear stemware and back at the vase. "Did you have only the flutes and the vase in this style of glass?"

"Yes." I stepped forward to admire the piece. "No other glassmaker knows how to produce the opalescence and even my father rarely makes it."

"Has he produced opalescent stemware, such as the champagne flutes, before?"

I tilted my head and thought. "Not that I know of, but I am not often in the shop."

Mr. Holmes lifted the vase to his nose and, to my bewilderment, sniffed it. "Hmm. No help there. Help me put everything back, would you, Doctor Watson?"

I was thankful that Dr. Watson looked as baffled as I felt, but he said nothing and simply helped Mr. Holmes repack everything except the vase. Mr. Holmes turned to me and said, "I am sorry for the inconvenience, Signorina Grisanti. Do let me know when your brother returns." He bowed over my hand and he and Dr. Watson took their leave.

I stared at the door after them and then picked up the vase and sniffed it. I smelled nothing.

Some hours later Orazio sauntered into the room. "Well, little Rosa, how do you like your first ocean voyage?"

"I am frightened. Dottore Watson and Signore Holmes said—"

He crossed the room in one stride and grabbed my wrists. "What did you tell them?"

"Nothing!" I twisted in his painful grasp. "I had nothing to say. I do not understand what is happening. Orazio, they said the champagne was poisoned."

He dropped my wrists and stepped back, smiling. "Did they now?"

"How can you smile when the Depretis have been murdered?"

He laughed. "Why, my dear sister, do you think we are on this boat?"

The successive shocks I received that night had hardened my nerves, or perhaps I had already begun to accept the truth. With a click, the pieces came together in my head, along with something I had not told Mr. Holmes. I knew how my father made the glass. I could not let Orazio guess at my thoughts and I forced myself to answer him as the foolish girl he thought me to be, "I'm supposed to get married."

He turned, smiling, relief written on his face. "Yes, my beautiful Rosa. That is true." He kissed me on the forehead. "I am exhausted and it is long past time that you retired for the evening."

I twisted my fingers together, faint with the awareness of what my brother had done. Had his only target been Signore Depretis, perhaps I would not have felt as horrified, but the memory of Signora Depretis kissing my brother on his cheeks, thanking him for bringing her death, sickened me. The realization that I could, perhaps, have prevented it tore at my soul. "All the excitement has me overwrought. Do you think it would be all right if I walked on deck to cool my head?"

Orazio squeezed my hands. "I am too tired to escort you."

"Anita will serve." I smiled coquettishly, masking the anguish over what I must do. "Or did you want to dazzle the young ladies yourself?"

Laughing, my brother kissed my cheeks. "Go on, Rosa, but do not walk too late."

I called Anita and we went to the upper decks. You have asked about Mr. Holmes, so I will not trouble you with the thoughts of my long promenade. Know that the night air cooled my fevered temples and gave me the resolution I needed. Anita walked with me through the decks until we arrived at Mr. Holmes's stateroom. I blushed, thinking of how it looked for an unmarried young woman to seek a man at this hour and then in the next instant I shook my head at my foolishness. What mattered my reputation on such a night as this?

Still, the sounds of an unearthly violin haunting the night nearly undid me but I gathered my resolve and knocked on the door. It opened to a cloud of blue-smoke, swirling about like that in the chimney of my father's furnace.

"Miss Grisanti?" Dr. Watson seemed so shocked at my appearance that he forgot to speak Italian and his next sentence fell on uncomprehending ears.

Mr. Holmes tucked his violin under his arm and said in excellent Italian, "Be courteous, Doctor Watson. Signorina Grisanti doesn't have a word of English. Won't you come in?"

I shook my head. "I have come simply to tell you that my brother has returned. He knew the glass was poisoned, and it *was* the glass, Signore Holmes, not the champagne."

Mr. Holmes leaned forward on his toes. My breath caught at his eagerness, but I somehow found the air to continue speaking. "The opalescence is caused by arsenic powder blown with the glass."

"In the glass, not on the surface!" He spun happily and pointed his bow at Dr. Watson. "That explains why my tests failed to detect it."

I felt close to fainting. "But you surely suspected, else you would not have come to look at my dowry."

His bushy eyebrows arched and I blushed under his scrutiny. "Your observation is astute," he said. "Signore and Signora Depretis's symptoms began at dinner shortly after their champagne toast. The note of garlic, which Depretis noticed in the champagne, led me to suspect arsenic. The champagne combined with arsenic would have produced arsine gas, which was consistent with the Depretis's symptoms, but there was no arsenic residue in the bottle, so I turned my attention to the flutes. Your mention of your father's involvement with politics provided a motive, but I could not deduce the method."

Dr. Watson stepped forward, asking. "You must know what this means for your father and your brother?"

"I do." I looked down and wrapped my arms about myself, feeling the hard bones of my corset and wishing they could protect me. "My father has chafed against the government since Italy annexed Venezia in 1871 and my rapid engagement to Mister Boerwinkle must be a sham to give us reason to be here. I am certain that Orazio would have presented these flutes at another time, but took the opportunity to discredit the Comazzolo family. I know what is at stake and—" my voice faltered but I drew my head up higher. "I will not be a pawn. Their treachery is dishonorable."

From my readings of Dr. Watson's papers, I suspect this is one of the few times Mr. Holmes was ever taken aback—not at my answers, but that a young girl could have changed so, in the hours since he had interviewed me. "Signorina Grisanti, you are a noble woman. I thank you."

"I will walk on deck awhile longer." I turned to go, conscious that I had betrayed my brother and my father—but had they not betrayed my youthful ideals more? Had they not traded my hope for death? Over my shoulder, I asked, "Will you be able to complete your business before I return?"

"Yes." The smoke swirling in the room created the illusion of mist sweeping over his eyes.

I walked on deck for hours, before returning to my empty cabin. The too-tidy room betrayed signs of a struggle, which some kind soul had neatened. A folded piece of paper waited for me on the table by my lacework. I enclose it now, to complete your record of this remarkable man.

My dear Signorina Grisanti,

I applaud the fine intellect that brought you so swiftly to understand the intricacies of the situation. I regret that I have received a telegram indicating your betrothed, Mr. Boerwinkle, is also in league against the current Italian government. With this first step, it seems certain they intended to shift the ruling party of Italia to the Left. Your father and brother have been taken into custody for the assassination and will be duly tried."

With these facts, it seems apparent you cannot return home, nor can you continue your voyage. Dr. Watson and I are departing the ship tomorrow and wish to offer you safe conduct."

I await your reply,

Sherlock Holmes

I wept. I wept for the truth of his words, for the loss of my home, and for the loss of my innocence. I wept till Anita came to me and held me in her arms, singing to me and comforting me for the lost child that I was.

We departed the ship the next day. On Mr. Holmes's urging, I changed my name to Eve V--- and I never saw my family again. Until I received your letter, I had seen the name Grisanti only once, in a newspaper report of the arrest and execution of my brother, Orazio Rinaldo Paride Grisanti. I would not read a paper for years after—lest I see a notice of my father's trial, and know that I had killed him as well.

Now you have my account to add to the ones Dr. Watson left of Mr. Sherlock Holmes and so, I will close by signing my old name, for the whole affair belongs to a girl much different from me.

Sincerely yours,

Rosa Carlotta Silvana Grisanti

Salt of the Earth

MELIA ADJUSTED DORA'S SALT-SUIT, feeling as if it were futile because the two-year old would have the sweatband off her head the instant Melia's back was turned. She caught her daughter's hand reaching for the soft, green mesh. "No. You have to leave that on."

Dora twisted away from Melia and pulled the sweatband off. "No." She threw it on the ground and reached for the high thin turtleneck that caught the sweat from her face.

Melia's ex-husband, Theo, leaned against the doorway, waiting to take the children to his house. "Just let her leave it off."

"Daddy!" Dora toddled to her father with her arms raised.

Theo scooped Dora up, ignoring Nikolas, who seemed oblivious as he rocked in place, staring at a sunbeam on the wall.

Melia's smile felt tight. "We don't waste salt."

Out of the corner of her eye, Melia watched Theo while she checked Nikolas's salt-suit. Even though he was six, he sometimes took his cues from his little sister. His light mesh suit still covered him from chin to toe, ready to retain any salt if he sweated in the warm New Gaean sun.

Theo tickled Dora into a trill of laughter. "You've got enough salt to spare."

Melia picked the sweatband off the floor. "Because we don't waste it." She settled the band on Dora's head.

Theo bounced Dora on his hip. "You don't want to wear that do you, A-Dora-ble?"

"No!"

They had never agreed on disciplining the children. It was as if Theo took a perverse pleasure in watching Melia undo the damage he caused. Given a choice, she wouldn't let him take either child, but it was his week for custody. "We reclaim our salt, just like everybody else on New Gaea."

"But you've got plenty in the 'Salt Baron's' storehouse."

Melia held her breath, biting down on the words she wanted to shout. Dad's salt money had supported Theo for years. Her great-great grandfather's luck in discovering a salt deposit on this sodium-poor planet had started her family's fortune, but they retained that money because they weren't wasteful. She let her breath out slowly. The only way to end an argument with Theo was to relent, to let him think he had won. "Please. It's important to me."

He smiled at her over Dora's head. "I'll remember that."

Melia turned from his mocking face and knelt in front of Nikolas, inserting herself into her son's line of sight. "Nikolas? It's time to go with Daddy." She looked for a sign of life behind her son's eyes. "Nikolas?" The rocking slowed a little.

Theo said, "Just leave him. He won't even notice when I'm gone."

Melia bit the inside of her lip. Theo had never been able to deal with Nikolas's autism. "If you want me to contact my attorney, I'd be more than happy to make that a permanent arrangement."

"I bet you'd like that." He shifted Dora to his other hip. "Just get him ready."

It was probably just as well. She had spent most of the last year getting Nikolas adjusted to the new schedule; he knew that every seventh day he switched between his parent's houses. Breaking the routine now would upset him. "Nikolas. It's time to go."

His eyes flicked to the clock and then back to the dust motes in the sunbeam. He shook his head once, and then began rocking again.

Melia looked over her shoulder at the clock and sighed. They still had three minutes before the scheduled time.

"For Pete's sake." Theo strode over, still holding Dora. "Nick. Let's go. Now."

"Just give him a minute."

"I don't have time for this."

Melia pressed her fingers between her eyebrows, as if that would stop her impending headache. "Please."

"Then let's go." He reached down and took Nikolas's hand.

Nikolas screamed as if the world were ending. He pulled away from Theo, leaning back with his whole body. Theo let go of his hand and Nikolas dropped to the floor, still screaming.

"Hush, hush." Melia was by his side in an instant. She watched the tears flow down Nikolas's face, knowing that the salt in them was lost. Damn Theo. He knew better than to touch Nikolas without warning.

"Oh for the love of Pete." Theo pulled a salt candy from his pocket and held it out to his son. "Here. Want a Salti?"

The screams stopped as if a switch had been thrown. Nikolas took the Salti, and removed the paper wrapper with precise motions. He put the candy into his mouth and folded the wrapper in half, then half again and then dropped it on the floor.

"Me too, me too." Dora called.

"Sure, Adorable." Theo stripped the paper off one and popped it into his daughter's mouth.

Melia picked up the wrapper, and put it in her pocket to drop in the reclaimer later. She got off the floor, feeling every joint ache with sudden weariness. "Don't give them too many."

Theo snorted. "You control them your way, I'll control them mine."

Melia opened her mouth to retort, but Nikolas stood up, abruptly, and went to stand by the door. She looked at the clock. "Time to go."

"Well. I wouldn't want to break his schedule." Theo stopped by Nikolas and turned to smirk at her. "See you next week."

TRAFFIC IN DELFIE CITY was crawling. Scattered thunderstorms dumped heavy rain randomly, followed by brilliant blue sky. The few pedestrians had slickers pulled tightly over their salt-suits to keep the salt from washing down the gutters.

During the drive, Melia replayed every moment of the conversation with Theo a dozen times, filling in all of the I-should-have-saids with bitter rhetoric. By the time she arrived at the Seven Seas Salt Factory, she was ready to bite someone. The receptionist at the front desk only gave her a half smile as Melia stormed past.

Her dad looked up from the dehydrator lamp he was adjusting when she burst onto the factory floor. He raised his eyebrows. "How's Theo?"

"He grabbed Nikolas's hand!" Melia crossed her arms holding in the desire to hit something. "Lot's Wife! He knows Nikolas hates to be touched."

Sighing, her dad screwed the cover back over the lamp. "We can go back to court if you want to try for sole custody again."

"If I thought it would do any good, I would, but he'll just put on another show of how much he loves *his* children."

"It's good for them to spend time with their father."

"Is it?" She glared into the shallow pan of water under the heat lamp. A mosaic of crystalline salt shimmered down the length of the pan, except under this lamp.

Her dad cleared his throat. "Feel up to a blind tasting before you leave?"

"Sure."

Dad was trying to distract her, and Melia was more than willing to get Theo off her mind. Her dad led her up to the tasting room and set three tiny dishes of salt in front of her.

Moistening the end of a toothpick in neutral water, she dipped it in the first plate, catching some of the crystalline grains on the end. Melia touched her tongue to the salt and closed her eyes. "Sweet, with a little bit of a caramelized quality, nuances of . . . tobacco?" She opened her eyes. "Pure human reclaimed?"

Her dad was grinning at her, so she must be right. "Go on. Try the next."

She got a clean toothpick and sampled the next plate. "Oooo . . . this is that new salt lick in the South Valley, isn't it? I like the traces of magnesium you're leaving in. Very tangy."

He was bouncing on his toes with pride at her palette. "And our final sample?"

At the first taste, Melia frowned. A bitter aftertaste clung to her tongue. "Potassium chloride. Oh, come on, Dad. Don't tell me you're going to start blending too."

"You liked the magnesium."

"That's because it retains the terroir, the essential characteristics of the place the salt came from. This? This is just polluting it for profit."

He held up his hands in surrender. "Okay, okay. So go find a new source for us."

"I do my best."

THE PLANTS OF NEW GAEA rose to staggering heights around Melia. Unlike the lowlands surrounding Delfie City, this part of the continent had ferns that would have seemed at home in the Cretaceous period back on Earth. The giant fernwood trees dripped in the constant humidity and smelled of spicy loam. She had searched most of the last week, piloting the rover between the trunks, but she had yet to find a new source of sodium.

Her salt-suit stuck to her skin as the sweat just sat on her body. Some of the fernwoods from this region had shown faint traces of sodium blight. She had hoped it was a sign of a deposit, but it looked like nothing more than a groundwater leach from an earlier colonist's graveyard. After four hundred years, the bodies would not retain enough sodium to make exhuming them worth the furor from the historical societies.

If she could find even sodium carbonate, she could extract the sodium in the lab and then combine it with chlorine to make salt.

Her phone rang with a recording of Dora's laughter. For a moment it seemed as if her daughter had stepped into the fern forest with her. She toggled it on, glancing down to see her dad's icon. She grinned. He couldn't stand being back in the factory.

"What's up?"

"Melia—" His voice shook like an old, old man. "How long will it take you to come home?"

"What's wrong?" Her heart stopped. "Is it Mom?"

"Theo just called. Nikolas and Dora are in the hospital."

The soil sampler dropped from her hand. Melia pressed the earpiece deeper into her ear as she turned to the rover. "What—?" *What happened? What do you mean? What did he do to my children?* "What's wrong with them?"

"I don't know. They've been vomiting, so he's been keeping them in bed, but this morning he couldn't get Dora to wake up."

Melia felt cold. "And Nikolas?" The rover recognized her as she approached and opened its door.

Her dad was silent for a moment. "We aren't sure. He won't talk, and stares at the wall, but . . . that's normal."

"No, it's not." Melia bit the words off as she backed the rover out of the clearing. She left her tools lying under the dripping canopy of ferns. "He has a routine; if he doesn't follow it, something is very, very wrong." Theo should have called her the moment they got sick.

She could hear her mom's voice in the background asking Dad a question. Melia should have left the kids with Mom. She would have sent status reports every half hour.

Her dad said, "Your mother wants to know when you'll be home."

"Closest main road is L-90. I'm a good six hours away from that. Late tonight. Early tomorrow."

"Tell me the closest town, and I'll send an aero to get you."

Melia could not breathe for the bubble of fear pressed against her throat. They could not be dying. She swallowed. "Campsol. Have it meet me at Campsol."

THE AERO that met her was automated. In the silence of the cabin, Melia's fear screamed around her. Why hadn't Theo called her? He should have called her. Please let them be all right. Why hadn't Theo called her when they got sick?

The phone rang once during the flight, laughing with Dora's voice.

She shut her eyes, without answering it, and listened to Dora laugh. She could do nothing to get there faster, and as long as she didn't know better, her children were alive.

Let me be on time.

When the aero landed on the roof of the hospital, her dad was waiting for her by the lift, hunched over. He looked old.

Melia flung herself out of the aero and ran to him. He wrapped his arms around her, holding her close. She buried her face in his shoulder, as if he could still fix everything.

He stroked her hair. "I'm so sorry."

Melia trembled, rejecting the reasons for his apology. There were other things he could be sorry about. He was sorry she had to come back for a false alarm. He was sorry she was upset. He was—

"Dora didn't make it."

He was wrong.

She had heard Dora laughing on the aero. How could a little girl who laughed like that be gone? It wasn't possible.

He said other things to her as they rode the lift down. Melia nodded whenever he paused; his words were almost meaningless. "Salt overdose . . . Theo thinks the kids might have thought the supplements were Salties . . . Dora's so much smaller…"

A long tunnel seemed to be between her and the outside. Was that what it was like for Nikolas?

Nikolas.

"How is Nikolas?"

Her dad stopped with his mouth open. He had been speaking, but she had no memory of what he had just said. He cleared his throat. "The doctors say he'll be fine. They were worried about brain damage, but think he's out of the woods."

Brain damage. As if her sweet boy didn't have enough to cope with.

The lift opened on a lobby filled with people. It seemed as if her entire extended family was there. Theo's grandmother sat in a corner next to Melia's aunt. They were holding hands, with their heads bent together.

Theo's grandmother held a tearsheet under her eyes, delicately catching each tear that streamed down her face. Was she going to make a huge show of how much salt she collected for the memorial service?

The conversations stopped as people saw her. A cousin took a step forward, but Melia's dad shook his head, waving him off. She wanted to thank him for that, but her tongue had frozen in her mouth.

He led her down the hall to a private room. Thank God her children had a room of their own.

The room was dimly lit. Her mom turned as they entered. The lines in her face seemed deeper than Melia remembered. At her side, the hospital bed seemed to swallow Nikolas.

Melia's heart twisted. His face was puffy and slick with sweat. The sheets under him were damp. His eyes were closed. His right hand fluttered against the sheet in the pattern he made for distress.

What had happened to her son?

Theo stepped between her and Nikolas.

The tunnel protecting her shattered. All of the anger she had swallowed boiled up and over. Theo had killed her child.

She launched herself at Theo, swinging her fists wildly, beyond words. He had taken her children from her. Dora was dead. It was his fault. His fault. "What did you do to them?"

Theo tried to catch her hands. "I didn't do anything!"

Over his shoulder she saw Nikolas. His eyes were open and he was watching them.

Melia dropped her hands.

She pushed past Theo. Nikolas looked at the ceiling when she got to the side of his bed. He hummed through his nose and his right hand beat against the bed.

She wanted to hold his hand, to brush the hair back from his forehead, but she clutched the rail on the edge of the bed so hard that her fingers ached.

"Nikolas?"

He closed his eyes.

He must blame her for not protecting him.

"Melia," Theo said, "I don't know what happened."

She held on to the side of the bed. She had lost it once, but she would not do that again in front of her child. Her only child. She held her breath till the possibility of sobs passed. Breathing shallowly, fighting for her voice, Melia said, "I would like some time with my son."

She squeezed her eyes shut, like Nikolas, and listened to the murmurs around her. Theo's mother sounded as offended as always, but his father seemed to understand. She waited until the last footstep left the room and the door closed.

Then she opened her eyes. Nikolas's eyes were still closed, but his hand had stopped beating its rhythm on the sheets. She took that as a sign of forgiveness.

THE EXTRACTION ROOM at Seven Seas was intimate, dominated by the flushing machine. Beyond the window in the extraction room door, Melia could see the main factory floor. The workers appeared to go about their business, but she kept catching them as they looked away from her.

She turned back to Dora. The hospital had pumped Dora full of fluids as they tried to restore her electrolyte balance, leaving her skin swollen like a water balloon. Even so, her tiny body looked lost in the flushing machine.

Melia found herself wanting to look for the sweatband, which Dora must have thrown on the floor. She brushed Dora's hair back from her forehead.

Picking up the first of the tubes she needed to flush the salt from her daughter's body, she held the sharp metal tip of the siphon over the artery in Dora's thigh. She had reclaimed the salt from hundreds of bodies, but her mind balked at pushing the siphon into her daughter.

Melia turned slightly so she couldn't see Dora's face, so that the body in the flushing machine looked like any other. She placed the needle again. And stopped. This was still wrong. She had wanted to be the one to extract her daughter's salt; she wasn't here to extract a stranger's.

Looking at Dora's face, she pushed down on the siphon. It slipped into Dora's thigh with a slight pop. Melia watched Dora's face for any sign of a flinch, even though she knew there would be nothing.

She picked up the flush tube. Her hands were shaking, but she pushed it into a vein in Dora's other thigh. A little of the tension eased at the back of Melia's throat to have that accomplished.

Her little girl was on her way back to the great salt sea where life began.

Melia turned the machine on. As the pumps began to flush Dora's body, washing the salt from her veins and bones, Melia sank into a chair against the wall. She rocked slightly as she listened to the pump hum.

MELIA'S HOUSE was too quiet. She kept feeling like Dora was just in another room, napping. She had to turn off the newsfeeds because she kept seeing Dora's name. The media could not let go of the extravagance of her death by salt overdose.

The morning of Dora's memorial service, Melia poked her head into the kitchen to tell Nikolas's sitter that she was leaving. His plate was on the table, with the vegetables cut exactly the way he liked them, but the room was empty.

Wrong. Something was wrong when he broke his routine. She called him, knowing he wouldn't answer, but hoping.

"He's up here, ma'am."

Following the sitter's voice to the front door, Melia found Nikolas, rocking slightly. The sitter stood beside him, shifting uncomfortably, so she seemed to rock with Nikolas.

Melia took a breath to brace herself for the fireworks that would go off about the break in his routine. This was not the right time of day for her to be leaving the house. This was his lunch time.

The sitter said, "I'm sorry, ma'am, I know we should be having lunch, but he won't come."

Melia crouched next to Nikolas. "Do you need something?"

He turned his face slightly closer to her, but still didn't meet her gaze. His right hand fluttered in his distressed rhythm. He licked his lips before whispering, "Dora."

Melia waited a moment to see if he would say anything else, then asked, "Do you want to go to her memorial service with me?" She had not been sure that he understood or even noticed that Dora was gone.

Nikolas jerked his head once in a quick nod, still looking sideways at the wall.

"All right, then."

She led him down to the garage, keeping a careful distance from him. Nikolas was silent on the way to the memorial service, not even rocking as they drove through the streets. The road in front of the chapel was thronged with tourists and paparazzi anxious for news about the Salt Baron's granddaughter.

The security system recognized Melia's vehicle and passed her through the barricades. She went around the car to let Nikolas out. When she opened the door, he slipped out to stand quietly on the pavement next to her. In the throng of people, Nikolas huddled closer to her than he usually stood to anyone. Melia chewed on the inside of her lip. The crowd could overwhelm him. "Nikolas, you tell me when you need to leave, all right?"

He didn't answer, but she rarely got a response to that question. He might, just might, grunt before melting down.

As they went inside, the people surrounding them all had tearsheets under their eyes catching tears for Dora. Melia wondered which ones were really shedding tears, and which had bought pre-salined sheets to demonstrate their shared grief.

The reclaimer by the entrance to the chapel was already full of the tearsheets.

Every person she passed seemed to want to clutch her hand and express the same banal condolences as the person before. Melia kept nodding and thanking them for their thoughts, but her attention was on Nikolas. She diverted the people who wanted to pat him on the head, but could do little to protect him from the closeness of the crowd as they worked their way across the lobby. Her dad saw her and arrowed through the crowd to shepherd them across to the private family waiting room.

He stopped outside the door. "Theo is inside."

"I won't say anything."

He squeezed her arm once before opening the door.

At first, she only saw her mom and grandma. Her mother looked as if she had been crying off and on for days. Grandma was patting her hand.

Theo's father stood up when she came in. Mr. Lathouris's eyes were as red as her mom's. He had a wad of tearsheets in his hand, and she had no doubt that he had saturated them all himself; he had always been so good with the children.

Nikolas screamed.

He had his hands over his ears and was staring at Theo.

"What the—?" Theo flung his hands out in exasperation. "Why did you bring him?"

"He wanted to come."

"That's great, Melia. What did he do, tap it out in code?"

Melia ground her teeth together to keep the silence she had promised her dad. She knelt between Nikolas and Theo, hoping that cutting into his line of sight would help. "Nikolas? Do you want a Salti?"

He jerked his head in a *no* and continued to wail.

Nikolas had never been frightened of Theo before. What had changed?

"Shut him up! People can hear him."

"Theo!" Mr. Lathouris took his son by the arm and pulled him to the side, whispering angrily.

Theo jerked his arm free of his father's grasp. "For Pete's sake, I'm not staying here to listen to this." He stalked to the door and spun dramatically to glare at Melia. "Make sure he's better behaved than this when I come pick him up." Before she could respond, he slammed out the door.

Nikolas's screams cut off the moment the door closed.

Melia stared at him and then at the door. Mr. Lathouris apologized for Theo but Melia barely heard him. What was Nikolas trying to tell her?

"Melia, it's time to go in." Her dad crouched down next to them. "Is he going to be all right?"

"I'm not sure. I don't know what set that off." She turned to look up at Theo's parents. "Why don't you all go in, and I'll stay out with Nikolas."

Mr. Lathouris said, "I think Theo has probably gone home."

Melia tried to smile at him. He knew his son well. Even if Theo wanted to come into the funeral, he wouldn't be able to back down from his dramatic exit. "Nikolas? Do you want to go in to the memorial service?"

He nodded.

When she stood up, Nikolas followed her to the door like cattle to a salt lick.

She went through the motions of the service with the rest of the family and went to the rail when the priest held out the weeping cup. Melia took a sip of the saline, holding the sweetness of her daughter's salt in her mouth.

The flushing machine had recovered much more salt than she had expected from Dora. How had her little girl ingested that much salt?

Her breath caught in her throat as she sat down. Was that why Nikolas was afraid of Theo?

Nikolas rocked in his seat, while the congregation shuffled past to taste their grief at the weeping cup. Melia leaned as close to him as she dared. "Did Daddy give you the salt?"

Nikolas stopped rocking. His right hand fluttered. Then his head jerked once.

Yes.

What had happened? She could imagine Theo messing up Nikolas's schedule and then trying to soothe him with salt. A spoonful would do no harm. Two might have been all right. But Dora would have begged for anything that Nikolas got and she was too small to eat as much as Nikolas. It didn't matter if he hadn't planned on it.

Theo knew what the lethal dosage was. He knew what the symptoms were and he let her children lie in bed, dying, for a week. Because he couldn't admit he had made a mistake.

And he was coming for her son in three days.

MELIA DROPPED Nikolas off at the house with the sitter and went to the salt factory. She measured out some of the salt from Dora and entered the lab. Working methodically, she isolated the sodium from the salt's sodium chloride. With the pure silvery element, she went through each of the steps, combining it with hydrazine hydrate to make a small quantity of sodium azide.

She packed the crystals in an airtight jar so there was no chance of water touching them. Then Melia carefully wiped all equipment with oil to catch any stray granules. Melia did not want to chance killing any of Seven Seas' workers if the sodium azide got wet. Just a few grains would be enough to make a cloud of odorless poison gas. It would dissipate quickly, and leave only the signs of a sodium deficiency, which was common enough on New Gaea. The oil kept it inert, but water would kill.

When Melia was certain the room was clean, she picked up the jar and left the lab.

THEO OPENED the door himself, when Melia knocked. He looked astonished to see her. Before he could say anything, before she could have a second thought, Melia held the jar out to him. "I brought you some of Dora's salt."

He stared at the jar for a moment before taking it. "Thanks."

"Since you missed the weeping cup, I thought you might want to make one yourself . . . " Her voice trailed off. She had given him the salt, and now she just wanted to get away from him.

Theo leaned against the door. "Forgive and forget, huh?"

As if it were that simple. "No. But I found a way to move past it."

He seemed to recognize that she wouldn't bend, but he still said, "Do you want to come in and share it with me?"

Melia shook her head slowly. "I can't. Nikolas needs me."

She drove home to her son. After she sent the sitter away, Melia sat with Nikolas. He stood in the living room, with his head cocked to the side watching dust motes in the sun. She held her phone in her lap, as she watched them float with him, and waited for Dora's laughter.

American Changeling

HALF-CONSCIOUSLY, Kim put a hand up to cover her new nose ring. It pissed her parents off no end that she could tolerate touching cold iron and they couldn't.

Iron still made her break out sometimes, but didn't burn her. It had taken forever to find someone to make an iron nose ring, but the effort would be totally worth it.

"Kimberly Anne Smith," Mom's voice caught her in the foyer as surely as if she'd been called by her true name. "I've been worried sick. Do you know what time it is?"

"Eleven forty-nine." Kim dropped her hand and turned to face Mom, her Doc Martens making a satisfactory clomping on the hardwood floor. "I'm here. Home before midnight. No one with me." Sometimes she thought about bringing friends home to show them what her parents *really* looked like after their glamour dropped.

Everyone thought Mom was so pretty, so Betty Crocker, and Dad was all Jimmy Stewart. Whatever. Maybe if people saw that her parents were freaks like her they wouldn't look at her with such pity.

"I specifically asked you to come home straight after school, young lady. I tried calling your cell I don't know how many times. You have no idea how worried I've been."

"I was hanging out with Julia and Eve on Hawthorne."

Mom took a step closer, wearing pearls, even at home. "What's that in your nose?"

Kim blew her dyed-pink hair out of her face. "It's called a nose ring." Having people stare at her for the piercings and hair and leather was way better than having them stare at her because she looked prematurely old like a Progeria victim.

From the den, her father called, "Is she home?" A piece of ice clinked against glass. She so did not want to deal with Dad if he'd been drinking. He got maudlin about the old country and if she had to hear one more story about how life was so much better in Faerie, she'd scream.

"Yes!" Kim shouted. "I'm home and I'm going to bed so I don't have to look at myself."

She ran up the stairs two at a time, Utilikilt swinging against her legs. Mom hollered up the stairs at her, but Kim didn't care. She hopped over the salt line on her threshold, slammed the door to her room and threw herself on the bed without even bothering to turn on the lights. What was the point?

The mantel clock downstairs chimed midnight.

Kim's mom knocked on her door. "Kim? Come out honey, your father and I need to talk to you."

"Why don't you come in?"

"If you'll sweep the salt aside."

Rolling her eyes, Kim dragged herself off the bed and opened the door. With midnight, the glamour masking her mother's appearance had dropped. Mom had shrunk and twisted, aging one hundred years in the stroke of the clock. Gone was her carefully coiffed platinum hairdo in exchange for sparse, dry hair. The hall light gleamed off her scalp. Her nose nearly touched her chin, where a wart sported more hair than was on the rest of her head.

The thing that burned Kim like cold iron was that, aside from her dyed hair, she knew she looked just like her mother. All changelings were born looking old. That might be fine if you lived in Faerie with other people of your species, but here, Kim was just a freak. "What."

Mom smiled, showing her scraggly teeth, but her chin trembled and her eyes were moist. "We've had a message. From the old country. Come downstairs so we can talk about it."

Despite herself, Kim stepped over the salt line, into the hall. The only time she could remember Mom crying was when their dog had died. She'd held Buffy's head and wept like her heart had broken. Dad had said the golden retriever had been the first mortal thing Mom had ever loved. Death wasn't common in Faerie.

Seeing her on the verge of tears now freaked Kim out. She followed Mom downstairs without speaking.

Dad sat in his easy chair, holding a glass of whiskey loosely in his left hand. The reading lamp lit his arm and lap, but left his face in shadow. On the walnut end table beside him lay a piece of parchment at odds with the magazine-perfect living room.

The cream Berber carpet and the cranberry French toile curtains and the tan leather couch all seemed dirty and smudged by the introduction of this one thing from Faerie. It forced itself into her vision with a crisper focus than anything of mortal origins.

Her father set his drink down and leaned forward into the light. Like her mother, he looked scary ancient. His gray wool sweater hung from his shoulders as if he were a first grader playing dress up. His broad, pitted nose was bright red. Dad wiped his hand across his face and covered his eyes for a moment.

He inhaled deeply and dropped his hand. "This is difficult." Dad picked up the parchment. "We knew it was coming, but . . . Do you want to sit down?"

"No, sir." Kim bit the inside of her cheek, uncertain about what was going to come next.

Even though her parents had always told her they'd come to the mortal world for the sole purpose of conceiving her, even though her childhood had been filled with fairy tales in which she was the chosen one, even seeing their glamour, Kim had never fully believed them. Because the alternative, that she was the first fairy born into the mortal world since the gate closed, was crazy. She gestured at the parchment. "Can I see it?"

Dad handed it to her and took another sip of his whiskey while Mom dabbed at her eyes with a tissue.

To Mossblossom, daughter of Fernbrooke and Woodapple

Right trustie and welbeloved, wee greete you well.

Grat is the task which wee must aske of you, but wee know you will fulfill it in such a way as may not onely nourish and continue our love and good will towards you, but also encrease the same. Our good and most loving Subjects, your worthy parents, have striven to raise you out of the sight of certaine devilish and wicked minded enemies of ours. These enemies who style themselves the Unseelie Court, have most wickedly and unnaturally conspired to have stirred up (as much as in them lay) a generall rebellion throughout our whole Realme. It pleases us to . . .

"I don't get this." Kim lowered the parchment. "I mean, she can't even spell."

Her mother winced and took the parchment out of her hands. "The Faerie Queen is using the high court language from before the gate closed during Bloody Mary's reign. Your father and I had to learn modern English as a second language, of course we were both very young, but—"

"Fern, we need to get moving." Dad nodded at the brass and mahogany mantel clock. "She wanted us at Saint Andrew's after mass."

"What?" Kim scanned the parchment again, but the spelling was so poor she had trouble making any sense of it. The cathedral was five blocks from their house, and though she knew it held the key, they weren't supposed to open the gate until her sixteenth birthday which was still months away. "But it's after midnight."

Her mother sniffed. "If you'd come home when I asked this wouldn't be a problem."

"Yeah, well, you didn't tell me why."

"I didn't want to distract you at school. Your grades have already been slipping and—"

"Oh, as if that matters. What? My SAT scores will get me into the best schools in Faerie?"

"Stop it." Draining his whiskey, Dad stood and pulled the letter from her hands. "The Unseelie Court know about you."

That cut her retort off. The rebel faeries who formed the Unseelie Court had nearly torn the realm apart three hundred years ago when they closed the gate. The only people through since then had been a handful of changelings, like her parents, who'd worked a complicated magic to change places with mortals. "When you say *know* . . . ?"

He snapped the parchment at her. "There's a traitor in the Queen's Court. She knows not who it is, but it is clear that they have found out about you and the plans to reopen the gate. If we give them any time at all, they will send a changeling and kill you rather than let that happen."

"Woody, you're frightening her."

"What would you have? A child not frightened, but without the information to make good decisions? Fern. We can't go into the church with her. She has to know that the Unseelie have likely alerted the Catholics and that someone might be there."

"Let's just go and get it over with." Kim flipped the hood of her sweatshirt up to give herself at least a semblance of privacy. Underneath everything, a film of sweat coated her body. Her joints ached with anticipation. "Opening the gate is what I'm here for, isn't it?"

EVEN THOUGH it was only five blocks to the church, her parents drove in case they needed to make a quick getaway. They stopped the Prius across the street from Saint Andrew's and got out with her. Farther down the block, the laughter of late-night hipsters drifted down Alberta Street. Mom put her hands on Kim's shoulders and kissed her forehead. "I want you to know that your father and I are very proud of you, no matter what happens."

Kim's heartbeat rattled through every bone of her body. She knew their allergies meant that her parents couldn't go into the church with her, but for a second, she wished they could. "Any last words of advice?"

Her dad leaned in close enough that she could smell the whiskey on his breath. "Just be safe. You see a priest, you hightail it out of there. We'll figure out some other plan."

"Right . . . " It had only taken the Faerie Queen five hundred years to cook this one up. Before she could chicken out, Kim got out of the car and crossed the street to the cathedral. She'd read everything her parents could find about the place, knew all about its French Gothic style of architecture, had studied the floorplan until it was printed on the inside of her eyelids, but she had never set foot on the property before.

Once, when she was six, she'd run the five blocks from their house to the cathedral. Her mom caught her just before she got there. Kim had wanted to work the magic so she could get the key out of the altar. She'd thought her reward would be to get wings like the fairies on TV. Mom had set her straight, explaining that there might be alarms set if any of Faerie blood approached. Since then, she'd always walked down the other side of the street rather than chance it.

Not tonight though. Tonight, she walked straight up the marble steps and pulled out the keys Dad had gotten hold of years ago. It would suck if they'd changed the locks. She put the keys in the lock, braced for something to scream or an alarm to go off.

The door wasn't even locked. All Dad's effort to get the keys and she didn't even need them. Kim hauled open the heavy door and slipped into the nave. She had been to the church's website dozens of times, but the photo galleries had not conveyed the arcing height of the ceiling. Despite the simple beauty of the oak carvings, which adorned the plaster walls, her pulse ratcheted up to quad-espresso rate.

Her parents had refused to teach Kim any spells but those she needed to open the gate, because glamour would interfere with her ability to handle iron. Well, after tonight, baby, that restriction would be lifted and she'd be working it like any good Fae.

Kim sauntered down the middle of the church. Beyond a few guttering candles visible in the side chapel, the building was still and empty. At the altar, Kim put her hand on the cold marble.

All around her, wood splintered as the oak carvings forced their mouths open and shrieked.

Panicked, Kim lifted her hand off the altar, ready to run out of the church—but if she did, her chance to get the key out of the altar was blown. Whoever had set the alarm already knew she was here.

She pressed her hand back on the altar, crooked her little finger into a fishhook and shouted the words she'd learned as a nursery rhyme:

"Stone, stone, earth's bone,

Once hid, now shown!"

Under her hand, the center of the stone burst. Its halves tilted and thudded to the ground. In the exposed middle, was a small, ornate iron casket, no larger than a paper-back. Above her, the carvings still screamed bloody murder.

A door on the side of the church slammed open and a priest, tousled white hair sticking out like a halo, ran into the sanctuary.

Kim grabbed the casket, leaped over the broken altar, and sprinted down the aisle with the reliquary tucked under her arm like a football.

She hauled open the church door. Yelling incoherently about thieves and sacrilege, the priest chased her. Kim vaulted down the steps of the cathedral, momentum carrying her forward to her knees. The pavement tore through her striped stockings.

Before Kim could rise, the priest grabbed her. "What did you do?"

Kim tried to shrug free, but the priest had a grip like a bulldog. "Let me go!"

"Stealing is a sin and what you've done to the altar . . . " His other hand grabbed for the iron reliquary.

Kim kicked and twisted to keep him from taking the Key.

Out of nowhere, her father punched the priest in the nose. He staggered, blood streaming down his face.

Dad yelled, "Get in the car!"

Kim tore down the sidewalk. Hipsters and neighbors gawked in the street.

Dashing into the road, Kim headed for her parents' car. When she stepped off church property, the carvings went silent. The cessation of noise rang like tinnitus.

Their Prius pulled away from the curb. Her mom leaned out the window, "Hurry!"

Kim opened the back door and scrambled into the seat. Dad half fell in after her. As people ran for the car, Mom peeled out, which Kim didn't even think a hybrid could do.

Mom dodged the on-lookers and drove down Alberta to the I-5 on-ramp. Kim stared out the rear window at the crowd milling around.

"Do you have it?" her mother asked.

Kim turned around to face the front. "Yeah. It's what I was born to do."

"Don't get cocky." On the seat beside her, Dad had his head down, trying to catch his breath.

Mom peered at her in the rearview mirror. Seeing only her eyes, it was easy to forget how old she looked right now. "We still have to get to Stonehenge to open the gate."

Kim leaned forward. "I didn't bring my passport with me."

"No, no, dear. The replica at Maryhill. We should be able to use it as a mirror with the real one."

"Oh." That was a change from the original plan. Kim had been looking forward to going to England, but she'd practiced the ritual every summer at the replica.

"Dammit." Dad leaned against the seat, still gasping for breath. His face was swollen and puffy.

"Dad?"

He tried to smile, but his breath wheezed in his throat. "Allergies. It'll pass."

It sounded like he could barely breathe. His left hand had swollen to water balloon tightness. "Mom . . . ?"

Dad put his hand on her knee. "Don't, you'll worry her for no reason."

"What is it, dear?

Kim bit the inside of her cheek. "How much farther is it?"

"Mm . . . an hour and a half, I think. Why don't you take a nap, hm? It's been a long day for you and not over yet."

As if napping were an option. "You should have seen me. It was ten types of awesome. The rhyme worked like you said and boom!" Kim leaned forward and rested her chin on the seat. "How did they make the carvings scream? I mean, this church was built way after the wall went up, right?"

Kim's mother tapped the steering wheel. "Well . . . you know how, according to the rules, things may only cross between if there's a one-to-one exchange. The carvings could be like that. They could be something someone prepared in Faerie and exchanged for the ones here. Or, I suppose there could be an Unseelie agent sent as a changeling. Or it might have been Catholic magic of some sort. We've never been able to really study the spells built into their rituals."

Dad's breath was more labored now. His face lolled against the window.

"Dad?" Kim whispered.

In the passing light from a truck, his skin had a distinct blue pallor. Kim put her hand on his shoulder. "Dad?"

Nothing.

"Mom?" Kim kept her hand on his shoulder, as if she could hold him here. "Something's wrong with Dad."

Mom didn't answer, and Kim thought for a moment that her mother had not heard her, but the Prius slowed and pulled to the side of the interstate.

Still silent, her mother grabbed her purse and got out of the car. Kim could not swallow or breathe or do anything except keep her hand on her dad's shoulder.

Mom pulled the back door open, her face impassive. As the door opened, Dad started to slump out. Kim tightened her hand on his sweater and hauled him back.

"Fool. Foolish, foolish man." Mom's hand trembled as she touched his face. Her breath hitched visibly.

Kim stared at Dad, whose face had all the wrinkles puffed out of it. She did not recognize this moon-faced man in her arms. "What is it? Is he under a spell or what?"

"No. His allergies . . . "

A hard laugh escaped Kim. "Allergies? I've seen your allergies before; he's not sneezing, Mom. He can't even breathe."

Her mother didn't answer, but rummaged in her purse and pulled out a vial and a pack of handiwipes. "He hit the priest, didn't he?"

"Yeah, but . . . What? Holy blood is dangerous?" She hated the scorn coming out of her, but the anger was easier to manage than fear.

"Perhaps. Wipe the blood off his hand." Mom ripped the handiwipe open and handed it to Kim. "We don't fully understand the way Catholic magic and Faerie magic interact. I don't know what spells their priests are under, but I do know this is the sort of protective spell one would lay." She lifted Dad's head and held the vial to his lips.

Kim stared, fascinated, as Mom tried to get some of the amber liquid past his swollen lips. Her mother said, "Kim, I asked you to do something for me and I need you to do it."

"Sorry." When she touched her dad's hand, Kim flinched. The flesh was turgid with pressure but gave slightly under her hands, like a rotting pumpkin.

"How come this didn't happen to me? I mean, I cast a spell and, you know, desecrated an altar." She couldn't tell if the blood was the priest's or Dad's from where the skin had broken on his knuckles. "Oh, and stole."

"You didn't steal. Fae don't steal things. The Key belongs to us."

"Still." Kim passed the handiwipe between her father's fingers. "Why Dad and not me?"

Mom capped the bottle of whatever and tucked it into her purse. "We had you baptized."

"What?"

"Think of it as an inoculation against allergies." Mom slid out of the car. "Ride up front with me."

"What about Dad?"

Mom stood by the side of the car, her skirt flaring every time a car passed them. She bent down so Kim could see her face. "If we get the gate open fast enough, the Faerie Queen will heal him. He doesn't have much time. I need you to start thinking."

Kim swallowed. "Yes, ma'am." She got out on the passenger side and closed the door as gently as possible to keep from jarring Dad.

Sitting in the front seat, as her mother drove, Kim replayed the events in St. Andrew's. It wasn't her fault touching the altar set off an alarm. And Dad should have known better than to hit that priest. Right?

She prodded her scraped knee. He shouldn't have tried to protect her. And now he might die. The pain did nothing to distract her. Dad had to get better. Kim dug her nails into the raw flesh. The Faerie Queen had to fix him.

ON A BLUFF overlooking the Columbia Gorge, the monument loomed out of the dark, silhouetted by moonlight. The water below caught the moon and tossed its silver light like a ball on the surface of the river. This replica of Stonehenge had been built as a World War I memorial by a railroad industrialist. He'd built it out of "modern" materials, concrete and rebar, but made it look like Stonehenge had when new. The monoliths ringed the center, none fallen on their sides. Even so, it had an air of being decrepit beyond its years. The concrete had its share of graffiti and had crumbled in places.

They'd left Kim's father in the car because Kim's mother was worried the spell would think he was an offering in addition to the Key.

Kim huddled against the side of a monolith and tried to stay out of the wind. She ran her fingers across the sculpted surface of the reliquary as if she could read its history in braille. The heavy cross embossed on its surface bumped under her fingers in a constant reminder of what Kim had to undo.

In the middle of the monument, her mother did something on the flat altar. Kim wanted to yell at Mom to hurry and, at the same time, tell her to slow down. As soon as Mom finished prepping the altar, it would be Kim's turn. What if she didn't get it right? Dad could die. She clutched the reliquary.

Mom gestured frantically. "Kim, quickly now."

She joined her mother at the altar stone and put the reliquary in the middle of it. How many times had she pretended to do this while playing in her backyard? She felt split into two halves, the one which knew exactly what to do and the one which was sure she'd screw up. Inhaling to steady herself, Kim pressed her thumb against the catch holding the reliquary shut and let it prick her finger. She bit the inside of her lower lip as the blood welled up on her thumb.

This had been Bloody Mary's genius; the reliquary would only open to one of pure Faerie blood, but it was made of iron and would burn all Fae who touched it. She had collaborated with the Unseelie Court to close the gate in order to prevent the Faerie Queen from aiding her enemies during the Wyatt Uprising. The Unseelie stooped to her aid, ironically, to keep mortals and their taint out of Faerie. The reliquary was a perfect blend of Catholic and Faerie magics.

Carefully, Kim slid the catch aside, exhaling in a rush of relief as the lock opened. Her thumb stung where the iron had cut her, but no more than with a sunburn. Kim could feel her mother, more than see her, shifting with impatience at her side.

Digging her fingernails into the crack between the covers, Kim pried the reliquary open.

She had expected a flash of magic like in the *Lord of the Rings* movies, but nothing even glowed. Inside the reliquary lay a mat of dried leaves. Kim held her breath for fear of disturbing the thing lying on them.

Curled in a fetal ball lay the tiniest skeleton Kim had ever seen. All her life she had heard of the other breeds of Fae but had never seen anyone besides her parents. With birdlike bones, this skeleton could only belong to a pixie, the most delicate of the Fae.

Kim slid her hand under the leaves and they disintegrated. Shaking, she picked up the pixie's skull. Dried to almost nothing, it felt like papier-mâché and was no bigger than her thumb. She set the skeleton on the altar piece by careful piece. Most of the bones were still attached with mummified tendons and leathery skin. She did not like to think about how hard it would have been if she'd had to piece the hands together.

"Don't miss a single bone." Mom leaned forward, as if she could stick her own hand in the reliquary and fish around.

"I know." Kim scowled. They'd spent enough time telling her bedtime tales about little changelings who didn't follow the rules. Kim sifted the ashy remains of the leaves until she was confident she had all the bones.

Bowing her head over the remains, Kim held her hands over them in benediction and said the words she had been taught.

"Child of Faerie, blessed are ye in your innocence. Return ye to the state from which our ancestors preserved us, free from the knowledge of the tree of good and evil. I release ye from your bonds to the mortal world. Go in peace."

Light, golden as sunset bloomed out of the arch behind and cast her shadow across the altar. Now this was more like it. This was magic.

Her mother hissed, "Bow. The Faerie Queen is coming."

Kim's mother lowered herself into a deep curtsy. Kim tried to follow suit, but her legs gave way and dropped her on the ground. Her scraped knee sent a bright flash of pain up into her forebrain and snapped her attention to the fact that this was happening. She was about to meet the freakin' Faerie Queen.

For the first time in five hundred years, faeries set foot on mortal soil without needing to take a human in exchange. A retinue of faerie men and women stepped through the gate. Kim's heart sank as she looked from beautiful Fae to Fae. This was worse than high school; the disdain was apparent even on their inhumanly beautiful faces. Every one of them was beautiful and she . . . She looked like ass.

Her mother even looked panicky at the sight of these beautiful Fae.

The light frothed over, spreading to all the arches of the monument.

The interior lit up like Kim was standing center stage in the auditorium at school. Trumpets sounded. If silver were a sound, then it bugled out of the arch. The light boiled within the confines of the stone.

The radiance in all the other arches coalesced into a horde of other Fae. They sent up a cheer as they streamed through into the mortal world.

None of her parents' stories had prepared Kim for the full diversity of faeries. She'd known about the different species of Fae, but did not realize they came in every shade of skin known to humanity and then some. Brown, black, green, blue and red—some with tall pointing ears, others with noses drooping to their chins. The sight of a scattered few who were as ancient in appearance as she was, relieved her somewhat. She wouldn't stand out like a freak in Faerie after all.

Amidst the horde stampeding into the space, strode a woman who made every model ever born look dull and ordinary. She was made of beautiful.

Kim's mother turned from the group of Fae who had come through the first arch and gasped. "Majesty!"

This was the Faerie Queen? Then who were these other guys? The Queen saw them and her perfect face blanched in horror. Kim's mind caught up. The Unseelie court had found them.

A tall elven man with fox-red hair, drew his sword and stepped between the Queen and the Unseelie. "Majesty, we are ambushed."

Only then did Kim realize that each of the first group of Fae carried a weapon and wore a red band on their sleeves. Before she had time to register more than that, the Unseelie court fell upon the Queen and her retinue. Metal clashed against metal and sparks flew.

Her mother shrieked and scrambled toward the Queen. Kim turned to follow her, but an Unseelie man with leaf-green hair stopped her with a sword to her chest.

Kim bent back across the altar to get away. One of her hands landed on the reliquary. Desperate for a weapon, Kim swung it up and swiped at the him. The corner nicked his cheek.

His skin sizzled and peeled as if she had hit him with a flaming poker. Holy shit. Iron raised welts on her parents' skin, but nothing like this. Kim didn't waste any time wondering *why*, she just started laying into the Unseelie faeries attacking her.

Kim wielded the reliquary as if it were a book in a room full of jocks. At first the Unseelie retreated from the cold iron but the reliquary gave her a shorter reach than their swords and daggers.

Another beautiful, lean Unseelie man, with eyes like ice nearly took her arm off but a gnome stopped his blow with a shovel. Kim retreated, dodging blows that pushed her farther from the Faerie Queen. The Unseelie man drove the point of his sword over the gnome's shovel and into his chest. Wrenching it free, he stepped toward Kim.

Kim staggered and fetched up against the hard surface of one of the monoliths. He had the sword leveled at her before she had time to draw breath. As he thrust it at her, she raised the reliquary to block. The shock of impact sent tremors through the bones of her hands.

She tried to swipe at him, but he twisted the sword under the reliquary and flicked it out of Kim's hands.

A squeak of horror escaped her throat as the piece of iron flew out of her grasp.

The Unseelie smiled the coldest smile Kim had ever seen. "What now, changeling child?"

He pressed the sword against her chest lightly but with enough force to pin her against the concrete block. "By the powers, you reek like a mortal. If the Unseelie Court didn't have use for you, I'd gut you like the spell-less outcast you are."

Kim tried to twist away from the sword but he pressed it forward, cutting through her shirt and into her breastbone. She grunted at the sudden pain.

And then she got pissed. "I'm not spell-less, you bastard."

Kim pressed her hand flat against the concrete behind her. "Stone, stone, earth's bone; Once hid, now shown!"

The concrete exploded. Chunks spun through the air, slamming into the mob. The blast knocked Kim flat, forcing the air from her lungs. She rolled frantically to get away from the falling concrete and rebar.

Her chest burned, screaming for air but she could not draw a breath. Kim pawed at her throat as if she could open it by hand.

Howling, the Unseelie man pushed a block off his chest. A host of other Unseelie, bloodied and furious turned toward where Kim lay. She dragged air in with a terrified wheeze. A part of her brain wondered if this was what her dad felt like.

Her anger rekindled. Her dad was dying because of these traitors.

Kim grabbed the first thing she laid her hand on—a twisted length of rebar torn from the stone. Her hand stung from its rough surface, but Kim didn't care. She rose to her feet and ran at the Unseelie as he was dragging his sword from under another chunk of cement.

Double-handed, Kim brought the rebar down on his wrist. The rod passed through his arm in a crackle of flesh. He screamed and fell, leaving his hand still clutching the hilt of his sword.

No blood dripped from the wound. The blackened skin had cauterized as the rebar had passed through. Kim stared at the rod in disbelief. Of course . . . it was iron. She had, like, a freakin' light-saber against these guys. And since she'd grown up here, it only stung her a little.

Kim dove forward, hacking with the rebar. Even a glancing nick with the iron made their skin bubble and peel. The Unseelie retreated before her.

This was the best weapon, ever.

Gnomes, changelings, and other of the Queen's Fae came to her side and formed a phalanx, cutting through the host of Unseelie. Kim fought without grace, but the terror that her weapon brought turned the tide quickly to the Queen's favor.

Time lost its meaning until Kim found herself standing, rebar in hand, next to her mother.

And the Faerie Queen.

"Bravely done, good Mossblossom."

For a moment, Kim wondered who she was talking to, and then remembered her Faerie name. "I—thank you, your Majesty." There was probably something else she should say, but Dad didn't have time for formalities. She pushed away the possibility that he was already dead. "So, could you—"

The fox-haired Fae stepped in front of her. "I am Oreyn, the Queen's champion and I, too, thank you for your service, but I must ask you to release your weapon near the Queen."

"Oh." Kim looked at the length of iron stupidly and let it drop to the ground. "Okay. But listen, my dad needs help."

Oreyn shied as the rebar rolled toward his toe. "Of course." He stepped past it and put his hand on Kim's shoulder.

She had never been this close to anyone like him. He smelled of honeysuckle and salt. His cheeks bore no trace of fuzz and had the poreless perfection of porcelain. He lifted his left hand and put a knife to her throat.

"Oreyn! What means this?" The Faerie Queen's shout came at the same moment as a wordless cry from Kim's mother.

Oreyn spoke three quick words in some language Kim did not recognize.

The world inverted, spun and sharpened into a painful clarity. The replica of Stonehenge had vanished, replaced by crisp trees and a stark blue sky.

The iron ring in Kim's nose burned. As it seared her flesh, she screamed.

Kim didn't care about the knife at her throat. The thing burning her had to stop. She grabbed it. Her fingers flared with pain.

She jerked them away.

Oreyn laughed and let his knife fall. "The touch of iron is worse here, is it not?"

Sick, twisted traitor. *He* was the one who had told the Unseelie Court about her. *He* was why her dad was dying.

Tears filling her eyes, Kim let the sleeve of her shirt fall over her fingers. With that slight protection, she yanked the ring out of her nose. The skin tore, but the pain was nothing to what she had felt.

Kim drove the point of the tiny piece of iron into Oreyn's throat. Flame curdled the skin around it.

He shrieked.

As he tried snatching it, the fire leaped from his throat to his hands and then to his sleeves. His screams turned to hoarse wheezes. Arms outstretched, he staggered toward Kim.

She dodged, then turned and fled deeper into Faerie's perfect woods. Careening through the trees, Kim ran until her legs collapsed under her. With her arms wrapped around her head, Kim lay on the ground and sobbed.

SHE WOKE in an unfamiliar bed. Every thread in the silk sheets chafed, as if her skin were too sensitive from a fever. Light filtered through carved filigree windows and caressed rich tapestries. Kim squinted to hold out as much of the too-crisp vision as possible. Her head ached from all the intricate detail.

"Kim, honey?" Her mother's voice drew her gaze to the side.

She had thought Mom seemed old before, but worry had added new lines to her forehead. Or maybe she could see more in Faerie. "Dad?" Her voice cracked on that one syllable.

"Right here." From her other side, Dad took her hand and held it firmly. "How do you feel, little girl?"

She whispered, "I want to go home."

Her dad froze. "You are home, sweetie"

"Hush, Woody." Mom patted her hand. "Let's go."

They helped her stand. Then Kim's mother spoke in the same language Oreyn had used. The world twisted, spun and Kim staggered into her living room.

The soft toile fabric and Berber carpet looked as they had left it. The clock on the mantle said it was just after seven. Outside the window, dawn was beginning to light in their yard.

Her mother said, "Why don't you run on up to bed?"

Without words to even think about everything that had happened, Kim nodded. Later there would be time to talk, but she felt too battered for thought. Kim hugged her parents for a long time and dragged herself up the stairs to her room.

She hopped over the line of salt, then turned. Squatting, she brushed the barrier aside.

Kim turned out the lights and crawled into bed.

She left the door open.

The White Phoenix Feather: A Tale of Cuisine and Ninjas

VIOLA LEANED ACROSS the white tablecloth of Luigi's Interstellar Cafe and Pub. "When I said the ninjas were no match for us, I meant it. Joe will have the White Phoenix Feather by dessert." She checked the edge of her fish knife. She hated clients like this. "Quit gaping and finish your soup."

Anthony Cardno stirred his habanero spinach bisque, mixing the crème fraîche into the soup in marbled swirls. "I don't doubt your skills."

A dark shape scuttled past the wall of tinted glass, silhouetted by the lights illuminating the ships waiting at New Rushmore's spaceport. Crap. She hadn't expected any ninjas until later. "May I have your soup?"

"My soup?"

Without explaining, she hailed a passing waiter. "Two brandies. Neat."

The native species of New Rushmore were more akin to spiders than humans and had acquired their nickname from their middle arms, which ended in a long curved spine as though they were holding a katana.

They were a real pain in the ass.

A ninja dropped from the ceiling, bladed arms extended. Viola hurled Cardno's habanero spinach bisque, splashing it in the ninja's face. He screamed as the fiery soup spattered his eyes. Viola punctured his airway with her fish knife and stepped back as he sagged to the carpet.

The diner closest to them slid her chair back to avoid the pool of ichor, but otherwise ignored them. Everyone else continued with their meals and studiously ignored the fight, only a raised eyebrow or curled lip expressing their opinion.

A new ninja leaped down, blades at ready. Viola groaned and looked for the waiter. Ninjas always traveled in pairs.

With the prompt service she'd come to expect at Luigi's, the waiter appeared with the brandy she'd ordered. She tossed it and the table's candle at the new ninja.

He flambéed.

This caused some consternation among the other diners as the ninja staggered away from her table and into their zones. Yanking the tablecloth off the table, without disturbing the stemware, Viola tossed it over the flaming ninja and knocked him to the ground. She rolled him over and trussed the creature securely as smoke trickled out from the edges of the tablecloth. It would be unfortunate if the smell lingered.

Straightening, she tossed her hair back and raised a single finger to summon her waiter. He appeared like a wraith at her side. "Madam?"

Viola held up her fish knife. "I'm so sorry, but I'm afraid I need a new knife."

With a bow, he took the ichor glazed blade in an immaculate white napkin and almost smiled. "Of course."

She seated herself at the table where Cardno gaped blatantly at her. Around them, the busboys of Luigi's moved in a silent frenzy of activity, trundling off the ninja corpses and resetting their table with a new cloth in the quiet efficiency that made this her favorite spot to escort their gastronomy clients. As the snowy white cloth draped across her legs, her waiter laid a new fish knife at her place.

"Thank you. I think we're ready for the salad course." Viola paused to check with Cardno. "Unless you wanted some more soup?"

He sputtered something in the negative and shook his head. Amateur. A true gastronome would have wanted to sample the chef's offering despite the interruption in service. With a bow, the waiter vanished into the hush of the dining room. Viola took a sip of her 2148 Frameworks Viognier, savoring the touches of slate and pear on her palate. She swallowed, enjoying the lingering anise on the finish, and eyed Cardno who picked up his own glass—Cabernet, 2152 Coastal Highlands—and buried his nose in the glass rather than meet her gaze.

"There is something you have not told me."

He lowered his glass and tried a smile. In another place, she might have found the thirty-year-old actor charming, with his dimpled cheeks and tousled brown hair cut in a retro-Regency style, but his pretensions at being a gastronome disgusted her. Gastronomy might be fashionable, but it was clear that, no matter how successful the star might be, he did not understand food. "I should have thanked you, straightaway. That was nicely done."

Viola set her glass carefully on the table and swirled the straw pale liquid around the glass. "I meant, that you have an opportunity to explain why ninjas are attacking you now."

"Because of the White Phoenix Feather—"

"Spare me. It's not here yet and they stand to gain nothing by attacking you rather than trying to stop Joe." She leaned back in her chair as their waiter appeared with the salad course. "So, what I want to know is why?"

Viola picked up her salad fork and lifted a slice of the roasted persimmon, without releasing Cardno from her gaze. Licking his lips, he moved the escarole and sea beans around on his plate, destroying the chef's composition. She waited, savoring the fruit as she did. In her opinion, the balsamic vinegar played nicely with the caramelized natural sugars on the fruit and the goat cheese gave a tart complement to the subtle flavors, but she expected nothing less at Luigi's. At last, after her second bite, Cardno put down his fork without tasting the salad. "All right. I have been holding out on you."

Viola raised an eyebrow, waiting for him to tell her something that she did not know.

"I might have . . . It is possible that I mentioned something about the

White Phoenix Feather to my girlfriend." He wet his lips. "She's very discreet."

Picking up her salad knife, Viola tilted the blade to flash light in Cardno's eyes as she cut a slice off the persimmon. The knife was too dull to do any serious damage, without being inventive, but she was still satisfied when he flinched. "I see. So . . . at this point, the ninjas clearly know that the White Phoenix Feather is being sought, which compromises Joe's mission. Was our contract not perfectly clear?"

"I'm sorry. I should have told you."

"You apologize for the wrong thing." Viola took a bite of her persimmon. "You should not have told your girlfriend. Then you would have had nothing to tell me."

He shriveled. "But she wouldn't have told anyone."

"Of course not." Viola said, though she believed no such thing. She signaled the waiter. "But you must understand that ninjas are everywhere on this planet. Simply because you do not see one is no indication that it is not present."

He scoffed openly. "Even if they overheard, they're harmless."

Viola raised her eyebrow and indicated the scorched spot on the floor. To be sure, ninjas normally ignored humans and were even sometimes useful, but the White Phoenix Feather changed everything. She turned to the waiter. "Might I have some fresh ground pepper?"

As if he had anticipated her request, which at Luigi's was a certainty, the waiter offered her tall wooden grinder, a new immaculate napkin over his arm. "Certainly, madam."

"Thank you." She nodded, not taking her gaze away from Cardno, who flushed red. "Ninjas are everywhere." Viola took the pepper-grinder from the waiter and stood on her chair. Sweeping the wooden grinder over her head, she twisted the top, flinging ground pepper in an arc. A muffled sneeze came from behind the ceiling tile. She leaped toward the sound, thrusting the grinder upward like a club and dented the tiles. From behind the tile, came a squawk and a moment later, a ninja dropped into the dining room.

Sighing, Viola clubbed it with the grinder and the ninja toppled over. She handed the grinder back to the waiter and seated herself again. "As I said, ninjas are everywhere but do not usually pay attention to us unless something prompts their attention, such as an attempt upon the White Phoenix Feather."

"But you talk about it freely here—" Cardno sputtered.

"Because the meal has begun. As our contract states, bragging rights prior to the meal add an additional hazard fee, however, we can discuss that later." She swept her napkin back into her lap. "Meanwhile, it is clear that we must anticipate a visit from a samurai."

His face paled. The ninjas were the male of the species. The much larger and more colorful females had acquired the nickname of samurai. They were less common and significantly smarter than the males of their species. Each samurai kept a stable of males, collecting them from other females and trading them with their favorites in the way a human might show dogs. Simple-minded and loyal, the ninjas could be set to tasks for which they would be rewarded with an opportunity to breed with the samurai. Viola prided herself on helping with their natural selection by removing so many ninjas from the breeding pool.

Wiping his face with his napkin, Cardno asked, "Why do you think a samurai will come?"

"Because ninjas always travel in pairs. There was only one in the ceiling." She laid her fork and knife at precise angles across her salad plate, signaling that her waiter could take them. She really must leave him a good tip. His service was excellent thus far and she had told the maitre d' that this dinner would only cause a minimal intrusion. "How is your salad?"

Cardno shook his head and pushed the plate away from him, without trying it at all. Viola clenched her jaw in an effort to control her urge to reprimand him. She was perfectly willing to accept their money with certain *very* strict contractual guidelines and speaking of the White Phoenix Feather was strictly forbidden before dining for very good reasons.

As the ninjas were not ninjas, the White Phoenix Feather was not truly a feather. It was a frond-like growth which samurai only sprouted during mating season. The pheromones from it gave ninjas the urge to prove themselves in battle in order to earn the right to mate with the samurai. In humans . . . in humans eating it produced a euphoria and a temporary reversal of aging. Much like fugu fish on Earth, the danger involved in eating White Phoenix Feather was part of the allure, albeit from ninjas rather than toxins. There were levels of danger and one's enjoyment and subsequent bragging rights were dependent on those. Viola's company specialized in Extreme Dining. Her job was to sit at a table and look decorative, while protecting the clients. In order to maintain the illusion of risk, she brought no weapons to the table.

But the presence of a samurai would change everything. Their arrangement with the samurai from whom Joe harvested the White Phoenix Feather was profitable and normally left Viola with only ninjas to deal with during dining. While the smartest ninjas were no more intelligent as a well-trained dog, the samurai were fully sentient. The samurai they dealt with used these dinner engagements as a way to clear her stables of lesser ninjas.

But Cardno's indiscretion meant that *another* samurai would attempt to get the Feather. With it, she would potentially be able to steal the entire stable of ninjas that would be drawn to it. While ninjas were plentiful, a samurai without a stable had no resources. Viola could not jeopardize their business partner in this way.

She considered her options as the table was cleared for the entree. She had ordered salmon roasted on a Lekejera-wood plank with sea urchin ceviche, wasabi risotto, and sauteed radishes. If a samurai were about to join them, she needed to add another item to her order. Raising her finger, she hailed a waiter.

"May I add the fondue to my order?"

The waiter bowed, "Of course, madam. Would you like that with your entree or before?"

"Before, but don't hold the entrees. Bring them out when they are ready. Also a baguette, if you don't mind. Unsliced."

"Seeded or plain?"

She settled back in her chair and considered. "Seeded, please." It should provide a better grip.

Cardno continued to gawk at her. Viola favored him with a smile and sipped her wine. "Since you are already paying for it, you might as well let your fans know that you are Dining on White Phoenix Feather this evening."

"Now, wait a minute. I didn't say anything about being willing to pay extra. I told one person—maybe."

Viola set her glass down. "Oh? Then shall I let you handle the samurai by yourself?"

"If it comes." He scowled like a petulant child. "How do I know that you don't set all this up to scam people?"

Always . . . always when they made a mistake, the wealthy tried to blame it on someone else. "I assume you checked our references before hiring us."

"Yeah. They said you have an arrangement with a samurai. That's how come you can always get the White Phoenix Feather."

Smoothing the tablecloth, Viola took a moment to calm herself before she answered him. "This is true. However, this will not be that samurai. This will be one of her rivals and she will not be friendly" A flash of yellow and red at the door caught Viola's attention. "Ah. There she is."

"She?" Cardno turned his seat to see what had attracted Viola.

"The samurai. They are always female." Without standing, Viola turned toward the kitchen entrance, looking for the waiter. She might have to stall until her order arrived. The samurai stalked through the dining room, too large to fit through the ceiling tiles the way a ninja would. Perhaps Viola should not have sent her salad away, so she had an extra knife. "Are you still going to contest the charges?"

"This is extortion."

"We did sign a contract, which listed these charges, however, I am perfectly happy to restrict myself to the activities we originally discussed. I will note, however, that the samurai will attempt to kill

269

you in order to claim the right to the White Phoenix Feather." She slid her fish knife across the table. "You may want this."

The samurai choose that moment to charge, unlimbering her bladed arms as she did. She let out a high-pitched shriek as she bounded through the dinner tables. Cardno flinched, almost knocking his aluminum chair over. From the acrid stench that rose, he had just wet himself. Viola took that as permission to engage the samurai. Snatching the fish knife off the table, she stood. She lifted her chair and thrust the back between the samurai and Cardno. The blade came down on the chair, skidding along the metal. Viola thrust the fish knife into the samurai's wrist, twisting as she did.

The creature yanked back, howling with rage. The knife wrenched out of Viola's grasp, but the samurai's wrist hung limp. Viola kept her grip on the chair and snatched up a fork. This would be an excellent time for the waiter to arrive with her fondue. Luigi's normally had such prompt service. Without the fondue, she was forced to make do with the fork.

Viola spun swiftly and attempted to bury the fork in the samurai's neck, while she was distracted by the knife in her wrist. The creature used her other blade and blocked the fork with ease. Viola slid under her guard and aimed a kick at the samurai's leg. The samurai swept the blade down and Viola barely got the chair between her and the samurai. She dodged to the side in time, losing the fork.

Cardno had ordered squid-ink pasta with fresh peas so he did not have anything sharper than a butter knife. Snatching it, Viola faced the samurai again. With the chair held as a shield, she flipped the knife, aiming for the samurai's eyes.

As the blade left her open hand, the waiter appeared and placed the fondue and baguette on the table. Without waiting to see if she had hit the samurai, Viola snatched the baguette and thrust it into the fondue's spirit lamp, lighting it. She lunged at the samurai with the flaming loaf. Briefly distracted, the samurai blocked with her sword, slicing through the bread. In that moment of distraction, Viola dropped the chair and flung the fondue on the samurai. Molten cheese coated the creature's face and upper torso in a blinding mass. Viola snatched one of the long fondue forks from the table as she ducked behind the samurai. Pinning the creature's sword arm, Viola shoved the fondue fork against the samurai's chin.

In their hissing language, she said, "Do you yield?"

The creature stood for a moment, utterly still, and then spat an assent.

Viola stepped back. She disliked killing samurai but had found it necessary twice, both times with young ones who would not yield. The samurai stalked out of the dining room, cradling her injured wrist.

Shaking more than she would like to admit, Viola turned to the waiter. "Thank you. The fondue was exactly as I had wished."

He bowed. "I'll clear your settings then for the entree, if you are ready."

"That would be lovely." She glanced to Cardno who sat, shell-shocked in his seat. Standing as she was, the stain on his trousers was obvious. "Perhaps you might show my companion where the restrooms are?"

Only raising an eyebrow, the waiter nodded. "Of course."

As he led Cardno to the facilities, Viola righted her chair and sat. By the time the staff and busboys had repaired the damage and removed the samurai, the waiter returned with Cardno, who had been given a clean set of trousers. Thank heavens. The stench would have seriously interfered with the aromatics of her salmon.

She smiled as he sat, but chose not to say anything. He picked up his wine glass and drank the entire contents without pausing to savor the bouquet. He asked for a bottle of Cabernet, without specifying which one, without noting that a Cab of any providence would overwhelm his entree. When the wine arrived, Cardno downed his first glass as though it were a mass-produced soda. They proceeded through the entree with Cardno chattering in increasingly animated tones to which Viola said nothing.

The salmon was exquisitely succulent and had picked up deep resinous notes from the plank on which it had been fired. Pity she hadn't had it when the samurai had been here. The wood made an effective shield. To her relief, no more ninjas appeared. The rest would arrive with dessert.

Cardno continued to ramble about the film he was involved in and the starlet who shared his scenes as he finished the bottle of house wine by himself. As the waitstaff cleared the entrees, the diners at the other tables all turned, subtly, to watch them. No doubt they understood what was coming next. Viola settled back in her chair with the cognac she had ordered and swirled the glass, enjoying the caramel and apple notes. Cardno fidgeted with his napkin.

"Well?" He tossed the napkin down. "Where is it?"

"Joe will be here."

As she lifted her glass to hide her scowl, the waiter stepped out of the kitchen. She stiffened at the sight of what he carried. Joe normally presented the White Phoenix Feather himself, resplendent in a white silk dinner jacket. If he sent the waiter in, instead, something had gone horribly wrong.

The waiter carried a plate sealed with a clear glass dome. Inside was a bowl of sweet cream gelato, adorned with the White Phoenix Feather. The frond trembled with every step. Pure white at the tip, it shaded to a deep vermillion red at the base, tinged with yellows as though lit from within.

The waiter bowed as he presented the dish, setting it in front of Cardno with a flourish.

He leaned over and whispered in Viola's ear. "Pardon, Madam. Your partner wished me to let you know that he was in good health but not presentable for dinner." It was not the first time, by far, that Joe had been injured while delivering the White Phoenix Feather, but this contract had been for a minimal risk dinner. That's why the dessert was in the hermetically sealed tray until the last possible moment. In the normal course of events, if Joe kept it sealed until serving, the diner could usually finish it before ninjas arrived. Of course, that reduced the risk, so most true gastronomes had it served without the covering.

Cardno was no gastronome. He did not even wait for the waiter to step fully back, before yanking the cover off the White Phoenix Feather. Aromas of coriander, honey, and autumn leaves rolled out, underlaid by the subtle musky fragrance of the samurai's signature. Viola inhaled slowly, savoring the fragrance.

"Huh." Cardno stared at it. "How am I supposed to eat this?"

"With the chopsticks." Viola nodded to the ebony ones under the dome, carefully chosen to serve as a contrast to the White Phoenix Feather.

Cardno picked them up and struggled with his grip. Viola had to bite the inside of her cheek to keep from stabbing him with her fork. He didn't even know how to hold a pair of chopsticks?

"Is it okay if I just pick it up with my fingers?" His cheeks were quite flushed, more from the wine, than from embarrassment, she suspected.

"You may do whatever you see fit, of course."

He reached for the White Phoenix feather and stopped. "Oh, I should totally get a pic of this." Patting his pockets he fished out his handy and started to pass it to Viola. "No, wait. That's a terrible idea."

Then—in Luigi's Interstellar Café and Pub—he addressed the table next to them. "Would you mind taking a pic of us together?" Bad enough that he was ignoring the food, but he couldn't even ask a waiter? He had to disturb someone who was *enjoying their meal*? Viola shook with rage. Had he no respect for the sanctity of Dining?

No. No of course, he didn't. "If you don't eat that soon, more ninjas will arrive."

He flashed her a sloppy smile. "You just defeated a samurai with a breadstick. I'm not worried about a couple of ninjas."

Thankfully, the waiter intercepted the camera and took their photo so she did not have to be part of any further intrusions into the other diners' meals. When she saw Joe again, she was going to insist that they institute a better screening process. If she had to—

Two ninjas dropped from the ceiling. She grabbed the chopsticks and slammed them into each ninja's throat as they straightened from their landing. "Will you eat?"

Cardno settled back in his chair and took her picture. "Hey . . . I'm paying you to protect me while I dine. I want to get all the buzz I can out of this."

Viola was going to kill him.

He nodded over her shoulder. "Behind you."

Viola spun, raising her arm to sling the cognac at the ninja—but it wasn't a ninja. It was her waiter. She managed to not hit him in the face and instead splashed the drink over the front of his spotless white shirt. Flushing, Viola stepped back in unholy shock. "I'm—I'm so sorry."

"It is quite all right, madam." He held out a short glass of whiskey, a single malt from Islay, judging from the aromas of butterscotch and cherry. "With the compliments of Luigi."

With reverence, Viola took the glass and lifted it to her nose, savoring its complex peatiness. Luigi had graced her with, not just an Islay, but a Glenmorangie aged in honey willow casks imported from Beta Five. "Thank you. You anticipate my needs as always."

As she placed the scotch on the table in front of her, Cardno frowned at the glass. "What's that for?"

"For me." She rose as a ninja dropped from the ceiling. "It's going to be a long evening."

Viola hefted her chair and reflected that she would have to leave the waiter a very good tip. He was a true artist who understood what his patrons needed at any given moment.

She might lack the will to shield Cardno any longer, but a good single malt was worth protecting.

We Interrupt This Broadcast

DOUBLED OVER with another hacking cough, Fidel Dobes turned away from his 1402 punchcard reader. The last thing he needed was to cough blood onto the Beluga program source cards. Across the cramped lab, Mira raised her head and stared with concern. He hated worrying her.

Fidel's ribs ached with the force of the cough. He held a handkerchief to his mouth, waiting for the fit to pass. For a long moment, he thought he would not be able to breathe again. The panic almost closed his throat completely, but he managed a shuddering breath without coughing. Then another. He straightened slowly and pulled the cloth away from his mouth. In the glob of sputum, a bright spot of scarlet glistened.

Damn. That usually only happened in the morning. He folded the handkerchief over so it wouldn't show, turned back to the 1402 and continued loading the source cards into the sturdy machine. Its fan hummed, masking some of the ragged sound of his breathing.

Mira cleared her throat. "Would water help?"

"I'm fine." Fidel thumbed through the remaining manila cards to make certain they were in the correct order. He had checked the serialization half a dozen times already, but anything was better than meeting Mira's worried look. "The TB won't kill me before we're finished."

Mira pursed her lips, painted a deep maroon. "I'm not worried about you finishing."

"What are—" No. He did not want the answer to that question. "Good."

She sneezed thrice, in rapid succession. On her, the sneezes sounded adorable, like a kitten.

"You still have that cold?"

She waved the question away, turning back to the 026 printer keyboard to punch a row of code into another card. Her dedication touched him. The Beluga program was huge and the verifier had tagged a score of corrupted data cards. He did not have time to send the cards back to one of the card punch girls upstairs—as if this were even an official project—and still be ready for broadcast. He had only one chance to intercept Asteroid 29085 1952 DA before it hurtled past the Earth's orbit.

It had been a risk bringing Mira into the project, but when she asked for details he'd implied that it was classified and she left it at that. As far as the government was concerned, she had the security clearance necessary for the clerical work for which he'd *officially* employed her but then, the government didn't know about Fidel's Beluga program. They knew that he used this forgotten corner of the Pentagon's basement to do research on ways to control spacecraft through computers. The additional program that he had devised to fit into the official project was something he had managed to keep hidden from everyone. So many times he had wished for someone to confide in and had nearly told Mira. But fear kept the words inside. Despite the years that he had known her, despite the strength of her mind, he feared that if she knew what he had created, he would lose her.

Ironic, that he now kept her close to be certain she was safe.

Fidel loaded the next set of cards into the feeder and stopped. On the top card, someone had drawn a red heart. He brushed the heart with his index finger; it was a smooth and waxy maroon, like a woman's lips. The next card had an imprint of lips as if she had kissed the card. The one after that was blank.

He looked up across the lab, to Mira. She met his gaze evenly with a Mona Lisa smile.

Suddenly too warm, Fidel broke eye contact and loaded the cards, the nine edge face down. What kind of life would he have been able to give her anyway? Not a long life together, not happily ever after. Nine months in a sanatorium had done nothing for him except give him time to read the news out of Washington and brood.

Only his correspondence with Mira had kept him sane—knowing that she had agreed with him about the outrages against humanity. And what a relief it was to know that his was not a lone voice crying out: How dare they!

He had known what the Manhattan Project was when he had worked on it, but they were only supposed to use the A-Bomb once. The threat of it was supposed to be deterrent enough, and yes, yes, he had known that it would involve a demonstration. For that, he had remorse, coupled with acceptance of his sins.

The second town. Nagasaki. That had been unnecessary. And now . . . the new project. Launching bombs into space and holding them there, ready to rain terror on any country that disagreed with the United States. As if that were a surprise coming from President Dewey, an isolationist president who defeated Truman on the strength of his reputation as a "gangbuster." His idea of foreign policy was to treat every other country like the gangs of New York. Well, no more. Fidel put the last of the cards in the 1402. "I'm ready to generate the object cards when you are."

Mira nodded and did not look up from the 026. The clacking of the machine's keys filled the room with chatter as she re-keyed Fidel's code.

Her fine black hair clung to the nape of her neck. Fidel wet his lips, watching her work. The delicate bones of her wrists peeked from the sensible long-sleeved shirt she wore. Her fingers deftly found the keys without apparent attention from her. Mira stifled another sneeze, turning her head from the machine without breaking her rhythm. His heart ached watching her. Mira must be kept safely away from DC. "Is everything still on for our trip tomorrow?" he asked.

She laughed without looking up from her work. "This is the third time you've asked in as many days," she said. "Yes, I'm all packed."

"Good."

The punch machine clattered as she continued to work. "I'm glad you're getting away from DC for a few days."

"So am I. Happier that you're coming with me."

Her hands stopped on the keys and a frown creased her brow. "Fidel—"

"What?"

"Nothing. I'm just glad you're getting away. DC isn't good for you."

Without thinking, he laughed and plunged into a fit of coughing. His lungs burned with every breath reminding him of the gift he was leaving the world.

He had run the calculations, punching the cards over and over to check his theory against numerical fact. Blowing up Washington would get rid of the corruption and greed, but it would rekindle the tensions of the second World War and lead to a destruction the likes of which man had never seen. An asteroid crashing into the city would seem like an Act of God. The shock waves and ash thrown up would affect the entire world. People would rally together, coming to the aid of a country shocked and devastated. It would be the dawn of a new Age of Enlightenment.

Fighting to control the coughing, Fidel pressed his handkerchief against his mouth to stifle the sound until he could breathe. "I'm okay," he said.

"I'm sorry." The distress in Mira's voice forced him upright.

He tucked the handkerchief in his pocket without looking at it. "Don't be. As you say, DC isn't good for me."

She twisted her fingers together. "Why don't you rest while I finish up. I can run the last compile on my own and you can check the listing for errors afterwards."

"I—"

"Please, Fidel. I worry about you."

He had nothing he could say in response. She was right to worry about him and at the same time worry would do no good. His fate was sealed. Nodding, he settled in his chair. "All right. Let me know if you need anything."

While Mira worked, Fidel let his head droop forward until his chin rested on his chest. If he could just close his eyes for a few minutes, he might be able to chase off the fatigue for a while longer.

~

A HAND TOUCHED his shoulder and Fidel lurched upright in his chair. Mira stood beside him, a stack of punchcards in her hand. "Sorry to wake you."

"No. It's fine." Fidel stood, trying to mask his fatigue and confusion. How long had he been asleep? The urge to check the cards one more time pulsed through him, but he'd done that enough and Mira was more than competent. "How did it go?"

"I haven't run it yet. I . . . Will you check this?" She handed him the stack of cards, a few stuck out at ninety degrees from the others as flags. "They match the listing but I don't think they're right."

He waited for enough of his drowsiness to drop away for her sentence to make sense. How could the cards be wrong if they matched his code? She was a smart girl but it was impossible that she could be critiquing his programming. Frowning, Fidel accepted the cards and sat down at his desk again. Flipping through the cards, he compared each to the lines of code he had originally written. The code handled the timing of the rocket's navigation. It was scheduled to start the takeover on March 1, three days from today and everything matched up. Mira hovered next to the desk, twining her fingers together.

To reassure her, he jotted the numbers on the back of an envelope and redid the calculations leading in and out of that code. "I don't see any errors here."

"What about leap day?" Mira asked.

Numb, Fidel stared at her. A blue vein beat in her neck as she stood on first one foot then the other. Leap day. Which meant that the rocket would not fire until a day late, by which point the asteroid would be gone. He shoved aside the pile of papers on his desk to uncover the ink blotter calendar there, as though Mira had made leap day up. Twenty-nine days. And he had only accounted for twenty-eight of them.

"My God." His hands shook as he picked up the cards and began to recalculate. One chance to save the world and he had almost missed it.

"Then it *is* an error." Mira nodded, pressing her lips together.

"Yes, thank you for catching that." His pencil flew over the paper. The changes were minor since the only bug in the code was how long the program lay dormant before triggering. The launch date, though, was unchanged; only the interval between had altered. Which meant that he had to make these changes quickly. "Start keying these as I hand them to you."

The lab vibrated with the sound of Mira's keypunch machine as she replaced the six cards she had flagged. As she finished them, he flipped through the deck to check the serialization one more time and nodded, grunting in satisfaction.

"Well . . . " he said. "Shall we?" Fidel winced at the banality of his own words. Perhaps he could write something in his journal that sounded more appropriate to the moment.

Straightening, Fidel let his hand drop to the 1402.

Mira ducked her head and lifted one hand to rub the base of her neck as if she were pained. "Fidel—"

He lifted his finger and waited for her to continue. She bit her lip studying the cards in the machine. He waited. "Yes?"

"Are you . . . are you sure?"

"Sure about what?" His heart sped and he glanced at his desk, but the drawer with his journal was locked and it was only there that he had recorded his thoughts. She could not know.

She touched the cards. "Sure . . . Sure that your calculations are all correct?"

"I believe so." He had gone through the cards often enough that he felt certain and time was running out. He put his finger back on the start key. "Thanks to the error you caught."

"No . . . " she said. "I mean the other calculations. The ones about the asteroid."

His throat started to close. "Asteroid?"

Mira nodded, tears brimming in her eyes. "I read the cards."

"You read them?" He seemed only able to ask questions.

"So many people . . . " she said, trailing off as she choked back tears. "That's why we're leaving the city tomorrow isn't it?"

He removed his hand from the key and wiped it over his face. She was never to have known. Such a soft and gentle heart should never be a party to what he was unleashing on the world. "I'm sorry. I thought I'd divided the cards up among the punchcard girls. I didn't think any of you had the whole program."

"I—I was interested in what you were doing so I printed a second copy of the listing when we ran it."

"I see." Fidel pressed his fingers against the center of his forehead, rubbing them in a circle. "Then yes, I am certain. Did you tell anyone what you read?"

"No." She grimaced. "It's just . . . This is what you faced when you worked on the Manhattan Project, isn't it?"

"Yes." He put his finger on the start key. "I had . . . I had initially planned to stay in the city when it happened. The TB, you know. I thought it would be faster this way."

A muscle pulsed in the corner of her jaw. "Why did you change your mind?"

"You. I wanted to see you safely out of the city. I wanted to know that I had not killed you."

She covered her mouth, eyes bright with tears, and turned away.

"Do you . . . " he began. All of the work he had done, all of his calculations—he would give it all up for her. "Do you want me to call it off?"

Her voice was hoarse. "No. It's just . . . all those people."

"It can't be helped. But the new world, Mira. Oh, it will be chaos and the world will suffer at first but the dawn that follows . . . "

She straightened and turned back to him, placing her soft hand over his where it rested on the keys. Compressing her mouth, she gave a small nod and pressed down on his hand.

Fidel pushed the start key with a harsh click, and the machine began feeding the cards, whirring and clunking as it joggled the cards and then fed each piece of the program into it. From there it would get loaded into the magnetic memory tapes of the N5 rockets scheduled to launch in the morning, carrying a nuclear warhead to orbit. On March 1, his program would activate and override the rocket's programming. The rocket would appear to lose communication with ground control, but it in reality it would be hurtling toward Asteroid 29085 1952 DA. Fidel's program would cause it intercept the asteroid and redirect it to Earth and Washington.

No one else could program this. No one else would even think it was possible to hit a target so small in the vastness of space, but for Fidel, the numbers had always danced at his command.

Mira kept hold of his hand as they sat down to wait for the program to compile. He kept his focus on the machine rather than what mattered to him. She sat silently by him, shoulders hunched as though against the clatter of the card reader.

When the last one rattled through the machine and dropped into the finish tray, Fidel let out a long, careful, sigh. "It is finished."

She squeezed his hand. "I thought it was just beginning?"

"More like a hard reset," he said. He held her hand, tracing the lines of her palm with his thumb, grateful that he would not have to spend his remaining months alone before the TB took him.

Mira echoed his sigh and then sneezed, daintily. A cough followed, hacking and wet. He looked at her in alarm.

Mira waved her hand to brush his concern away. "It's nothing, just a tickle in my throat."

But he knew what he had heard. "Are you certain?"

She pressed her fist against her mouth and stared at the floor for a long moment. Lifting her head, Mira looked at him with bright eyes, chin firm. "Maybe we both should stay in DC."

Fidel gripped her other hand harder and bowed his head. In his efforts to protect her, he had killed her anyway. "Yes," he said, "perhaps we should."

Rockets Red

WATCHING HIS MOTHER kneel awkwardly in her rented space suit, Aaron worried his lower lip inside his own helmet. She did not touch the fireworks, but her arm twitched like she wanted to. Or was that twitch because of the Parkinsons? He should have told her to stay on Earth, but she was so damn excited that he landed the Mars gig for Parkhill Pyrotechnics.

God. When had Mom gotten so small?

He turned away and scanned the horizon of Mars as if it were business as usual to be working here. The stars were amazing. He had dim memories of seeing them on Earth when he was a kid, before the asteroid hit. They sparkled like a silver peony aerial shell, with the dome of Landing a steady glow against the sky. The streets of the colony had been packed with people celebrating the twentieth anniversary of Arrival Day. Hard to believe it was 1974 already.

Over the speaker, Mom's voice crackled, "You adjusted the perchlorate balance?"

"Yep."

She threw her arms into the air like an Olympic gymnast. "Triumph! I— Oh!"

Off-balance with unfamiliarity in the light Martian gravity, the sudden movement tipped her to the side. Aaron hopped forward and caught her before she could pitch over onto the small array of pyrotechnic devices.

"Sorry." She patted his hand clumsily. "I was just so pleased I remembered my chemistry."

"It was always second nature for you."

"On Earth. The mix has to be different up here." She nodded to the firework. "Did you think about using an oxygen chamber around the fuse instead?"

He rolled his eyes, grateful that his helmet kept his expression from being too obvious. Clearly, some things hadn't changed. "Mom—The show is in an hour and a half. If I've screwed up, you aren't going to fix it by quizzing me."

"Well. Well . . . I'm proud of you. Your great-granddaddy would have split a side if he'd have known Parkhill Pyrotechnics would have a show on Mars someday."

"Thanks. I—" He shouldn't have taken the time to walk her past the fireworks staging area. He knew how she got. Always wanting to help out, even in retirement. "Listen, we should get a move on so I can load the program."

She clambered to her feet. Aaron caught her arm and helped steady her. Even in the bulky suit she was tiny. "You and your punchcards. It seems so lonely."

"It's safer. If you're in a bunker, there's darn little that can go wrong."

"I'm just saying—"

"Can we not have this argument again?" He thumped the bag of punchcards slung over his shoulder. "There was no way I could have brought a team of twenty up to Mars. If I still did things the old-fashioned way, I'd never have landed the contract."

"You're right. Of course, you're right."

"I'm sorry. I shouldn't have snapped."

"No, no. It's good for me to remember that I'm just a tourist these days." She turned away from the town to face the dome of the Bradbury Space Center. "Let's go watch your show."

IN LANDING, the city lights reflected off the interior of the dome and would have made the fireworks nearly invisible. The Bradbury Space

Center on the other hand, with its vast space for interplanetary rockets, could hold the whole town but, more importantly, it was easier to darken. Just turn off the work lights and you had an unobstructed view of the sky.

Through the thick glass of the airlock's window, Aaron could just see the banners proclaiming "1954-1974" inside the hangar. The interior of the space center had been swathed with red, green, and blue bunting for the celebration.

He held the door for his mother as she ducked into the chamber after him, kicking the ubiquitous red dust off her boots. Aaron shifted the satchel over his shoulder while he waited for the air to cycle.

With a hiss, the door finally opened and they stepped onto the hangar floor.

People were already filling the hangar with a cheerful buzz of conversation. Some folks had even brought blankets and carried sacks with picnics, like everyone was trying to recreate a holiday from Earth. Heck . . . the mayor had even erected a bandstand and rounded up a horn section from somewhere. Darn good thing they'd have music, too, given that between the dome and the thin atmosphere the fireworks made more of a snap than a bang.

People thought fireworks were about the flash and bang, but if his mom had taught him anything it was that they were about building community. For one night, everyone breathed with the same breath, with the intake of *Oh* and the exhale of *Ah*.

Aaron popped the seal on his helmet and pulled it off, switching from the steely recycled funk of suit air to the steely recycled burnt hydrocarbon funk of the hangar. Burning things, at least, smelled comfortably familiar if you just mixed in a little sulfur stink.

His mother's hands fumbled with the latch on her helmet. The suit's heavy gloves made her normally nimble fingers clumsy. No . . . No, it wasn't just the suit. He'd never get used to thinking of her as fragile.

"Here." He handed her the satchel with the punchcards in it. "Let me help."

Her mouth quirked to the side in a sheepish grin. The external speaker on the suit crackled. "I'll blame it on the suit instead of getting old."

"Fair assessment—" He tugged on the latch and grunted. "Darn thing's stuck."

"Triumph! It's not me!" His mom again flung her arms up in celebration.

With the movement, the catch on his satchel released and the bundle of punch cards came out, flying in a high inertial arc in the light gravity.

"Shit!" His mother jerked away, reaching for the punchcards.

For a moment, Aaron was more stunned that she had cursed than about the cards.

The cards—Shit. He turned and jumped, to try to catch them, but his gloved hand just batted at the bundle. The rubber band holding them slipped and the cards sprayed around them like a Waterfall Shell expanding. Each individual card tumbled free and fluttered to the ground. They dropped so slowly, it almost seemed as if he could catch them.

Not that it would do any good. They were already hopelessly out of sequence.

"Oh, sweetie. I'm so sorry." His mother stared at the cards, still falling to the blackened hangar floor.

He took a breath, trying to not completely lose it in front of his mother. There was nothing that could be done and she would already feel bad enough. He had to keep it together.

But the show was in an hour.

A barrage of curses ran rapid-fire through his mind, but he just took another breath of the recycled air and turned to his mom. "Let's get you out of that suit first, okay?"

"But—your program."

He held up a finger to silence her and turned the corners of his mouth up in a smile. "No way we can pick things up in the gloves. So let's get that sorted out first."

Pick things up? There were two hundred and fifty individual cards. Forget about picking them up, how was he going to re-sequence them fast enough? His sequencer was back in Landing proper and that was a good quarter hour away from the hangar by train. Then he'd have to get to his hotel and back and . . . Shit. Aaron put his hand on the latch of his mother's helmet and gave it a quick tug. The darn thing popped free immediately, as if it had never been stuck.

"Well, turtle feathers." His mother scowled and pulled the helmet off. "If it had done that in the first place . . . " Her voice trailed off as she stared at the cards.

Behind them, the airlock cycled open, and a family of five stepped into the hangar.

"Careful—" Aaron held up his hand to direct them around the pile of cards, but the smallest of the suited figures bolted away from the group, running toward the bandstand. The little booted feet kicked up the punchcards like dried leaves. *Turtle feathers* was not a sufficient level of expletive. Aaron compressed his lips to hold everything else in. Instead he gestured to the cards and asked the rest of the family to go around.

When he turned back, his mother was on her knees, gloves discarded, and picking up cards.

He yanked his own off and dropped to the hangar floor beside her. Picking up a card, he pointed to the notched corner. "These should all be facing the same way to load them into the computer."

"How do we know what order they go in?" She rifled through the ones she'd already picked up, and reoriented the cards that were upside down.

"See these last three columns of holes? That's the sequence number." A jump in numbers would cause the computer to throw an error. Damn it. He sagged on his knees. There was no way he could run the program out of sequence.

And what if one went missing? Or was folded?

God. That would jam the machine. He could just picture it choking on an early card and the entire sequence just sitting there on in the middle of a field of red, without detonating. His claims that he could actually get fireworks to go off on Mars, with the thin atmosphere and the complications of the gravity—all of that was about to look like shameless boasting. His professional reputation would be ruined.

And the deposit. All that money to haul stuff up here. He'd have to eat the expenses and give them the deposit back. It would be the end of the family business.

Aaron's hands shook as he snatched cards off the floor.

"Can we do it the old-fashioned way?"

"What? Run across the airless plains of Mars and light fuses?" He grimaced an apology for letting the sarcasm slip out. She looked just miserable and that wasn't what she'd meant anyway. "Sorry. No. There's no way to manually drive the electronic initiator without the computer."

"I am so sorry." His mother looked down at the cards in her hands and shook her head. "It takes me five minutes just to count the holes to figure out where they are in sequence."

"I know." He snorted. "If we had a team like Grandpa's then maybe we could sequence them faster."

His mother's head snapped up. "You are brilliant."

"Mom . . . " She'd always had faith in him, and this time he was going to fail, and she'd feel responsible. "It's not your fault."

"It is. And I'll fix it." She jumped to her feet and ran to the bandstand.

"What the . . . "

She took long bounding strides and in a moment was talking to the mayor. Even from where Aaron was, he could see Mom turn on the charm. A moment later, the mayor handed her the microphone.

"Ladies and gentlemen!" Her Southern twang sounded more apparent over the hangar loudspeakers. "Do y'all want to see some fireworks tonight?"

They cheered. God. How many times had he heard Mom pump up a crowd before they started a show on Earth. The roar went up from their bellies, full of enthusiasm for this new life.

And he didn't have a show to give them.

"Then we need your help! My son, Aaron Parkhill, has programmed a brilliant show for you but . . . " she let her voice drop to a conspiratorial whisper and held the microphone closer so it sounded like she was sharing a secret with each person individually. "But . . . I dropped the cards. What I need y'all to do is to help us get them back in order so the show can go on." She held a card over her head. "On the right side, there's a line of holes. That's the number of the card. Go over there to where Aaron is—Wave honey."

Sheepishly, feeling like he was twelve again, Aaron got to his feet and waved.

"Go over there, grab a card, and sort yourselves into a line. Remember when you were in school and had to sort yourself by height? Just like that." She gave a wink. "I used to be the tallest girl in my class. Wouldn't know it to look at me now. Oh . . . And y'all know that rhyme?

'Here he lies molding
his dying was hard,
they shot him for folding,
an IBM card.'"

A wave of laughter went up. Aaron turned in a circle, watching the scattered individuals join together.

"So, careful with those cards. Now . . . can y'all help us out?"

They gave another cheer and the band struck up a march.

In moments, people were coming over and grabbing cards. They were laughing and sliding into line, trading places with their neighbor as someone with a higher number joined them. Good lord—he'd just handed a card to Elma York, one of the first astronauts to land on Mars. And there was the mayor snatching up a card. Was *everyone* helping?

Aaron handed out the cards till he just had one left. Number 92. He went down the line full of people laughing and chatting as if this was the best game they'd ever played. His mother stood at position 67, giggling with a little girl who held her card in both hands.

Just like that—the cards were sorted. He'd been worried that this was the end of Parkhill Pyrotechnics. It hadn't been the end when his mom retired and it wouldn't be the end now. His mother had managed to turn a disaster to a success. He'd thought she'd gotten small with age, but he was wrong. His mother was still a giant.

She built something better than fireworks. She built community.

Laughing, Aaron threw his hands into the air like an Olympic gymnast. Like his mom. "Triumph!"

The Lady Astronaut of Mars

DOROTHY LIVED in the midst of the great Kansas prairies, with Uncle Henry, who was a farmer, and Aunt Em, who was the farmer's wife. She met me, she went on to say, when I was working next door to their farm under the shadow of the rocket gantry for the First Mars Expedition.

I have no memory of this.

She would have been a little girl and, oh lord, there were so many little kids hanging around outside the Fence watching us work. The little girls all wanted to talk to the Lady Astronaut. To me.

I'm sure I spoke to Dorothy because I know I stopped and talked to them every day on my way in and out through the Fence about what it was like. *It* being Mars. There was nothing else it could be.

Mars consumed everyone's conversations. The programmers sitting over their punchcards. The punchcard girls keying in the endless lines of code. The cafeteria ladies ladling out mashed potatoes and green peas. Nathaniel with his calculations . . . Everyone talked about Mars.

So the fact that I didn't remember a little girl who said I talked to her about Mars . . . Well. That's not surprising, is it? I tried not to let the confusion show in my face but I know she saw it.

By this point, Dorothy was my doctor. Let me be more specific. She was the geriatric specialist who was evaluating me. On Mars. I was in for what I thought was a routine check-up to make sure I was still fit to be an astronaut. NASA liked to update its database periodically and I liked to be in that database. Not that I'd flown since I turned fifty, but I kept my name on the list in the faint hope that they would let me back into space again, and I kept going to the darn check-ups.

Our previous doctor had retired back to Earth, and I'd visited Dorothy's offices three times before she mentioned Kansas and the prairie.

She fumbled with the clipboard and cleared her throat. A flush of red colored her cheeks and made her eyes even more blue. "Sorry. Doctor York, I shouldn't have mentioned it."

"Don't 'doctor' me. You're the doctor. I'm just a space jockey. Call me Elma." I waved my hand to calm her down. The flesh under my arm jiggled and I dropped my hand. I hate that feeling and hospital gowns just make it worse. "I'm glad you did. You just took me by surprise, is all. Last I saw you, weren't you knee-high to a grasshopper?"

"So you do remember me?" Oh, that hope. She'd come to Mars because of me. I could see that, clear as anything. Something I'd said or done back in 1952 had brought this girl out to the colony.

"Of course, I remember you. Didn't we talk every time I went through that Fence? Except school days, of course." It seemed a safe bet.

Dorothy nodded, eager. "I still have the eagle you gave me."

"Do you now?" That gave me a pause.

I used to make paper eagles out of old punchcards while I was waiting for Nathaniel. His programs could take hours to run and he liked to babysit them. The eagles were cut paper things with layers of cards pasted together to make a three-dimensional bird. It was usually in flight and I liked to hang them in the window, where the holes from the punch cards would let specks of light through and make the bird seem like it was sparkling. They would take me two or three days to make. You'd think I would remember giving one to a little girl beyond the Fence. "Did you bring it out here with you?"

"It's in my office." She stood as if she'd been waiting for me to ask that since our first session, then looked down at the clipboard in her hands, frowning. "We should finish your tests."

"Fine by me. Putting them off isn't going to make me any more eager." I held out my arm with the wrist up so she could take my pulse. By this point, I knew the drill. "How's your Uncle?"

She laid her fingers on my wrist, cool as anything. "He and Aunt Em passed away when Orion 27 blew."

I swallowed, sick at my lack of memory. So she was THAT little girl. She'd told me all the things I needed and my old brain was just too addled to put the pieces together. I wondered if she would make a note of that and if it would keep me grounded.

Dorothy had lived on a farm in the middle of the Kansas prairie with her Uncle Henry and Aunt Em. When Orion 27 came down in a ball of fire, it was the middle of a drought. The largest pieces of it had landed on a farm.

No buildings were crushed, but it would have been a blessing if they had been, because that would have saved the folks inside from burning alive.

I closed my eyes and could see her now as the little girl I'd forgotten. Brown pigtails down her back and a pair of dungarees a size too large for her, with the legs cuffed up to show bobby socks and sneakers.

Someone had pointed her out. "The little girl from the Williams farm."

I'd seen her before, but in that way you see the same people every day without noticing them. Even then, with someone pointing to her, she didn't stand out from the crowd. Looking at her, there was nothing to know that she'd just lived through a tragedy. I reckon it hadn't hit her yet.

I had stepped away from the entourage of reporters and consultants that followed me and walked up to her. She had tilted her head back to look up at me. I used to be a tall woman, you know.

I remember her voice piping up in that high treble of the very young. "You still going to Mars?"

I had nodded. "Maybe you can go someday too."

She had cocked her head to the side, as if she were considering. I can't remember what she said back. I know she must have said something. I know we must have talked longer because I gave her that darned eagle, but what we said . . . I couldn't pull it up out of my brain.

As the present-day Dorothy tugged up my sleeve and wrapped the blood pressure cuff around my arm, I studied her. She had the same dark hair as the little girl she had been, but it was cut short now and in the low gravity of Mars it wisped around her head like the down on a baby bird.

The shape of her eyes was the same, but that was about it. The soft roundness of her cheeks was long gone, leaving high cheekbones and a jaw that came to too sharp of a point for beauty. She had a faint white scar just above her left eyebrow.

She smiled at me and unwrapped the cuff. "Your blood pressure is better. You must have been exercising since last time."

"I do what my doctor tells me."

"How's your husband?"

"About the same." I slid away from the subject even though, as his doctor, she had the right to ask, and I squinted at her height. "How old were you when you came here?"

"Sixteen. We were supposed to come before but . . . well." She shrugged, speaking worlds about why she hadn't.

"Your uncle, right?"

Startled, she shook her head. "Oh, no. Mom and Dad. We were supposed to be on the first colony ship but a logging truck lost its load."

Aghast, I could only stare at her. If they were supposed to have been on the first colony ship, then her parents could not have died long before Orion 27 crashed. I wet my lips. "Where did you go after your aunt and uncle's?"

"My cousin. Their son." She lifted one of the syringes she'd brought in with her. "I need to take some blood today."

"My left arm has better veins."

While she swabbed the site, I looked away and stared at a chart on the wall reminding people to take their vitamin D supplements. We didn't get enough light here for most humans.

But the stars . . . When you could see them, the stars were glorious. Was that what had brought Dorothy to Mars?

~

WHEN I GOT HOME from the doctor's—from Dorothy's—the nurse was just finishing up with Nathaniel's sponge bath. Genevieve stuck her head out of the bedroom, hands still dripping.

"Well, hey, Miss Elma. We're having a real good day, aren't we, Mr. Nathaniel?" Her smile could have lit a hangar, it was so bright.

"That we are." Nathaniel sounded hale and hearty, if I didn't look at him. "Genevieve taught me a new joke. How's it go?"

She stepped back into the bedroom. "What did the astronaut see on the stove? An unidentified frying object."

Nathaniel laughed, and there was only a little bit of a wheeze. I slid my shoes off in the dustroom to keep out the ever-present Martian grit, and came into the kitchen to lean against the bedroom door. Time was, it used to be his office but we needed a bedroom on the ground floor. "That's a pretty good one."

He sat on a towel at the edge of the bed as Genevieve washed him. With his shirt off, the ribs were starkly visible under his skin. Each bone in his arms poked at the surface and slid under the slack flesh. His hands shook, even just resting beside him on the bed. He grinned at me.

The same grin. The same bright blue eyes that had flashed over the punchcards as he'd worked out the plans for the launch. It was as though someone had pasted his features onto the body of a stranger. "How'd the doctor's visit go?"

"The usual. Only . . . Only it turns out our doctor grew up next to the launch facility in Kansas."

"Doctor Williams?"

"The same. Apparently I met her when she was little."

"Is that right?" Genevieve wrung the sponge out in the wash basin. "Doesn't that just go to show that it's a small solar system?"

"Not that small." Nathaniel reached for his shirt, which lay on the bed next to him. His hands tremored over the fabric.

"I'll get it. You just give me a minute to get this put away." Genevieve bustled out of the room.

I called after her. "Don't worry. I can help him."

Nathaniel dipped his head, hiding those beautiful eyes, as I drew a sleeve up over one arm. He favored flannel now. He'd always hated it in the past. Preferred starched white shirts and a nice tie to work in, and a short sleeved aloha shirt on his days off. At first, I thought that the flannel was because he was cold all the time. Later I realized that the thicker fabric hid some of his frailty. Leaning behind him to pull the shirt around his back, I could count vertebra in his spine.

Nathaniel cleared his throat. "So, you met her, hm? Or she met you? There were a lot of little kids watching us."

"Both. I gave her one of my paper eagles."

That made him lift his head. "Really?"

"She was on the Williams farm when the Orion 27 came down."

He winced. Even after all these years, Nathaniel still felt responsible. He had not programmed the rocket. They'd asked him to, but he'd been too busy with the First Mars Expedition and turned the assignment down. It was just a supply rocket for the moon, and there had been no reason to think it needed anything special.

I buttoned the shirt under his chin. The soft wattle of skin hanging from his jaw brushed the back of my hand. "I think she was too shy to mention it at my last visit."

"But she gave you a clean bill of health?"

"There's still some test results to get back." I avoided his gaze, hating the fact that I was healthy and he was . . . Not.

"It must be pretty good. Sheldon called."

A bubble of adrenalin made my heart skip. Sheldon Spender called. The director of operations at the Bradbury Space Center on Mars had not called since—No, that wasn't true. He hadn't called *me* in years, using silence to let me know I wasn't flying anymore. Nathaniel still got called for work. Becoming old didn't stop a programmer from working, but it sure as heck stopped an astronaut from flying. And yet I still had that moment of hope every single time Sheldon called, that this time it would be for me. I smoothed the flannel over Nathaniel's shoulders. "Do they have a new project for you?"

"He called for you. Message is on the counter."

Genevieve breezed back into the room, a bubble of idle chatter preceding her. Something about her cousin and meeting their neighbors on Venus. I stood up and let her finish getting Nathaniel dressed while I went into the kitchen.

Sheldon had called for me? I picked up the note on the counter. It just had Genevieve's round handwriting and a request to meet for lunch. The location told me a lot though. He'd picked a bar next to the space center that *no one* in the industry went to because it was thronged with tourists. It was a good place to talk business without talking business. For the life of me I couldn't figure out what he wanted.

I KEPT CHEWING on that question, right till the point when I stepped through the doors of Yuri's Spot. The walls were crowded with memorabilia and signed photos of astronauts. An early publicity still that showed me perched on the edge of Nathaniel's desk, hung in the corner next to a dusty ficus tree. My hair fell in perfect soft curls despite the flight suit I had on. My hair would never have survived like that if I'd actually been working. I tended to keep it out of the way in a kerchief, but that wasn't the image publicity had wanted.

Nathaniel was holding up a punch card, as if he were showing me a crucial piece of programming. Again, it was a staged thing, because the individual cards were meaningless by themselves, but to the general public at the time they meant Science with a capital S. I'm pretty sure that's why we were both laughing in the photo, but they had billed it as "the joy of space flight."

Still gave me a chuckle, thirty years later.

Sheldon stepped away from the wall and mistook my smile. "You look in good spirits."

I nodded to the photo. "Just laughing at old memories."

He glanced over his shoulder, wrinkles bunching at the corner of his eyes in a smile. "How's Nathaniel?"

"About the same, which is all one can ask for at this point."

Sheldon nodded and gestured to a corner booth, leading me past a family with five kids who had clearly come from the Space Center. The youngest girl had her nose buried in a picture book of the early space program. None of them noticed me.

Time was when I couldn't walk anywhere on Mars without being recognized as the Lady Astronaut. Now, thirty years after the First Expedition, I was just another old lady, whose small stature showed my origin on Earth.

We settled in our chairs and ordered, making small talk as we did. I think I got fish and chips because it was the first thing on the menu, and all I could think about was wondering why Sheldon had called.

It was like he wanted to see how long it would take me to crack and ask him what he was up to. It took me awhile to realize that he kept bringing the conversation back to Nathaniel. Was he in pain?

Of course.

Did he have trouble sleeping?

Yes.

Even, "How are you holding up?" was about him. I didn't get it until Sheldon paused and pushed his rabbit burger aside, half-eaten, and asked point-blank. "Have they given him a date yet?"

A date. There was only one date that mattered in a string of other milestones on the path to death but I pretended he wasn't being clear, just to make him hurt a little. "You mean for paralyzation, hospice, or death?"

He didn't flinch. "Death."

"We think he's got about a year." I kept my face calm, the way you do when you're talking to Mission Control about a flight that's set to abort. The worse it got, the more even my voice became. "He can still work, if that's what you're asking."

"It's not." Sheldon broke his gaze then, to my surprise, and looked down at his ice water, spinning the glass in its circle of condensation. "What I need to know is if *you* can still work."

In my intake of breath, I wanted to say that God, yes, I could work and that I would do anything he asked of me if he'd put me back into space. In my exhale, I thought of Nathaniel. I could not say yes. "That's why you asked for the physical."

"Yep."

"I'm sixty-three, Sheldon."

"I know." He turned the glass again. "Did you see the news about LS-579?"

"The extrasolar planet. Yes." I was grounded, that didn't mean I stopped paying attention to the stars.

"Did you know we think it's habitable?"

I stopped with my mouth open as pieces started to tick like punch cards slotting through a machine. "You're mounting a mission."

"*If* we were, would you be interested in going?"

Back into space? My God, yes. But I couldn't. I couldn't. I—that was why he wanted to know when my husband was going to die. I swallowed everything before speaking. My voice was passive. "I'm sixty-three." Which was my way of asking why he wanted *me* to go.

"It's three years in space." He looked up now, not needing to explain why they wanted an old pilot.

That long in space? It doesn't matter how much shielding you have against radiation, it's going to affect you. The chances of developing cancer within the next fifteen years were huge. You can't ask a young astronaut to do that. "I see."

"We have the resources to send a small craft there. It can't be unmanned because the programming is too complicated. I need an astronaut who can fit in the capsule."

"And you need someone who has a reason to not care about surviving the trip."

"No." He grimaced. "PR tells me that I need an astronaut that the public will adore so that when we finally tell them that we've sent you, they will forgive us for hiding the mission from them." Sheldon cleared his throat and started briefing me on the Longevity Mission.

Should I pause here and explain what the Longevity Mission is? It's possible that you don't know.

There's a habitable planet. An extrasolar one and it's only few light years away. They've got a slingshot that can launch a ship up to near light speed. A small ship. Big enough for one person.

But that isn't what makes the Longevity Mission possible. *That* is the tesseract field. We can't go faster than light, but we *can* cut corners through the universe. The physicists described it to me like a subway tunnel. The tesseract will bend space and allow a ship to go to the next subway station. The only trick is that you need to get far enough away from a planet before you can bend space and . . . this is the harder part . . . you need a tesseract field at the other end. Once that's up, you just need to get into orbit and the trip from Mars to LS-579 can be as short as three weeks.

But you have to get someone to the planet to set up the other end of the tesseract.

And they wanted to hide the plan from the public, in case it failed.

So different from when the First Mars Expedition had happened. An asteroid had slammed into Washington, DC and obliterated the capitol. It made the entire world realize how fragile our hold on Earth was. Nations banded together and when the Secretary of Agriculture, who found himself president through the line of succession, said that we needed to get off the planet, people listened. We rose to the stars. The potential loss of an astronaut was just part of the risk. Now? Now it has been long enough that people are starting to forget that the danger is still there. That the need to explore is necessary.

Sheldon finished talking and just watched me processing it.

"I need to think about this."

"I know."

Then I closed my eyes and realized that I had to say no. It didn't matter how I felt about the trip or the chance to get back into space. The launch date he was talking about meant I'd have to go into training *now*. "I can't." I opened my eyes and stared at the wall where the publicity still of me and Nathaniel hung. "I have to turn it down."

"Talk to Nathaniel."

I grimaced. He would tell me to take it. "I can't."

I LEFT SHELDON feeling more unsettled than I wanted to admit at the time. I stared out the window of the light rail, at the sepia sky. Rose tones were deepening near the horizon with sunset. It was dimmer and ruddier here, but with the dust, sunset could be just as glorious as on Earth.

It's a hard thing to look at something you want and to know that the right choice is to turn it down. Understand me: I wanted to go. Another opportunity like this would never come up for me. I was too old for normal missions. I knew it. Sheldon knew it. And Nathaniel would know it, too. I wish he had been in some other industry so I could lie and talk about "later." He knew the space program too well to be fooled.

And he wouldn't believe me if I said I didn't want to go. He knew how much I missed the stars.

That's the thing that I think none of us were prepared for in coming to Mars. The natural night sky on Mars is spectacular, because the atmosphere is so thin. But where humans live, under the dome, all you can see are the lights of the town reflecting against the dark curve. You can almost believe that they're stars. Almost. If you don't know what you are missing or don't remember the way the sky looked at night on Earth before the asteroid hit.

I wonder if Dorothy remembers the stars. She's young enough that she might not. Children on Earth still look at clouds of dust and stars are just a myth. God. What a bleak sky.

When I got home, Genevieve greeted me with her usual friendly chatter. Nathaniel looked like he wanted to push her out of the house so he could quiz me. I know Genevieve said good-bye, and that we chatted, but the details have vanished now.

What I remember next is the rattle and thump of Nathaniel's walker as he pushed it into the kitchen. It slid forward. Stopped. He took two steps, steadied himself, and slid it forward again. Two steps. Steady. Slide.

I pushed away from the counter and straightened. "Do you want to be in the kitchen or the living room?"

"Sit down, Elma." He clenched the walker till the tendons stood out on the back of his hands, but they still trembled. "Tell me about the mission."

"What?" I froze.

"The mission." He stared at the ceiling, not at me. "That's why Sheldon called, right? So, tell me."

"I . . . All right." I pulled the tall stool out for him and waited until he eased onto it. Then I told him. He stared at the ceiling the whole time I talked. I spent the time watching him and memorizing the line of his cheek, and the shape of the small mole by the corner of his mouth.

When I finished, he nodded. "You should take it."

"What makes you think I want to?"

He lowered his head then, eyes just as piercing as they had always been. "How long have we been married?"

"I can't."

Nathaniel snorted. "I called Doctor Williams while you were out, figuring it would be something like this. I asked for a date when we could get hospice." He held up his hand to stop the words forming on my lips. "She's not willing to tell me that. She did give me the date when the paralysis is likely to become total. Three months. Give or take a week."

We'd known this was coming, since he was diagnosed, but I still had to bite the inside of my lip to keep from sobbing. He didn't need to see me break down.

"So . . . I think you should tell them yes."

"Three months is not a lot of time, they can—"

"They can what? Wait for me to die? Jesus Christ, Elma. We know that's coming." He scowled at the floor. "Go. For the love of God, just take the mission."

I wanted to. I wanted to get off the planet and back into space and not have to watch him die. Not have to watch him lose control of his body piece by piece.

And I wanted to stay here and be with him and steal every moment left that he had breath in his body.

ONE OF MY FAVORITE restaurants in Landing was Elmore's. The New Orleans-style café sat tucked back behind Thompson's Grocers on a little rise that lifted the dining room just high enough to see out to the edge of town and the dome's wall. They had a crawfish étouffée that would make you think you were back on Earth. The crawfish were raised in a tank and a little bigger than the ones I'd grown up with, but the spices came all the way from Louisiana on the mail runs twice a year.

Sheldon Spender knew it was my favorite and was taking ruthless advantage of that. And yet I came anyway. He sat across the table from me, with his back to the picture window that framed the view. His thinning hair was almost invisible against the sky. He didn't say a word. Just watched me, as the fellow to my right talked.

Garrett Biggs. I'd seen him at the Bradbury Space Center, but we'd exchanged maybe five words before today. My work was mostly done before his time. They just trotted me out for the occasional holiday. Now, the man would not stop talking. He gestured with his fork as he spoke, punctuating the phrases he thought I needed to hear most. "Need some photos of you so we can exploit—I know it sounds ugly but we're all friends here, right? We can be honest, right? So, we can exploit your sacrifice to get the public really behind the Longevity Mission."

I watched the lettuce tremble on the end of his fork. It was pallid compared to my memory of lettuce on Earth. "I thought the public didn't know about the mission."

"They will. That's the key. Someone will leak it and we need to be ready." He waved the lettuce at me. "And that's why you are a brilliant choice for pilot. Octogenarian Grandmother Paves Way for Humanity."

"You can't pave the stars. I'm not a grandmother. And I'm sixty-three not eighty."

"It's a figure of speech. The point is that you're a PR goldmine."

I had known that they asked me to helm this mission because of my age—it would be a lot to ask of someone who had a full life ahead of them. Maybe I was naive to think that my experience in establishing the Mars colony was considered valuable.

How can I explain the degree to which I resented being used for publicity? This wasn't a new thing by a long shot. My entire career has been about exploitation for publicity. I had known it, and exploited it too, once I'd realized the power of having my uniform tailored to show my shape a little more clearly. You think they would have sent me to Mars if it weren't intended to be a colony? I was there to show all the lady housewives that they could go to space too. Posing in my flight suit, with my lips painted red, I had smiled at more cameras than my colleagues.

I stared at Garrett Biggs and his fork. "For someone in PR, you are awfully blunt."

"I'm honest. To you. If you were the public, I'd have you spinning so fast you'd generate your own gravity."

Sheldon cleared his throat. "Elma, the fact is that we're getting some pressure from a group of senators. They want to cut the budget for the project and we need to take steps or it won't happen."

I looked down and separated the tail from one of my crawfish. "Why?"

"The usual nonsense. People arguing that if we just wait, then ships will become fast enough to render the mission pointless. That includes a couple of serious misunderstandings of physics, but, be that as it may . . . " Sheldon paused and tilted his head, looking at me. He changed what he was about to say and leaned forward. "Is Nathaniel worse?"

"He's not better."

He winced at the edge in my voice. "I'm sorry. I know I strong-armed you into it, but I can find someone else."

"He thinks I should go." My chest hurt even considering it. But I couldn't stop thinking about the mission. "He knows it's the only way I'll get back into space."

Garrett Biggs frowned like I'd said the sky was green, instead of the pale Martian amber. "You're in space."

"I'm on Mars. It's still a planet."

I WOKE out of half-sleep, aware that I must have heard Nathaniel's bell, without being able to actually recall it. I pulled myself to my feet, putting a hand against the nightstand until I was steady. My right hip had stiffened again in the night. Arthritis is not something I approve of.

Turning on the hall light, I made my way down the stairs. The door at the bottom stood open so I could hear Nathaniel if he called. I couldn't sleep with him anymore, for fear of breaking him.

I went through into his room. It was full of gray shadows and the dark rectangle of his bed. In one corner, the silver arm of his walker caught the light.

"I'm sorry." His voice cracked with sleep.

"It's all right. I was awake anyway."

"Liar."

"Now, is that a nice thing to say?" I put my hand on the light switch. "Watch your eyes."

Every night we followed the same ritual and even though I knew the light would be painfully bright, I still winced as it came on. Squinting against the glare, I threw the covers back for him. The weight of them trapped him sometimes. He held his hands up, waiting for me to take them. I braced myself and let Nathaniel pull himself into a sitting position. On Earth, he'd have been bed-ridden long since. Of course, on Earth, his bone density would probably not have deteriorated so fast.

As gently as I could, I swung his legs to the side of the bed. Even allowing for the gravity, I was appalled anew by how light he was. His legs were like kindling wrapped in tissue. Where his pajamas had ridden up, purple bruises mottled his calf.

As soon as he was sitting up on the edge of the bed, I gave him the walker. He wrapped his shaking hands around the bars and tried to stand. He rose only a little before dropping back to the bed. I stayed where I was, though I ached to help. He sometimes took more than one try to stand at night, and didn't want help. Not until it became absolutely necessary. Even then, he wouldn't want it. I just hoped he'd let me help him when we got to that point.

On the second try, he got his feet under him and stood, shaking. With a nod, he pushed forward. "Let's go."

I followed him to the bathroom in case he lost his balance in there, which he did sometimes. The first time, I hadn't been home. We had hired Genevieve not long after that to sit with him when I needed to be out.

He stopped in the kitchen and bent a little at the waist with a sort of grunt.

"Are you all right?"

He shook his head and started again, moving faster. "I'm not—" He leaned forward, clenching his jaw. "I can't—"

The bathroom was so close.

"Oh, God. Elma . . ." A dark, fetid smell filled the kitchen. Nathaniel groaned. "I couldn't—"

I put my hand on his back. "Hush. We're almost there. We'll get you cleaned up."

"I'm sorry, I'm sorry." He pushed the walker forward, head hanging. A trail of damp footsteps followed him. The ammonia stink of urine joined the scent of his bowels.

I helped him lower his pajamas. The weight of them had made them sag on his hips. Dark streaks ran down his legs and dripped onto the bath mat. I eased him onto the toilet.

My husband bent his head forward, and he wept.

I remember wetting a washcloth and running it over his legs. I know that I must have tossed his soiled pajamas into the cleaner, and that I wiped up the floor, but those details have mercifully vanished. But what I can't forget, and I wish to God that I could, is Nathaniel sitting there crying.

I ASKED GENEVIEVE to bring adult diapers to us the next day. The strange thing was how familiar the package felt. I'd used them on launches when we had to sit in the capsule for hours and there was no option to get out of our space suit. It's one of the many glamorous details of being an astronaut that the publicity department does *not* share with the public.

There is a difference, however, from being required to wear one for work and what Nathaniel faced. He could not put them on by himself without losing his balance. Every time I had to change the diaper, he stared at the wall with his face slack and hopeless.

Nathaniel and I'd made the decision not to have children. They aren't conducive to a life in space, you know? I mean there's the radiation, and the weightlessness, but more it was that I was gone all the time. I couldn't give up the stars . . . but I found myself wishing that we hadn't made that decision. Part of it was wishing that I had some connection to the next generation. More of it was wanting someone to share the burden of decision with me.

What happens after Nathaniel dies? What do I have left here? More specifically, how much will I regret not going on the mission?

And if I'm in space, how much will I regret abandoning my husband to die alone?

You see why I was starting to wish that we had children?

In the afternoon, we were sitting in the living room, pretending to work. Nathaniel sat with his pencil poised over the paper and stared out the window as though he were working. I'm pretty sure he wasn't but I gave him what privacy I could and started on one of my eagles.

The phone rang and gave us both something of a relief, I think, to have a distraction. The phone sat on a table by Nathaniel's chair so he could reach it easily if I weren't in the room. With my eyes averted, his voice sounded as strong as ever as he answered.

"Hang on, Sheldon. Let me get Elma for— Oh. Oh, I see."

I snipped another feather but it was more as a way to avoid making eye contact than because I really wanted to keep working.

"Of course I've got a few minutes. I have nothing but time these days." He ran his hand through his hair and let it rest at the back of his neck. "I find it hard to believe that you don't have programmers on staff who can't handle this."

He was quiet then as Sheldon spoke, I could hear only the distorted tinny sound of his voice rising and falling. At a certain point, Nathaniel picked up his pencil again and started making notes. Whatever Sheldon was asking him to do, *that* was the moment when Nathaniel decided to say "yes."

I set my eagle aside and went into the kitchen. My first reaction— God. It shames me but my first reaction was anger. How dare he? How dare he take a job without consulting with me when I was turning down this thing I so desperately wanted because of *him*. I had the urge to snatch up the phone and tell Sheldon that I would go.

I pushed that down carefully and looked at it.

Nathaniel had been urging me to go. No deliberate action of his was keeping me from accepting. Only my own upbringing and loyalty and . . . and I loved him. If I did not want to be alone after he passed, how could I leave him to face the end alone?

The decision would be easier if I knew when he would die.

I still hate myself for thinking that.

I heard the conversation end and Nathaniel hung up the phone. I filled a glass with water to give myself an excuse for lingering in the kitchen. I carried it back into the living room and sat down on the couch.

Nathaniel had his lower lip between his teeth and was scowling at the page on top of his notepad. He jotted a number in the margin with a pencil before he looked up.

"That was Sheldon." He glanced back at the page.

I settled in my chair and fidgeted with the wedding band on my finger. It had gotten loose in the last year. "I'm going to turn them down."

"What—But, Elma." His gaze flattened and he gave me a small frown. "Are you . . . are you sure it's not depression? That's making you want to stay, I mean."

I gave an unladylike snort. "Now what do I have to be depressed about?"

"Please." He ran his hands through his hair and knit them together at the back of his neck. "I want you to go so you won't be here when . . . It's just going to get worse from here."

The devil of it was that he wasn't wrong. That didn't mean he was right, either, but I couldn't flat out tell him he was wrong. I set down my scissors and pushed the magnifier out of the way. "It's not just depression."

"I don't understand. There's a chance to go back into space." He dropped his hands and sat forward. "I mean . . . If I die before the mission leaves and you're grounded here. How would you feel?"

I looked away. My gaze was pointed to the window and the view of the house across the lane. But I did not see the windows or the red brick walls. All I saw was a black and gray cloth made of despair. "I had a life that I enjoyed before this opportunity came up. There's no reason I shouldn't keep on enjoying it. I enjoy teaching. There are a hundred reasons to enjoy life here."

He pointed his pencil at me the way he used to do when he spotted a flaw in reasoning at a meeting, but the pencil quivered in his grip now. "If that's true, then why haven't you told them no, yet?"

The answer to that was not easy. Because I *wanted* to be in the sky, weightless, and watching the impossibly bright stars. Because I didn't want to watch Nathaniel die. "What did Sheldon ask you to do?"

"NASA wants more information about LS-579."

"I imagine they do." I twisted that wedding band around as if it were a control that I could use. "I would . . . I would hate . . . As much as I miss being in space, I would hate myself if I left you here. To have and to hold, in sickness and in health. Till death do us part and all that. I just can't."

"Well . . . just don't tell him no. Not yet. Let me talk to Doctor Williams and see if she can give us a clearer date. Maybe there won't be a schedule conflict after al—"

"Stop it! Just *stop*. This is my decision. I'm the one who has to live with the consequences. Not you. So, stop trying to put your guilt off onto me because the devil of it is, one of us is going to feel guilty here, but I'm the one who will have to live with it."

I stormed out of the room before he could answer me or I could say anything worse. And yes—I knew that he couldn't follow me and for once I was glad.

DOROTHY CAME not long after that. To say that I was flummoxed when I opened the door wouldn't do justice to my surprise. She had her medical bag with her and I think that's the only thing that gave me the power of speech. "Since when do you make house calls?"

She paused, mouth partially open, and frowned. "Weren't you told I was coming?"

"No." I remembered my manners and stepped back so she could enter. "Sorry. You just surprised me is all."

"I'm sorry. Mr. Spender asked me to come out. He thought you'd be more comfortable if I stayed with Mr. York while you were gone." She shucked off her shoes in the dust room.

I looked back through the kitchen to the living room, where Nathaniel sat just out of sight. "That's right kind and all, but I don't have any appointments today."

"Do I have the date wrong?"

The Lady Astronaut of Mars

The rattle and thump of Nathaniel's walker started. I abandoned Dorothy and ran through the kitchen. He shouldn't be getting up without me. If he lost his balance again—What? It might kill him if he fell? Or it might not kill him fast enough so that his last days were in even more pain.

He met me at the door and looked past me. "Nice to see you, Doc."

Dorothy had trailed after me into the kitchen. "Sir."

"You bring that eagle to show me?"

She nodded and I could see the little girl she had been in the shyness of it. She lifted her medical bag to the kitchen table and pulled out a battered shoe box of the sort that we don't see up here much. No sense sending up packaging when it just takes up room on the rocket. She lifted the lid off and pulled out tissue that had once been pink and had faded to almost white. Unwrapping it, she pulled out my eagle.

It's strange seeing something that you made that long ago. This one was in flight, but had its head turned to the side as though it were looking back over its shoulder. It had an egg clutched in its talons.

Symbolism a little blunt, but clear. Seeing it I remembered when I had made it. I remembered the conversation that I had had with Dorothy when she was a little girl.

I picked it up, turning it over in my hands. The edges of the paper had become soft with handling over the years so it felt more like corduroy than cardstock. Some of the smaller feathers were torn loose showing that this had been much-loved. The fact that so few were missing said more, about the place it had held for Dorothy.

She had asked me, standing outside the fence in the shadow of the rocket gantry, if I were still going to Mars. I had said yes.

Then she had said, "You going to have kids on Mars?"

What she could not have known—what she likely still did not know, was that I had just come from a conversation with Nathaniel when we decided that we would not have children. It had been a long discussion over the course of two years and it did not rest easy on me. I was still grieving for the choice, even though I knew it was the right one.

The radiation, the travel . . . the stars were always going to call me and I could ask *him* to be patient with that, but it was not fair to a child. We had talked and talked and I had built that eagle while I tried to grapple with the conflicts between my desires. I made the eagle looking back, holding an egg, at the choices behind it.

And when Dorothy had asked me if I would have kids on Mars, I put the regulation smile on, the one you learn to give while wearing 160 pounds of space suit in Earth gravity while a photographer takes just one more photo. I've learned to smile through pain, thank you. "Yes, honey. Every child born on Mars will be there because of me."

"What about the ones born here?"

The child of tragedy, the double-orphan. I had knelt in front of her and pulled the eagle out of my bag. "Those most of all."

Standing in my kitchen, I lifted my head to look at Nathaniel. His eyes were bright. It took a try or two before I could find my voice again. "Did you know? Did you know which one she had?"

"I guessed." He pushed into the kitchen, the walker sliding and rattling until he stood next to me. "The thing is, Elma, I'm going to be gone in a year either way. We decided not to have children because of your career."

"We made that decision together."

"I know." He raised a hand off the walker and put it on my arm. "I'm not saying we didn't. What I'm asking is that you make this career decision for *me*. I want you to go."

I set the eagle back in its nest of tissue and wiped my eyes. "So you tricked her into coming out just to show me that?"

Nathaniel laughed sounding a little embarrassed. "Nope. Talked to Sheldon. There's a training session this afternoon that I want you to go to."

"I don't want to leave you."

"You won't. Not completely." He gave a sideways grin and I could see the young man he'd been. "My program will be flying with you."

"That's not the same."

"It's the best I can offer."

I looked away and caught Dorothy staring at us with a look of both wonder and horror on her face. She blushed when I met her gaze. "I'll stay with him."

"I know and it was kind of Sheldon to ask but—"

"No, I mean. If you go . . . I'll make sure he's not alone."

DOROTHY LIVED in the middle of the great Mars plains in the home of Elma, who was an astronaut, and Nathaniel, who was an astronaut's husband. I live in the middle of space in a tiny capsule filled with punchcards and magnetic tape. I am not alone, though someone who doesn't know me might think I appear to be.

I have the stars.

I have my memories.

And I have Nathaniel's last program. After it runs, I will make an eagle and let my husband fly.

Acknowledgements

Special thanks to Jennifer Jackson of the Donald Maass Literary Agency, Beth Pratt, Howard Lyons, and the original editors who first published these stories.

EDITORIAL NOTE: The stories collected herein are arranged in somewhat, although not exact, chronological order by date of publication (which may or may not coincide with the order in which they were written).

"The Bound Man" © 2005 Mary Robinette Kowal. First publication: *Prime Codex: The Hungry Edge of Speculative Fiction,* eds. Lawrence M. Schoen & Michael Livingston (Paper Golem LLC).

"Chrysalis" © 2007 Mary Robinette Kowal. First publication: *Aoife's Kiss,* December 2007.

"Rampion" © 2005 Mary Robinette Kowal. First publication: *The First Line,* Spring 2005.

"At the Edge of Dying" © 2009 Mary Robinette Kowal. First publication: *Clockwork Phoenix 2: More Tales of Beauty and Strangeness,* ed. Mike Allen (Norilana Books).

"Clockwork Chickadee" © 2008 Mary Robinette Kowal. First publication: *Clarkesworld Magazine,* June 2008.

"Body Language" © 2009 Mary Robinette Kowal. First publication: *Orson Scott Card's Intergalactic Medicine Show,* #15, November 2009.

"Waiting for Rain" © 2008 Mary Robinette Kowal. First publication: *Subterranean Magazine,* Fall 2008.

About the Author

Mary Robinette Kowal is a novelist and professional puppeteer. Her debut novel *Shades of Milk and Honey* (Tor 2010) was nominated for the 2010 Nebula Award for Best Novel. A loving tribute to the works of Jane Austen, but set in a world where magic is an everyday occurrence, the novel was the first of the Glamourist Histories. Its sequel, *Glamour in Glass,* was followed by *Without a Summer,* and *Valour and Vanity* (a *Kirkus* and NPR book of the year). The fifth and final volume, *Of Noble Family,* was published earlier this year.

In 2008 she won the Campbell Award for Best New Writer. Her short story "Evil Robot Monkey" was nominated for a Hugo in 2009. "For Want of a Nail" won the 2011 Hugo for short story. "The Lady Astronaut of Mars" was honored by the 2014 Hugo for novelette.

Among other venues, her stories have appeared in *Asimov's, Clarkesworld, Subterranean Magazine,* and several "year's best" anthologies. Her debut collection, *Scenting the Dark and Other Stories,* was published in 2009 by Subterranean Press.

Kowal is also an award-winning puppeteer. With over twenty years of experience, she has performed for *LazyTown* (CBS), the Center for Puppetry Arts, Jim Henson Pictures, and founded Other Hand Productions. Her designs have garnered two UNIMA-USA Citations of Excellence, the highest award an American puppeteer can achieve.

When she isn't writing or puppeteering, Kowal brings her speech and theater background to her work as a voice actor. As the voice behind several audio books and short stories, she has recorded fiction for authors such as Kage Baker, Elizabeth Bear, Cory Doctorow, and John Scalzi.

Mary lives in Chicago with her husband Rob and over a dozen manual typewriters. Sometimes she even writes on them.

~